AYELET GUNDAR-GOSHEN was born in Israel in 1982. She holds an MA in Clinical Psychology from Tel Aviv University, has been a news editor on Israel's leading newspaper and has worked for the Israeli civil rights movement. Her film scripts have won prizes at international festivals, including the Berlin Today Award and the New York City Short Film Festival Award. *One Night, Markovitch* won the Sapir Prize for best debut. Her second novel, *Waking Lions*, will be published by Pushkin Press in 2016.

ONE NIGHT, MARKOVITCH

AYELET GUNDAR-GOSHEN

Translated from the Hebrew by Sondra Silverston

PUSHKIN PRESS

London

Pushkin Press
71–75 Shelton Street
London WC2H 9JQ

Original text © 2012 Ayelet Gundar-Goshen

Published by arrangement with the Institute for
the Translation of Hebrew Literature

English translation © 2015 Sondra Silverston

One Night, Markovitch was first published in
Israel as *Layla Echad, Markovitch*

This translation first published by Pushkin Press in 2015
This edition first published by Pushkin Press in 2015

0 0 1

ISBN 978 1 782271 63 5

Set in Monotype Baskerville by Tetragon, London
Printed by CPI Group (UK) Ltd, Croydon, CRO 4YY
Original front cover design by Alysia Shewchuk

www.pushkinpress.com

For Yoav

Even a fist was once an open palm with fingers.

YEHUDA AMICHAI

BEFORE

1

YAACOV MARKOVITCH WASN'T UGLY. Which is not to say he was handsome. Little girls didn't burst into tears at the sight of him, but neither did they smile when they saw his face. He was, you might say, gloriously average. Moreover, Yaacov Markovitch's face was remarkably free of distinguishing features. So much so that your eyes could not linger on him, but slipped onward to other objects. A tree on the street. A cat in the corner. It required an enormous effort to keep looking at the barrenness of Yaacov Markovitch's face. People do not enjoy making enormous efforts, and so they only rarely looked at his face for any length of time. This had its advantages, and the unit commander was aware of them. He looked at Yaacov Markovitch's face for exactly the amount of time he needed, then dropped his gaze. You will smuggle weapons, the unit commander said. With that face, no one will notice. And he was right. Yaacov Markovitch probably smuggled more weapons than any other member of the Irgun, and never came close to being caught. The British soldiers' gaze slid over his face like oil on a gun. If the Irgun members valued Yaacov Markovitch for his daring, he didn't know it. Few spoke to him.

When he wasn't smuggling weapons, he worked in the field. In the evening, he sat in the yard and fed leftover bread to the pigeons. Very quickly, a flock took to gathering there regularly, eating from his hands and perching on his shoulder. The village children would have laughed if they had seen that, but no one passed by the stone fence. At night, he read from the writings of Jabotinsky. Once a month, he went to Haifa and paid a woman to sleep with him. Sometimes it was the same woman, sometimes a different one. He didn't dwell on her face and she didn't dwell on his.

Yaacov Markovitch had one friend. Zeev Feinberg was, first of all, a mustache. Not blue eyes, not bushy eyebrows, not sharp teeth. Zeev Feinberg's mustache was famous in the entire area, and, some said, in the entire country. When an Irgun member returned from a trip to the south, he talked about "the blushing girl who asked whether the sultan with the mustache was still with us". Everyone laughed, but Zeev Feinberg laughed harder than any of them. And when he laughed, his mustache shook above his upper lip, it jiggled and wobbled, as happy as its owner had been between that girl's thighs. It was clear that Zeev Feinberg was not born to smuggle weapons; his mustache preceded him like a pair of marching black exclamation marks. You had to be blind and stupid not to see him. And while the British were indeed stupid, it would be too optimistic to assume they were blind as well. But though he could not smuggle weapons in, Zeev Feinberg knew quite well how to drive Arabs out, and he spent many nights patrolling the village.

Few were the nights that Zeev Feinberg spent alone. When it became known that it was his night to stand guard, a group would immediately gather. Some wanted to hear about the adventures of his mustache between women's thighs, others wanted to talk about the political situation and the damn Germans, and still others simply wanted his advice on raising cattle, weeding fields and extracting wisdom teeth—some of the areas in which Zeev Feinberg considered himself an expert. Girls would come as well. Though Zeev Feinberg was a loyal guard, his finger always on the trigger, it was nonetheless important to remember that God gave men ten fingers, and not for nothing. The fragrance of fields after rain, a smidgen of danger—a rustling there, an Arab or a wild boar—and the moans could sometimes carry all the way to the walls of the houses. Sometimes Yaacov Markovitch would join them, carrying his worn copy of Jabotinsky's writings under his armpit, the smell of sweat rising from its pages. Zeev Feinberg welcomed him happily, as he did everyone else. He was so used to the company of people that he didn't know how to be unsociable, even if he had wanted to. He didn't really even hate the British, and when he killed someone, he did so reluctantly, albeit with great efficiency. The first time they spoke was when Yaacov Markovitch returned in the middle of the night from a journey to Haifa.

"Halt," Zeev Feinberg thundered at him in the darkness. "Who are you and where do you come from?"

Yaacov Markovitch felt his legs tremble but answered in a steady voice, "I am Yaacov Markovitch. I was with a woman."

Zeev Feinberg's laughter woke the chickens in the coop. When they sat down together he continued to ask questions, and Yaacov Markovitch replied eagerly. He talked about the woman's nipples, which were extremely nice, and agreed to describe in detail her rear end and her legs without demanding even one lira from Zeev Feinberg for the information that had cost him half his weekly wage.

In the end, Zeev Feinberg leaned towards Yaacov Markovitch and asked, "Tell me, how wet was she down there?"

Zeev Feinberg's mustache tickled Yaacov Markovitch's cheek, but he didn't dare move. No one had ever looked at his face for such a long period of time.

Finally, realizing that he could hesitate no longer, he replied, "What do you mean?"

"What do I mean?" Zeev Feinberg's mustache whipped Yaacov Markovitch, pushing him backwards. His blue eyes gaped with such great shock that they almost swallowed up Yaacov Markovitch, together with the writings of Jabotinsky. "I mean her vagina, comrade. How wet was her vagina?" The very sound of the word made Yaacov Markovitch dizzy, and he sat down on a rock. Zeev Feinberg sat down beside him. "You do realize, I hope, that there can be different degrees of wetness? There are moist ones and there are wet ones, and there are the ones that—aie aie aie—you can drown in, like in the Black Sea. It depends, of course, on the woman's nutrition and the weather, but mostly on the passion between the man and the woman." Then Zeev Feinberg asked again how wet she was there, and Yaacov Markovitch had to admit that he hadn't noticed even a tiny bit of dampness. "Nothing?"

"Nothing. Dry as the fields at the end of August."

Now Zeev Feinberg was silent for a while, and then finally said, "In a case like that, comrade, I suggest that you find out whether she has other men. You're probably familiar with the law of the preservation of matter. The body of a person contains a limited amount of liquid, and I suspect, my friend, that your woman there in Haifa is using hers up in the presence of another man."

Yaacov Markovitch breathed a sigh of relief and declared that it was all clear to him now: the woman in Haifa had said that he was the fourth one that night, and, based on his knowledge of the law of the preservation of matter, it was indeed logical not to find water there. Zeev Feinberg burst out laughing and Yaacov Markovitch had to join in. He didn't know what he was laughing about, nor did he wish to know. It was so pleasant to laugh beside that man whose mustache filled the valley and whose laughter reverberated throughout the entire country. If there had been any mockery in Zeev Feinberg's laughter, it faded immediately, while the laughter went on for a long time. He laughed and laughed, until a small stain appeared at his crotch, and when he saw it he laughed even harder. From that night on, Yaacov Markovitch and Zeev Feinberg were friends.

Yaacov Markovitch saved Zeev Feinberg's life twice, both times on the same night. Back from one of his trips to Haifa, he was hurrying to the guard post because for the first time in his life he had seen two breasts that were not the same size. Still wondering what Zeev Feinberg would say about that, he saw a young Arab crouched in the bushes, the barrel of his rifle aimed at a moving mass, apparently Zeev Feinberg astride a woman. It's tempting to say that Yaacov Markovitch didn't hesitate. But until that night he had only smuggled weapons and, except for having smashed the heads of rats that destroyed the crops, he had never killed a living creature. Nonetheless, he overcame the trembling in his legs, gingerly picked up a smooth white stone, and in one strong blow smashed the Arab's head. A shot pierced the darkness and Yaacov Markovitch's eardrum. He ran his hands over his body to see whether he'd been hit, and found that this time Zeev Feinberg's pistol had missed. "It's me," he shouted, "don't shoot!"

Zeev Feinberg's mumbled thank-yous were lost in the stream of vomit. One look at the Arab lying on the ground, and Yaacov Markovitch's stomach overflowed. The Arab's blood glistened in the moonlight and his exposed brain tissue horrified Yaacov Markovitch. The crickets, in any case, continued to chirp. Yaacov Markovitch closed his eyes in despair, slammed the doors of his mind before the images of the Arab and his spilt brain, and clung as tightly as he could to the breasts of the woman from Haifa. When he opened his eyes, he saw a different pair of breasts before him, remarkably symmetrical. Rachel Mandelbaum, half naked, stood shaking beside Zeev Feinberg. She had been so stunned that she forgot to cover herself, and now appeared before him in all her glory, weeping at the sight of the Arab's corpse. When he looked at Rachel Mandelbaum's breasts, Yaacov Markovitch's penis stiffened. The stiffer it got, the weaker his mind became, until it completely let go of the image of the crushed Arab. The realization slowly penetrated his mind that he was staring at the breasts of Rachel Mandelbaum, even though he was absolutely not Avraham Mandelbaum. That realization caused Yaacov Markovitch to stop looking at Rachel Mandelbaum's breasts and, turning to Zeev Feinberg, he said, "Avraham will kill you."

Those in the know and the uninformed were divided on the question of how many people Avraham Mandelbaum had killed. Some said ten, others fifteen. Still others spoke dismissively about the exaggerations, stating firmly that it was no more than four. They finally compromised on a typological number: seven. Although everyone assumed that they were talking about Arabs, one Englishman at the most, none could swear to it. Flies thought twice before approaching Avraham Mandelbaum. Cats did not rub against his legs. If there had been a guillotine in the village, Avraham would have been chosen to operate it. Since there wasn't, he was forced to settle for the job of ritual slaughterer. Only a few knew that at night he cried in his sleep, mumbling Polish words of longing, muttering mysterious phrases about a white lamb, a sugared apple, malicious children. Rachel Mandelbaum heard and understood, and got quietly out of bed. She had got off the ship quietly too, five years earlier. She had stood silently in the Haifa port, waiting for something to happen. She had exhausted all her resourcefulness in order to survive the journey to Palestine, and now that she had arrived, she no longer had the strength for anything else but to stand and wait. She didn't wait long. After half an hour, Avraham Mandelbaum went up to her and introduced himself. He bought her a fruit drink at a kiosk and took her to his house. Rachel Mandelbaum followed him like a duckling newly hatched at the gates to the port, trailing after the first thing it sees.

Later, she asked herself what he had been doing at the port on the day the ship arrived. He hadn't been carrying anything and hadn't bought anything the entire time he was with her that day. He had no relatives, so Rachel Mandelbaum assumed that he hadn't gone there to welcome anyone. That's where she was wrong. Every few weeks, Avraham Mandelbaum went to the port to see the ships come in. When the hunger is great enough, anticipation alone can go a long way to filling the emptiness in your stomach. Avraham Mandelbaum would watch the people getting off the boat, their faces greenish, their limbs pale, and try to identify a familiar feature. After a while, they would disperse and Avraham Mandelbaum would return home. The day he saw Rachel, he knew right away, but waited thirty tormenting minutes to be sure. No one came. She didn't take a step. In her green dress she looked to him like a bottle that had been thrown out to sea and washed up on the shore, and he, the lonely survivor, would pick it up and read what was inside it. He took her home and married her, but he never succeeded in deciphering the words that were in the bottle.

Rachel Mandelbaum, formerly Kenzelfuld, took off her green dress and made it into a curtain. From her red ball gown she made two tablecloths and a pillowcase. Five months from the day she'd got off the boat, almost nothing was left of the city girl. The whole house was full of memorials to her former life, and they faded, they unraveled, until it seemed as if those pieces of cloth had always been here, in Palestine. The other women observed her with a combination of admiration and puzzlement. On the one hand, it was definitely good to see how well she blended in, not like those pampered young women who came there thinking they were at a holiday resort near Zurich. On the other hand, they wondered at how serenely she turned the most fashionable items into curtains, God help us, how, in her hands, the crème de la crème of Vienna became a towel in her husband's butcher's shop. Rachel Kenzelfuld also abandoned the German language. The moment her foot trod the ground of the Haifa port, she swore to speak only Hebrew. When she didn't know a word, she chose to be silent, even if the person she was talking to also spoke German. When officials from the leadership came to visit, one of them got wind of the fact that the beautiful woman in the butcher's shop doorway had also been born in Austria. He immediately showered her with an emotional stream of words, to which she responded with a mute stare. Rachel entrenched herself in silence and the embarrassed entourage hurried away. The women, who had learned to like the serious young girl, were quick to praise her devotion to the Hebrew language. The story of the impudent new immigrant who had taught the official the "Jews speak Hebrew" lesson spread rapidly, and many people greeted Rachel in the street. She returned the greeting with a slight accent. Her true reasons remained hidden, perhaps even from her. With some profound inner sense, she knew that if she allowed even the smallest crack, the mourning for her previous life would rise up and flood the entire country. The dresses, the balls, the light reflecting off cobblestoned streets, the snowflakes—all those were locked securely behind bars. One look back and, like Eurydice, she would stumble all the way down to the sweet, the oh-so-sweet European Hades.

During the day Rachel Mandelbaum helped her husband in the butcher's shop, the blood wafting around her like perfume. At night she sat in bed and knitted very tightly, to keep even one thought about the past from infiltrating into the present. But once a month she put down the knitting needles and slipped quietly out of bed. Avraham Mandelbaum muttered in sleepy Polish and

Rachel stroked his head with a practiced hand and went outside. Outside: Palestine is asleep. The ground is breathing heavily, its breath fragrant with the scent of earth and hay and orchards. And waiting for her out there is Zeev Feinberg. She closes her eyes and he kisses her neck. His mustache scratches her delicate, translucent skin. But Rachel doesn't move her neck away. Just the opposite: she rubs against the stiff hair again and again. And from beyond the orchards, the straw, the port, the great ocean, a memory comes to her of an Austrian soldier's beard, Johann was his name, and the smell of wine that rose from his lips as they kissed her, and the blood in her veins as he spun her in a never-ending Viennese waltz. At those moments, Rachel Mandelbaum's eyes grow moist, and so does her vagina.

2

ON THE NIGHT Yaacov Markovitch crushed the Arab's head, Rachel Mandelbaum's eyes hadn't had time to grow moist. Several moments earlier, Zeev Feinberg had taken off her blouse and hurriedly thrust his face between her breasts. The Austrian soldier, Johann, had never managed to visit between her breasts, so the touch of Zeev Feinberg's mustache there did not arouse any feeling in her except for, perhaps, a slight stinging. Rachel Mandelbaum wondered whether it was appropriate to move Zeev Feinberg's head from her breasts to her neck, but before she had time to come to a decision she heard the sickening sound of a skull being crushed. Rachel knew that sound very well. Despite its infrequent occurrence, from the moment your ear absorbs it there can be no mistaking it ever again. One clear night in Vienna, as she walked from her home to the café in the square, Rachel Kenzelfuld saw three boys pushing an old Jew. They passed him from one to the other as if he were a ball, and Rachel was shocked to see the expression of innocent pleasure on their faces, an expression so typical of children at play. Then one of them pushed the old man clumsily, and he stumbled and fell on the sidewalk, smashing his head on the curbstone. The Jew was no longer a game, but only a broken toy, a ball emptied of air. The boys looked at him in alarm. Several moments later, one of the boys swallowed his saliva and said, "Let's go. We'll find another one." They went on their way and she on hers. A week later, she boarded the ship. At night, when her stomach was on the verge of bursting from nausea and longing, she remembered the noise of the shattering skull.

When Yaacov Markovitch said, "Avraham will kill you" to Zeev Feinberg, Rachel Mandelbaum understood that she was standing bare-breasted in front of Yaacov Markovitch. A quick glance at his face was enough to see that Yaacov Markovitch did not even have the shadow of a mustache, so Rachel Mandelbaum found nothing to justify her nakedness. She covered herself quickly, upset by the thought that now three men in the village knew the mole she had above her right breast. If she had understood Yaacov Markovitch's train of thought, she might not have been upset. Compared to the asymmetrical breasts of the woman from Haifa, Rachel Mandelbaum's breasts were a divine creation, and Yaacov Markovitch decided that they definitely merited the sacrifice of a slaughtered Arab. Nonetheless, he thought, a slaughtered Arab is more than enough, and there was no need for the additional sacrifice of Zeev Feinberg, who had finally stopped thanking Yaacov Markovitch and was now cursing like a Russian sailor.

"Idiot, imbecile, damn the bitch that gave birth to you." At first Yaacov Markovitch thought that Zeev Feinberg was talking to the Arab, but when he began to tear out the hair of his mustache with his bear-sized hand, he realized that he was cursing himself. "Thirty men will be here within three minutes, and that still won't be enough to pry Avraham Mandelbaum's hands off my throat. Aaah, you suckling pig, today you go to the slaughter." Zeev Feinberg resumed tearing out his mustache and Yaacov Markovitch felt as if a wonder of the world was being destroyed right before his eyes, as if he were watching the conflagration of the library in Alexandria.

"Leave your mustache alone," he roared, frightened by the sound of his voice, "we'll face him together."

Zeev Feinberg finally let go of his mustache, to the relief of Yaacov Markovitch and Rachel Mandelbaum. The terror on his face was replaced by an expression that, from a certain angle, looked like scorn. He was a head taller than Yaacov Markovitch, and almost twice as wide. Yaacov Markovitch's seventy-eight kilograms would not win that battle, which had actually ended before it began. Yaacov Markovitch saw that expression and bitterness filled his heart. In the distance, they heard the voices of men who had been startled from their sleep by the sound of the shot. Avraham Mandelbaum was undoubtedly leading the pack.

"Run," Yaacov Markovitch roared. Zeev Feinberg remained where he was. "I'll say that I came back from Haifa and saw the Arab attacking Rachel. You were patrolling the northern fields at the time, heard shouting and fired into the air. Now go, go!" Under his mustache, Zeev Feinberg's lips opened in shock. It didn't take long for him to leap onto his horse and gallop off. Rachel Mandelbaum looked at Yaacov Markovitch as if she were seeing him for the first time. Lofty words in German came into her mind, but she didn't know their Hebrew form, so she remained silent. And perhaps that was a good thing. It was not for her that Yaacov Markovitch had dared to put himself in so much danger. Rachel Mandelbaum's breasts might be round and lovely, but Zeev Feinberg's mustache was one of a kind. It was the only mustache that rose in a welcoming smile whenever Yaacov Markovitch appeared.

The men surrounded Yaacov Markovitch in a semicircle. He had never been looked at by so many eyes at the same time. He repeated his story for the second time, glancing at Rachel every few sentences for confirmation. Her nods seemed excessive to him, and he was afraid they would be damaging to them. A man doesn't shout in the streets that two and two are four when saying it quietly is enough, but Rachel's head was going up and down with almost religious fervor. Avraham Mandelbaum noticed it too. He thought that the flush on his wife's cheeks was too bright, and even though he couldn't distinguish between cheeks colored pink by grievance and cheeks colored pink by pleasure, her lips were too swollen, the way they were during intercourse. When Zeev Feinberg finally arrived astride his horse, Avraham Mandelbaum's eyebrows contracted like two black goats pressing together in the cold night air.

"You took a long time getting here," one of the men noted.

"I circled the fields to see if there are others there."

Murmurs of agreement rose from the crowd and Yaacov Markovitch finally allowed himself to exhale normally.

"And you," Avraham Mandelbaum said to his wife, "what were you thinking when you went out wandering at this hour?"

Rachel Mandelbaum lowered her gaze to the ground and said, "Insomnia."

The moon reappeared through the clouds, illuminating Rachel Mandelbaum like a spotlight on a stage. She was so fragile, with her downcast eyes and torn nightgown, that not a man there didn't want to take her in his arms and protect her in his bed, and if it hadn't been for Avraham Mandelbaum, they would most likely have done so. Avraham Mandelbaum was the only man who didn't look at his wife, but kept his eyes on Zeev Feinberg's fly, which was gaping like a mouth open in a scream. Zeev Feinberg, wiping away a tear of sympathy for Rachel Mandelbaum's pain, saw her husband staring at his crotch and quickly zipped up.

"I'm a little embarrassed to say that when I heard the shot, I was about to pee for the sixth time tonight. That's how it is, when there's no one to talk to, you keep your mouth busy drinking. I spend whole nights like this, drinking and peeing, drinking and peeing."

The men burst out laughing, Rachel Mandelbaum smiled politely. Avraham Mandelbaum was silent.

A day later, around 7:30, someone pounded on Yaacov Markovitch's door. Zeev Feinberg stood in the doorway. "Pack quickly. He found out." On their way to Tel Aviv, as the clattering of the train drowned out the growling of Yaacov Markovitch's stomach (breakfast in his house was out of the question), Zeev Feinberg told him what had happened. "In the morning, Avraham Mandelbaum decided to have sex with his wife. He removed her nightgown and saw a terrible rash on her chest. An allergic reaction to the friction of the mustache rubbing against the delicate skin she had there. Aie aie aie, such beautiful skin! Pure milk. Except for the mole. You saw the mole?" Yaacov Markovitch said that he hadn't seen a mole, but would be happy to learn how Zeev Feinberg had been saved from the slaughterer's knife. "That's just it, he couldn't decide which knife to use. It took him five minutes to choose the right one, enough time for Rachel to run to my Sonya and tell her to warn us. Except that Sonya isn't like Avraham Mandelbaum, she's a lot less picky." Zeev Feinberg lifted his shirt and showed Yaacov Markovitch five long, bloody scratches. "My God, that woman has the strength of ten men." Yaacov Markovitch nodded appraisingly. Zeev Feinberg began to compare Sonya to a series of mammals, from wolf to hyena, but Yaacov Markovitch simply stared enviously at the five bleeding canals that had been dug in Zeev Feinberg's chest. "For a woman to feel that much for you, that's something I never thought was possible." At that moment Zeev Feinberg stopped talking about the wild bitch that had given birth to Sonya and nodded. "She has a heart the size of a dove, and a vagina of sweet water." Here Zeev Feinberg launched into a detailed description of Sonya's vagina, its sweetness, its pinkness, and the warm, cheerful moistness with which it welcomed him. "And she may not have breasts like Rachel, but she can make you laugh until your balls twist themselves around each other." At that point Zeev Feinberg burst into such roaring laughter that the train accelerated, and he finally sighed and said, "When we go back, I'll marry her. Really and truly."

Zeev Feinberg's eyes were full of purpose, and Yaacov Markovitch almost believed him. Then he dropped his gaze from Zeev Feinberg's eyes to his mustache, remembering how it curled when, from the corner of his eye, he saw a woman smile, how it quivered like a cat's delicate whiskers did when a mouse drew near. And he also remembered the cat that waited at the butcher's shop door for Rachel Mandelbaum's generous handouts. It was sated and fat, but nonetheless tormented an injured bird that happened to cross its path, not for the sake of the hunt, but out of habit. Zeev Feinberg was a true revolutionary. A Communist in every sense of the word. He distributed his love equally, showing no preference for one woman over another. "I'll marry her," Zeev Feinberg repeated, and also slapped his thigh with his hand, as if declaring the matter closed, "This time I'll marry her."

When the train entered Tel Aviv, Zeev Feinberg was regaling Yaacov Markovitch with a detailed description of the wedding banquet, where herring, sweet challah and pot roast had already been served. Yaacov Markovitch ate with his ears, but they apparently led to someone else's stomach. His own stomach had been empty for several hours now. Finally, he dared to stop Zeev Feinberg and ask where they were going and if there was food there.

"We're going to see Froike," Zeev Feinberg said, "and if I know him, you won't leave hungry."

Yaacov Markovitch froze. "You mean the deputy commander of the Irgun?"

"The one and only."

"How do you know him?"

Yaacov Markovitch's squad commander had spoken about the deputy with awe, and he himself had never dared to even dream of a meeting with that man who, as far as he knew, was ready to swallow a grenade and eject it from his anus if it would help save the country.

"We came on the ship together," Zeev Feinberg said, and kept walking.

But there was, of course, more to it. Four hundred other people had arrived on that ship, but none of them had formed the kind of relationship that Zeev Feinberg and the future deputy commander of Irgun had. They shared a love of women, jokes and chess, which, although common to many other people, was rarely as powerful. Since the ship was small—some fifty single women, close to thirty good jokes and one chess set—they decided to leave behind their European possessiveness and divide everything equally. They retained their previous fanaticism about only one thing: winning. When the ship reached the shores of the country, the two men were engrossed in a stormy game of chess. When Zeev Feinberg heard the captain's cry, he put his bishop down on the board and stood up. The future deputy commander of the Irgun gave him a deadly look. A razor had not touched his face since he left Europe, and now he looked again like the yeshiva boy he had once been, except that his eyes said that he had already sampled the taste of sin and he was not sated. "He who begins a good deed must complete it," he admonished Zeev Feinberg, "We've waited 2,000 years, we can wait another fifteen minutes." Surrounded by the tumult of boats being lowered into the water, the two men continued to play. Neither looked at his watch. Those two men had already tasted so many sweet mouths that neither was especially anxious to run his tongue over the earth of the Holy Land. When twenty more minutes had passed, the captain burst into the room. "If the British catch you, you'll be able to play chess all the way back to Europe!" The future deputy commander of the Irgun seemed to be seriously weighing the possibility. Finally, he relented and said, "I hope you can swim with one hand, Feinberg, because with the other, you'll be holding your pieces."

With bursting rucksacks on their backs and chess pieces in their hands, they hurried to the deck. Each held his own pieces, repeating to himself over and over again their positions on the board. Then the captain told them to help a pregnant woman and her two small daughters. They almost refused. In the end, it was decided: in a choice between the rucksack, the three illegal female immigrants and the chess game waiting to be finished, the rucksack lost. Zeev Feinberg took the pregnant woman and the black chess pieces. The future deputy commander of the Irgun maneuvered courageously between the pair of weeping girls and the white pieces, keeping all of them from vanishing in the waves. When they reached the beach, they parted from the grateful woman, brushed the wrinkled cheek of the Holy Land with a polite kiss, and were horrified to discover that they had forgotten where the pieces had stood on the board. They sat all night on the beach in their wet underpants, chests bare, arguing about the right placement. When the British arrived in the morning, the two men looked to them as if they had been on the beach forever. In the end, they left to explore the country, each in his underpants. Zeev Feinberg went north, and the future deputy commander of the Irgun headed for Tel Aviv, where he became the present deputy commander of the Irgun. At one of their meetings, when Zeev Feinberg asked how a person who had almost left behind a pregnant illegal immigrant in favor of a castle had become the co-ordinator of the Zionist project for smuggling illegal immigrants into the country, his friend replied that all he did was exchange one obsession for another. "In this too, there are black pawns and white pawns. And in this too, I hate to lose."

Yaacov Markovitch and Zeev Feinberg sat in front of the desk of the deputy commander of the Irgun. The former—cowering in embarrassment, his body seeming to withdraw into itself. The latter—arrogant, legs stretched forward, limbs relaxed. Even though his gaze was constantly drawn to the deputy commander of the Irgun, Yaacov Markovitch could not help noticing the essential difference between the way he and Zeev Feinberg were sitting. Yaacov Markovitch thought: there are people who walk through the world as if they were there by mistake, as if at any moment someone would put a hand on their shoulder and shout in their ears, "What is this? Who let you in? Get out, fast." And there are people who don't walk through the world at all. Just the opposite, they sail through it, slicing the water in two wherever they pass, like a boat full of confidence. It wasn't envy that Yaacov Markovitch felt towards Zeev Feinberg right then. It was a more complex emotion. Yaacov Markovitch sat in the office of the deputy commander of the Irgun looking at the extended legs of Zeev Feinberg, embarrassed by his own bent legs, and wondered how many other offices he would sit in with his legs withdrawn under him, and whether he would ever stretch his limbs with such liberty in the presence of other people. It was those questions that pushed him suddenly to straighten up, extend his hand to the deputy commander of the Irgun who, until that moment, hadn't said a single word to him, and say, "Yaacov Markovitch, at your service."

In the silence that ensued, he realized his mistake. The two men had apparently been engrossed in discussing several extremely important subjects: an audacious plan to defend the Holy Land, an especially complicated sexual position, a brilliant chess move they needed to practice—and Yaacov Markovitch's declaration did not fit in with a single one of them. The deputy commander of the Irgun looked appraisingly at Yaacov Markovitch, like the village doctor examining feces, and then turned back to Zeev Feinberg. "So how big is her mole?" The deputy commander of the Irgun was a well-known mole aficionado. His rivals claimed that he preferred them to the actual body of a woman. When Zeev Feinberg told him about the incident that had begun with Rachel Mandelbaum's breasts and ended with Avraham Mandelbaum's knife, the deputy commander of the Irgun ignored the knife—he'd had more than enough of those—and focused on the breasts. Zeev Feinberg didn't care. On the contrary—he admired his friend for knowing how to tell the wheat from the chaff, and returned happily to Rachel Mandelbaum's breasts. But then something strange happened: the more he conjured up Rachel's plump breasts, the more they looked to him like Sonya's breasts. And even though Rachel's breasts were more beautiful than Sonya's—plump and sweet and very, very firm—the image of Sonya's breasts made him so happy that he didn't want to drive them away. So it happened that he described Rachel's breast to the deputy commander of the Irgun while he was seeing Sonya's breasts in his mind's eye, until he was suddenly seized by the fear that he might get confused and begin describing Sonya's breasts to his friend, not Rachel's, and that was something he did not want to do.

Zeev Feinberg stopped speaking. For the first time since he met the deputy commander of the Irgun on the ship's deck, he felt that he possessed something he had no intention of sharing. Yaacov Markovitch was also silent. He was still cursing himself for his earlier remark. Despite his agitation, he noticed the change that had taken place in Zeev Feinberg: until now, he had recreated his conquests like someone musing to himself, still savoring the previous night's meal. But this time he spoke with genuine longing in his eyes: it is not a satiated man who praises his meal, but a hungry one, mad with yearning. The brightness that spread over Zeev Feinberg's face as he was supposedly recalling Rachel Mandelbaum's breasts was greater than the happiness he felt when he was actually with her. In light of his previous failure, Yaacov Markovitch needed all of his courage to open his mouth and say, "You will go back to Sonya someday." Zeev Feinberg looked at him, stunned. Then he smiled. If he had been alarmed at first by the clarity with which Yaacov Markovitch read his most secret thoughts, his fear turned immediately into relief—his friend could read the mysteries of his mind, the hieroglyphs he had long ago lost hope that anyone but he could decipher.

At first, the deputy commander of the Irgun mistakenly thought it was an upset stomach. Only later did he understand that the sharp stab in his stomach was actually envy. Because there was something there, between those two men sitting in front of him, something he himself had no part in. And even though this Yaacov Markovitch was nothing more than a worm—Zeev Feinberg must certainly see that; how could he not?—this worm was spinning a web of thin silk, winding it around his friend and leaving him outside.

Even though he was not a great fan of pain, certainly not in his stomach, the deputy commander of the Irgun was happy about the pain his envy had caused, like a person who finds something he's lost. It had been many years since he'd felt that kind of pain. While his job had made him well acquainted with all the pain a person could inflict on his fellow man—with a blow to the diaphragm, a nose-crunching punch, a ripped-out fingernail and a definitely unpleasant cut near the genitals—he had almost forgotten about the existence of other kinds of pain. The pain of fullness. Only someone who has been filled with something other than himself can feel the pain when it is gone.

When he left the yeshiva in Poland and went to the big city, the pain of fullness almost killed him. He walked along the main street, and everything was empty of God. Cleansed of God. Filthy with secularity. A loaf of bread was nothing more than a loaf of bread. There was not a drop of the Divine Spirit in a glass of wine. The world stood before him as it was, stripped of angels, shaking with cold, offering no promise of warmth. On his first night in the big city, the deputy commander of the Irgun missed God with all his heart and soul, and the drumming in his head pounded and pounded, like the drums at a pagan festival. In his hostel room he shaved off his beard in the darkness of the night. He couldn't see anything. The blood from the cuts clotted his hair and it fell to the floor, clump after clump. He should have waited for morning, but he knew that if he waited, the longing would drive him straight back to the morning prayer service. So he kept shaving his beard and, when he finished, he set to work on his scalp with shaking hands, Delilah hands, and then his eyebrows, and then his body hair. At dawn he found himself naked and alone before the void.

The years passed. The hair of the deputy commander of the Irgun grew back and his heart hardened. Sitting in his office across from the two men, he unconsciously ran his fingers over the tips of his dense, porcupine hair. When he became aware of this, he immediately dropped his hand. Such a gentle move-ment, so sentimental, was unbecoming to the deputy commander of the Irgun. To correct the distorted impression, he chose an utterly masculine movement, typical of deputy commanders of organizations whoever they may be, and pounded the desk. Zeev Feinberg and Yaacov Markovitch turned to look at him, the former curiously, the latter with awe. Since he had pounded the desk for no good reason, the deputy commander of the Irgun was now forced to think quickly of something to say. "Well then, you both seem to be in serious trouble." Yaacov Markovitch and Zeev Feinberg nodded in agreement.

He, the deputy commander of the Irgun, had the rare ability to say obvious things in such a way that made them sound remarkably fresh. "That Mandelbaum, will he come all the way to Tel Aviv?"

"To Tel Aviv?" Zeev Feinberg said, raising his voice, "he'll pursue us to the Red Sea if he has to!" The deputy commander of the Irgun and Zeev Feinberg burst out laughing. Yaacov Markovitch groaned faintly.

"Get me out of this, Froike," Zeev Feinberg said, "I like what I have between my legs too much to give it up to the slaughterer's knife."

"Of course I'll get you out of this, Feinberg. What are friends for if not to save each other's balls? Even though I'm not so sure about this friend of yours here. As it is, he doesn't seem to make much use of them." The deputy commander of the Irgun burst into laughter. Zeev Feinberg joined him in what the deputy commander of the Irgun considered enthusiastic agreement, and what Yaacov Markovitch deemed a polite gesture. When they'd finished discussing the limited use Yaacov Markovitch made of his testicles, the deputy commander of the Irgun grew serious and leaned over the desk towards them. "Feinberg, I'm sending you to Europe."

The expression on Zeev Feinberg's face, had it appeared on anyone else's face, would have been called "confused". But Zeev Feinberg, 120 kilograms of daring and muscle, not including the mustache, was not a man accustomed to being confused. The confusion, finding nothing to hold on to, slid rapidly off his face. It dripped from his blue eyes, from the mouth now smiling as it had before, and from the thick eyebrows. Only in his mustache did it find a crack in which to nestle, and so the confusion hung on the edge of the right side of Zeev Feinberg's mustache, which, upon hearing the word "Europe", jutted up oddly.

"By God, Froike, if this is another one of your herring schemes, I'll rip out your tongue." The deputy commander of the Irgun and Zeev Feinberg burst into conspiratorial laughter. Yaacov Markovitch tried mentally to fill in what was missing, and the story he wove in his imagination was probably infinitely more impressive than the one that had actually occurred in reality.

"No, Feinberg, I swear, not another herring." The deputy commander of the Irgun wiped away the moisture that the laughter had brought to the corners of his eyes, casually disproving the myth that deputy commanders of the Irgun do not shed tears. "This is the story: Europe has closed its gates, that you know, and the door isn't really open here either. But we have found a breach: marriage. A Jewish girl in Poland or Germany who marries a young man from Palestine can leave Europe without any problems. A Jewish boy from Palestine who comes back with a new wife from Europe can enter the homeland without any arguments. Over the last few months, we have recruited young men to travel to Europe and marry a woman there. When they return, they'll divorce the woman and that's that—another new immigrant in the Holy Land, another young man blushing after a thank-you kiss. And who knows, maybe more than that. I personally am willing to bet that at least two of those couples will stay married. A sea voyage tends to bring people closer, which you know, and not everyone can overcome the boredom of the journey with a chess game. So congratulations, Feinberg, you're about to get married."

While the deputy commander of the Irgun was speaking, the confusion began another assault on Zeev Feinberg's mustache. Upon hearing that last sentence, it no longer limited itself to the tip of the right side of the mustache, but spread across the length of the entire monument, causing many dozens of hairs to jut out in various directions and giving Zeev Feinberg the appearance of an out-of-control broom.

"Married?" Yaacov Markovitch could swear that he heard a quaver in Zeev Feinberg's voice. "There's no other way?"

"It's just on paper, Feinberg, just on paper. But if I were in your place, I'd leave my signature on that piece of paper!"

Zeev Feinberg ignored the wink of the deputy commander of the Irgun. He'd only just finally decided to devote himself to Sonya—to only one woman, for God's sake!—and the devil in the form of the deputy commander of the Irgun had come and whispered in his ear. The voyage from Europe to Palestine took eleven days. No man could resist the temptation. And even though he knew that the vaginas of European girls were as dry as the Siberian steppes, and even if they were filled with water, it would be as cold as the waters of the Rhine; he also knew that he would immerse himself in that snowy water and return to Sonya shivering with cold and guilt. Oh Sonya, the amber goddess of Palestine. Though she had also been a European iceberg once, the Mediterranean sun had warmed her spirit and imbued her skin with the scent of oranges (historical truth requires a note that Sonya's skin was far from being amber-hued, and never tanned, but went directly from milky white to sickly red—but Zeev Feinberg never noticed that).

"Find yourself someone else, Froike, I'm not going." The deputy commander of the Irgun looked at Zeev Feinberg, who spoke quickly before he could change his mind. "You've made a very tempting offer here, and a rescue, there's no doubt about that. But I'd rather stay here. You must have a well-hidden weapons cache somewhere, a camel in whose stomach you can smuggle explosive materials, fellahin that need to be driven away from their village in the Jerusalem hills where someone has to stay to guard their ruins. I'll take one of those jobs. Mandelbaum won't find me."

"He will," Yaacov Markovitch said, his eyes cast down. One night, when sleep evaded him, and his wages weren't enough for a woman in Haifa, and Jabotinsky's writings did not extinguish his loneliness, he went out for a walk around the village. On the way back, he passed the butcher's shop. Through the curtain, he saw Rachel Mandelbaum walking around the living room of her house. Mending a blouse, patting the dust from an embroidered pillow, sipping tea, her eyes on the void. Rachel Mandelbaum walked around her house, but her shadow danced in the yard. As she walked the length of the living room, the shadow moved to the flower bed at the front door. When she patted the pillow to remove the dust, the shadow patted the walls of the house. When she sipped tea, the shadow froze in place and stretched. After a while, Yaacov Markovitch noticed that he wasn't alone. On the stone fence that surrounded the yard sat Avraham Mandelbaum, looking at his house from the outside, guarding his wife's shadow. As if the slaughterer was afraid that the shadow would do what its owner dared not do: get up, run all the way to the Haifa port and board a ship sailing to Europe. When Yaacov Markovitch recalled the expression on the butcher's face as the wind made Rachel's shadow dance on the flower bed, he knew that Mandelbaum would find them. "No concealed weapons cache, no hiding place in a camel's stomach, and no trip to the Jerusalem hills. We'll travel to Europe together. And as for the women, don't worry: I'll save you from yourself."

3

T HEY BOARDED THE SHIP four days later. The sea was calm
and the sunset banal. Yaacov Markovitch was slightly disappointed. He was a practical man, not a sentimental fool, and
yet he harbored the hope that on the first day of their journey
the forces of nature would rally to present an opening scene
worth noting. A flock of storks would hover in the sky, a slippery
dolphin would approach the shore, the dying sun would have a
unique hue. Because, after all, this was not simply a voyage to
Europe; this was the beginning of his life's journey. From the day
he was born, Yaacov Markovitch had felt he was nothing more
than a minor character in other people's stories, a sub-plot, a
distant moon that received its light from a sun. He was the son
of his parents and the subordinate of his squad commander and
the friend of Zeev Feinberg. For the first time in his life Yaacov
Markovitch felt that he, Yaacov Markovitch, was living a life worth
telling about. Everything that had happened until now had been
merely a sketch, the mindless scribbling of an artist a moment
before he sits down purposefully at his easel. That was why he
no longer thought about his house in the village and did not
miss the people who lived there, sorry only that, in his headlong
flight, he had left behind the writings of Jabotinsky, and he also
felt sorry for the pigeons.

When he puked up his guts after half an hour of sailing,
Yaacov Markovitch observed his reflection in the water. Among the

floating bits of vomit he saw the average eyes, the run-of-the-mill nose, the tediously ordinary jawline. But on his forehead he saw something new, a firm line not previously there. When that line had appeared, he didn't know. Had it been when he smashed the Arab's head with a rock, or when he lied so brazenly to Avraham Mandelbaum, or perhaps when he insisted, actually argued, with the deputy commander of the Irgun, who refused at first to let him join the voyage? Whatever the reason, it was a clear sign. Yaacov Markovitch looked at the new line on his forehead, the crack through which the man he was meant to be would emerge at any moment. He wiped the remnants of vomit from the corners of his mouth and headed for the deck.

He quickly learned that he had been mistaken. Life on the ship was different from life in the village in almost every way, but when it came to Yaacov Markovitch, it was the same. The passengers' glances slid off his face and continued onward, like the drops of urine the men peed every night from the deck into the sea. No one hated him, no one mocked him—nor did anyone seek the protection of Zeev Feinberg's savior, Yaacov Markovitch, killer of Arabs, deceiver of slaughterers. If he had thought he would hatch from the shell of his cocoon-like youth, he now discovered that it had not been a shell, but his skin. When Yaacov Markovitch sought his friend's advice on this subject, he discovered that it was a lost cause: Zeev Feinberg had been crowned uncontested king of the voyage even before the ship had left the shore. He had strolled along the pier surrounded by a group of young men, drooling puppies who wanted to lap up more and more stories from the person known as the best friend of the deputy commander of the Irgun. And Zeev Feinberg gave them what they wanted. He told stories until his throat was dry, sang lewd songs until his tongue grew blunt, and made his listeners laugh, drowning out their laughter with his own, driving flocks of migrating birds from their route. Even though he had not been appointed leader of the mission—the deputy commander of the Irgun had given that position to a young man by the name of Katz several months earlier—there could be no doubt about who the acting commander was. If Zeev Feinberg had given an order to take a three-day detour to the coast of Greece to watch the local girls swim in the nude, the captain would have obeyed, and Zeev Feinberg would most likely have done that if his heart had not been aching with yearning for Sonya. Instead, he continued to talk and sing and laugh, only occasionally feeling as if his voice had departed from his body, was sailing forward without him, and Zeev Feinberg himself was far, far away. At such moments Zeev Feinberg was tired of being Zeev Feinberg. Yaacov Markovitch had never seen this before; how could a person grow tired of being Zeev Feinberg?

They always met on the deck at sunrise. Yaacov Markovitch came up to make sure that the sun had indeed risen, Zeev Feinberg was on his way to his bed after a night of drinks and stories. They sat beside each other in the silence, Yaacov Markovitch mustering strength for the day to come, Zeev Feinberg gathering courage to face his nightmares. At such moments the atmosphere was so congenial that they never dared to speak in its presence.

The days were alike, but passed nevertheless. As they drew closer to Europe, a quiver of restlessness circulated among the passengers, intensifying so much that it seemed as if the entire ship were dancing on the surface of the water in excited anticipation. They talked about it at breakfast and dinner, while standing on deck and lying in bed. They talked about Europe so much that when they finally saw it they were all silent, as if they didn't believe that there was an actual continent behind their words. Yaacov Markovitch stood on the deck and looked at the land. It seemed to him that the ship was moving faster than usual, drawn to the port by some sort of magnetic force. The third pole, the European pole, around which all the passengers had been circling, materialized before his eyes. Zeev Feinberg stood beside him, eyes closed, refusing to enjoy a view of that cradle of pleasure, the thought of which was enough to soften your heart and stiffen your penis. He rolled Sonya's name around on his tongue again and again, holding on to it to assuage temptations and witches. But from a distance his tongue seemed to taste the butter and the cocoa, the tender venison and the hardening nipples of women, and Zeev Feinberg gave one final sigh, "Sonya," and uttered her name no more.

At the same time, Sonya stood on the shore of Palestine and looked at the sea. Zeev Feinberg finally opened his eyes and saw the ground of Europe grow nearer. Sonya stood with open eyes, and saw nothing but water. Eleven days earlier, on exactly the same morning the ship left the Haifa port, Sonya was driven by a strong feeling to go and look at the sea. That fateful coincidence might have been considered evidence of the magical connection between a pair of lovers, if the same feeling hadn't driven Sonya to the shore on the previous three days as well. That behavior of Sonya's contained nothing of the highly praised women's intuition that wakes a mother in the middle of the night with the knowledge that her son has been wounded in battle, or causes her to hurry and bake a cake, mysteriously certain that he would return that day. It wasn't intuition, but devotion. When Zeev Feinberg scratched his nose, her nostril did not itch. When he had diarrhea from a gastroenteritis epidemic on the ship, Sonya slept soundly. She did not feel it when the ship reached Europe and did not prophesy the date on which she would leave the Haifa port; she only knew that she had to wait for him to return, and she knew that when he did—he would return from the water.

Sonya's girlfriends scoffed at her for waiting. Zeev Feinberg is a good man, there's no one like him for amusement, but no mustache is worth standing on the shore all day wearing an Anna Karenina face. Sonya shrugged and continued to stand there, hurling hot curses at Zeev Feinberg. Because even if she was doomed to wait, even if she was cursed with the humiliating tendency of women everywhere to find a piece of sand on which to stand and look at the sea, waiting for their man to return, at least she had the strength to be angry about it. And so she cursed Zeev Feinberg with all her heart and soul, loudly and resolutely. His illustrious mustache was, in her words, "a collection of black worms", and his penis—famous throughout the valley—was dragged through the mud daily. Sometimes she called it "a scallion", sometimes "a stunted squash", sometimes she declared it "a hothouse for lice", and one day she announced that such foul meat was unfit for human consumption. People quickly gathered to hear Sonya abuse Zeev Feinberg. She was no less passionate about it than she was about waiting for his return.

The young men from the village worshiped her. And not because she was beautiful. The distance between her eyes was a millimeter greater than the distance considered pleasing. The sun had scattered freckles across her face, and her aquiline nose would have reinforced the words of every German propagandist. Average height, reasonable breasts, a rear end there was nothing to say about except that it existed. Nonetheless, they came every day to watch her standing on the shore. The shy ones with yearning glances, the brave ones with clever remarks, urging her to forget Feinberg and give herself to one of them. While they might not have mustaches, and their laughter didn't rustle the leaves of the fruit trees, they at least were here, and that was nothing to sneeze at. Sonya thanked them from the bottom of her heart, and went on cursing Zeev Feinberg. The women, for their part, began to curse Sonya. Questions like, "But what does she have?" filled the air like a swarm of wasps. Some said that her devotion cast a spell. Deep in his heart, every man, even if he isn't a sailor, wants a woman to wait on the shore for his return. Cheap romanticism, nothing more. Devotion, in and of itself, does not cast a spell; its magic depends on who the devotee is. A charmless pumpkin standing on the shore would end up covered in hyssop or would be transformed into a lighthouse. Others talked about the orange scent. In truth, Sonya's skin did give off the scent of oranges, a heavy, sweet fragrance that is unmistakable. Anyone who stood next to Sonya at work and took a deep breath would immediately feel as if he were in the Jaffa port surrounded by crates of oranges. The orange scent was intoxicating, but so was the fragrance of jasmine and figs. Many women whose skin was redolent with a unique scent were scattered throughout the country: everyone knew that one from Degania who had to wear gloves to keep the insects from being drawn to the honey of her hands; and there was a girl from Rishon LeZion who, according to the stories, gave off such a strong scent of myrtle that people with allergies began to sneeze. The orange scent is all well and good, but it's a long way from that to mad love.

What the devotion and oranges did not explain, the fire might. The flame that blazed inside Sonya defrosted frozen limbs, warmed innards, made fingertips tingle. On rainy winter days, when water trickled down faces and filled shoes with mud and despair, people looked at Sonya and were warmed. And in summer, when the entire village was covered with a thin sheet of dust and the houses were glazed with a powdery confection of sand and suffocation, Sonya was the only one whose colors did not fade. She wasn't beautiful, they knew that, and yet they turned their faces towards her the way sunflowers turn to the sun.

One day, when she was still standing on the beach, Avraham Mandelbaum came to visit her. She didn't see him at first. She was fully engaged in a detailed description of the way she would pull out all of Zeev Feinberg's nails when he returned. When she recognized the slaughterer, she was afraid that upon hearing her words he might adopt some of the ideas for himself. But she calmed herself with the knowledge that a skilled slaughterer like Avraham Mandelbaum did not need her advice on how to deal with flesh and nails, and asked him why he had come. Ever since the day that Yaacov Markovitch and Zeev Feinberg had fled, they had avoided each other on the street. Avraham Mandelbaum wrung his thick hands in embarrassment, and Sonya thought that if it hadn't been for his height of almost two meters and his weight of more than 160 kilograms, you could see him as a child. With downcast eyes and a hesitant voice, he said that he had come to catch her anger.

"It's not the flu, you know."

"Yes, but even so." Then he said that for many days he hadn't felt any anger, not even a little, towards Zeev Feinberg. No matter how much he tried to blow on the fire of his rage to rekindle it, to make it burn by picturing in detail Zeev Feinberg lying with his wife, he did not have even an ember of anger in him.

"If that's the case, what do you have there instead?"

"Sometimes, in the butcher's shop, when I finish cutting up an animal, I sit among the pieces of meat and try to reassemble it in my mind. Sometimes it works, and then I see them become one again, like in a vision of the end of days, the meat on the table and the innards in the garbage pail and the skin tossed on the floor and the head that I always wrap in a rag so that Rachel won't see it, because it makes her nauseous. And sometimes it doesn't work, and I sit down on the stool surrounded by pieces and ask myself where the lamb is."

Sonya thought that this was undoubtedly the longest conversation she had ever had with Avraham Mandelbaum. Perhaps she even guessed that this was the longest conversation Avraham Mandelbaum had ever had in his life.

"I don't think I understand, Avraham. What's the connection between the lamb and Zevik?"

"I can't find it, Sonya. I can't find the anger. When I went to Feinberg's house that morning, I was ready to skin him alive. But when I went home, I didn't want to kill anyone anymore. I was tired."

For the first time since she had been standing on the shore, Sonya looked away from the sea. She turned to Avraham Mandelbaum and took his hands, a slaughterer's hands. Her eyes were far enough away from each other to divide between them what she felt: her right eye was all sadness, her left eye was all compassion.

"It's not my anger that you need, Avraham. Make your own. Make yourself something of your own."

At night, the deputy commander of the Irgun visited Sonya. Before leaving for Europe, Zeev Feinberg had made him swear to go north and tell her that he had gone on a voyage, "and the most important thing", Feinberg had stressed, "is to tell her that I'll be back". The deputy commander of the Irgun did not tell Sonya the purpose of his journey, but merely mentioned briefly that it was the only way "to save his ass, which I understand is quite precious to you". Then he looked straight ahead through the window at the night, to which he could shortly return, his ears perked to gather the murmurs of her gratitude. When the murmurs were late in coming—what happened to "What would we do without you?", where was "He owes you his life, and so do I"?—he narrowed his eyes and looked at her again. Much practice and childhood strabismus had made him an expert in this sort of slit-eyed detection. An outside observer might mistakenly think—here are a man and a woman sitting in the living room, the woman looking at the wall and the man at the window. With regard to the woman, that observer would be right, but with regard to the man, his observation would be far from the truth. The deputy commander of the Irgun looked at Sonya with the same concentration he applied to the study of a topographical map of the route of the next night's raid. He memorized every inch of her face: the wide-set eyes, the number of equally and unequally spaced freckles, the wide chin. He also saw the furrow of the wrinkle between the nose and the lip, and discovered that when she smiled, she did it by slightly raising the left corner of her mouth, a movement that might be considered charming. The sum total of it was quite ordinary, definitely not a reason to bother making the long trip from Tel Aviv. The deputy commander of the Irgun felt sorry for Zeev Feinberg, a wasted breeding bull who had chosen to settle in such a godforsaken area, where not only did the land close its womb, but the women were definitely mediocre as well.

He turned back to the window. In another moment, he would part from her. In another moment, he would walk out of the door. The way to Tel Aviv would be dark and cold, and all sorts of sights would dance in his mind, the kind a person sees only when he is out alone in the night. He had already begun to stand up when he heard Sonya's voice:

"You know him from the ship, right?"

The deputy commander of the Irgun said yes, he knew Zeev Feinberg from the ship, and now, if she would forgive him, it was late and he had to be going.

Sonya gave him an amused, tough look, an exact copy of the look he wore when speaking to his men, and said, "If you put him on a ship, the least you can do is tell me about what he did on the previous one."

"Why?"

"If I can't see him in the present, at least I'll hear something about his past."

The deputy commander of the Irgun sat down again, his expression angry. He had never liked rehashing past escapades. What was the point of chewing on the cud of the past when you could be chewing on the meat of the future? Talking about memories wears them away, like a shirt that is washed over and over again until its color is gone. But he soon discovered that when he told Sonya stories about being on the ship with Zeev Feinberg, they became infused with a life of their own, appearing before his eyes in colors brighter than ever before. At first he attributed this to his rare storytelling skills, but was quickly forced to admit that it was not his doing. It was Sonya. Every pore of her body seemed to absorb his words. When he told her how he left his family and went to the city, and from there to the ship, her eyes filled with compassion. When he described how he almost drowned in a storm, her nostrils quivered in a small spasm of fear. When he told the jokes he had taught Feinberg, she shook with laughter. And something in the deputy commander of the Irgun shook as well. The past was no longer the past when he recounted it to Sonya. Her attentiveness was so total, her participation so sincere, that what he had previously considered cold, bland leftovers of memories became warm and spiced again, filling his stomach with joy. They sat there until late into the night. He regaled her with the jokes they'd told on the deck, even the crudest ones, and was shocked to see that she did not blush with shame, but smiled broadly with pleasure. He described in detail Feinberg's brilliant chess moves, and his own sophisticated counter-attacks, and even though she didn't understand a thing, she clapped her hands happily at every crucial moment. So as not to hurt her, he avoided talking about their peccadillos with the women, but when she gave him a knowing look he broke down and related the details to her. There was the woman they tried to dupe into thinking they were brothers, and when she didn't believe it they claimed that they both had the same birthmark on their penises, and persuaded her to check. And there was the one who filled her corset with socks at the beginning of the voyage, and when it was so cold that she had to wear them at night, her breasts smelled like feet. And the one who said she wouldn't give herself to Feinberg until he shaved off his mustache, and in response the deputy commander of the Irgun said he wouldn't stay with her until she grew a mustache. Finally, he told Sonya about the night they reached Palestine. Her wide-set eyes moved closer together with shock, and he could barely finish a sentence without an interruption from her: "With the girls in one hand and the chess pieces in the other?" And "What did the British say when they saw you?" And in the end, the words that brought joy to the heart of the deputy commander of the Irgun: "But how were the pieces really arranged on the chess board?"

He left her house at dawn. After so many hours of talking about Zeev Feinberg he longed to see his friend, who was now an ocean away. He spent the entire trip back to Tel Aviv reminiscing about their sea voyage. And the deputy commander of the Irgun was so busy missing Zeev Feinberg that it took him another two whole days to realize that he missed Sonya too.

In the days that followed, the deputy commander of the Irgun smelled citrus fruit wherever he went. Again and again his legs took him to the Jaffa port, where the vendors were taken aback to see him sniffing the crates of oranges with a yearning look. He occasionally thought that he must be wrong, that it was impossible for a woman's body to give off such a scent, maybe there had been a bowl of clementines in the room. But in his heart he knew—there had been no clementines or grapefruit. In the end, desire got the better of him: he bought a crate of oranges, put them in his office at headquarters, and did not allow anyone to eat any of them.

While the oranges rotted away in the office of the deputy commander of the Irgun, Sonya blossomed at her post on the beach. The sea air did her good. The sun shone between her breasts. The stream of curses she hurled at Zeev Feinberg brought a constant blush to her cheeks. But more than anything, it was the futility of what she was doing, the arbitrariness of her expectations, the magnificent illogic that stirred her blood and filled her body with vitality.

At the end of a week, when the deputy commander of the Irgun returned and knocked at her door, he felt like a man lost in an orchard. He mustered all his verbal prowess in an effort to deny it, to persuade himself that he was in no way sinning against his best friend Feinberg. They had always shared everything that crossed their path—women, stories, bottles of liquor—why should this woman be any different from the previous ones? But he knew, he knew despite himself, that different she was. Finally, when the scent of oranges threatened to drive him mad, he decided that the entire matter had blown up beyond all proportion. Sonya was just another lady friend for Zeev Feinberg (who was undoubtedly on his way to Palestine now, sharing the beds of the women on the ship), and he would be only too happy for the deputy commander of the Irgun to visit her in his absence. Clearly Zeev Feinberg would appreciate the devotion of his friend, who had traveled all the way to the north to spend a bit of time with the woman whose eyes were set a millimeter too far apart to be considered pleasing.

When he reached the door to her house, he almost changed his mind. He spent close to an hour in the shadows, watching the oil lamp in the living room. Then he decided to move from darkness into light and knocked on the door. Sonya's voice asked, "Who's there?" The deputy commander of the Irgun hesitated for a moment, wondering how to reply to that question, and then said, "Ephraim".

When Sonya opened the door, she didn't recognize him. Nothing remained of the man she had met a week earlier. The confidence and the arrogance had vanished completely, replaced by a stumbling awkwardness that reminded her of a lamb's first steps moments after birth. She gave herself to him unhesitatingly, although his gratitude embarrassed her. He was too handsome to beg for any woman's kindness, and the fact that, of all of them, she was the only one whose kindness he did beg for aroused discomfort more than pleasure in her. In any case, her conscience did not torment her. She felt neither the joy of revenge nor the guilt of betrayal. Only the physical calm of sexual release. Three weeks had passed since Zeev Feinberg had fled from the terror of Avraham Mandelbaum, and while Sonya's body left no great impression on those who saw it, it was no small source of pleasure for Sonya herself. There was no reason to let it gather dust. Since Zeev Feinberg's departure, she had spent her evenings sitting on the armchair, sipping tea to moisten her throat, dry from the day's invectives, and dipping a pink finger into a jar of honey. That very same finger would wander along the lower part of Feinberg's stomach, skipping over to her own thighs. Now, in his absence, her body was orphaned and bored. True, Feinberg had come to her a number of times in her sleep, and she took her turn coming to him as she lay in bed at dawn, but the musings of imagination are nothing like the caresses of reality. However wild the lovemaking was in her mind, it left no marks on her body. And Sonya loved the marks almost as much as the act of love itself. Standing in the field at noon, she would steal a glance at a scratch that Feinberg had left on her breast, at a bite mark that adorned her stomach. Thus, as the sun blazed down on her head, she would take comfort in the reminders of the previous night, regards from the moon. Now her nights were silent and her body free of marks. That was why the presence of Zeev Feinberg's best friend in her bed seemed right to her: one had left and the other had come to fulfill his obligations. Before they went to sleep, the deputy commander of the Irgun even put up the shelf that Zevik had promised to put up.

Like Zeev Feinberg before him, the deputy commander of the Irgun discovered that Sonya's body was a well of sweet water. He drank from it and was not sated. But when he woke up the next morning, the bed was empty. He searched for Sonya between the four walls of the house and on the paths of the village to no avail—she had already taken her place on the shore and was cursing and abusing Zeev Feinberg with renewed strength, vociferously, passionately and resolutely.

4

A FTER YAACOV MARKOVITCH and Zeev Feinberg disembarked, they felt dizzy as they walked on the pier. Since
that is a well-known phenomenon among sea voyagers, they did
not attribute any importance to it. But their heads continued to
spin on the next day as well. And the day after that. Finally, Zeev
Feinberg said that it wasn't the ship that caused it, but the land
they were standing on. They drank coffee at a small table that
groaned under the burden of Zeev Feinberg's weight. The upper
part of his body covered the entire surface, and his curly head
adorned the center of the table like a decorative plant forgotten by its pruner. In light of this takeover of the table, Yaacov
Markovitch was forced to hold his cup of coffee, Zeev Feinberg's
cup, two small forks and one cream cake. This exemplary dem-
onstration of balance would most certainly have earned him a
few coins if it had appeared in the adjacent square, where Zeev
Feinberg had divested himself of a dozen coins, dropping them
into the hat of a mime artist who stood frozen in place for an
entire fifteen minutes. Yaacov Markovitch had watched the mime
with a growing sense of unease, and almost grabbed him by the
shoulders to shake him and shout, "Move, man! Don't stand there
like a golem while everything is constantly changing, be different,
different!" But Zeev Feinberg was filled with hope at the sight
of that miracle of stability, that ability to turn your back to the
bustling street, to the passers-by trying to get you to join in their

laughter, their stories, tempting you with a clever remark. His tongue must certainly be burning there, inside that scaled mouth.

The minute they turned away from the mime, Zeev Feinberg's head began to spin again. "Let's sit down," Yaacov Markovitch said, and that's how Yaacov Markovitch found himself holding a mountain of porcelain saucers and coffee and cake, while Zeev Feinberg was sprawled over the table with no apparent intention of straightening up. From among the abundance of his curls came a faint hum, and Yaacov Markovitch leaned forward to hear better. As he did so, the mountain in his hands became unbalanced and shattered on the polished floor of the café. The noise of the breaking dishes sounded to Yaacov Markovitch only slightly less loud than Kristallnacht. A grumbling waitress charged in their direction, holding a broom as if it were a spear. Yaacov Markovitch gave her an abashed smile, which did not go down very well. When she bent down to pick up the pieces, he looked at her breasts and felt like a baby. He always felt like a baby in the presence of those women, those personifications of efficiency, order and cleanliness, their aprons giving off the sour smell of milk and cake crumbs. Yaacov Markovitch was as attracted to café waitresses as he was put off by them, but they never gave him a second glance, except when he broke something; then their glances would slice through him with resentment even before they bent to pick up the pieces, their breasts peering out from under a mouth filled with angry mutterings. Still torn between the sweetness of her breasts and the sting of his shame, Yaacov Markovitch saw that Zeev Feinberg was still mumbling, his head on the table; in fact, he had not stopped mumbling from the moment he had begun.

"What did you say?"

Zeev Feinberg finally raised his head, completely ignoring the ruins of the cream cake and the broken dishes on the floor, gave a brief nod of appreciation at the waitress's breasts, and turned to Yaacov Markovitch. "I said that I'm not enjoying it here, Markovitch. I'm not enjoying it here at all."

Yaacov Markovitch allowed himself to be skeptical about his friend's remark. Over the five days that had passed since they got off the ship, Zeev Feinberg had gained five kilograms, slept with five women and emptied fifty liters of beverage into his stomach. He, like all the other men on the ship, had suffered some sort of bulimic attack, stuffing his senses with all the pleasures of the Continent before he would have to vomit them up and return to Palestine.

"Sounds strange to you, eh?" Zeev Feinberg said to Yaacov Markovitch as his eyes returned to the waitress's breasts. He could see a delicate tissue of bluish capillaries under the white skin. After gazing at that masterpiece for several moments, he turned back to his friend. "You see, Markovitch, coming back to Europe is like sleeping again with the woman you loved in your youth. You are so full of eagerness and longing that you can't see that that woman is gone. In vain you enter her body, in vain you look into her eyes. You might find a faint echo of the woman you loved, but nothing more. Ever since we got off the ship, the other fellows and I go to places from the past, drink drinks from the past. Whisper the same sexy things in girls' ears. In vain. That's why we're dizzy, my friend, that's why we've been walking around like drunkards from the minute we got off the ship. The difference in pressure between then and now pushes against our eardrums and destroys our balance!"

Yaacov Markovitch nodded slightly, his gaze wandering over the network of bluish capillaries at the waitress's breasts. Since he had never been fortunate enough to sleep with a woman he'd loved in his youth, he found it difficult to understand the defect Zeev Feinberg found in repeating such an act. But when the capillaries at the waitress's breasts suddenly joined together into the shape of the top of a tree that had stood in his parents' yard, he understood. He had spent most of his childhood years in a struggle with that tree, which looked to him like the tallest tree in the world. The scars on his knees were a detailed record of his relationship with that tree: this is when he crashed after trying to climb it on the right side, and this is where he was injured when he tried to vanquish it from the branch on the left, and this happened when he tried to charge the trunk with all the anger of a small boy attempting to conquer a tree and losing time after time. The nightmares of Yaacov Markovitch, the child, were no different from the nightmares of other children, but his good dreams always revolved around the branches of that tree. Every night he dreamed about the green treetop, the thousands of leaves untouched by human hands suddenly trembling when Yaacov Markovitch's head burst through the branches. The tree spoke to him in dozens of shades of green, and Yaacov Markovitch replied with words of affection. The countryside from the top of the tree spread to the four corners of the universe, and Yaacov Markovitch watched the polar bears in the south, saw oceans and mountains and castles whose turreted towers touched the sky. Below, beyond the birds' nests and the imps' hiding places, through the leaves and the branches, near the thick trunk, stood his parents. In the dream their faces were blurred, but their words were sharp and clear. His mother shouted, "Hold tight" and his father shouted, "Be careful", but they were both actually saying, "Yaacov, little Yaacov, how good it is to know that you've got so far."

They moved from that house when he was ten, and he went back to see it when he was twenty. Yaacov Markovitch, the grown-up, circled the peeling building quickly, ignored the roses in the yard and the blossoming of strangers' underpants on the laundry lines, and turned to his tree. At first glance he thought it had been replaced, that just as the new tenants had replaced the pictures on the wall and the clothes on the lines, they had also brought a new tree to stand in place of the old one. But when, horrified, he examined the texture of the trunk and ran his fingers over a leaf, he could not deny that this was the same tree. This time he did not have to struggle. In less than a minute he was peering down from the treetop, the branches groaning under his weight. Spread out below him were the adjacent yards, carpet after carpet of colored laundry and leaky roofs. There was no vestige of the polar bears and the imps, but in the neighboring yard he saw a famished cat trying futilely to catch a pigeon. Yaacov Markovitch climbed down from the tree and never went back to the yard.

Seven years later, in a fancy café whose peace and quiet he had disrupted, Yaacov Markovitch looked at the treetop that had taken shape fleetingly between the waitress's breasts. "You're right Feinberg," he said, "a person should not go back to a place he loved." He was about to suggest that they return to their rooms in the hostel and stay there until it was time to go and meet the women they had to marry, and that they should turn their backs on the present, which ruined the past, but at that moment Zeev Feinberg smiled under his mustache as if he'd made a decision, stood up and offered to help the waitress.

Her name was Ingrid, and she had a very complex inner life that Zeev Feinberg was not the least bit interested in. During the entire afternoon and the night following it that they would spend together, she would not say one word to him about the poems she wrote secretly, or about how much she missed her father, who left when she was six. One month after they met, she wouldn't remember his name and he wouldn't recognize her face if they met in the street (although his chances of recognizing her would increase if she were to bend down at the same angle she had bent down at in the café). So insignificant was their encounter that it could just as easily not have occurred. In fact, there's some doubt as to whether it actually did occur.

Nonetheless, one person was deeply affected by Zeev Feinberg's encounter with Ingrid, whose last name was not known. It was Yaacov Markovitch. As another cream cake was placed on the small table, Yaacov Markovitch walked alone to the hostel. In truth, he had walked alone to the hostel on all the preceding nights, but this time his steps were heavier. If any of the tenants of the hostel had looked at Yaacov Markovitch when he entered, they would certainly have thought—here's a man who ate a rich meal. His slow movements and his hand on his stomach seemed to say that. But Yaacov Markovitch's stomach was filled with loneliness, not food, and that was what made his steps heavy and sent him to his room. If he were in his house in the village, he would go out to the yard now and feed the pigeons. When a living creature eats from your hand, you don't feel lonely. But he didn't want to feed the European pigeons. They were too flamboyant for his taste, truly arrogant, and from a certain angle they reminded him very much of the iron eagle. And so Yaacov Markovitch went to bed. The night was cold and he warmed himself with a down blanket and self-pity, which defrosts frozen feet even faster than goose down. Again and again, the image rose in his mind of the breasts of the bending waitress and the bluish network of capillaries that he would have strummed like a harp player. He continued to strum all sorts of tunes on the waitress's breasts until they unraveled in his imagination into a giant book of music notation like the one his father used and only sometimes let him look at.

After he had studied every inch of the waitress's breasts, Yaacov Markovitch decided to seek other breasts to muse upon. At first, he summoned up Rachel Mandelbaum and the hostel landlady, but he quickly grew tired of flesh-and-blood breasts and stepped over into the wonderful Kingdom of the Possible. Tomorrow, for

example, he would meet twenty young Jewish damsels they had
come to rescue from their distress. Nineteen women grateful in
general, and one—the one he would marry—grateful specifically.
For the sake of proper order, Yaacov Markovitch lined up the first
nineteen in a row and examined them one by one, not devoting
too much time to their facial features. But when he reached the
twentieth girl, he didn't have the courage to look at her breasts.
It was only on paper, a rescue mission, for the duration of the sea
voyage only, and yet—she would be his wife. And it wasn't fitting for
a man to scrutinize his wife's breasts without her permission, as if
she were a bent-over waitress in a café. Instead, Yaacov Markovitch
examined her face at length. He was, at one and the same time,
the artistic painter and the enthusiastic observer, sketching her
features in his imagination and admiring them simultaneously.

If Yaacov Markovitch's face was ordinary, if it never caused a
passing glance to linger on it even fleetingly, then the face of the
girl in his imagination was the exact opposite. And since a person
cannot imagine what he has never seen, the face of his wife-for-
three-weeks was a remarkable jigsaw of facial features that he
knew. He gave her Gila Shatzman's lips, which were as plump as
a bursting fig, his mother's small and precise nose, Yona's cheeks,
which were so crimson that they drove bulls mad, and Fanya's hair,
which made him bury his hands deep in his pockets to keep them
from stroking it. Finally, all that remained were her eyes, which gave
Yaacov Markovitch no rest for two whole hours. Blue ones looked
cold and green ones mean and brown ones familiar. Ahuva's were
too big and Fanya's too small, and he could not remove the disappointment etched into his mother's eyes. Close to dawn, thrilled
by the solution he found, he gave her Sonya's eyes, after bringing
them a millimeter closer together. When he finally looked at the
whole facial composite, Yaacov Markovitch trembled with heat
that had nothing to do with goose down or self-pity. It was hope.

5

A T SEVEN the next evening, Yaacov Markovitch and Zeev
Feinberg left for the apartment in the eastern part of the city
where the meeting with the young women would take place. The
rest of the men walked at a distance from them, some in pairs,
others in small groups of three or four. Despite their attempts to
appear calm and speak slowly, the pungent fragrance of perfume
and shaving cologne gave them away. In the street adjacent to the
apartment, the groups had already joined together to become a
single block of restrained excitement. The official commander of
the operation, Michael Katz, studied their faces with dissatisfac-
tion. In his mind's eye, he saw himself leading a group of fearless
warriors to the apartment, the elite of the Irgun in Palestine.
He had hoped to present twenty poised young men to the pale
young women, young men tanned by the Mediterranean sun
and robust from working the land. But their suntans had faded
on the ship and a flush of embarrassment now spread over their
cheeks. The excited expectation on their faces made their arm
muscles, which were their pride, look like a costume worn by a
child. Basically, they were twenty young men a moment before
meeting twenty young women. When they entered the apartment, Michal Katz himself realized that his hands were sweaty,
and when he began to speak, he was horrified to discover that
he sounded like an announcer proclaiming that the ball was
about to commence.

"Ladies, I am Michael Katz, in charge of the operation for the Irgun in Eretz Israel." The ladies gave a general how-do-you-do nod, and Michael Katz allowed himself a quick glance at the harem assembled in the room. Most of the women sat crowded together on four faded sofas, and the ones who could not find a place sat on chairs that had been placed very close to the sofas, as if the women sitting on them wanted to be absorbed into the group of women who were sitting together. One woman was standing up, her back to him, looking out of the window. Five empty chairs stood against the wall, but since none of the men dared to take a seat that the woman at the window might want, they all remained standing. The Irgun representative in the city shook Katz's hand and began explaining details of the operation. In the six days since the ship had arrived, he had bribed almost every official in the city. The next morning, with a bit of luck, the soldiers would marry the young women, and the day after that, with a lot more luck, they would be on their way to Palestine. When they reached Eretz Israel, the marriages would be quickly dissolved, but of course they would always remain grateful to "the soldiers of the Irgun who rescued Jewish women from the iron vice of the enemy!" The final words were so rousing that all those present, men and women alike, burst into applause. Michael Katz also clapped his sweaty hands, but in his heart he cursed the representative for his eloquence. Zeev Feinberg took advantage of the general commotion to examine the women on the sofa, his mustache curling with pleasure as his eyes surveyed the room.

Yaacov Markovitch's gaze was also drawn to the sofas, but quickly moved to the woman standing with her back to the room. Michael Katz cleared his throat, a flowery speech on the tip of his tongue, one that would make the representative's words pale in comparison, but the representative once again beat him to the punch. "Since not much time remains before the actual marriages,

I have allowed myself to leave the rest of the evening for the couples, who were selected randomly, to get to know each other briefly. Who knows, maybe they will even manage to squabble a bit, the hallmark of every married couple."

Everyone laughed at the joke, and Michael Katz's speech died inside him. With an infuriating thrust of his tongue the representative had dealt a death blow to the formal seriousness that had pervaded the room, had destroyed the loftiness of the moment, leaving nothing for the acting commander of the operation to do but pull the list out of his pocket with great solemnity and read it in a voice he hoped would sound majestic.

"Gideon Gottlieb—Rivka Rosenberg."

"Yehuda Greenberg—Fruma Shulman."

As he read the names, Michael Katz's anger faded, and was replaced by elation. Each fictitious couple he announced looked to him like a sword and a shield, a bullet and a gun, a grenade and a safety pin—to sum up, like a couple fighting for the future of Israel. At such moments his mind was not troubled by thoughts of romance. He almost forgot that these were men and women, and thought only about armed resistance and illegal immigration, a phoenix that would rise again even if its head were cut off.

The soldiers of the Irgun, on the other hand, had forgotten for a while the future of the Jewish people and turned to examine what fate had handed them. When the name of one of the men was called, he stepped forward, and when the name of a woman was called, she got up from the sofa or chair. They shook hands formally and went to a corner of the room, which was filling up with chattering couples. Even though the men were in complete control of their facial expressions, it was impossible to miss the smile of victory on the face of Yehuda Greenberg as he shook the hand of Fruma Shulman, a hand that ended in a shoulder that was as white as milk, and, beneath it, breasts as sweet as whipped cream. Nor did the disappointment disappear from the face of Hanan Moskovitch, who had invested most of his money on shaving cologne and now stood near the door, hidden by the fat of Hava Blubstein. The smile on Zeev Feinberg's face did not dim even a little when he discovered that he would marry the short, mustached girl named Yaffa. He knew he would visit all of them anyway. He kissed her hand gallantly and led her to the window, leaving Yaacov Markovitch standing alone. When Yaacov Markovitch looked around, he saw that the entire room was full of conversing couples, and only one girl was left, her back to the room. That did not escape Michael Katz's attention either, and in an especially loud voice he announced, majestically, the last fictitious couple:

"Yaacov Markovitch—Bella Zeigerman."

Later, Yaacov Markovitch would flog himself for the look on his face at the moment the woman near the window turned around. The gaping mouth, the bulging eyes, they would haunt him wherever he went. In vain would he curse the jaw that had dropped as if it had a life of its own, the eyebrows that leaped towards the forehead. No one would have reacted differently if he had found himself standing in an apartment in the eastern part of the city looking into the face that only an hour before sunrise he had finally managed to complete in his imagination.

In the end, Michael Katz had to intervene. He waited several moments in the hope that Yaacov Markovitch would finally close his open mouth and walk over to Bella Zeigerman, but he showed no signs of doing so. And Bella Zeigerman, after deigning to turn around, did not look as if she intended to do anything further. There was a need here for radical intervention, a sharp and precise operational action that would break the strange spell that was there in the middle of the room. Realizing that, Michael

Katz spoke to Yaacov Markovitch in a friendly voice that had an undertone of warning: "*Nu*, Markovitch, won't you shake the lady's hand?" Yaacov Markovitch looked at him, shocked, as if the very idea was blasphemous. Bella Zeigerman smiled politely, and Michal Katz asked himself how it happened that, of all the girls, she would be the one to marry Yaacov Markovitch, while waiting for him at the far end of the room was the emaciated Miriam Hochman. With a visible effort, Yaacov Markovitch managed to pull himself together and extended a hand to Bella Zeigerman, holding her fingers as if he were lifting a chick that had fallen from a nest. Bella Zeigerman's gaze rested momentarily on his face. She was the most beautiful woman he had ever seen in his life. Bella Zeigerman's gaze moved onward.

Now they stood there in silence. Michael Katz understood that he had failed. Without another word, he turned towards Miriam Hochman, silently cursing all pathetic men and beautiful women. While Michael Katz planned to fulfill the obligation of his mission to carry on a polite conversation with his future wife, Zeev Feinberg parted from his own obligation and left Yaffa on the sofa, blushing about something he had just whispered to her. Now Zeev Feinberg wanted to see what the goddess of luck had given his friend, and once again noted that the bitch invariably gives nuts to people who have no teeth. Because Bella Zeigerman was, without the shadow of a doubt, the most beautiful woman in the apartment. And although, unlike Yaacov Markovitch, he didn't think she was the most beautiful woman he had ever seen, she undeniably belonged to the Olympus of goddess-like women which would never admit Yaacov Markovitch, even as a servant. Zeev Feinberg was sad for his friend because he saw Yaacov Markovitch's glance follow every movement of Bella Zeigerman's head, while Bella Zeigerman's glance sought anything that wasn't Yaacov Markovitch.

Almost unintentionally, the things that happened in that room were all the things that happen inside four walls when a beautiful woman is present. The men, who finally saw the face in front of the back, began to raise their voices as they spoke with their mates so that their jokes would reach her ears. Those who found an appropriate excuse—"I'll bring you a glass of water," "You probably want to get some air"—returned from their exile at the far end of the room and gathered around Bella Zeigerman. The women went to stand beside them, looking at Bella Zeigerman with a coldness she had become accustomed to, just as she had become accustomed to the European cold she had grown up in from the day she was born.

Against his will, Zeev Feinberg also found himself verbally courting Bella Zeigerman. Force of habit. He chose to recount his daring escape from the slaughterer's knife, a story that had already gained him a place of honor among the men and earned the cries of amazement he expected now as well, as it was being told for the third time. The men applauded at the right moments and the women, who were hearing the story for the first time, leaned so far forward with interest that Zeev Feinberg knew which of them plucked her mustache and which of them did not need to. During the long days on the ship Zeev Feinberg had polished the story into a piece of art, shortening unimportant details and lengthening Avraham Mandelbaum's knife. He stopped wisely when he heard the thunder of laughter, nodded at the sounds of amazement, and tried as hard as he could to drive away the vision of the silent mime in the city square.

In the end, Bella Zeigerman drove it away when she touched his arm and said, "But tell me, is it true?"

Zeev Feinberg looked at her face, his mind searching feverishly for a remark that would make her his. But suddenly he saw that Bella Zeigerman's eyes were not Sonya's eyes, and realized that he would never sleep with her. He decided, therefore, to help his friend.

"Absolutely true, miss. My friend Yaacov Markovitch, who saved me from the terror of the slaughterer, will testify to that."

As he spoke those words, Zeev Feinberg turned to look for Yaacov Markovitch, but he had disappeared a while ago, when his stomach had begun to ache. Bella Zeigerman frowned in an effort to remember.

"Yaacov Markovitch, the name sounds familiar."

"Of course it does, miss, he's your husband."

Already as a child she, Bella Zeigerman, had refused to accept the world as it was. Her silent complaint, had it been voiced, could be summed up in the question: What? This is all there is? Bella Zeigerman looked at pigeons in the square and at the street lights, examined the color draining from the sky as sunset approached and decided that this couldn't be all there was. A starched cotton napkin. A bottle of milk past its sell-by date. That isn't everything. It can't be everything. Another young woman might have been tempted to join a religious cult. Bella Zeigerman chose poetry. God in his goodness had nothing to offer but the world he had created: pigeons in the square and street lights and starched cotton napkins and bottles of milk. But, unlike God in his goodness, the poet did not restrict himself to six days of creation, but woke each morning to destroy worlds and create them anew.

That is why Bella Zeigerman loved poetry, and loved poets. When she lost her virginity in the bed of a poet, he compared the blood on the sheet to the blooming of a rose, and the pain between her legs grew suddenly sweet. Like a miracle-worker turning a staff into a snake, water into wine, that mortal man had transformed bodily fluid into a flower. Then the war broke out. The poet tried to create a just world with his words and disappeared from his home in the middle of the night. The other poets were also arrested, or fled, or gave in to the government's demands and created all sorts of worlds with their words, worlds that Bella Zeigerman had no desire to visit. After reading a translated poem written by a Hebrew poet in the Zionist newspaper, she decided to emigrate to Palestine. Her parents breathed a sigh of relief. Such a beautiful girl in such difficult times, that was a recipe for trouble.

When Bella Zeigerman became Bella Markovitch and boarded the ship, her parents stopped worrying, but Michael Katz's worries had only just begun. In the damp office on Bar Kochba Street in Tel Aviv, picturing himself commanding the operation, he had planned how he would dupe the Germans or outwit the British. He never thought that the greatest threat to the success of his plan would come from a Jewish girl who weighed in the neighborhood of fifty kilograms. As long as they stayed in the city, Bella Zeigerman's beauty did not have a fatal effect, because the city was large enough for the venom to disperse in its streets and fade without doing any damage. But now it throbbed like a wound in the heart of the ship, the men were drawn to it like flies and the women nested in it like maggots. The ship had sailed in the wrong direction for almost two days because the captain was looking at Bella and not his instruments. There were at least two skirmishes a day when the men mentioned her name. Hava Blubstein's sobs kept the entire ship awake when Hanan told her that, though she was his wife on paper, his heart belonged to Bella.

But even when Hava Blubstein finally fell asleep, along with the rest of the passengers, Yaacov Markovitch's eyes remained open. In fact he had barely closed them since Bella Zeigerman had turned around to face him in the apartment in the eastern part of the city more than two weeks earlier, as if he were afraid she would disappear on him in his sleep and he would never find her. He lay on his back, thinking, as the ship made its way to Israel, to the place where Bella Zeigerman would go on her way and he on his. She to Olympus and he to the village. He almost leaped towards the engine room to order the ship to halt. The adventure of his life would come to an end in another few days, and here he was, returning with an overflowing heart and empty hands.

Yaacov Markovitch wanted to ask Zeev Feinberg for his advice but, without lifting his head, he knew his friend was not in his bed. Since they had set sail from Europe, Zeev Feinberg had spent all his nights on the deck and Yaacov Markovitch assumed that his friend, as methodical as always, was visiting the women's beds in alphabetical order. He was wrong. Ever since Zeev Feinberg had looked into Bella Zeigerman's eyes, which were similar to Sonya's in everything, except that they were a millimeter closer than was considered beautiful, he wanted nothing but to be with her. Zeev Feinberg spent entire nights in the company of Bella Zeigerman telling her of Sonya's virtues and lamenting his past adulteries. Bella, unaccustomed to having a man sit beside her extolling the virtues of another woman, found his presence a refreshing novelty. There was no poetry in him, of that she had no doubt, but he was—unquestionably—the sort of person about whom poetry is written. With his blue eyes and thick mustache, he looked to her like a lesser Odysseus returning to Penelope, and though he had committed adultery on his travels, he had overcome his urge now, in spite of the Sirens' pleas. And plead they did, of that there was no doubt. The mustached Yaffa, though she knew quite well that she would be unable to keep him close to her when they reached Israel, nonetheless hoped that he would treat her kindly while they were still on the ship. And then there was Fruma Shulman, now Greenberg, whose whipped-cream breasts quivered in front of him wherever he went. And Miriam Katz, who at first was filled with pride that fate had married her to the commander of the operation himself, but in no time at all was seeking the proximity of the acting commander. Every night Zeev Feinberg went up to the deck, ignored the winks, responded with a polite nod to the offers, some implicit, some less so, and looked into Bella Zeigerman's eyes until his head became as clear as the water. Then he went down to his bed and slept the sleep of the just.

Yaacov Markovitch didn't know that. He was so immersed in his love for Bella Zeigerman that he spent every moment with his friend talking about her. He didn't ask Zeev Feinberg about his nights and the latter offered no details. After all, he finally had nothing to tell because, since he'd met Bella Zeigerman, he was as pure as a baby.

That night Yaacov Markovitch tossed and turned in his bed, but knew that however much he tossed and turned, he could not divert the path of the ship, which maintained its course straight to the rabbinical court. Finally, when he could no longer bear the voices in his mind, he set out in search of different voices. Perhaps he could listen to the chatter of the couples on deck, perhaps he would be lucky enough to meet Zeev Feinberg on his nocturnal journeys, and perhaps—his heart trembled just thinking about it—he might bump into Bella. Since they had boarded the ship he'd been with her for only several minutes, and the number of words they'd exchanged could be counted, to his great sorrow, on the fingers of one hand. Their longest conversation had taken place in a crowded waiting room the day after their first meeting, a few minutes before their wedding. The Irgun fighters and their fictitious wives had agreed among themselves not to wear fancy clothes as a way of differentiating between the sacred and the profane, between wished-for marriages and no-choice ones. But Yaacov Markovitch shone with a bright light that broke through the admonishing looks of Michael Katz and the chuckles of the men, and Bella Zeigerman, though she did not feel any unusual excitement, glowed in the light that beautiful women have, the light that burns other women and attracts men with its heat. While they were waiting for the rabbi, Yaacov Markovitch gathered all his courage and stood facing Bella Zeigerman. She was half a head taller than he was, so he consoled himself with the thought that she was merely looking straight ahead, which put her glance on the horizon, not on him.

"Are you excited about the journey to Palestine?"

That she would be excited about their marriage was something he dared not expect, but he hoped that the excitement she felt at the proximity of the Holy Land would project a bit onto the means of her reaching it, that is, onto him.

"Definitely. I've read a great deal about the oranges."

Here Bella Zeigerman stopped speaking, and Yaacov Markovitch decided happily that his wife, like him, was a fan of agricultural literature. On the narrow, crowded bookshelf in his house in the village, next to the writings of Jabotinsky, stood all sorts of guides—the mother of wheat and how to improve species, how to plow and plant grain, how to graft a tree without causing pain. Bella Zeigerman knew how to recite Goethe, but it is doubtful that she would be able to memorize, with the same degree of success, the list of insects that threaten to destroy grapevines. When she mentioned oranges, it was because she recalled a line from the Hebrew poet's poem that had been published in the newspaper—

> And the sun, as orange as the ripe orange on the tree
> Fills our hearts with courage on the road to victory.

She had folded the clipping carefully and inserted it into the locket that rested between her breasts. Before that, she had kept the picture of her poet lover in it, but it pained her to think of the picture living longer than the man. She had decided, therefore, to replace it with the words of the Hebrew poet, which were—thank God—a promise for the future and not a monument to the past. It is the nature of words placed close to the skin to bubble their way inward, and indeed the words of the Hebrew poet—flowery, lofty, saturated with the juice of citrus fruit—came into contact with Bella Zeigerman's skin and left a rash on it. Bella Zeigerman scratched a bit and looked with displeasure at her red skin, but did not take off the locket.

"I understand that you like oranges?"

Bella Zeigerman nodded firmly, a large, unequivocal nod that had a small question mark behind it. Did she really like oranges? She had eaten one for the first time the previous summer, and it had seemed wildly expensive to her and ten times inferior to the apple. But from the moment her eyes had fallen on the poem in the newspaper, she yearned for oranges with every fiber of her being. She begged her parents, who granted her one orange a day, even though that meant they had to give up other items. But now she tried to recall the taste of an orange and could not, because she had never actually experienced the taste of the sections she put in her mouth; it was always hidden by the taste of her anticipation. Bella Zeigerman ate the flesh of an orange every day with her eyes glazed, seeing vineyards and green fields, hills carpeted with orchards. And walking among the trees were miracle-workers, turning staffs into snakes, water into wine, blood into roses, and a Hebrew poet reaches out to pick an orange, and look, he holds the sun itself in his hand and gives it directly to Bella Zeigerman.

"Yes," Bella Zeigerman said to Yaacov Markovitch, "I like oranges very, very much."

Yaacov Markovitch promised to buy her oranges the moment they reached Palestine, and Bella Zeigerman fingered the locket on her breast and smiled, and Yaacov Markovitch was filled with joy.

Four days had passed since then. Yaacov Markovitch tried on a host of occasions to continue the conversation, lecturing Bella Zeigerman on the various kinds of oranges, on aphids and modern methods of increasing the yield. But Bella Zeigerman's gaze wandered from him to the sea. "What does she see there?" Yaacov Markovitch asked Zeev Feinberg when he saw him one night. "From the expression on her face, you would think there was a pod of whales in front of us!" But Bella Zeigerman had no interest in whales, just as she had no interest in aphids or improving the yield, or in real oranges. Bella Zeigerman looked at the water because it was opaque, like a mirror, exactly the right substance on which to sail the oranges of her anticipation, an orange trail that would spread from the small ship all the way to far-off Palestine.

Now, after completing 130 tosses and turns in his bed, Yaacov Markovitch realized that he could wait no longer. Only a few days remained until the end of the voyage, and if he wanted to win Bella, the first step he had to take was to get out of bed and look for her. Still wandering on the deck and wondering what the second step would be, Yaacov Markovitch saw the profile of Bella Zeigerman. She was sitting on a crate talking to a man who was sitting with his back to him. The moonlight touched her hair, coloring it with stripes of silver. At that moment, the man said something and Bella Zeigerman burst into laughter. Yaacov Markovitch's heart clenched, but did not break. Deep inside, he knew that only a divine miracle could have brought him together with Bella Zeigerman, so how did he dare to add to that miracle the expectation that she would give herself to him? But then the man turned his head and Yaacov Markovitch's heart broke, because even though he was entirely in darkness, the outline of Zeev Feinberg's thick mustache was discernible in all its curled glory.

6

O N THE LONG NIGHTS he spent trying to stop the ship with the force of his thought, it never occurred to Yaacov Markovitch that he had a partner. In the daytime the deputy commander of the Irgun fulfilled the duties of his office properly. He organized arms shipments and gossiped with senior staff at headquarters and served as the object of admiration for every soldier, male and female. But at night he lay in bed and prayed to the ocean currents to delay the return of Zeev Feinberg a bit. Since he was a rational person, the deputy commander of the Irgun knew that salvation would not come from the ocean currents, so he placed his hope in the human element. Twenty European women on one ship—there had to be one who would capture Zeev Feinberg's heart. Then, when he returned with another woman in his arms, perhaps Sonya would finally stop cursing Zeev Feinberg, for the opposite of love is not hatred and invective, but quiet indifference. But the deputy commander of the Irgun knew in his heart that it was not to be: Feinberg would not find another woman. How could he? After all, even he himself, despite his careful daily search for an alternative to his deaf love, had returned to knock on Sonya's door.

Three days before the ship was scheduled to return, as Sonya's hair lay spread out like a fan on his stomach, he asked her what she would do when Feinberg came back.

"I'll probably beat him black and blue."

"Maybe you don't have a reason, Sonya. Maybe, as they say, it's a blessing in disguise."

Sonya lifted her head. The spot where the velvet of her hair had warmed the stomach of the deputy commander of the Irgun now encountered cold air. She looked at the deputy commander of the Irgun in astonishment. A handsome, kind and brave man, just like Zeev Feinberg. One day they would both become the names of streets at busy intersections. Why stay with one and not the other? But that was precisely why she had to abide by her decision. Otherwise she would spend the rest of her days going from one handsome, kind, brave man to another handsome, kind, brave man. Like a person who covers large distances but never stays in one place long enough to grow a flower. Sonya lay back on the mattress. Her completely average body aroused an emotion in the deputy commander of the Irgun that was not the least bit average. He wanted to compose rhymes to her stomach and adorn her cheeks with words, but since he was more a military man than a poet, he found himself declaring that he would kill anyone who dared raise a hand to her. He luxuriated in her flesh until sunrise, and Sonya, after having given him her body as provision for the journey, opened the door and said, "Now go. Don't come back. And don't say a word to him." Then she kissed him for the last time and whispered, "Ephraim", and the deputy commander of the Irgun ceased being the deputy commander of the Irgun for a moment and went back to being Ephraim, for the last time in his life.

Three days later, the ship entered the Jaffa port. The people on the shore applauded and the women on the deck wiped sweat from their brows. It was hot here. Very hot. Fruma Greenberg's whipped cream breasts collapsed under large drops of sweat. Yaffa Feinberg's mustache glistened in the sunlight. The women drew their only consolation from the discovery that even a resident of Olympus like Bella Zeigerman had sweat glands under her armpits. Their happiness was premature: the two round stains on her dress only made it clear to the men that she was indeed human, not an optical illusion, and they now invested most of their energy in creating connections that would continue after the voyage. And so Bella Zeigerman disembarked with ten men fighting among themselves to carry her baggage, while their legal wives collapsed under the weight of their suitcases. The deputy commander of the Irgun, pale and stooped, stood on the pier and welcomed the arrivals. His handshake was as strong as ever, but the sight of his face frightened the soldiers, and a rumor spread that he had been wounded by a bullet during a mysterious operation several nights earlier. The story of the bullet, as far-fetched as it sounded, was much more logical that any attempt to attribute the look on the face of the deputy commander of the Irgun to a broken heart. Thus the heroism of the wounded commander coming to welcome his people was transformed from rumor to absolute fact, enhancing the status of the deputy commander of the Irgun, and hammering the last nail into the coffin of the person who once was Ephraim Hendel. Yaacov Markovitch was the last to disembark. On the final few days of the voyage he did not leave his compartment and everyone agreed that he had fallen victim to an uncommonly violent case of seasickness. But when the deputy commander of the Irgun shook Yaacov Markovitch's hand, he knew immediately that this was not seasickness, just as Yaacov Markovitch knew that it was not a bullet that had wounded the deputy commander. Yaacov Markovitch and the deputy commander of the Irgun looked at each other as if they were observing their reflections in a mirror, and though they exchanged not a word, each one knew all he needed to know.

When Michael Katz's flowery speech began, the deputy commander of the Irgun realized that he hadn't seen Feinberg. He looked around at the groups of men. Greenberg was there, and also Mosovitch; Gottlieb was exchanging highly meaningful winks with Braverman; and Markovitch stood near the platform looking bereft. There was no sign of Feinberg. Though he didn't want to interrupt Katz's speech, which he had obviously polished and reworked every single day of the voyage, the deputy commander of the Irgun could not restrain himself. While Katz was still talking about the homeland opening its arms to receive the newcomers, he interrupted him and asked, "And where's Feinberg?"

Katz looked angry at the interruption, but pulled himself together when he realized who was speaking. "He jumped off the ship while we were still moving," he said. "He forced us to sail to a spot that suited him, then he simply swam to the shore."

Actually, it hadn't been that simple. Zeev Feinberg was a robust fellow, but all those days on the ship had depleted his strength, and much time had passed since he had swum through the waves, a pregnant illegal immigrant in one hand and chess pieces in the other. When he jumped into the water, the cheers of the men in his ears and the sight of shocked women leaning over the deck warmed his body. But now the ship had disappeared from sight and the sea spread out before him, five kilometers at least before he reached Sonya. He didn't know that she was waiting for him on the shoreline, but nonetheless an unknown force had compelled him to leave the ship before it reached the port, at a spot—so he hoped—that was exactly opposite the path that led to the village.

The idea had entered his mind several days earlier, as he sat with Bella Zeigerman on the deck late at night. He had just finished singing the praises of Yaacov Markovitch in a futile attempt to ignite even the smallest spark of interest in her heart. Bella listened politely, but grew quickly bored by the talk about her first husband, that nice but so-forgettable man, and asked Feinberg what he would do when he saw Sonya. At the end of those long days at sea, Bella Zeigerman felt as close to Sonya as she did to the heroes of legends that had been read to her years ago. Because, truly, she had listened every night to the adventures of Sonya as told by Zeev Feinberg, and already knew how she had delivered a baby with her own hands, and how she had chased off horse thieves by hiding in the bushes and howling like a wolf.

Zeev Feinberg was forced to abandon his attempt to help Yaacov Markovitch, and moved on to other things. He talked about how he would bite Sonya's earlobe and how he would inhale the scent of oranges on her neck and how he would run when she wanted to hit him for his infidelities, which she was more than likely to do. The more he spoke, the worse he felt about the dreary hours he would spend on his way from Tel Aviv to the village, and in the end he came to a decision. "When we get close to Palestine, I'll tell the captain to sail along the shoreline up to the spot that leads inland to the village. Then I'll jump into the water and swim to her." Bella Zeigerman burst out laughing. The moon touched her hair, painting it with silver stripes, which Zeev Feinberg didn't even notice because he was completely engrossed in the plan of his return to Sonya. Suddenly he was seized by a fierce desire to tell the plan to Yaacov Markovitch. He would understand. The illogical did not seem illogical when told to Yaacov Markovitch, and though most of the ship's passengers never gave him more than a passing glance, he was still Zeev Feinberg's best friend.

Zeev Feinberg said goodnight to Bella Zeigerman and hurried to the compartment they shared, where he found the door locked and a note he could barely read: "Very sick. Do not disturb." On the days that followed, he knocked on the door again, at first to ask how his friend was, and later to ask for at least his extra underpants, but the door remained closed. In the end, Zeev Feinberg reconciled himself to the locked door and assumed that he would see his friend during the divorces. When he parted from

Bella, a moment before he jumped into the water, he made her promise to say hello to Yaacov Markovitch for him.

Zeev Feinberg swam vigorously towards the shore. When he got tired he floated on his back for a few moments, but he thought he could smell oranges, and quickly began swimming again. He swam and swam and swam and swam and swam, and then he swam and swam, and then he swam a bit more, and in the end he arrived.

At the same time, Sonya was standing on the beach looking at the water. During his last visit the deputy commander of the Irgun had said that the ship was on its way to the Jaffa port, and it was only habit that made her continue to look at the sea and not southward to the route that Zeev Feinberg would be taking. Waiting on the main road was different from waiting on the beach. Many people walk along the road, and the heart leaps each time anew, then sinks again, fluctuating between hope and disappointment like a ship being tossed in the waves. But no one arrived by sea, just a small crab or an oily seagull, inscrutable messengers whose language is unknown, so that the ear can find in it what it wishes to find. That morning Sonya watched the crabs' dance, the sight inspiring her curses against Zeev Feinberg. "I hope that one of these grabs your penis in its claws... When I get through with you, you'll walk on your side, like them, for the rest of your life." But her voice was weaker than usual and her curses had soured like old milk. After such a long period of waiting, Sonya's anger had faded. True, everyone talked about it, and it had become famous throughout the valley, but that had only made it so unreal that she hardly recognized it.

She hardly recognized Zeev Feinberg either. When he came out of the water—naked, wet, his muscles quivering from the strain and his eyes colored by the depths—she thought she was seeing some kind of Neptune. When he took the first step towards her on the sand the crabs fled, leaving her alone. When he fell to his knees in front of her, exhausted, humbled and grateful, the seagulls took off with a raucous cry. As Sonya looked at the man who had come out of sea her eyes filled with wrath and her mouth filled with words of reproach and anger, as if many days had not passed since she first stood on the beach. Sonya began to curse Zeev Feinberg vociferously. The crabs entrenched themselves in their burrows and the seagulls flew higher, but they couldn't escape the invective. Zeev Feinberg, however, did not try to flee, but rather knelt on the sand, his face raised to absorb the words, a blessed rain of curses and contempt. Finally, Zeev Feinberg stood up and kissed Sonya. His lips were salty from the water and her lips were sweet from the anticipation. He had only just taken his tongue out of her mouth when she began swearing and cursing again, like a bottle after its cork is removed. Zeev Feinberg laughed and picked her up, and Sonya cursed louder. And so they walked to the village, he carrying her in his arms and she cursing him every step of the way.

7

Avraham Mandelbaum had just finished slaughtering a golden calf when he saw Zeev Feinberg through the window, Sonya in his arms, walking down the main path. Feinberg was wearing nothing but a strip of cloth torn from Sonya's dress. At the sound of Sonya's cursing voice all the doors and windows rattled. Avraham Mandelbaum cleaned his knife well. He always cleaned his knife after a slaughter so that the blood of the dead animal would not mix with the blood of the animal that was about to die. On the other side of the butcher's shop, the head of the calf stared at him. Years ago, when he had just begun to work as a slaughterer, he thought he saw anger in the eyes of the dead animals and he didn't like to remain in their presence after dark. Then he thought that it wasn't anger, but rather acceptance, even compassion. Today he knew that there was nothing in the eyes of the calf but what he put there. He put compassion in them and closed the curtain. When he turned around he saw Rachel Mandelbaum, her hand on her stomach. The light was dim, he could barely see her face, but he thought she was smiling.

When he woke up in the morning, Zeev Feinberg was shocked to discover that Sonya was already dressed.

"Where to?"

"Work. Standing on the beach doesn't put bread on the table."

He took her in his arms and said, "Not today. Today you're coming to Tel Aviv with me."

"What do you have to do in Tel Aviv?"

"I have to get a divorce. And get married."

When Zeev Feinberg and Sonya reached Irgun headquarters, they found it noisy and bustling. In addition to the twenty fictitious couples, the building on Bar Kochba Street was filled with soldiers who hadn't been on the mission but had come to lie in wait for the new divorcees, and there were clerks and leaders, public figures and eccentrics. The deputy commander of the Irgun maneuvered among all of them with restrained majesty. On that day he shook more hands that ever before in his life but, as always, he made sure to pause for an additional fraction of a second, causing the other person to believe that there was genuine affection behind the handshake. He felt Sonya's entrance into the room before he saw her, because over the last six weeks he had learned to pick out the smell of oranges even on a busy street. Therefore he had several seconds to compose himself before turning around and facing her in her ordinary blue dress, part of a sweet routine that was not his. The early warning did not help. The deputy commander of the Irgun merely looked at Sonya and paled instantly. Zeev Feinberg, in any case, did not notice it, and hugged him with all his strength.

"My dear, good Froike! What can I say, I really owe you this time." The deputy commander of the Irgun mumbled the few appropriate words he kept in his mind for difficult times of this sort, when his soul was agitated but his mouth did its job. "What did you say? I can't hear you, friend! You have to learn from my Sonya; the whole village heard her screaming at me yesterday." The deputy commander of the Irgun did his best to smile, and since he was a man of many skills he was able to produce an absolutely believable imitation. Zeev Feinberg patted him on the back and kissed Sonya on the cheek, and the deputy commander of the Irgun fingered the pistol in his trousers and drew comfort. Of course he had no intention of hurting Feinberg or himself, but the cold metal cooled the blood in his veins and reminded him that there were many more Arabs to kill, and perhaps the victory of the homeland might sweeten the failure of love. Zeev Feinberg moved onward to the crowd, followed by Sonya, who lingered at the side of the deputy commander of the Irgun for another moment, during which he inhaled deeply of the fragrance of oranges and saw her lips, perfect in their simplicity, whisper, "Thank you."

The men were glad to see Feinberg, and the women stared at Sonya in astonishment. "To live like a Franciscan monk for someone like her?" Yaffa Feinberg burst into tears, and Sonya won the women over when she hurried to offer a handkerchief to her beloved's fictitious wife. She was still comforting the weeping Yaffa when Zeev Feinberg came over and took her hand.

"Come with me. There's someone I want you to meet."

Zeev Feinberg was forced to make his way through the circle of young men surrounding Bella Zeigerman. When they finally stood face to face, he and Sonya opposite Bella Zeigerman, her eyes lit up.

"So the sharks did not devour you in spite of everything."

Sonya exhaled derisively. "What shark would want to take a bite out of such a suckling pig?"

As the three of them laughed, Sonya and Bella appraised each other. Except for their identical eyes they had nothing else in common, but nonetheless they felt an immediate affection for one another. Zeev Feinberg began a formal introduction: "Bella Markovitch—my fiancée, Sonya."

"Markovitch?" Sonya asked with interest, "you're the one who married our Yaacov?"

"Not for long," Bella replied. "The rabbis will be here any minute. Soon, twenty divorced couples will be standing here." She must have spoken too loudly, because Yaffa Feinberg burst into tears again, managing to infect Hava Blubstein as well. Michael Katz saw that and sighed, yearning for the moment he would finally be rid of beautiful troubles like Bella Zeigerman and return to simpler matters like arms smuggling. Then he turned to see where the hell the rabbis were, and to steal a quick glance at the draft of his speech.

After consoling the weeping women, Sonya asked Bella Zeigerman where Yaacov Markovitch actually was, and she replied that she hadn't the slightest idea. "I think he was sick the last few days of the voyage. Yesterday I saw him at the port and gave him regards from our swimmer here. Right after that, they took us to the hostel."

Zeev Feinberg frowned in concern. "Poor fellow. He was really sick. How did he look yesterday?" Bella Zeigerman said that Yaacov Markovitch looked fine, but it would have been more accurate to say that she didn't remember. Since meeting him she had not spent much time looking at his face, and she obviously did not deviate from that practice on a day so full of upheaval as the previous day had been. From the moment she stepped off the ship she had been surrounded by dozens of young Jewish men, all of them looking to her like potential poets. Along with the rest of the women, she was taken to the hostel. The sun blinded her and she could hardly take in the sights on the street. Sweat dripped from her in waves. Unlike the other women, who were moaning about the heat, Bella Zeigerman was happy to sweat, as if all the tears of Europe were pouring out of her; layer after layer of frost and rot flowed from her to the sidewalk and drained into the sea. When she reached the hostel she fell asleep immediately, rocked by the voices of the women, who looked at her and whispered, "A princess". She slept all afternoon and all night, and did not wake up until Fruma Greenberg came to shake her by the shoulders and say, "Come on, Bella, we're getting divorced."

When the rabbis arrived they all applauded. Michael Katz waited until the noise died down and launched into his speech. "This an emotional day for us, a festive day—" But here an angry-faced, long-bearded rabbi interrupted him. "Please, a festive day this is not. Twenty couples getting divorced is not a reason to celebrate. We understand that lives have been saved here, so we do not create difficulties, but please—without festivities." While the stunned Michael Katz was considering the form his protest would take, the rabbi took a list out of his pocket and called the names of Fruma and Yehuda Greenberg. Fruma's whipped-cream breasts quivered in anticipation, and Yehuda looked at them longingly as the couple walked to a side room, accompanied by the rabbis.

For the next half-hour all went according to plan. Married couples entered the small room and emerged from it a few minutes later holding a divorce. Some of them left the room holding hands. Avishai Gottlieb and Tamar Eisenman, for example, agreed to celebrate their divorce at lunch. There were fewer people now. When Zeev Feinberg and Yaffa went in, only Bella and Sonya were left waiting outside.

"Where's Markovitch?" Bella wondered, a small line of worry creasing her perfect brow.

"Maybe he's still sleeping," Sonya tried. "Are you sure he looked healthy yesterday?"

Bella Zeigerman was still racking her brain when Yaacov Markovitch walked into the room. He was pale, and he had lost weight too, but he walked ramrod straight, like a soldier. Sonya ran over to hug him, but at that moment the door to the side room opened, emitting the weeping Yaffa, and Zeev Feinberg's voice boomed from within, "Sonya! Come inside! We're getting married!" Sonya kissed Markovitch's cheek and hurried into the room, her face radiant. Yaacov Markovitch and Bella Zeigerman remained alone. Noontime light shone through the window, reflecting off the painted tiles. Bella Zeigerman was painfully beautiful during all the moments that passed until the door to the side room opened. Zeev Feinberg came out carrying Sonya Feinberg, who was no longer cursing and swearing, but laughing loudly. Her laughter echoed from the walls and caused the rabbis to shift uncomfortably in their seats.

When Zeev Feinberg saw Yaacov Markovitch, his smile broadened. "You're well again! I'd hug you, my friend, but my hands, as you can see—are full." At that point Zeev Feinberg lifted Sonya into the air. "We're going out to get some wine to celebrate the occasion. Just promise me you won't disappear on me before we get back!" Zeev Feinberg did not wait for an answer. And why should he? He held in his arms the sole, basic answer to every question and event that might occur. And the answer was yes.

Yaacov Markovitch and Bella Zeigerman were alone in the room once again. He did not look at her and she did not look at him. Yaacov Markovitch needed all his strength not to look at Bella Zeigerman. Bella Zeigerman did not need any strength not to look at Yaacov Markovitch. Yaacov Markovitch and Bella Zeigerman made a terrible mistake by not looking at each other. Yaacov Markovitch erred by not taking the last opportunity to look at Bella Zeigerman when she was calm, composed and pleasant. Bella Zeigerman erred greatly by not looking at Yaacov Markovitch to see the change in him. Because even though today, as every day, he was still called Yaacov Markovitch, he was nevertheless different. Bella Zeigerman's mistake was more terrible than Yaacov Markovitch's. For she was like someone who wants to cross a river she knows, saying, "I know it flows slowly" and, taking no care, walks into it and drowns because it is winter and the water has risen. Bella Zeigerman did not look at Yaacov Markovitch, who had filled with murky water.

"Yaacov Markovitch," the rabbi's voice called from the side room. Bella Zeigerman walked towards the door. Yaacov

Markovitch stayed where he was. Bella Zeigerman turned around and looked at Yaacov Markovitch in surprise.

Yaacov Markovitch looked at Bella Zeigerman and said, "No."

"What do you mean, no?"

"We are not getting divorced."

For the first time since they'd met, Bella Zeigerman looked at Yaacov Markovitch's face for a long time. A very long time. She examined his face slowly, lingering on the decisive line on his forehead, the hard eyes, the ruler-straight back. Had they been there all this time without her having noticed them, without her having taken the pains to discover these warning signs with one penetrating glance at her husband's face? And perhaps—she thought in horror—perhaps they were all the result of the sea voyage, the rotten fruit of long days of futile anticipation? Now Bella Zeigerman tried to summon up the image of Yaacov Markovitch the first time she met him in the apartment on the outskirts of the city. Although she did not fully succeed in that mission, recalling only the way his mouth had gaped quite ridiculously at the sight of her, she was nonetheless sure that he hadn't had such flinty eyes then. The man had changed. She didn't know exactly when it had happened or why, but such questions do not trouble a trapped animal in any case. Bella Zeigerman looked at Yaacov Markovitch with doe eyes and said, "If you are a man of honor, let me go."

Yaacov Markovitch said to himself, she doesn't want me. And was surprised at how such a trivial fact could cause so much pain. Yaacov Markovitch thought: it is forbidden, forbidden. And for a moment he felt his heart softening, and the same swelling warmth between his knees that you feel after making a decision: return quietly to your home, return to your land and your loneliness. He would return to his home and to the woman from Haifa, who was actually many women, but was always a woman with her legs spread, and even if she tasted different each time, the bitter taste of shame in his mouth on his way home was always the same. He would return to his home and live his life—he would weed the field in the morning, feed the pigeons at noon, browse through Jabotinsky in the evening. The image of Bella Zeigerman would fade in parts: first the eyebrows, then the breasts, and finally the eyes and the earlobes. He would go and forget her more each day, but he would never forget his defeat: to be so close to living his life with a woman like Bella Zeigerman, and not to dare. That thought hardened Yaacov Markovitch's heart again, and again it beat with such defiance that it frightened even its owner. "No," Yaacov Markovitch's heart declared. "No, no, and again no." And that man, who until that day had been all hesitation, a single monotonous, ongoing line of "maybe", felt the "no" round out inside him, filling him. Now he knew that he would not let Bella go. He would live with her, and his life would be pure hell. But he preferred the certainty of hell to an eternity of doubt.

When Zeev Feinberg and Sonya came up the stairs with a bottle of wine they found only a pale Bella Zeigerman in the room, encircled by three black-clad rabbis. The paleness made Bella look like a corpse the rabbis were preparing for burial. Zeev Feinberg and Sonya unconsciously took a step back, the way a healthy person steps back from a sick one, the way a happy man steps back from a sad one. It was a small step, and yet Bella saw it because all her life people had wanted to move closer to her and this time they were trying to move away. Seeing that small step, Bella did something she had not done earlier—neither when Markovitch left despite her pleas, nor when the rabbis swooped down on her with drawn claws and distressing questions:—when she saw Zeev Feinberg's and Sonya's retreat, she burst into tears.

Seeing how shattered Bella was, Sonya hurried to embrace her. She looked into her tear-filled eyes and began to cry as well. Because Sonya's eyes were identical to Bella's and, from now on, one would not be able to cry without the other crying along with her. As they hugged and wept Zeev Feinberg's voice shook the room, one hand holding the now redundant wine bottle, the other clutching the rabbi's beard.

"What the hell is happening here?!"

Hearing his shout, Bella sobbed louder, and the rabbi was dumbstruck. It isn't every day that an angry giant like Zeev Feinberg grabs you by the beard, his eyes furious and his mustache blazing. The two other rabbis began screaming at Feinberg to let their colleague go, and their screams blended with Bella's sobs into an organ and violin duet. Then Sonya spoke in a clear, quiet voice that silenced the two rabbis and caused Zeev Feinberg finally to let go of the remains of the third rabbi's beard.

"It's Markovitch, Zevik. He won't give her a divorce."

Bella stopped crying and looked at Sonya—how had she deciphered the code of her sobbing? However, it wasn't from Bella that Sonya had learned what had happened, but from Markovitch. Unlike Bella, Sonya had looked into Yaacov Markovitch's face when he entered the room, and even though she was full to bursting with happiness and anticipation, she nonetheless saw that his face had hardened. Perhaps it was because she was entirely "yes" that she could feel the "no" taking shape in him. But right then, Zeev Feinberg had called her to come and get married, so Sonya stopped functioning as a seismograph for the feelings of others and abandoned herself totally to her own feelings. Now she blamed herself for the brazen gestures of love she had showered on Zeev Feinberg in front of Yaacov Markovitch. In their pride, they had thought that their openly displayed love was like blessed rain, while in fact it was corrosive acid on the heart of that lonely man.

Zeev Feinberg was having different thoughts. It was not himself that he blamed, and certainly not Sonya, but the seasickness that had attacked his friend and driven him mad. Although he was knowledgeable in all the pleasures of the flesh and all the arts of seduction, Zeev Feinberg was naive. He still did not realize that his friend had not locked himself in his compartment because he was ill, but because the conversation he saw between his wife and his best friend had broken him. Even if Yaacov Markovitch had said to him, "I watched you that night," Zeev Feinberg would not have been the least bit embarrassed because he knew that nothing had happened between him and Bella Zeigerman that night or any other night. Yes, Zeev Feinberg was a naive person who did not know that the things that happen in someone's mind are infinitely more important than the things that happen before his eyes.

The rabbis shifted uncomfortably where they stood. There were other weddings to perform that day, and people to bury, and somewhere there must be a young man who needed to be bar mitzvahed. How much more time would they spend in the company of these three—one woman beautiful enough to tempt the sages, the other one able to guess other people's thoughts, and the man, God help us. They began walking to the door. Zeev Feinberg saw, and rushed towards them. "The husband is sick, gentlemen, his head is spinning. But you can probably give the woman a divorce, after all, she won't stay married because of seasickness." The rabbis needed all their courage to reply that people stay married for reasons much more trivial than seasickness, and that a divorce can only be given with the consent of the husband. If Zeev Feinberg wanted to tear out their beards—let him. A divorce, at any rate, would not be granted here.

The rabbis left the room and Bella resumed crying, this time so hard that it was impossible to believe that such a small body could produce so many tears. Though Zeev Feinberg was already a married man, he was still unable to bear the sight of a woman crying. He poured her a glass of wine and stroked her hair as if she were a little girl, then promised her again that as soon as the last vestiges of his seasickness were gone, Yaacov Markovitch would immediately dissolve their marriage. And Bella Markovitch heard and believed, not because of the power of Zeev Feinberg's claims, but because of the power of her hope.

That evening Michael Katz walked to the house of the deputy commander of the Irgun, and his heart was heavy. An hour earlier Zeev Feinberg had come to his home with that ordinary girl he married and, with them, a weak creature who looked like Bella Zeigerman in every way, except that the color had drained from her face as if it had been wiped off with a rag. His expression serious, Zeev Feinberg told him that Yaacov Markovitch had left Tel Aviv without divorcing Bella Zeigerman, his completely ficti-tious but remarkably legal wife. "I assume that his seasickness has blurred his mind," Feinberg said, "and he'll definitely come here in another day or two to complete the process. In any case, you should report to Froike." Michael Katz looked at Zeev Feinberg resentfully. Wasn't it enough that he'd stolen command of the operation from him? Now he had to brag in front of him by saying the actual name of the deputy commander of the Irgun, a name that Michael Katz himself dared not speak.

"Why don't you tell him, Feinberg. After all, Markovitch joined the operation as your dowry."

"We stood at the door of the headquarters for three hours waiting for him to come back. It's time for us to leave for the vil-lage. Go to his house tonight, maybe by then he'll be back from the operation he must have gone out on. Sonya and Bella and I will wait in my house for a message from you." Feinberg said those last words with his back to Katz, walking towards the door. With his hand on the knob, he turned around. "And remember: Yaacov Markovitch is my friend. If you speak ill of him, I'll make sure you don't speak at all." Zeev Feinberg left. Sonya left. Bella Zeigerman left.

When the door closed, Michael Katz buried his face in his hands. Even if Markovitch were Feinberg's hanger-on, that hanger-on was his, Michael Katz's, responsibility. His first steps as commander would come to a dead halt if he couldn't even make a man like Markovitch carry out his orders.

With a heavy heart he set out to the house of the deputy commander of the Irgun. Twenty meters before the door of the house the smell of oranges reached the nose of Michael Katz. It filled the street, permeated the paving stones, encircled the garbage pails. A British ruse? A diversionary tactic of the Arab Legion? Michael Katz walked cautiously. As he knocked discreetly on the door, he peered all around to make sure no one was following him. Faces filled with surprise sprouted from the windows of the houses, nostrils dilated and noses inhaling the citrus smell. The entire street sought the source of the smell, eyes staring directly at the house of the deputy commander of the Irgun. When the door opened, the sight struck with all its force: hundreds, perhaps thousands of oranges rolled around on the floor. There were large and small ones, orange and green ones, some that had a leaf attached at the apex and some that had no trace of the tree from which they had come. The deputy commander of the Irgun turned to walk inside and Michael Katz followed, struggling to maintain his balance among the rolling obstacles. In vain. Just as the deputy commander of the Irgun finished moving oranges from one sofa to another and sat down, Michael Katz stumbled on one of the damned pieces of fruit and fell flat on the floor. When he raised his head in embarrassment the deputy commander of the Irgun looked at him with his orange-tinted face and said, "I assume that I have to explain myself."

"No!" Michael Katz shouted, still trying to haul himself up over a pile of oranges, "Absolutely not! I understand completely, sir, a brilliant ruse, to camouflage the smell of explosive materials with the smell of oranges, a truly magnificent idea! This way we can finally put one over on those British bastards!"

The deputy commander of the Irgun stared at Michael Katz, his expression unreadable. Then he smiled bitterly. Even the mad love of Ephraim Hendel, a madness that could not be ignored, that had filled his apartment with thousands of oranges—even that madness had been co-opted from Ephraim Hendel and turned into a further episode in the heroic saga of the deputy commander of the Irgun. The thought briefly crossed his mind that if he went totally insane from missing Sonya so much, everyone would say that the British had something to do with that too.

Michael Katz finally managed to stand up and now wanted a place to sit. The deputy commander of the Irgun made a place for him at his side on the sofa and Michael Katz's heart trembled with admiration and fear. Admiration for the exalted personage he was sitting next to, and fear of what he was about to say. Then Michael Katz began to describe Zeev Feinberg's visit and the things he had told him, ignoring Zeev Feinberg's warning and roundly vilifying Yaacov Markovitch. If the guilt were placed on Markovitch, there was hope that it would remove itself from Michael Katz. He might have commanded the operation, but he could in no way be considered responsible for such behavior. "And the terrible thing is that, in my opinion, Feinberg is wrong. It's not seasickness. He just isn't planning to let her go."

The deputy commander of the Irgun listened carefully. Michael Katz's fears began to subside. The terrible scenarios he had created in his mind had been proven false: the commander did not pound his fist on the arm of the sofa, did not raise his voice in rebuke, did not interrogate Katz with accusatory questions. The expression on his face looked more like curiosity and amusement than anything else, accompanied by a tinge of appreciation.

"So you think he'll continue to refuse."

"Exactly! Think about it—a worm like Markovitch who has miraculously been handed a ripe fruit like Bella Zeigerman… Uncommitted to the idea of nationhood, to this crucial moment in time, to the stain he is leaving on our noble operation in the eyes of history."

As Michael Katz continued to speak about the eyes of history, the deputy commander of the Irgun was thinking about eyes that had nothing to do with history. The ones that stole into its pages not to record themselves in the ink of courageous action, but surreptitiously to tear off a corner of one of them. The deputy commander of the Irgun, whose actions eternity had appropriated and used for the sole purpose of sanctifying the redemption of the country, could not help feeling jealous of Yaacov Markovitch, who was indeed a worm, but it is the way of worms to be free of the burden of history.

In the end, Michael Katz saw that his commander was not listening to him. The deputy commander of the Irgun was staring at the oranges in the room with dull eyes and the thought passed briefly through Michael Katz's mind that it was madness, not cunning, that had brought hundreds of oranges to this place. But Michael Katz immediately stifled his heretical thoughts, said goodbye to his commander and turned to go.

"Give him a week," the deputy commander of the Irgun said. "If he doesn't give her a divorce within a week, I'll go to the village."

8

T HEY FOUND HIM in the yard of his house, feeding the pigeons. How happy it had made him to see that the birds had waited for him, that they hadn't taken wing to other villages and other breadcrumbs. Now he was scattering handful after handful for them, unable to stop, because they were the only ones who had waited for him to return. The writings of Jabotinsky rested on his table, but he didn't want to read them again. What use were flowery language and big words to him? He had already had his great moment in life. Now all that remained were the breadcrumbs and the pigeons. And there were also the visitors. At first, Feinberg alone. Then Sonya. And then the deputy commander of the Irgun, who admonished him with his tongue and envied him with his eyes. They talked and asked and shouted and stamped their feet. They rebuked and cursed and threatened that he would be punished by both God and man. Yaacov Markovitch genially offered them tea and almonds and locked the gate when they left and clung to his "no" the way a drowning man clings to a plank.

Later, others came, with real planks in their hands. Michael Katz had thought up the idea, but the deputy commander of the Irgun did not object. As sympathetic as they might feel towards Markovitch, such a disgrace could not be allowed to continue. Michael Katz assembled the most violent men, the ones whose aggressive urges sizzled inside them and were about to erupt anyway, so it was better for someone to at least channel the flow in the right direction. A week earlier they had broken the legs of an Arab cart driver who blocked their way as he unloaded merchandise in the port. That kept them quiet for a while, but now Katz saw in their eyes the same hunger for action that drove them over the edge. This time he gave them Markovitch. They knocked on his door at about eight o'clock, and Yaacov Markovitch opened it with an expression that said he had guessed their reason for coming. The entire event took less than five minutes, and when it was over Yaacov Markovitch was left with two teeth short of a full set, a broken rib, a black eye and the promise of a return visit if he didn't give Bella a divorce. But as the blows rained down on him he thought about the reason for them, a reason in the shape of Bella, and Yaacov Markovitch took the blows with a grateful smile on his face.

Yaacov Markovitch lay on his back for a while, in the same spot the men had left him. Through his swollen eyes the stars looked especially large. An ordinary person finding himself outside at night is excited by the stars, but something urgent always calls him home. A child to feed, a sock to mend, something down-to-earth that cannot be put off. But that night Yaacov Markovitch knew he would put off everything. He would lie on his back and look at the small stars through his healthy eye and the large stars through his painful eye. He drew great serenity from the fact that, even though the world had turned upside down, the Big Dipper still appeared at its regular time and in its regular place. Finally, Yaacov Markovitch fell asleep within his pain. When he woke up, his body frozen and his head spinning, he saw that while he had been asleep strings of blood had run onto his chin. Still fuzzy, he thought the strings were saliva, the kind that had dribbled from his mouth when he was a child and fell asleep on his mother's lap of an evening. But when he regained consciousness he realized that he was not lying on his mother's lap but on the hard ground, and the taste of blood was nauseating and bland. Yaacov Markovitch looked angrily at the Big Dipper. It didn't care whether it shone down on a child dozing on a woman's lap or a man whose blood dribbles down his face as he sleeps. He no longer wanted to look at the stars.

At one in the morning, Yaacov Markovitch knocked on Zeev Feinberg's door. He said that he'd come to ask for an antiseptic and a bandage. In fact he'd come to him to have the affront to his person disinfected and his humiliation bandaged. Zeev Feinberg gave him the first but withheld the second. He didn't ask, "Who did this", and he didn't cry, "We'll go after them", he didn't even insult the bitch that had given birth to them after a one-night stand with a pig. Zeev Feinberg bandaged Yaacov Markovitch's wounds with a practiced hand, cleaned the liquid that had accumulated in his eye and pulled out a third tooth that was jiggling. And when he had finished he opened the front door and told him to leave.

The men kept their word. Every few nights Yaacov Markovitch knocked on Zeev Feinberg's door. Once he came in with a broken nose, another time he limped in on a leg that had been properly stomped, and still another time he remained in the doorway because he was afraid he would faint if he took another step. Each time Zeev Feinberg tended to him loyally and silently, then sent him on his way without another word. Sometimes Yaacov Markovitch found himself waiting for a visit from the men so he could go to his friend's house again, where the door was open to him now only in exchange for sacrificial blood. Sonya and Bella knew nothing about those nocturnal visits. When Yaacov Markovitch knocked on the front door they were deeply asleep, each woman with her dream (though sometimes the dreams of one dripped into the sleep of the other, as sometimes happens to people who live in the same house). But one day Sonya wanted to put some disinfectant on a cut she'd got while cooking and saw that the bottle of iodine was almost empty.

"Does he come here a lot?"

"Every third night."

Sonya turned her back on him. Zeev Feinberg sympathized with her. The tears that Bella had shed in Sonya's arms were enough to irrigate three orange groves; how could she find compassion for the man who had caused them? Zeev Feinberg looked at his wife's straight back, at her hand placing the iodine bottle on the table. He stood up to go over to her but bumped into the table, causing the bottle to tip over. Drops of iodine fell onto the tablecloth, spreading quickly into an expanding purple circle that seeped into the fibers of cotton until it changed from a circle into a monstrous butterfly. Zeev Feinberg looked at the butterfly, mesmerized. Suddenly he noticed the slight trembling of his wife's shoulders.

"Enough, dear, don't be angry." But when he touched her shoulders he realized that it wasn't anger that shook them, but tears.

"That poor man. That poor, poor man."

Michael Katz's men began to tire. Half a day just to get to the village, half a day to get back, and in between maybe five minutes of professional satisfaction. And anyway, that Markovitch was a very problematic target. He didn't defend himself, didn't try to return the blows, so you felt like you were beating a rag doll, not a person (not a doll, Michael Katz tried to explain to them, a reed, a reed that bends in the wind so it never breaks and is unvanquished in its wretchedness). Yaacov Markovitch did not see himself as a reed or a rag doll. Such metaphors had no place in the mind of a person beaten to the ground. Yaacov Markovitch kept only one image in his brain while he was being pummeled by the men, the image of Bella. Every fist that pounded him carried with it, apart from the pain, a reminder of the reason for its existence as well. Recalling the image of Bella's face was enough to anesthetize Yaacov Markovitch's pain.

In the end Michael Katz's men decided to go out on one more persuasion mission, during which, perhaps from an excess of motivation, Yaacov Markovitch's right arm was broken. When Zeev Feinberg saw the broken arm he could keep quiet no longer.

"But why, damn it, tell me why."

Yaacov Markovitch looked at him in surprise. During the last month he had grown used to his friend's silence, which at first had grated on his ears but in the end had enveloped him like a womb. Now that Feinberg had finally spoken to him, he realized how much he had missed the sound of his voice.

"Because I love her."

"But she doesn't love you, friend. She doesn't love you. How can you hold on to her for your whole life now, with only the power of Jewish law? She'll hate you so much that your blood will dry up and she'll cut your throat in the middle of the night."

"My blood was already dried up, Feinberg. That's what you don't understand. That's what you and Sonya and the deputy commander of the Irgun and all those thugs that come to visit me don't understand. That my blood was dried up. That nothing flowed in my veins but the waiting for something finally to happen. Did you ever have to wait for something to happen to you? No. People like you don't have to wait. Things come to people like you. How to walk. How to speak. How to laugh. But people like me have to wait for something to happen to them. And when it finally does, it ends right away. Bam! Here's the most beautiful woman you've ever seen. Bam! She's married to you. Bam! She's not! Bam! I need that beauty beside me, Feinberg. I need that beauty beside me because heaven doesn't send you something like that twice. If you don't hold on to her very, very tight, if you let her go because someone breaks your tooth or your arm, then you obviously don't deserve her. And she will love me, I'm telling you, in the end, she'll love me. I'll wait quietly and patiently, I'll work hard, I'll show her that I deserve her. In the end, she'll love me."

Zeev Feinberg sighed. He finished bandaging Markovitch's arm, which in the meantime had turned a shade of gray. Then he went to the front door and opened it. "You're my best friend, Markovitch. But you'll enter this house again only as a divorced man."

Bella had spent more than two months in Sonya and Zeev Feinberg's house. Every evening they left her and went to try and persuade her husband. Every evening they returned, their eyes downcast. She spent the days feeling sorry for herself, which is an excellent way to spend time, except that it ruins your complexion. Bella did not realize how much it had ruined her complexion until the deputy commander of the Irgun came to visit them, because she saw how much he looked at Sonya's face and never at hers. Bella was extremely upset and instantly stopped feeling sorry for herself. She used the newly available time for other things, and began to help with the housework. A week later the deputy commander of the Irgun arrived again, apparently only to try and convince Markovitch. If a commander's threats did not help, maybe the sound of a friend's voice would. Strange: when he said that, he was not looking at Bella Zeigerman but at Sonya. Bella, who was used to having all eyes on her, felt the lack of it the way a person feels the lack of his wallet when he discovers that he's lost it.

In the end, Bella realized that she had to leave. Feinberg and Sonya did not urge her to go, but a small cloud covered their faces when they looked at her, and they no longer tried to choke down their giggles at night. Nonetheless, when she told them of her intention Sonya protested.

"But where will you go?"

"What do you mean, where will she go?" Zeev Feinberg said in surprise, "to Markovitch! If he hasn't given her a divorce, then she's his wife. His home is her home. His money—her money. In that, at least, he has to act like a man of honor."

One Sunday morning Yaacov Markovitch awoke to the sound of loud knocking on his door. At first he was afraid that the men were back to beat him up, now of all times, when most of his wounds had healed. Still in his pajamas, he got out of bed and hurried to the living room. He opened the door, and standing in front of him was his wife. Bella Markovitch was even more beautiful that Sunday morning than she was on other mornings. It was cold outside, and Yaacov Markovitch closed the door quickly after she came in. He realized immediately that the cold had entered the living room. Yaacov Markovitch turned on the kerosene heater, thinking it would warm them. He was wrong. From the moment Bella Markovitch entered the home of Yaacov Markovitch, it never warmed up again.

9

B ELLA MARKOVITCH'S WAR against Yaacov Markovitch was
long and hard. If the name of that war is unknown it's not
because it lacked life-and-death battles, clever maneuvers or bitter
casualties. It was Bella Markovitch's bad luck that her war took
place at a time when everyone was fighting. The Jews in Europe
were fighting for their lives. The French for the last vestiges of
their honor. The Russians for their icy steppes. The British for
their empire. And when they fought, all the others fought as
well—the Chinese and the Japanese and the Indians and the
Africans. And at the same time, the regular wars were continuing—wolves fought to devour their victims, rabbits fought not to
become victims. Larger fish ate smaller fish. Birds of prey cast a
shadow over field mice. And at the same time, Bella Markovitch
kept fighting for her freedom. Though there was no mention of
that war in the official sources—not a word in the newspapers or
in nature books—the villagers nonetheless followed it breathlessly.

"Listen, she didn't sleep at home yesterday either."

"The lights were on in his house till a quarter to three."

"She'll kill him with all that flirting."

"And what did he do to her? A lot worse!"

The villagers were horrified by what Yaacov Markovitch had
done to Bella Markovitch. They were so horrified that they never
stopped talking about it for even a moment. When he passed them
on the street they shook their heads in condemnation, and when

they saw him in the fields they clicked their tongues in disapproval. When conversation around the table lagged, the mention of his name was enough to bring everyone to life with after-dinner fire. And when two farmers were having an argument that was escalating into a fully fledged fight, each one tried to find a way to slip Yaacov Markovitch into the conversation, and in no time at all they would be united in their condemnation and tongue-clicking. Yaacov Markovitch did the village a great favor by refusing to divorce Bella Markovitch: it was such a terrible thing to do that the villagers only had to look at him to feel instantly pure.

They also liked to look at Bella Markovitch, albeit for different reasons. Though they had not known her before Yaacov Markovitch had refused to give her a divorce, they could still imagine how that kind of beauty would have worked on them if it were unleashed. The men's desire and the women's jealousy would not have fallen short of those experienced by the ship's passengers, because although the village was surrounded by orchards, not the sea, many would have considered it an island of sorts. Europe was blessed to be large enough to contain beauty the likes of Bella Markovitch's. But Palestine was small, and the village even smaller. If Bella had entered it as a free woman, the men would have loved her and the women would have hated her. But since she entered it as she did, a magnificent animal living under lock and key, the men liked her and the women felt sorry for her. Affection and pity, those were the appropriate feelings for such a small village. The gods had finally punished Bella Markovitch for her beauty, and now people could bear it.

For the first time in her life she had girlfriends. Every day Sonya came with gifts. Seashells (if you just touched one of them, your mouth filled with the taste of salt and your ears with the sound of waves), and a lamb from the pen (Bella pressed her cheek against its damp nose and cried because she remembered the softness of the black velvet in the fabric shop), and a loaf of hot, slightly burnt bread that they ate right then and there, making fun of their hunger with hot brown laughter. After a month Rachel Mandelbaum also arrived, her stomach growing larger from day to day, and she carried it in front of her proudly, like a child holding a balloon he bought at a fair. "I thought you might like to learn Hebrew." Bella replied that she would like to very much, and after that Rachel did not stand alone in the butcher's shop. Avraham Mandelbaum would look at them in amazement, not understanding why his wife wanted to immerse herself in the imprisoned beauty's sadness. It never occurred to him that not just one imprisoned beauty was standing there in the butcher's shop but two, and he did not see that, when Rachel Mandelbaum immersed herself in Bella's sadness, she was washing off some of her own.

The joy of compassion helped lighten Rachel Mandelbaum's mood, but her pregnancy helped even more. As the days passed, Rachel's longing for the life she had lost was replaced by anticipation of the life she was going to live. She no longer thought about the Austrian soldier Johann, and no longer yearned for the glitter of snow. A baby girl was growing in her stomach, ten soft fingers and eyes serenely closed. When Rachel Mandelbaum felt sadness coming on, she quickly drove it away with the blue eyes of the baby girl in her womb, and the sadness was no match for that blueness. For days at a time Rachel looked into those blue eyes of her baby girl, inhaled her sweet scent, heard her laughter. The baby's laughter struck her stomach in waves, and they rose and washed over her face, small ripples of smiles that warmed Avraham Mandelbaum's heart and even gave Bella pleasure. That disappeared when Bella returned to Yaacov Markovitch's house. She never called that building home, only "Markovitch's house", two words that conveyed clearly that, while she slept and ate and bathed there, it was not her home. She didn't sweep the living room, to which Markovitch had been banished, and she didn't clean the bedroom, where she lived. If she picked flowers on her way back, she threw them away before entering the house. She left her dresses creased in her suitcase, even though the white wardrobe Markovitch had installed for her stood with doors gaping in anticipation. Every now and then she spent a few nights in a different bed, not out of sexual desire but with the cold calculation of an accomplished general. Bella Markovitch had sworn to make Yaacov Markovitch miserable even if she had to make herself miserable in the process and so, even though she missed Rachel and Sonya fiercely, she occasionally left the village for several weeks without saying a word, only to increase his pain.

Yaacov Markovitch did not search for her. He worked in the field and fed the pigeons and poured tea into the glasses of Zeev Feinberg and Sonya, who occasionally came to plead with him, and into the glass of the deputy commander of the Irgun, who came on weekly persuasion visits, spending less and less time with Markovitch and more and more time giving reports when Sonya was present. During that period, though he didn't move from where he sat, Markovitch's mind would wander through the country. He saw Bella in the arms of workers in the Jaffa port, swimming in the waters of Lake Kinneret with the fisherman of Tiberias, leaning on the wall of Jerusalem in the embrace of a British officer. He saw her putting socialism into practice on kibbutzim, riding a horse through the orchards, driving Hasidim mad in the Galilee, learning the art of the recorder from a Bedouin. He listened to her moans, saw her body arch and tore chunks of bread from the loaf with such anger that the pigeons no longer wanted to eat from his hand. Nonetheless he did not go after her, but left the kerosene lamp burning because he was afraid she would return in the dark and not find the house. Yaacov Markovitch did not know how much he disappointed his wife: when she came back and saw the glimmer of light in the distance she hoped that the house was burning down with him inside, but when she came nearer she found the house still there and its owner inside, living, breathing and intransigent.

When Bella came back from her travels, the burning jealousy that had roasted the walls of the house vanished and the coldness returned. Yaacov Markovitch found himself lighting the fire even at the end of April and wondered whether the temperature of the house would ever be suitable for human habitation again. Every time Bella disappeared, Markovitch poured rivers of sweat and fantasies. Every time she returned, Markovitch shivered with the frost that blew through the rooms. The stone walls that he was so proud of, that sheltered the house from winter cold and kept out the summer heat, those walls had fallen under the spell of evil magic that had only one purpose: to make Yaacov Markovitch's life difficult every single minute. If he brought fruit from the orchard to the kitchen the cold damaged it, making it inedible. And if he threw off his blanket with his tossing and turning at night he woke up with a cold and a cough, as if he had been sleeping outdoors. Bella, meanwhile, adjusted to the whims of the house without any problem, almost as if she had summoned them there herself. True, the cold cut through to her bones too, and sometimes she wondered how it was possible for there to be a snowstorm inside when it was so warm outside, but she liked the thought that the house was a replica of the natures of its inhabitants. A house with walls that are not indifferent to the people they contain. The greater her hatred for the man in the house grew, the more affection she felt for the house itself. She continued to call it "Markovitch's house", but she often stroked a cool wall with her hand, and once even pressed a soft cheek against a door frame.

In the evening, when Markovitch fed the pigeons bread-crumbs, Bella tasted some crumbs of her own: she took off her locket, removed the newspaper clipping and read the words of the Hebrew poet, the words that had seduced her into coming here, to Palestine.

And the sun, as orange as the ripe orange on the tree
Fills our hearts with courage on the road to victory.

Was the sun really as orange as an orange? Sometimes, when she went walking with Rachel and Sonya right before sunset, they would see the flaming ball on its way to the sea. Sonya would say, "Look at them, like two lovers about to meet," and Rachel would say, "Like a suicide about to sink to his death," and Bella would say, "Like an optical illusion, an optical illusion, that's all. They're millions of kilometers apart, that's what we always forget." At those moments the sun was orange, like an orange, but not at other moments. Sometimes it was red, like the evil eye of a dying bull, and sometimes, on those smoggy days she despised, the sun was the color of a runny egg white. She could never guess, from looking at the sun one day, what color it would be the next. That was not true about the Hebrew poet's words, which were fading on the newspaper clipping at a regular, almost imperceptible pace. At first, the dark black turned black. Then dark blue. Then a gray tone crept in. On the day when the "c" in the word "courage" faded, Bella decided to seek out the Hebrew poet. She said not a word to Yaacov Markovitch when she left, but when he saw that she was taking all her dresses with her he understood that she might never return. In her absence he allowed himself to do what he did not do in her presence: he took a plain nightdress that she had left behind and fell asleep with it in his arms. Sometimes he was afraid she might return in the middle of the night and find him holding an item of her clothing without her permission, but he could no longer fall asleep if the sleeves of the nightdress were not wound around his arm. Anyone peering through Yaacov Markovitch's window would certainly wonder whether he had lost his mind. Yaacov Markovitch himself sometimes wondered exactly the same thing.

10

THAT MORNING, Rachel Mandelbaum woke up with a craving for grapes. It was hot, and her tongue felt like sandpaper against her palate. Avraham Mandelbaum had left early for Haifa. He would return at night with new knives. When he left, the rooster in the yard crowed with joy, and all the animals in the village breathed a sigh of relief. The slaughterer is gone, won't be back till evening. The sheep bleated more loudly. The chickens became brazen. And Rachel Mandelbaum lay in her bed and thought about how much some grapes would sweeten her mouth now. The baby girl in her stomach kicked in approval. She too, it seemed, wanted grapes. And perhaps from the outset it was the baby's craving and not the mother's. Either way the desire was very great, and it sent Rachel out of bed.

Her breasts were full and heavy, and milk often oozed onto her nightdress. When Avraham Mandelbaum noticed it he looked away quickly, but the brightness radiating from his face filled the room. Now Avraham Mandelbaum was on his way to Haifa, and Rachel Mandelbaum wanted grapes. She was prepared to kill for grapes. Rachel Mandelbaum put on her very wide dress and went out into the field to look for a bunch forgotten on the vine.

Since becoming pregnant, Rachel Mandelbaum did not leave the house very often. Once, jealousy had made Avraham Mandelbaum watch her every move. Now it was concern. When she went into the fields Rachel Mandelbaum realized that she had not gone walking alone for quite a few days. The baby girl in her stomach kicked again to remind her that she wasn't alone now either. Rachel Mandelbaum stroked her stomach and whispered, "*Sha, sha*," partly to soothe the baby, partly to soothe herself. How beautiful the field looked to her that morning, even though it was nothing but thorns and soil. But, from looking at the thorns, she could guess the kind of flowers that would bloom, the way she could guess what her baby girl would be like from the kicks against the wall of her womb. She would weave those flowers into a crown for her daughter that she would place on her silky, golden hair. Though Rachel had thick black hair, and Avraham Mandelbaum's hair was brown and frizzy, she nevertheless knew that her baby girl's hair would be golden, like wheat, and she knew that looking at it would fill her like bread. She would have a girl, small and beautiful, and she would clothe her in dresses and knit a scarf for her neck. If Avraham Mandelbaum gave her nothing but that, it was enough.

Rachel walked for more than an hour among the paths in the fields. The heat distorted her perception: wherever she thought she saw a vine, it turned out to be dry earth. Finally she sat down under a carob tree, exhausted. Now she no longer wanted grapes, only water. Clear, fresh water that would soften the sandpaper in her throat. Rachel Mandelbaum tried to stand up, but couldn't. The carob tree spun around her, its fruit brown, admonishing tongues: why did you come out to the fields alone? In your ninth month—how irresponsible. You wanted grapes, you couldn't control yourself. Rachel Mandelbaum closed her eyes so she wouldn't see the carobs or hear their rebukes. The rebukes were quickly silenced. Now she could only hear her heart beating between her temples. You're dehydrating, she whispered to herself, and the pounding between her temples joined in: de-hy-dra-ting, de-hy-dra-ting, de-hy-dra-ting. The rhythm and the meaning of the word, at first so ominous, began to take on the sound of a lullaby, and Rachel rocked with it until her eyes closed. She woke up in a puddle of water. She looked up immediately to bless the clouds that had taken pity on her, but the sky was painfully blue. Not from above had the water come, but from below, from her own body. Rachel reached between her legs with two trembling fingers. It can't be. It's too soon. And then a sharp stab of pain unlike any she had felt before seized Rachel, causing her voice to shake and making it clear to her that yes, it can be.

A woman was about to give birth beside a carob tree, and evening was falling. Her husband was gone and would not return until nightfall. Her parents were far away, across the sea. The path was empty. Rachel Mandelbaum listened to the sounds. A branch breaking nearby, thorns moving as a field mouse scurried through them. The madness of the birds as evening approached. But the sound of human footsteps, the sweet sound of human footsteps, she heard only in her mind. Or perhaps not? Because now she heard the steps clearly, the sound of thorns snapping under soles, a man's breathing. She couldn't be imagining them. And there, at the bend in the road, Yaacov Markovitch appeared, looking worried. He hadn't seen Bella for more than two months. He continued to sleep with her nightdress in his arms, but the cloth had lost the scent of its owner and all that remained was a scentless nightdress. When he realized that it didn't matter how much he strained his nostrils, how close he put the cloth to his nose, it no longer held even the smallest trace of the body that had worn it, he got out of bed and knocked on Zeev Feinberg's door. "From now on, I'll guard the fields at night. There's no need for shifts anymore. I don't sleep anyway."

Zeev Feinberg opened his mouth to speak, then changed his mind and nodded. The next day the villagers learned that they were exempt from guard duty at night, thanks to Yaacov

Markovitch, and while they hadn't the slightest wish to show him any gratitude, they nonetheless resumed nodding at him when they passed him on the main street. Frequently the nod lasted only until Markovitch passed, when it was replaced by the sound of tongue-clicking. Thus, the villagers could be grateful and condemning at the same time. Yaacov Markovitch patrolled the village every night, a rifle in his hand, his eyes searching. Bella might return suddenly, and he would protect her against Arab rioters and Jewish lovers; he would escort her to their home in the thick darkness and tell her how beautiful the night was. He left for his patrol earlier each night; he hurried out when the sun had only begun to sink, before the walls began to trick him with optical illusions. Because at twilight, when shadows grew longer, the house would launch its attack: making Markovitch think he heard the steps of a woman approaching the door, moving a branch of the bougainvillea to make it look like a silhouette through the curtain. Yaacov Markovitch saw and yearned, and when he could no longer bear the yearning, he went out on patrol early.

When Rachel Mandelbaum saw Yaacov Markovitch she moaned loudly, a sound that combined despair, hope and labor pains. For one happy moment Yaacov Markovitch thought that the woman under the tree was none other than Bella, but when he saw the mound of her stomach he realized his mistake. Yaacov Markovitch barely had time to feel his disappointment because Rachel's words reached his ears: "Markovitch, I'm giving birth."

Yaacov Markovitch had helped birthing cows many times, and when he had smuggled weapons to the south he had even watched a camel being born. But Rachel Mandelbaum was far from being either a cow or a camel, and he was a farmer, not a doctor. Those thoughts led Yaacov Markovitch to say, "I'll get help," and begin to run, but after less than ten meters he again heard her moan. Though Rachel Mandelbaum's voice was different from the voices of cows about to calve, Yaacov Markovitch turned back, because he recognized from the sound that the moment was very near. Yaacov Markovitch knelt at Rachel Mandelbaum's side and wiped the perspiration from her brow. He gave her some water to drink and held her hand and whispered soothing words that even he did not know if he believed. Rachel Mandelbaum's labor pains came more frequently now, and she held Yaacov Markovitch's fingers so tightly that he was afraid they would break. But he didn't take his hand away, and only said, "Push, push," because he remembered the voice of the midwife ordering his mother, "Push, push," coming from the other room, and remembered the tension on the face of his father, who was with him in the living room, and he remembered the terrifying silence that filled the house when his mother finished pushing and the baby was out, and there was no crying. Perhaps Yaacov Markovitch might have wondered a bit at that memory, the memory of the night after which the house grew silent and his father began to avoid his mother and his mother began to avoid life itself, but Rachel Mandelbaum's screams nailed him to the present and kept him there. Now she screamed loudly and Yaacov Markovitch hoped that in one of the houses in the village someone would hear and say, "Hurry up, to the fields!" But the houses in the village were filled with the clamor of clicking tongues and nasty remarks and nods and embraces, and no one noticed that it wasn't the wind moaning outside, but Rachel Mandelbaum.

After hours of labor Rachel Mandelbaum's screams took on a new form, a German one. The lock she had placed on her lips to keep that language inside on the day she got off the ship was smashed by every stomach-stabbing pain until it burst open. Rachel could not express such cutting pain, such terror, in any language but German. From the moment her mouth filled with the taste of that language, she could not stop it. In the breaks between the pains, which were growing shorter, she wept in her mother tongue for all the things she had left behind and were gone forever. The halls where the dances were held, the cobblestone streets, the Austrian soldier Johann in his beautiful velvet jacket, the Jew with the shattered skull who had sent her from Vienna to the ship, and Avraham Mandelbaum, who took her from the port to be a slaughterer's wife. Yaacov Markovitch wanted to cover his ears because he knew he was witnessing an inner torrent, a subterranean stream erupting suddenly from the ground in front of an uninvited witness. He felt more embarrassed in the presence of Rachel Mandelbaum weeping for her past in German than he had felt on the night he'd seen her breasts. Because now he was seeing her stark naked.

The moon had begun to shine when Rachel Mandelbaum stopped crying and called out in German, "She's coming!" Yaacov Markovitch peered embarrassedly between Rachel Mandelbaum's legs. His embarrassment turned into joy when he saw the small, red head bursting into the world. He grabbed the baby's head and shouted at Rachel, "Push! Push!" and Rachel pushed and pushed, and then the baby finally emerged, and for one terrible moment there was silence.

For only one moment, because right then the small lungs filled with a bitter cry. Yaacov Markovitch took a penknife out of his pocket and cut the umbilical cord, wrapped the baby in his shirt as it continued to cry, and then put the crying baby boy into its mother's arms. He thought how right the baby was to cry, because he remembered Bella and the cruelty of the world; and then he thought how wrong the baby was to cry, because he once again felt the touch of his head in his hands at the moment he was born, and was filled with compassion.

Rachel Mandelbaum clutched Yaacov Markovitch's shirt, from which a human cub, red with crying, was screaming at her. For close to nine months she had waited for this moment, the moment she would hold her golden-haired, blue-eyed, pale-skinned, fragrant baby girl in her arms. Lying in Yaacov Markovitch's shirt was a black-haired baby with Avraham Mandelbaum's face. The face of the baby girl had been so alive in her mind after all the time she had spent in her company that she almost handed the boy to Markovitch and said, "It's a mistake." Instead she gave Markovitch back his shirt with her son inside it and whispered, "Take care of him until I get my strength back." But she actually meant, "Who is this boy that grew in my stomach while my heart yearned for another?" So exhausted were Yaacov Markovitch and Rachel Mandelbaum—she from the efforts of giving birth and he from the efforts of helping her—that they fell asleep on the spot a few moments later. When the villagers arrived, led by Avraham Mandelbaum, the baby was sleeping in the arms of Yaacov Markovitch.

Avraham Mandelbaum raced forward, the villagers several meters behind him. The gap could be attributed to Avraham Mandelbaum's fervor, but also to the fears of the villagers. Although they wanted to help the slaughterer find his pregnant wife who had disappeared, none of them wanted to be in close proximity to him if the search turned into a tragedy. During the months of Rachel's pregnancy the villagers had learned to like Avraham Mandelbaum, who had begun to hum when he was at work in the butcher's shop and had begun to pick violets for Rachel to make her happy. At first they ridiculed the change, imitating the clumsy slaughterer's humming and picking violets that they gave to their wives, gesticulating extravagantly. But it is the power of humming that, even if it is ridiculed, it catches on, and in no time at all the villagers were humming Avraham Mandelbaum's happy tune wholeheartedly. And it is the power of violets that, even if they are given facetiously, their scent fills the house, and the villagers thanked Avraham Mandelbaum in their hearts for reminding them of that. But when Avraham Mandelbaum burst out of his house that evening roaring, "Rachel", the humming was gone and the violets had vanished without a trace. There was a wild, primitive look on the slaughterer's face, and the villagers hesitated in their doorways. It wasn't until they heard the cries of Zeev Feinberg that their hesitation disappeared. Not because of what was said, which was quite laconic, but because of the identity of the speaker. If Feinberg dared to leave his house and stand beside Avraham Mandelbaum, how could all the other men not?

They circled the village in groups, but found no trace of Rachel Mandelbaum. On the way they looked for Yaacov Markovitch— perhaps the guard had seen something—but he too had disappeared. Some of the men replaced their fear for Rachel with their anger against Yaacov Markovitch, hissing, "Some guard he is," but held their tongues when they walked past Zeev Feinberg. Finally they reached the carob tree. They almost didn't see Rachel Mandelbaum and Yaacov Markovitch, who were sleeping off their exhaustion, but the small bald spot on Markovitch's head shone brightly enough in the moonlight for Zeev Feinberg to notice it and shout, "Over there!"

Avraham Mandelbaum rushed forward, the others behind him. When the searchers found the baby sleeping in the arms of Yaacov Markovitch, and Rachel Mandelbaum asleep with empty arms, they were confused. Avraham Mandelbaum knelt beside Rachel, howling with tears. Rachel Mandelbaum startled awake and looked at the face, red with strain and tears, and wondered whether the baby had grown up so quickly that he already looked exactly like Avraham Mandelbaum. The villagers drew back, embarrassed at the sight. But even as they stepped back, even as they began walking towards their homes, they could not help but hear the slaughterer's wails: "I thought you left me. That you went to the port. To Europe. That you left me." Rachel Mandelbaum closed her eyes again and whispered, *"Sha, sha." Sha* to Avraham Mandelbaum and his fear, *sha* to the baby who was so much like him that it woke up now and began to cry, *sha* to the villagers whispering in the distance. Perhaps if all of them were quiet she could hear again the laughing voice of the golden-haired, blue-eyed baby girl she had carried in the womb of her imagination for nine months, the baby girl who was no longer there.

Yaacov Markovitch knew that he was no longer needed. His knees hurt from kneeling beside Rachel Mandelbaum for so long, and his fingers still hadn't regained their flexibility after the pressure he had put on them. Nevertheless he was happy, because he was holding in his arms, wrapped in his shirt, a baby that he himself had delivered from its mother's womb. Never had he felt such fullness before. Zeev Feinberg knelt beside him and placed his hand on his naked shoulder. "You've done a great thing today." Yaacov Markovitch looked at his friend, and tears filled his eyes. "Really, Markovitch, there's enough crying going on here. Come on, give this bundle to Rachel—unless you're planning to take him for yourself too—and let's go. I'm hungry."

They began walking towards the village, and the crickets chirped a wedding song to them. Zeev Feinberg could not stop extolling Markovitch's bravery. "I want you to know that few men can go through that. I, for example, can kill a man with my bare hands if there's no choice, but seeing a vagina in that condition would make me pass out." Yaacov Markovitch hoarded the words in his memory, provisions for the journey, the way a person chews on a piece of honeycomb for hours after he has sucked all the sweetness out of it. When they reached Zeev Feinberg's house, they stopped. Feinberg shifted uncomfortably where he stood, and Yaacov Markovitch felt that, for the first time since they had met, his friend looked embarrassed.

"I can't let you in, Markovitch. I told you I wouldn't do that until you release Bella, and I meant it." Yaacov Markovitch put his hands in his pockets and turned to go. He hadn't taken three steps when he heard Feinberg call to him, "Where are you running off to, friend? If we can't eat inside, we'll eat outside."

The bread was hard and the cheese had known better days. "You can't expect a woman like Sonya to bake bread," Feinberg said. "At best she'd burn the bread, at worst she'd burn you." But there was one pomegranate in the house that had ripened before the others, and it was now festively cut open in the yard. Zeev Feinberg took more seeds in his hand, which was already red with juice. "Small and sweet," he said and put the seeds in his mouth, "small, sweet sins. That's how it should be, Markovitch, small, sweet and harmless. Not like you, who have never hurt a fly in your life, and all at once you commit a sin that sticks in the throat, a sin you can't vomit up or swallow, only choke on. Have you ever heard of anyone choking on a pomegranate? No. And you never will."

Yaacov Markovitch also took a handful of the pomegranate seeds. The fruit was sweet, and so was his conversation with Feinberg, but Bella's nightdress was sweeter still. When he said that to Feinberg, he looked scornfully at him. "Going to bed with a nightdress and hoping you'll wake up with a woman in it? You must have fallen on your head. It'll never happen, not in a year, not in twenty."

"So in another thirty, or forty. You know what, Feinberg, maybe never. But I hope, and that's something too. And maybe if I hope enough, if I hope really hard, that hope will turn into something real. Look at us, look at this country. Two thousand years we've been hoping for her, waiting for her, sleeping at night with our arms around the sleeves of her nightdress, because what is history if not the sleeves of a nightdress that has no smell? And you think she wants us? You think this country returns our love? Nonsense! She vomits us up time and time again, sends us to hell, beats us down without mercy. With the Romans and the Greeks and the Arabs and the mosquitoes. So you think that someone here says, 'If she doesn't want me, I should go?' Someone here says, 'There's no point in holding a country by force if she's been trying to get rid of you from the minute you came to her?' No. You hold on to her as hard as you can and you hope. You hope that maybe she'll finally look around and see you and say—that one. That's the one I want."

11

I N HER SEARCH for the poet, Bella came to Tel Aviv. Perhaps it would be more accurate to say—the city called her to it. Their previous encounter had been brief and bitter. This time it was longer and sweeter. She began her visit in the home of the deputy commander of the Irgun, who ignored her low-cut dress and the charm of her lips, but looked at length into her eyes. Bella knew that it was not her he was looking at. The nights she had spent on the ship's deck with Zeev Feinberg had taught her to recognize when she herself was the object of desire or merely a substitute when no other choice was available. When the deputy commander of the Irgun looked into her eyes, Bella knew whom he wanted to see there, and kindly allowed him to look without interruption. When his eyes had had their fill, he suggested that she stay in his apartment. He was about to leave on a top-secret mission anyway, and he didn't know how many nights he would be gone. Why shouldn't she stay there for the time being? Bella Markovitch looked carefully around the apartment. Though there was nothing lacking, there was something lacking that she could not put her finger on. Only three days later did she realize that the apartment was lacking anything that could be considered unique to it: a picture on the wall, a faded rug he didn't want to throw out, an object reminiscent of the past. The apartment of the deputy commander of the Irgun was not the home of a private individual for whom objects and sentiments were bound together. The flowers she picked and a piece of her embroidery did not help; the house turned away from the personal as if it were alien to it: the flowers withered and the embroidery looked so ridiculous that she put it in her bag. But sometimes, when a strong wind gusted in from the sea and shook the walls, Bella imagined that she smelled the faint scent of oranges rising from the sofas and the floor tiles, a scent that faded the moment she smelled it.

She found the poet where everyone said she would find him. At the table in the far-right corner of the café near the sea. The entire facade of the place bespoke self-importance. The chairs, the wooden tables and the ashtrays united to proclaim to the observer that a mistake had placed them here, in the sand, and not on the streets of Berlin. The patrons of the café did not join in that proclamation, but neither could they ignore it. Thus they sat rebuked on the chairs, treated the wooden tables with respect and used the ashtrays with reverence. They knew who they were expected to be like and they knew that they were not like them, no matter how hard they tried. They could wear clothes made in Europe, eat cakes baked from European recipes, blow their noses in embroidered handkerchiefs from Europe and recite verses written by European poets. But they could never do those things with the same effortlessness, the same natural nobility of those who really and truly were children of Europe. Of those who were not Jewish. The coveted, insufferable ease of the Poles or the Germans or the Austrians could not be imitated. Even here, in Palestine, it was unmistakable. If a foreign guest came to the café, everyone spotted him immediately. He did not sip his coffee in any unique way, or blow his nose into a handkerchief with any unusual charm, but the comfort with which he inhabited his body waved above him like a flag. And his shoulders bore only the weight of his own voyage and his own memories, and not 2,000-years-of-exile-and-who-knows-what-is-yet-to-come. The patrons of the café would look at that foreigner, whose worries were his own, whose memories were his own, whose fears were his own, and think, how nice it is for him to be only a person. Then they stole glances at the people sitting at the other tables who, even if they were alone, always had at their side the Jews murdered in pogroms and tortured to death in the Inquisition and exiled by their governments and slain in the rebellion against Rome, and the thirty-six righteous men as well, why not. The entire Jewish people crowded around the tables in the café, even when they were empty.

The poet's table was always more crowded than all the other tables, even though he always sat there alone. He had not yet given up hope that one day, if only something would happen to Bialik, he himself would become the national poet, hence he spent his days making himself worthy of the role. He wrote about the three Patriarchs and the Four Mothers, about the Exodus from Egypt and the vision of dry bones. And, in order not to lose his relevance to the here and now, he wrote about every pogrom, every murder, every crime, extolling and versifying the hopeless. Thus he invited to his table long lines of slaughtered, hung and beaten Jews, and gave them all fleeting glances, enough to capture the right metaphor on paper. And if he felt that his pen hand was growing tired, that the flame of his memory was beginning to extinguish, he simply thought about the literary supplements that rejected his poems, and tears immediately welled up. At such times, when the hardships of the Jewish people blended with the rejections of him as a poet, he wrote his best poems.

A person who devotes his life to the wonders of poetry does not always find time for minor matters of hygiene. The poet's hair rested on his forehead in oily strands, shell-less snails trailing their way to his scalp. When Bella approached him his face was bent over a page, and so she spent several moments looking only at his hair, a view that did not flatter him. When he raised his tormented eyes to her Bella recalled a similar look on the face of her dead poet, and she knew: he was searching for a rhyme. The eyes shifting back and forth, the mouth slightly open to receive the tip of a bitten pencil, the entire body tense with expectation, as if his back itched him terribly and he were just waiting for a hand that would finally be so kind as to find the right spot and scratch it hard. Bella smiled at the searching poet, and he ceased his searching. He had been on the verge of a breakthrough, had almost found the right rhyme for the word 'homeland' (the final candidates were 'hot sand' and 'swampland'), but there were many rhymes out there and only one beautiful woman at his table. True, many beautiful women had sat at his table: Rachel, who wept for her sons, and Esther, who saved her people, and Yael, with her prominent bosom and the head of Sisera in her hand. But an actual woman, flesh and blood and not a single drop of ink, had not stood at his table for a long time.

"Would madam like to sit?" His voice disappointed her. When she read his words in the newspaper clipping she always heard them loud and strong, as if they were being declaimed by a Shakespearean actor with a booming voice and a powerful gaze. But when he spoke his tone was tentative and there was a certain nasality in his voice, as if he had swallowed a kitten that was now speaking from his throat. Nevertheless, she sat down. Even if his hair was snails and his voice nasal, he was still one of those people who performed miracles, transforming blood into a rose, water into wine, the sun into an orange.

"I read one of your poems."

Perhaps she should have been suspicious when he knew immediately which poem she was referring to, should have understood from his reaction that only one of his poems had ever been published, but Bella was tired of suspicion. Instead she let the

poet recite other poems from his notebook and improvise various rhymes appropriate to her face. Much time had passed since
anyone had praised Bella's face in verse, and she had almost
forgotten the beneficial effects of love poems on the complexion.
The annoying dryness of her lips vanished as if they had been
rubbed with olive oil, and the black bags under her eyes shrank as
if they had never been. After speaking at length about her face, it
was only natural that he would take it in his hands and kiss her.
His breath smelled of chopped liver, but Bella, still grateful that
the annoying dryness was gone from her lips, did not reject him.

They left the café and took a walk through the streets of the
city. The poet had never experienced an outburst of such intense
creativity as the one he had as he walked with Bella. Everything
seemed worthy of having a poem written about it: a piece of
wrapping paper on the street, a hedgerow in front of a house, an
old man leaning on his cane. And even though he should write
something about all of them (for the first time in his life, poems
that had nothing to do with the hardships of Jews were budding
inside him), even though his hands tingled the entire time and his
fingers sought a pen to hold, he plunged them into his pockets
and continued to walk in the world instead of writing about it.

Bella Markovitch lay on her back in the poet's bed, vaguely
bored. Long minutes had passed since she had last looked at him
sucking her nipple with almost religious fervor. Now he thrust
his head between her legs and, recalling the chopped liver smell
of his breath, Bella cringed slightly. Nonetheless, she did not get
up. In order to leave a place you had to believe that you would
be happier in another place. As she lay on her back in the poet's
bed, Bella could not picture such a place. For so long she had
yearned to meet the man behind the words, for so long she had

believed that, if not for Markovitch, everything would have been as it should. And now Markovitch wasn't here and a Hebrew poet was. But the lump of tears in her throat refused to disappear.

The poet finally finished what he was doing and lay on his back beside Bella. Since she could no longer bear the smell of his breath, she asked him to bring her something to eat. He went to the kitchen and returned with a sectioned orange on a plate. Bella looked at the fruit with interest. She had not eaten an orange since boarding the ship, even though Yaacov Markovitch left one at the door to her room every night because he remembered her saying that she loved the taste. Bella Markovitch had thrown Yaacov Markovitch's oranges out of the window, hurled them into the fields, the way Persephone had thrown away Hades' pomegranates. She refused to let Yaacov Markovitch give her the first orange she would eat in Eretz Israel and swore to abstain from eating the fruit until the moment was as sweet as it was. Now, with an orange being handed to her by none other than the poet who had seduced her into coming here with oranges, she could not resist. When Bella reached out for the orange fruit the poet recalled the lines of the only one of his poems to be published and declaimed:

And the sun, as orange as the ripe orange on the tree
Fills our hearts with courage on the road to victory.

Bella smiled and took a bite of the fruit. She immediately began to cry. To no avail did the poet try to elicit the reason for her tears, and she simply mumbled over and over again: "And I don't even like oranges."

The longer Bella's trip lasted, the less Yaacov Markovitch slept. Until finally he was driven out of bed even before dawn. He took a loaf of bread and went out to feed the pigeons, but even they were asleep. So he waited for sunrise and headed for the slaughterer's house. Avraham Mandelbaum welcomed him with a warm handshake, which Mandelbaum thought was friendly and Markovitch found bone-crunching. The hand-shaking began the day after Rachel gave birth. Early one morning, Markovitch heard someone pounding on his door and got up quickly. Still wondering whether the men from Tel Aviv had returned to beat him up, he saw Avraham Mandelbaum in the doorway, holding what once had been a lamb.

For a moment they stood facing each other as each recalled the last time Avraham Mandelbaum had knocked on Yaacov Markovitch's door. That time Mandelbaum hadn't been holding a lamb but a knife, and Markovitch hadn't opened the door because he had fled with Zeev Feinberg on the train, where they had talked pleasantly about the mole on Rachel Mandelbaum's left breast. After a moment Avraham Mandelbaum's happiness overcame his embarrassment, and he extended his sheep-free hand to Yaacov Markovitch. "*Mazal tov* to us," Avraham Mandelbaum said, and Yaacov Markovitch, whose hand was now being crushed in the slaughterer's, thought how good it was that this encounter with Avraham Mandelbaum was taking place in a time of peace.

"I've brought you a thank-you gift," Avraham Mandelbaum said, "we'll eat it together." Yaacov Markovitch thanked him from the bottom of his heart and suggested that they eat the gift in Mandelbaum's house, beside the new mother and the baby he wanted so much to see. Avraham Mandelbaum cast his gaze downward and stammered something about Rachel's weakness, and Yaacov Markovitch was generous enough to nod as if he were deeply convinced. Yaacov Markovitch and Avraham Mandelbaum shared the meat of the lamb, which was as rich and plush as velvet, and also shared the velvety silence, which was smooth and dense and soft. Yaacov Markovitch did not ask himself how many people Avraham Mandelbaum had killed, and Avraham Mandelbaum did not wonder about when Yaacov Markovitch would finally release the poor woman he had married. If they did think about anything beyond the lamb it was the red-faced baby they had met the previous day, about its spread fingers, its downy head, its cries of defiance, "I'm here, I'm here, I'm here." And since the baby would not have been here if not for Avraham Mandelbaum and Yaacov Markovitch—one created it with his sperm and the other pulled it into life with his two hands—the fact of its existence was testimony and affirmation of their own existence.

When they finished eating, Avraham Mandelbaum stood up and turned to go home. After taking several steps he turned around. "Maybe you should come home with me anyway. Rachel is tired, so it'll have to be a short visit, but you must see the baby." With full stomachs and satisfied smiles on their faces the two men walked to Avraham Mandelbaum's house. But when they reached the stone fence that surrounded the house their expressions darkened. Issuing from the walls of the house were the sounds of a baby crying fiercely—desperate, inconsolable crying, crying that no longer held any hope that it could change anything, and persisted only out of habit. Anyone hearing it could have no doubt: the baby in the house had been screaming for a long time, perhaps from the moment Avraham Mandelbaum walked out of the door, because its exhaustion and sadness were unbearable. Yaacov Markovitch followed Avraham Mandelbaum across the yard and through the front door, straight to the room in which Rachel Mandelbaum was sitting and staring with glazed eyes at the screaming baby.

Rachel Mandelbaum made no sign to indicate that she was aware of her husband's return. It was not easy to ignore the presence of someone like Avraham Mandelbaum, whose body filled half the room, but when the slaughterer entered his home he lost so much weight and size that nothing was left of him but the shadow of a giant. Avraham Mandelbaum gave his wife a pleading look, of the sort not meant for the eyes of strangers. Yaacov Markovitch felt like an outsider in most places, and certainly in that living room where a husband, a wife and a baby were wallowing in their sorrow. And so he retreated, preparing to leave, but the baby's crying stopped him. Only yesterday he had helped him emerge from his mother's womb; how could he leave him in his anguish now? Yaacov Markovitch crossed the living room and stopped in front of Rachel Mandelbaum, the baby's cradle between them.

"Pick him up."

"I can't."

"Then I will."

Yaacov Markovitch bent over the cradle and picked up the baby. Rachel Mandelbaum closed her eyes in relief. For an entire day she had sat and looked at the child, swearing not to take her eyes off him until she finally felt all the things she had been told she would feel when she became a mother. Softness, compassion, a closeness she had never known before. She stared at the small face until her eyes hurt, wanting to find in it what a woman was supposed to find in the face of her baby—sublime beauty, overwhelming sweetness, an expression that would kindle unconditional love in her. But the face that stared back at her looked more than anything like a small monkey, and when she thought that even female monkeys show maternal affection to abandoned human babies, she felt so intensely guilty that once again she could not move from where she sat.

When Yaacov Markovitch picked up the baby it began to cry more loudly. Avraham Mandelbaum wrung his hands in concern, but Yaacov Markovitch smiled with satisfaction. If the baby cried louder at the touch of a person's hands, that meant he had not lost his faith that hands had the power to give him what he wanted, for after all a person does not demand something from someone he believes is unable to give it to him. The baby demanded consolation and Yaacov Markovitch wanted to give it to him. When he saw that the baby was not calming down inside the walls of the house he gestured for Avraham Mandelbaum to go with him, and went out to the yard. As soon as they were outside the baby's cries grew weaker, and when they went from the yard to the street the crying stopped completely.

Yaacov Markovitch and Avraham Mandelbaum walked side by side. When they had walked to Mandelbaum's house earlier, it had been only the two of them united in a pact of silence. Now their pact was enlarged to include three: Yaacov Markovitch, Avraham Mandelbaum and a mollified baby that was being passed from one to the other. Yaacov Markovitch chuckled. "You're holding him the way rabbis hold the Holy Book on Simchat Torah." Avraham Mandelbaum did not reply, only held the baby tighter and slowed down, because he saw that Yaacov Markovitch had to take three steps for every one of his. They walked for a long time, their feet carrying them through the streets of the village to the paths in the fields, and finally to the carob tree. At the sight of the tree Avraham Mandelbaum's brow furrowed and his eyes glittered with anger.

"God knows how many hours she lay here until you came. Alone, completely alone. It's no wonder she's lost her senses." Yaacov Markovitch, an expert in loneliness, knew very well that there was no difference between a carob tree and a made-up bed. A person can be alone anywhere, even in the heart of a crowd. But he didn't say a word. If Avraham Mandelbaum chose to channel his grief to a tree, he would not put up any obstacles.

"Hold him a minute for me." Once again Yaacov Markovitch found himself holding the human cub as Avraham Mandelbaum approached the carob tree. The slaughterer examined the ground near the trunk, where the thorns had been crushed by the weight of his wife lying there to give birth. He felt the rough bark of the tree with his large hand. "Alone," he said, "all alone." And then he began beating the carob tree with his fists. Mercilessly. The branches shook, as did Yaacov Markovitch. With the tenth blow all the fruit of the tree fell at once, a deluge of carobs raining down on Avraham Mandelbaum's head. The slaughterer continued to pound the tree with his fists, now red with blood, pounded and pounded and slammed his body into the trunk. Only when the tree had collapsed and the trunk split open, exposing its naked roots, did Avraham Mandelbaum finally stop taking revenge for the shame of his wife's aloneness. He wiped his hands on his trousers and went to take the baby, but changed his mind and left him in Markovitch's arms. They returned on the same route they had taken there.

12

BELLA MARKOVITCH spent an entire year in the home of the poet. Several days after their first meeting she got used to the chopped liver smell, and now smelled it only when they fought. Every morning, after the poet left for work, Bella packed all her clothes in a bag and was ready to leave the house. Sometimes she opened the door and walked down a few steps of the staircase, sometimes getting as far as the end of the street. And sometimes she didn't do even that, but only stood in front of the closed door for several moments before she unpacked the bag.

The poet knew nothing about that morning ritual. When he returned from his job at the newspaper, after spending most of his day writing obituaries and an occasional congratulatory item, he found Bella bathed and fragrant. He took her to cafés and films, strolled along the avenues with her and even agreed to dance with her, because although he hated dancing, he loved the looks people gave him when then they saw a man like him dancing with a woman like her. But one day he found out how great the gap was between her happiness at night and her sadness during the day. It was on a morning in February, when the buildings on the street press up against one another because of the cold. The poet, who had left his apartment with only a thin jacket and the ardor of love to preserve his body heat, realized very quickly that the ardor passed and his shoulders shook. He turned around at the corner and headed back to the house, where he would wrap himself in a warm coat and another hug from his beloved. As he neared the building, he saw Bella standing in the doorway, her expression clouded, her suitcase in her hand. The poet froze where he stood. The man inside him wanted to break away from that spot, to run towards her, to kneel before her and beg her to stay. But the artist in him ordered him to remain where he was and watch, to engrave in his mind the features of her face on the day she left, a face unaware that it was being observed, a face he could write poems about until the day he died. As the artist and the man struggled with each other, Bella turned around and went back into the house and the poet walked to work, confused, hurt and freezing.

And from that day on, he resumed writing poetry. He no longer wrote about the Jewish revival or sang the praises of agricultural crops and the landscape of the country. All his poems—simple, spare, touching—were about the possibility that one woman might leave one home. It wasn't great poetry, far from it, but neither was it terrible poetry, and that was something new. The day the poet watched Bella as she stood in the doorway of the house became the day he moved from being a failed poet to a mediocre poet. At the time there were more than enough great poets in the country; nor did it lack terrible poets. The great ones were idolized, the terrible ones pitied. But the mediocre poet was a source of much happiness. His poems were printed in newspapers but his books were rejected by publishers; he was invited to address unimportant conferences and everyone knew they would not have to name a park after him, only a bench at the most.

Bella did not read the poet's poems. Since the day she had tasted the orange sections she had lost faith in words. In the past she had loved poets because she thought they had the power to create worlds that people would want. Today she knew that those worlds were nothing but round soap bubbles, like the ones that rose from the water when she washed the poet's laundry in the sink. Lovely, colorful bubbles that your body wants to cradle itself in, but they burst immediately in a spray of water, leaving behind only dirty socks and shirts that had to be scrubbed with soap.

Women began to want to be close to the poet. Beautiful women. His earlier poems, the Zionist poems about redeeming the land, had left them indifferent. Now their eyes filmed over with tears when they read his poems to his beloved. The poems touched the most delicate chords of their souls—their desire one day to be the object of a poet's love. Bella could feel it when she walked hand in hand with the poet of an evening. No longer did he wait for her every smile, but spread smiles of his own; no longer did he stare into her eyes, but looked around at other women, from the redhead to the brunette, from the brunette to the buxom one. When they returned to the poet's apartment, Bella still felt the nausea she had felt in the morning. That day she had not packed her things, but remained near the toilet from one bout of vomiting to the next. She vomited up the cake she had eaten the previous night in the café, and the expressions of the women who had watched her as she ate. She vomited up the Hebrew poet, who now preferred writing about her leaving to actually being with her. She vomited up all the orange sections she had eaten in Europe without tasting them because her tongue had tasted only the anticipation of seeing the country the oranges had come from. And she vomited up the country itself, bits of food that had not been properly digested, khamsin and sand and wretchedness and futile hopes.

When she had finished vomiting Bella lay down on the bed and suddenly felt as light as a bird in flight. Even the burning in her esophagus was pleasant. Now she knew that she was free to do whatever she wished. Yaacov Markovitch could rot in his house in the village; she herself would live here, in Tel Aviv. That very day she would leave the unfaithful poet and find herself a true love. A good, simple person who had no room in his life for poetry, whose feet were planted firmly on the ground. A doctor. Perhaps a clerk. A modern man who did not consider marriage at all important. And she also decided to register at the teachers' college, to teach the children of Israel not to submit to baseness and infidelity, which apparently were deeply rooted in the men of this country. They would speak to her in an embarrassed, admiring voice and she would teach them everything they needed to know. Mathematics, history, geography. She would teach them about the towering Himalayas and the history of the Jews in the kingdom of Spain. About the sum of the angles in a triangle and the anatomy of a flower. The only thing she would not teach them was poetry. The falseness of words was too dangerous for young people. They would treat her with respect and she would never raise a hand to them. When she walked in the street with the doctor, or the clerk, mothers would come up to her to shake her hand and thank her.

As light as a bird, except for the faint burning in her esophagus, Bella Markovitch lay on her back and made plans without knowing that the next morning she would again find herself leaning over the toilet, and the day after that as well. She would endure more than two weeks of nausea and vomiting before she realized that vomiting was not the mind's way of cleansing itself of its past, but the body's way of heralding the future.

Bella did not tell the poet about her pregnancy. She packed her belongings one morning and left the house, not lingering on the threshold or the street corner. But four blocks away from the poet's apartment she stopped, because she didn't know where she would go. She did not want to stay in Tel Aviv. There were too many poets walking around the streets. Jerusalem seemed too holy. She liked Haifa, but there too the danger of being a bastard would pursue the child. Perhaps she would knock on the gates of a kibbutz. She had heard that there they did not adhere to the rules of religion and marriage, sharing love as they shared food. But who would want to take in a pregnant young woman who couldn't tell the difference between rice and wheat? Bella stood where she was for a long time. People crossed the length and width of the street, Bella's thoughts with them. From Tel Aviv to Haifa. From Haifa to Jerusalem. From Jerusalem to a kibbutz. And since none of those destinations seemed right, she moved on to others. Petah Tikva, Tiberias, Rishon LeZion. Bella's thoughts wandered through the country, passing the village and hurrying away from it. Not there. No, not there. But the harder she tried to distance herself from the village, the more she returned to thinking about it. She thought about the spring Sonya had taken her to, the fig tree that guarded the entrance to it, behind which they had swum naked and combed each other's hair. She thought about the balcony of Rachel Mandelbaum's house, where a child was undoubtedly playing now, where her child could play too. Finally she thought about Yaacov Markovitch, a vile man who had a good income and a large house.

On a cold March night, Bella returned to Yaacov Markovitch's house. She returned as she had left, without saying a word to him. When Bella entered the house Yaacov Markovitch was working in the fields. Every once in a while he automatically raised his head above the hoe in the hope that he would see her tall figure on the road. For two whole years he had raised his head that way, above the hoe, and the movement caused constant pain in his neck, making him more stooped than he was. Nonetheless, he persisted in raising his head about once every twenty minutes, in a movement that was more habit than hope. On the day Bella returned, Yaacov Markovitch raised his head above the hoe and saw the figure of a woman walking in the distance. His heart began to flutter like a bird, but his head silenced it firmly. For the first few months after Bella left he would run out of the field every time he saw a woman on the road. Short or tall, thin or fat. He knew quite well that none of them was Bella, but his legs moved from where he was standing, covered the field in a run, hurried along the road, stopped in embarrassment in front of the woman they wanted to meet, who now, face to face, did not resemble Bella Markovitch in the slightest. Every now and then, when boredom overcame pity, one of the village boys wrapped a piece of cloth around his trousers and went mincing his way along the road. Yaacov Markovitch raised his head above the hoe and saw a sturdy figure in the distance, walking like a woman and wearing a skirt, and though he knew that something was not kosher—he even heard the giggles of the boys hiding in the bushes—he nonetheless walked towards the figure with hopeful eyes.

"You're making a fool of yourself," Zeev Feinberg told him when he saw him return to the field pursued by jeering whistles. "She won't come back."

Yaacov Markovitch replied, "We'll see," but stopped running to every woman he saw. Now he simply looked up to examine the figure in the distance. If it resembled Bella he would take off at a run, if not he would stay where he was. And since few women resembled Bella, certainly not the Bella in his memory, Yaacov Markovitch rarely left the field. On the day Bella returned he saw her on the path. His heart, as always, wanted to fly to her, but his feet remained unmoving. The woman on the path walked heavily and slowly. Her hips were full and her shoulders slightly stooped. Bella's gait was agile and aristocratic, her hips slender and her back straight. Yaacov Markovitch continued to work in the field.

When he entered the house he found her there. Fuller, more stooped, but still the most beautiful woman he had ever seen in his life. Her beauty worked on him now just as it had the first time he saw her, when she turned from the window in the apartment in Europe. He once again froze, once again felt as if someone had assembled all the fragments of his dreams into a single whole that stood before him now. The lips as plump as a bursting fig, the nose small and resolute, the eyebrows arched like the windows of a mosque. And those eyes, though they looked at him now with unmistakable loathing, were filled with the same life.

"You've come back."

Bella's arched eyebrows rose slightly, as if to say that the fact of her return was known to her and there was no need to announce it again. Yaacov Markovitch still stood on the threshold, while Bella sat and embroidered on the sofa. Despite himself Markovitch felt like a stranger in his own home, as if he were an unwanted guest disrupting the owner's peace and quiet. So he took another step into the house and began to speak again in a voice he hoped would sound authoritative: "You've come a long way. I'll make you something to eat." Bella Markovitch did not reply and Yaacov Markovitch hurried to the kitchen. He brewed tea and sliced bread, and after a slight hesitation added an orange that he peeled. For a moment, as he stood in the kitchen, a cup of tea in one hand, a plate of bread, cheese and a sectioned orange in the other —for one moment Yaacov Markovitch thought that everything was going to work out.

When he returned to the living room he saw that it was empty. Bella Markovitch had taken her embroidery and gone. At first he was terrified that she might have left again, but then he saw her bag in the bedroom, and a note beside it. "From now on, you will go back to sleeping on the sofa in the living room. You can take the nightdress with you."

*

Yaacov Markovitch did not have to wait long to discover where she had gone. Zeev Feinberg's cry of surprise could be heard clearly throughout the village: "You're back!" The cry contained not only happiness but also a question neither Feinberg nor Markovitch dared to ask, the latter standing alone in his living room and the former standing at his front door hugging Bella and calling, "Sonya, look who's here." Sonya gave Bella a quick glance and immediately guessed why she had returned. Not because of Bella's body, which still kept its secret; it was her eyes that told her. Bella's eyes, which resembled Sonya's in all things except that they were set apart at exactly the distance considered pleasing, now held something more. It was neither softness, nor sweetness, nor any of the things that people expect to see in the eyes of a pregnant woman. On the contrary: there was something in Bella's eyes now that was hard and determined, the knowledge that another person depended on her for its existence. That knowledge had seeped into her mind as she was making her way to the village, and by the time she arrived it had already become part of her. Another person depended on her for its existence, a secret person that only she knew, a baby. That word pleased her so much that she rolled it around on her tongue over and over again, never getting her fill of it, hoping that its sweetness would be enough to make up for the taste of everything else. Sonya hugged Bella with two strong arms and whispered, "*Mazal tov.*" At first Bella was terrified that her secret was not as well kept as she had thought, but immediately relaxed, for Sonya's eyes were not like other people's eyes.

That night, Bella stayed in Sonya and Zeev Feinberg's house until late. The joy of seeing friends blended with the fear of the moment she would have to return to Markovitch's house. So she remained sitting on the sofa, listening eagerly to Feinberg's stories (about a bear that would have eaten a three-year-old child if he hadn't fought it with his bare hands), smiling at Sonya's corrections (not with bare hands, but with a rifle; not a three-year-old child, but a thirty-year-old man; and not a bear, but a boar). Finally she knew that she could not wait any longer, and said goodnight. The closer she came to the house, the more hesitant her steps became. As she opened the door she had a sudden attack of nausea and hurried to the bathroom. She knelt over the toilet for twenty minutes. When she stood up it was not because the nausea was gone, but because she had decided to act despite its presence.

Yaacov Markovitch was asleep on the living room sofa. The banishment from his bed to the sofa did not bother him in the slightest. Since Bella had gone the bed had been a torture chamber for him, not a place of rest. He had spent his nights with open eyes, in tense expectation of the sound of Bella's feet at the door. In the end he preferred the frozen night air to the heat of anticipation-soaked sheets and spent his nights guarding the village. The night Bella returned was the first night in two years that Yaacov Markovitch slept soundly. Bella approached the sofa. She did not look at him, neither when she took off her blouse nor when she removed her skirt. She unhooked her bra and stepped out of her underpants quickly, like a person who has decided to immerse herself in freezing water and knows that if she hesitates she will never do it. Bella Markovitch took a deep breath and slipped under her husband's sheet.

Yaacov Markovitch did not wake up immediately. He had slept alone all his life, and his body was quick to dismiss the touch of the soft skin as yet another deceptive dream. But when several seconds had passed and the touch was still there, joined now by a woman's breath, he opened his eyes. Bella Markovitch was lying beside him, her eyes closed, her body bare. Yaacov Markovitch dared not move. So great was this miracle that he knew clearly that a small mistake would be enough for it to vanish as if it had ncver been. He did not even risk looking at her, but simply lay there with closed eyes and inhaled her fragrance, which held hints of dew and honey. After several moments had passed he opened his eyes again. She was still there. Naked. Lush. Abandoning her body to his staring eyes. Even naked, she remained proud. A perfect marble statue that multitudes flock to see, surreptitiously running a brazen hand over it when the guard isn't watching; but its beauty is the statue's alone, no matter how many look at it. Now he didn't know where to look first: the ivory shoulders he had lain in wait to see when she walked around the house and bent to pick up something were now lying beside him. Beneath them rose a pair of perfect breasts, two round pomegranates crowned by nipples pointing to the sky. Further down was a rounded, honeyed stomach, its navel a gold coin. And below that. Below that. Yaacov Markovitch looked at the triangle of Bella Markovitch's sex and grew dizzy. He closed his eyes again. When he opened them they darted away from Bella Markovitch's sex—how much joy can a person bear?—and looked at her thighs. Recently they had been causing Bella great sadness, because she had discovered that they were covered with bluish veins and the beginnings of cellulite. But in the night darkness Yaacov Markovitch did not see those defects, and in truth it is doubtful that he would see them in the light of day either. Not because his sight was impaired. Yaacov Markovitch's sight was no worse than that of most people, in the sense that his too tried to provide its possessor with what he wished to see and conceal everything else. But Bella's feet were exactly the sort of thing with which the eye tries to make its owner happy—small, curved, a masterpiece of planning and execution.

When he finished surveying her body from head to toe, he began to survey it from toe to head. He derived special pleasure from looking at her face. Although he had looked at it many times—whether in the flesh or in the imagination—it nonetheless looked different to him now that it was joined to her naked body. The face was a consequence of the body, just as the body was the promise embodied in the face. The redness of her lips matched the blush of her nipples. The curve of her chin complemented the curve of her foot. The arch of her eyebrows hinted at the triangle of her sex.

Behind closed lids Bella waited for the touch of Yaacov Markovitch's hands, as tense as someone waiting for a tooth to be pulled. She swallowed her tears before they could flow out of her eyes and give away her secret. So much salt. She hoped it would not hurt the baby. As soon as she thought of the baby the images rose in her mind once again: an infant crying with hunger and she is unable to feed it; a pupil she cannot buy books for; a teenager branded with the word "bastard" wherever he goes. If only she could do it, she would have a way out of the dead end she faced and seduce Markovitch with her own hands, but since she couldn't, for long minutes she couldn't, she did the only thing she could: "I'll sleep with you if you want."

A fraction of a second passed before Yaacov Markovitch grasped the meaning of the words. The gap between the tone of her voice and the meaning of her words confused him. In his efforts to reconcile them he told himself that she was embarrassed, ashamed about her earlier actions. The men who were sent to beat him, the scornful looks of the villagers, the revenge taken by the house that he had built with his own hands—all those things were certainly nagging at her conscience and hardening her voice. Because now Bella Markovitch understood how much Yaacov Markovitch loved her, understood that feelings for him, even if they did not exist, could be created through hard work and much dedication, and here she was, lying in his bed and waiting for him to forgive her. Yaacov Markovitch, a smart fellow, almost convinced himself that this was the case, until he touched his wife's shoulder with his trembling hand.

There was no mistaking Bella Markovitch's revulsion. Her body took possession of its owner. Her plump fig lips pulled back, her eyelids squeezed shut, the arch of her eyebrows flattened out completely. Yaacov Markovitch withdrew his hand and sat up. For a long while, he thought with his eyes closed. He thought about the months that Bella had spent far away from him with a man she had surely left behind when she returned, about the defeated way she had walked on the road leading to the village, about her slightly fuller body. When he opened his eyes again he saw Bella looking at him, her body wrapped in the sheet.

"You don't have to be afraid," he said. "You came back because of the baby, and I will take care of it. And now, leave this bed and don't come back to it until you want to."

From that day on the house returned to its normal temperature. And the bougainvillea stopped behaving oddly, to Yaacov Markovitch's great happiness, since he had been thinking about uprooting it. The living room retained its sadness because furniture could not be happy in a house that had no love in it, but at least it stopped freezing its occupants. Yaacov Markovitch had no illusions that those things were done for him. A baby was growing in his wife's stomach, and the house ended its war against Markovitch in order to make it easier for the baby to flourish. Not only the house mobilized to help Bella's pregnancy; Yaacov Markovitch himself wanted to take care of her and make her days easier. He considered the child collateral, a guarantee that she would stay. He was prepared to support the child for its entire life if only it would ensure that its mother would stay with him.

13

Yaacov markovitch and Avraham Mandelbaum never spoke again about the night the slaughterer demolished the carob tree. After Bella's return, Markovitch went to the butcher's shop every day to choose a small piece of meat for his pregnant wife. The slaughterer gave him the meat at half the price, along with a handshake that left feeling in only half of his fingers. When Markovitch left the slaughterer's shop, villagers stopped to look at him and wonder. Now he felt their eyes on him wherever he went. The same eyes that, in the past, had not given Yaacov Markovitch more than a passing glance now studied him for a long time and followed him all the way to his house, until he closed the front door on them and went in to see how Bella was. And even then, after he had closed the door, the eyes stayed where they were, flashing beyond the closed door, straining to penetrate the layers of white-painted wood and find out, once and for all, why Yaacov Markovitch's wife had returned.

The rumors did not begin immediately. That year, people had other things on their minds. The advance of the Allied forces, the amount of ammunition the damn Germans had, the Arabs' schemes. Matters of the highest importance. But here, below them, a beautiful woman's stomach was swelling, and after a month and a half no one could walk in the streets of the village without seeing it. And so it happened that great concerns were replaced by small questions and, in the end, by petty matters of the sort that cause only quarrel and contention but are nonetheless pleasing to the palate.

"It's not his, the baby."

"How do you know?"

"Did you forget how she used to disappear at night?"

"But since she came back, she hasn't disappeared even once."

"Maybe she came back with a surprise in her belly."

At first the words were spoken behind closed doors, in a whisper, when the lamp was turned off and a couple wished to placate each other with a bit of gossip. From the bedroom they moved to the dinner table; perhaps they would add spice to the soup. And from the dinner table they wandered outside, to the orchards and the fields, to amuse weary ears. Finally the rumors took on a financial character, after Michael Nudelman promised to give twenty liras to anyone who could verify the details of that business with Yaacov Markovitch. At the time, Nudelman was a young man and Yaacov Markovitch was a grown man, but Michael Nudelman compensated for the difference in age with a difference of twenty centimeters in height and width. Michael's younger brother, Haim, took up the challenge. He waited for Markovitch on his way home from the butcher's shop, keeping his hands in his pockets and his expression one of feigned innocence.

"Greetings, Markovitch."

Yaacov Markovitch nodded and continued walking. He remembered Michael and Haim Nudelman very well from the evenings they sashayed along the dirt road in their idiotic imitation of a woman's walk, waiting for him to come running towards them, pathetic and hopeful.

"Bringing some meat for the little woman?" Now Haim Nudelman was actually walking beside him, his acne glowing on his face like star clusters. "It's very good for the baby, the meat.

Especially if it's going to be born anemic. Are you yourself anemic, Markovitch? No, of course not, I can see your face getting red now. Maybe the little woman is anemic? She definitely doesn't look it, not with those pink cheeks of hers. So maybe someone else is anemic, eh Markovitch, maybe the father—"

Now Haim Nudelman's stream of words stopped, due to Yaacov Markovitch's completely surprising punch. It had to be a surprise, because if it wasn't there was no chance that a man of Yaacov Markovitch's height and weight could knock down a man with Haim Nudelman's physique. Now Yaacov Markovitch bent over Haim Nudelman and waved the bleeding piece of meat he'd got from Avraham Mandelbaum in his face.

"If you or anyone else ever has doubts about who the father of her baby is, I'll make sure your face looks like this steak before it's cooked."

That night Yaacov Markovitch took part in a brawl for the first time in his life. He himself had been hit in the past, of course, but this time he fought back like a real man, beating Haim and Michael until he heard the glorious sound of a rib cracking from the force of his fist. He was defeated, naturally, but when the brothers left him battered and bruised on the main road they could not ignore the smile on his face. When he had hobbled back to his house, Bella came out to greet him. "Scum," Bella said, and Yaacov Markovitch's heart fluttered with joy because he had never seen such intense loathing on her face that had not been directed at him. The next day he came home from the field early. He found her embroidering in the living room, wearing a bathrobe.

"Get dressed, we'll go out for a walk."

Bella looked up from her embroidery. "Much has changed between us, Markovitch. But still, the only walk I'm ready to take with you is to the Rabbinate."

"Whatever you say. But the rumors about the baby being a bastard won't stop until you prove that you came back for me, that you wanted to be with me."

Bella Markovitch contemplated his words for several moments, and finally stood up with a sigh. "Then we'll go for a walk."

From that day, Yaacov and Bella Markovitch made sure to go out for an evening stroll along the village street. Bella walked close to Yaacov Markovitch but never gave him her hand, and in fact barely looked at him unless they passed other people. Yaacov Markovitch spoke little, and Bella was grateful to him for that. Sometimes they met Sonya and Zeev Feinberg. They could recognize them from a distance because Sonya and Zeev Feinberg leaned so close to each other when they walked that they looked like a single person walking on four legs and laughing in two voices. Yaacov Markovitch focused on the way his two friends moved and on their voices, avoiding their gaze, for if he hadn't he would have seen a thin veil of sadness gnawing at Zeev Feinberg's blue eyes. For an entire year he had not taken precautions with Sonya, but had lain with her for reasons that had shifted from desire of the flesh to hope for the future. But Sonya's stomach remained maddeningly flat, and he searched in vain for the lovely curve of the beginning of life. For the last several weeks he could no longer touch his wife without thinking of such words as ovum, sperm and womb, words that belonged in biology books and not in the mind of a man licking a beloved vagina.

Zeev Feinberg dared not articulate his fears, and since they remained unspoken they grew, as fears tend to do. Zeev Feinberg's mustache was the first to be affected, a seismograph that recorded every change in the mind of its owner. Whenever Feinberg saw Sonya's sanitary pads the curl of his mustache was damaged and gravitational force exerted a greater influence on its hair. He began to get angry about small things. A window left open, burnt food. And Sonya, who in normal times would pull out his mustache at such comments, saw the state of his mustache and decided to restrain herself. Zeev Feinberg realized that his wife was willing to endure things she had never accepted before, and pressed even harder. Not out of meanness, and certainly not out of cruelty. Most people, when given a chair, choose to put their weight on it rather than carry it on their own legs.

As the birth date grew closer, the relationship between Yaacov and Bella Markovitch improved. While Bella still avoided Yaacov Markovitch's company, except for their walks, and continued to lock her door every night, she did stop sleeping with a knife in her bed. And while Bella's sleep was becoming sounder, Yaacov Markovitch's sleep was eluding him once again. Since Bella's return he no longer tossed and turned in his bed, tormented by jealousy and uncertainty—now he lay on the made-up sofa, his body consumed by desire. He had refused Bella's offer to sleep with him when she returned because he could not bear the idea of sleeping with her if she had no desire for it. She was his wife, not a whore from the city, so he would sleep with her only when she herself wanted him to, with no negotiations or other benefits. But the touch of her naked body was burnt into his skin, and his mind wandered again and again to the golden triangle of her sex. During the day he forcibly pushed away thoughts of her, but the moment he went to bed he could not help abandoning himself to them. Since Bella had returned, Yaacov Markovitch's nights were dominated by a constant erection. Very quickly night-time hours were no longer enough for his organ, and it began to embarrass its owner in the middle of the day. Seeing a red fruit—whether a plum, a strawberry or an apple—was enough to make Yaacov Markovitch's trousers balloon and his cheeks flush. Every piece of fruit reminded him of Bella's nipples, every hill of wheat sang to him the song of her triangular mound. When the slaughterer sliced meat for him, Yaacov Markovitch would swallow his saliva so loudly that Avraham Mandelbaum looked at him with concern. Whenever Zeev Feinberg met Yaacov Markovitch, his eyes were drawn to the crotch of his friend's trousers, for though Yaacov Markovitch's face was its usual self there was nothing at all usual about his constant erection.

"Why don't you go to Haifa? If you drink enough and want it enough, you can manage to believe that one woman is really another." Yaacov Markovitch took his friend's advice. Once every few weeks he went to release his sexual tension with the woman in Haifa, but as soon as he put a foot in the door of his house his penis stiffened in joyful anticipation.

Zeev Feinberg's penis, meanwhile, was growing limp. If, in the past, his mustache curled at the sight of every curvaceous breast or sumptuous behind, when they appeared before him now he remained indifferent. Only when he saw a pregnant woman did his eyes regain their glitter, and he looked at her stomach with longing. If, in the past, he had prided himself on never getting a girl into trouble, slept with all of them but never embarrassed a single one, now he was constantly worried that it wasn't caution that had protected him from unwanted father-hood but something else. And that thought was so threatening that it brought out a nastiness he did not know existed in him, and now it was directed entirely at Sonya. He taunted her at every opportunity and preferred night guard duty to their bed. When she spoke his eyes wandered around the room, and when she laughed he gave her one look and her voice fell like a bird that had been shot from the ground. Bella saw Sonya's pain and was angry. Finally she went looking for Feinberg when he was working in the field.

"You married a lioness and now you're turning her into a plucked chicken. Why?"

Zeev Feinberg looked at her in astonishment. The weeping beauty he had known was gone, and in her place stood a woman with a large stomach and red cheeks whose eyes flashed and hands clenched into fists. "Some things, Bella, are between a husband and his wife."

"Not in this village, Feinberg. Every farmer might work the land alone, but you do everything else together. No one knows that better than I do."

Zeev Feinberg put his hand on her clenched fist. "Go home Bella, all this strain is not good for the baby."

He spoke the final word with such sadness that it gave Bella the chills.

News of Yaacov Markovitch's constant erection finally reached the ears of the deputy commander of the Irgun. "This is neither the time nor the place," the voice of the revered commander boomed. "This country is on the way to war, and our arms smuggler in the north, a person handpicked especially because he doesn't stand out in any way, is walking around the streets with a flagpole in his trousers?" Michael Katz nodded and pointed out that, for a long time now, he had wanted permanently to remove Yaacov Markovitch from the ranks of the Irgun because of the scandal of his marriage, which had still not been resolved. But the deputy commander of the Irgun said that marriage was one thing and guns were another. "Expelling Yaacov Markovitch is all well and good in times of peace, but not when a war is about to break out. Take care of his problem and send him out on the next mission." Michael Katz left headquarters cursing and grumbling. He could speak four languages and pretend to speak eight. He knew how to disassemble a gun blindfolded and reassemble it with one hand tied behind his back. But he most definitely did not know, nor did he want to know, how to take care of a problem like Markovitch's.

In the end he bought string that he tied into a loop and headed for the village. When Yaacov Markovitch opened the door for him Michael Katz saw the size of the problem immediately. Yaacov Markovitch was no longer gloriously ordinary. Even if he stood behind a counter, his red face would glow with the intense redness of a person with sinful thoughts.

"That is of no interest to me, Markovitch," Michael Katz said, gesturing with disgust at the farmer's trousers. "There is a cache that has to be transferred to Metulla, and you will be the one to transfer it. So take this—" here Katz tossed the string at Markovitch—"and tie down whatever needs to be tied down. You leave tonight."

"My wife is about to give birth," Markovitch said, "I'm staying here."

"Let's hope that the child knows how to write verse like his father," Michael Katz replied, and began to tell Yaacov Markovitch about the Tel Aviv poet whose bed Bella had shared for a whole year. "What a charming couple they made, she with her long legs and he with his long sentences." Yaacov Markovitch wanted to slam the door in his face but froze where he stood. Wicked animals leaped from Michal Katz's mouth in herds and flocks and galloped into the house. Katz told him about the cafés where Bella held the poet's hand, and about their evening strolls along the avenues. He described the charming way she danced and the smile that came to the faces of those who were fortunate enough to hear her laugh. Slowly Yaacov Markovitch's house filled with Bella's past, until there was no room left for Yaacov Markovitch himself. When Bella returned from her visit to Sonya she found the house empty and Michael Katz at the door, a string wound around his finger.

"Where's Markovitch?"

"He went out. An urgent mission."

"Where to?"

"I am afraid, madam, that I am not at liberty to answer that."

Bella Markovitch had gained many kilograms since Michael Katz last saw her. Her hair was messy and her forehead sweaty, but Michael Katz could not keep from trembling slightly when she gave him a withering look and asked again, "Where to?"

"The north. A week, at least."

Michael Katz looked at Bella Markovitch's unreadable face and still found it remarkably beautiful. As aristocratic as always, he thought; even now she won't let on how happy she is that I have released her, if only for a week, from that worm. One more look at Bella Markovitch's face and Michael Katz was tempted into saying that it was a very dangerous mission, and in fact there was no way of knowing whether Yaacov Markovitch would return from it or not, so it was a lucky thing that Bella had returned here, to this house, which must certainly be worth something, instead of remaining in Tel Aviv, destitute.

"What a shame," Bella said, "that I didn't ask you to come into the house earlier." Michael Katz looked at her in surprise. "If I had, I could throw you out now."

Bella entered the house and closed the door in Michael Katz's face. She found the silence in the living room pleasant. She stood there for several minutes, examining the room as if she were seeing it for the first time, empty of her husband's presence. Finally she sat down on the sofa. There was a bundle of carefully folded bedclothes under one of the pillows. A pillowcase, a sheet and a blanket and, among them, her old nightdress. Bella raised it to her face and inhaled the smell of a laundry soap she didn't recognize, mixed with the smell of a body that was not hers. Yaacov Markovitch had spent so many nights embracing the sleeve of that nightdress that his smell had stuck to the smell of the fabric. And now he was gone. Bella Markovitch threw the nightdress at the wall. Then she threw the pillowcase and the sheet. She lay down on her back on the sofa, her stomach rising above her, her eyes closed. She had lain there that way seven months ago, ready to endure the touch of that terrible man in order to buy security for the baby in her stomach. He gave her security and spared her his touch, and she was grateful to him for that, but she despised him for all the rest. If he died now. If he died now. She didn't wish for it to happen. She didn't hope for it not to.

Three days after Yaacov Markovitch left, the deputy commander of the Irgun arrived in the village. The children who heard the noise of the engine ran to welcome him and returned in tears because the deputy commander of the Irgun ordered them to help their parents and questioned them about their homework with such a murderous look on his face that they almost wet their pants. The children who didn't hear the noise of the engine also cried because they had missed the visit of the person everyone whispered about, the one who had given a live grenade to every child who came out to welcome him—or that, at least, was what they had been told by the children who met him. The mothers wiped their children's noses with the hems of their blouses, patted weeping heads and wished with all their hearts that visits from pillars of the country would take place only after dark.

The deputy commander of the Irgun left the car in the center of the village, where it would be well oiled by the people's gazes, and walked towards Yaacov Markovitch's house. He would have liked to hesitate before knocking on the door. He hadn't seen Bella since the night she left his apartment in Tel Aviv and went out in search of a poet. He didn't know for certain why she had returned to Markovitch, or how she had reacted to his departure. A minute or two of situation assessment might have helped, but the children had followed him at a distance to Bella's house and were now watching the deputy commander of the Irgun with admiring eyes. The deputy commander of the Irgun knew that the education of the younger generation would be severely damaged if they saw hesitation on the part of the older generation, so he knocked on the door with a sure hand and a fearful heart.

Bella Markovitch did not open the door right away. Her steps were heavy and her body overflowing. But when she finally opened it her face was remarkably beautiful and her eyes, so like Sonya's, gave the deputy commander of the Irgun chills that had nothing to do with the coolness of the morning.

"I have come to find out how the lady of the house is feeling."

"The lady of the house is feeling fine," Bella replied, and would have slammed the door in his face if she hadn't remembered how kind he had been to offer her his apartment to stay in. So she asked him to come in and made him a cup of coffee. While she was pouring, Bella asked what Michael Katz had said to Markovitch that had made him leave in such a hurry. The deputy commander of the Irgun took a moment to reply.

"He most probably talked to him about this crucial moment in history, about the supreme importance of his mission. War, after all, is liable to break out at any moment now."

"And this?" Bella pointed to her stomach and said, "This isn't liable to break out at any moment?"

"That's exactly why I'm here," the deputy commander of the Irgun replied, "to be at your side in the event that anything happens while your husband is on his mission."

Bella Markovitch tilted her head back and burst out laughing. Blue capillaries snaked under her delicate white skin.

"Be at my side? For that, you could have sent any one of your underlings. But to be at her side—for that, you had to come."

The deputy commander of the Irgun lowered his gaze. He was still searching his mind for an escape route when Bella put her hand on his arm.

"Forgive me. I know you didn't mean me any harm by sending Markovitch on the mission. Maybe you even thought I would benefit from it. I would have thought so too, at least until not too long ago."

The deputy commander of the Irgun kept looking at the floor, dividing it in his mind into so many squares, multiplying and subtracting its size, wondering whether it could serve as an arms cache, trying despite himself not to ask the only question he wanted to ask: how did you know that I came for her? But he himself had not known until Bella had asked. He had decided to visit Yaacov Markovitch's indentured wife at a time when her husband was endangering himself at his command. Not for a moment did he realize that it wasn't Bella he wanted to see, but Sonya. He hadn't seen her for more than a year, and he was also avoiding Feinberg as much as possible. Every time the deputy commander of the Irgun shook Zeev Feinberg's hand, he couldn't help thinking about the body that hand had touched earlier, and from the moment he thought about that body he could no longer resist temptation and hurried to the market, where he annihilated his yearning in oranges. But oranges were expensive, and there was too much work to do that he could not stop in the name of mad love, so the deputy commander of the Irgun avoided his best friend and tried as hard as he could not to look north. Fantasies of Sonya trailed after him for several months, but in the end they stopped, like stray cats absently petted that pursue the petting hand for a while longer before giving up. Now the deputy commander of the Irgun was a few houses away from the woman he loved and he felt the pulse of her life in his body. She's walking in the kitchen. She's watering the garden. She's pushing unruly strands of hair behind her ear. He could have gone on like that for an entire day if Bella had not groaned suddenly and grabbed his hand. "Call Feinberg and Sonya. It's starting."

Zeev Feinberg arrived first. He burst into the house with his mustache pointing up and his eyes primed for battle. Sonya arrived shortly after him, panting from the run. Then the group of children, ordered to bring them there by the deputy commander of the Irgun, charged in. They were quickly thrown out of the house and returned to their positions around the fence, waiting for the moment the deputy commander of the Irgun would entrust them with another mission.

The deputy commander of the Irgun prepared himself for the extremely painful sight of Sonya and Feinberg's love. The previous times he had seen them together, Sonya's face had been radiant and Feinberg's smile had reached all the way to his eyes. But now Sonya looked like a candle that had been blown on, and Feinberg's face was sad and hard. The deputy commander of the Irgun studied them for a long time as they knelt beside Bella, one on her left, the other on her right. He looked at Sonya when she left to boil some water and watched Zeev Feinberg's eyes when she returned. Through their efficient movements, their soothing words and Bella's moans, a surprising, even revolutionary intelligence picture began to take shape. For Zeev Feinberg did not look into his wife's eyes even once, and Sonya's voice, that deep, warm, throaty voice, sounded as weak as that of a person lost on the road whose calls for help go unanswered.

"Take deep breaths, Bella, the doctor will be here soon with the children."

"He won't come, he won't come," a child shouted from the door, "his wife said he went out to treat a man with a fever in the village."

The deputy commander of the Irgun and Zeev Feinberg looked at each other over Bella's stomach. "I'll take her in my vehicle," the deputy commander of the Irgun said, "you stay here in case Markovitch comes back."

"Seriously, Froike, the way you drive? With all those jolts and turns the baby will be born in the car! I'll take her." The deputy commander of the Irgun wanted to protest, but he saw how reverently Feinberg was wiping the sweat from Bella's brow, and saw his right hand pinching his mustache in a way that was reserved for especially serious cases.

"Why don't we all go then?" the deputy commander of the Irgun asked.

"No." The voice was so weak that, for a moment, the deputy commander of the Irgun thought that Bella was speaking, not Sonya. "Zevik will go with Bella. We'll stay here."

If Zeev Feinberg was puzzled by his wife's decision, he didn't show it. He just kept wiping the sweat from Bella's brow and occasionally stole a glance at her stomach. The deputy commander of the Irgun, on the other hand, gave Sonya a long look and then took the keys out of his pocket and said, "Get going."

Five minutes later the deputy commander of the Irgun and Sonya were alone, she emptying the bowl of boiled water into the yard, he trying to find something to keep his hands busy. When she sat down beside him on the sofa he began to breathe through his mouth, only because he didn't know how he would respond if her fragrance reached his nose. "Just imagine, Ephraim, it's so quiet here now, and tomorrow, the day after at the latest, this house will be filled with laughter and a baby's crying." Sonya didn't wait for his reply, and it didn't come, because the deputy commander of the Irgun had heard her speak his name and from that moment on he heard nothing else. When she kissed him he turned his head away from her.

"Wait," he said, "first I'll take it off you."

"Take what off me?"

"The sadness."

Then he kissed her face from her chin to the top of her forehead, a hundred little kisses that covered her skin. The hollow above her lips, her cheeks, her nostrils, her eyes. With every kiss the deputy commander of the Irgun inhaled the air on her skin, contaminated with doubts, and when he felt that kisses were not enough to remove the mask of clay that had hardened on her face he began to lick it—long, wet strokes of his tongue on her cheeks, her eyes, her nose, her ears. Only when she began to laugh in her throaty voice, only when she sounded once again like a purring lioness, only when she slapped him with all the strength in her arms and shouted, "Enough! You criminal!"—only then did he stop licking her face, take her head between his trembling hands and kiss her.

Yaacov Markovitch's squealing sofa almost buckled under their weight. The deputy commander of the Irgun was a large man, and Sonya was not skinny. True, the sofa was used to Markovitch's nocturnal tossings and erect penis, but this sort of lovemaking was double the weight on it, and that did not include the weight of the anticipation—more than thirty months, dozens of crates of oranges bought in the Tel Aviv port, and one hope. As much as the deputy commander of the Irgun wanted to immerse himself totally in the work of love, he could not help noticing the change that had taken place in Sonya since the last time he had slept with her. Then her body had reminded him of a huge amusement park, and they were two children who had come to taste its wonders. And now Sonya loved him fiercely, desperately, like someone whose major concern was not the pleasures of the body but the sickness of the soul.

Afterward, his body pleasantly languid, the deputy commander of the Irgun lay on his back and drew circles with his finger around Sonya's nipples. The faint smile on Sonya's lips was so sweet that the deputy commander of the Irgun mustered the strength to raise himself and kiss the corners of her mouth.

"I know what your answer will be, but I'll ask you anyway," he said.

"If you know my answer, why ask?"

"Maybe you'll surprise me. If not, I can at least tell myself that I tried to convince you to come with me. And maybe you really will come with me, Sonya? Why wouldn't you? You're not happy here. You can't lie to me. I saw it. You aren't happy."

"Happiness?" Sonya's gray eyes widened in surprise, "since when have happiness and love had anything to do with each other?"

They went on to speak of other things. Sonya listened intently when the deputy commander of the Irgun told her about the only letter he had received from his family in Europe, and about the difficulties of the last operation. She laughed when he laughed, grew sad when he grew sad, and for that entire time her right hand stroked her bare stomach. The stomach from which, in another nine months, Zeev Feinberg's first child would be born.

DURING

1

I N ALL THE HISTORY of the village, there had never been two children so emotionally bound together as Yaacov Markovitch's son and Zeev Feinberg's son. It is true that Zvi Markovitch had to wait all of nine months for Yair Feinberg to come into the world, but from the moment he arrived they were never apart. For nine months Zvi Markovitch waited for Feinberg's son, and refused to grow. His parents, who didn't know the reason for the delay, feared that he had been damaged at birth. He hardly cried, hardly crawled, turned over lazily, all the while staring expectantly into space. No matter how often Bella gave him her breasts, he did not want to suck the milk, and if his father made him a toy—like wooden beams joined into the shape of a star—he turned his eyes away from it. As if to say, "Not yet, the time hasn't come." Until he heard Yair Feinberg cry for the first time, the sound of a flock of birds splitting the air of the village and the thin film of his expectation. Oh yes, Zvi Markovitch opened his eyes then, deep, inscrutable blue pools, and he opened his mouth too, and when his mother heard the sound that came out of it she took his father's hand and said, "He laughed! He laughed!" He never stopped after that, except to eat. Yaacov Markovitch's house filled with children's laughter. His yard as well. When he worked in the field, a walk of several minutes from the house, he sometimes imagined that he heard, among the weeds, the echoes of laughter borne on the wind from his home.

Until, one day, Yaacov Markovitch was hoeing in the field and heard the sounds of war. That doesn't mean he heard mortar shells booming in the sky. There was not a single barrage, and the ground did not quake from the trampling of soldiers' boots. Nonetheless, Yaacov Markovitch put down the hoe and hurried back home. The emptiness of the fields on the way back made it clear that he was right. Everyone had heard. Everyone had hurried back to the village. The way horses stomp restlessly before a storm, the way birds grow silent half an hour before a natural disaster—that was how the people, with some inner sense that had evolved over the generations, felt the approach of an historical event.

There was a commotion in the village itself. Some people rushed to buy food, others hurried to hang laundry so that the war would not catch them without clean socks. Still others hastened to collect debts—at times like this, every penny counts. But it seemed that, whatever they were doing, they did it quickly. They drove quickly, spoke quickly, shook hands quickly, argued quickly and made up quickly. Even children's spankings were administered quickly, an effort to give them a brisk, concentrated lesson in good behavior before the war came to teach them other kinds of behavior.

Rachel Mandelbaum, with her slow, contemplative gait, stood out in this buzzing nest of ants. She walked on the street with measured steps, almost unaware of the hum of the men and women. When anyone bumped into her by mistake she mumbled, "Sorry," and kept walking, and they raised an eyebrow and went on their way. But when she saw Yaacov Markovitch, Rachel Mandelbaum stopped walking and dredged up a genuine smile from deep inside her. "Markovitch. If you're in a hurry too, then it must be true, war is on the way."

Yaacov Markovitch's eyes appraised the fragile creature standing before him. Since giving birth under the carob tree, Rachel

Mandelbaum rarely left her house. Her skin had grown pale, and now was so transparent that it was easy to see the tears gathering in the follicles near her lids. When he looked into her eyes—brown and sunken—he thought that they, not the slaughterer's knife, contained the thing that brought the animals in the butcher's shop to tears.

"It's true," he replied, "the war is about to break out. Maybe it already has. One way or the other, it's inevitable." Rachel's smile was nipped in the bud, and Yaacov Markovitch wondered whether he had been right to say what he had. Not because of the truth in it, of which there could be no doubt, but because of the emotional strength of the mind hearing it. Hearing the word "inevitable" made Rachel Mandelbaum's skin grow even paler, and now you could see her thoughts floating on the surface of the blood in her veins. She had come all this way to escape one war; how could it be that another one was waiting for her here? Above the hum of the villagers, carried over the fields, vineyards and the Mediterranean Sea, she heard the sound of the cracking skull that had sent her from Europe. Once again she looked into the face of the old Jewish man, coughing and praying, as the boys slammed him from one to the other on a street corner in Vienna. Now she was shocked to see in the old man's eyes the sorrow of the cows that watched Avraham Mandelbaum as he sharpened his knife. It was the look, exactly the look you have when awareness of the end opens like a black flower, its velvet leaves covering every vestige of reason.

Rachel Mandelbaum continued to think about the black flower, and Yaacov Markovitch had to clear his throat in order to get her attention back. But even when she looked at him again she saw nothing but the expression of bestial stupidity that appeared on the faces of the goats and the sheep, the ducks and the lambs, and now on the faces of all the people of the village. They smell their death, Rachel Mandelbaum thought, all these people hurrying to buy food and hang socks and slap their unruly children, all these people are no different from the animals at the door of the butcher's shop. At that thought Rachel Mandelbaum began walking faster, in fact breaking into a run and leaving Yaacov Markovitch confused where he stood.

But not for long. As Rachel Mandelbaum disappeared from sight Zeev Feinberg appeared, his steps rapid, his mustache erupting. Yaacov Markovitch saw his friend and hurried to join him, figuring that a man like Zeev Feinberg would certainly know how to act when the sounds of war fill the ear. He was wrong. Zeev Feinberg's ears were filled with the babbling of babies, and no external sounds entered them. Although his rapid steps and erupting mustache gave the powerful impression of a general, in reality the mustache was erupting with the joy of a children's song he was humming, and he was walking rapidly because he knew his son waited at the end of the road. "Markovitch! How good to see you. Listen, the baby is almost walking. An amazing thing at his age, amazing." Zeev Feinberg went on singing the child's praises, and Yaacov Markovitch went on nodding until he felt a slight pain in his neck. Finally, he dared to interrupt Feinberg's enthusiasm ("And his feces, it has almost no smell at all! Amazing!") and ask whether he'd heard anything about the war.

Upon hearing his question, Zeev Feinberg stopped talking and looked at Yaacov Markovitch in puzzlement. War. What with all the diapers, pots of hot water, lullabies, he had almost forgotten that word. Since Yair's birth, Sonya's orange scent had merged with the sweetish smell of breast milk. Zeev Feinberg walked through the rooms of the house like a drunkard, inhaling the blend into his lungs in deep breaths, and felt his insides grow sweet. The special blindness of people tricks them into seeing their own image in others. Thus a woman looking for a fight will imagine she sees scorn in loving eyes. And a man whose heart has turned to butter under the beneficial effects of the scents of oranges and breast milk will erroneously think that butter also resides in the hearts of others. Which is not so. While Zeev Feinberg counted and recounted the fingers of Yair's hands, there were others who were counting the bullets in their bags. When he squeezed red juice from pomegranates for the baby, others were learning how to cause a different kind of red liquid to explode from the bodies of their enemies. Zeev Feinberg did not see that because he was blind with love, and even now, as Yaacov Markovitch realized his mistake, all he could say was, "What a waste." Of course, immediately afterward he pulled himself together, buckled his gun belt and killed Arabs too, but at that moment, when gun-powder and scorched bodies assaulted his nostrils in vain, Zeev Feinberg once again inhaled the smell of oranges and milk, and his insides grew sweet.

2

I S IT POSSIBLE for a person to go through an entire war and emerge with a soul that is smooth and innocent, with sleep that is sound and deep? With a scratch or two on his body, but an undamaged heart? There are, of course, precedents in literature. The children of Israel left Egypt with the laments of a million Egyptian mothers in their ears, but their feet were untouched by a single drop of salt water from the sea or the mothers' tears. The sea split in half and they walked through the middle of it completely dry, and not one of them stopped to pick up a purple fish flapping on the sea bottom and return it to safe waters. Zeev Feinberg walked through the killing fields with strong legs and eyes that were closed even when they looked through rifle sights. Perhaps that was why he never missed.

On a hazy night in May, several months after he met Yaacov Markovitch on the street, Zeev Feinberg reported to his post in the north and looked into the darkness. If we want to be more accurate, we should admit that Zeev Feinberg allocated only half of his seeing power to his guard duty, devoting the other half to a detailed examination of Yair's face when Sonya rocked him to sleep. Divided sight does not help a guard to identify what he is seeing, so it was no wonder that only a long hour later did Zeev Feinberg see a figure approaching from the direction of the Arab village he was reconnoitering.

Adjusting the binoculars, he saw, despite the haze, that the man in the distance was slipping from tree to tree, constantly looking around. Every once in a while the man's hand went to the rucksack on his back, checking that it was firmly in place. At the sight of the bulging rucksack Zeev Feinberg tensed: he was definitely carrying a bomb in it, perhaps planning to place it on the bridge. When people clashed, the entire country knew no rest: trees were felled, bridges were blown up into the air, falling back to earth in a shower of small rocks that was quite destructive to all sorts of reptiles. Porcupines and jackals were sometimes thought to be people, and took bullets clearly not intended for them. Elsewhere blood blackened grass, and flowers withered under the weight of bodies. Yes, war is not a very pleasant business, and the young Arab sneaking his way forward with a bomb on his back was about to discover that, for Zeev Feinberg cocked his weapon. When he aimed his rifle at the enemy in the darkness, Zeev Feinberg felt nothing but the expectation that he would soon be able to lower his eyelids to the absolute minimum and continue to revel in the face of his son. Then came the shot, followed by the cry of a baby cutting through the night, and Zeev Feinberg dropped his weapon.

She was sixteen. Perhaps less. Her flat breasts and boyish body were what had tricked him into seeing a man. On her back, wrapped in a blanket, she was carrying a child that he had mistaken for a bomb. Zeev Feinberg stood over them, out of breath from running. Since the child's cry had driven him from his post and sent him running to the body he had shot, the child had not cried again. In the distance he heard the whispering of soldiers and the commander who were moving towards him. They walked slowly, unhurriedly. What they were about to see was not something you hurry towards. Zeev Feinberg knelt in front of the young girl's body. She lay with her face on the ground and her arms spread.

A child's hands jutted out through the blanket on her back. And for a moment, one blessed moment, Zeev Feinberg imagined he saw the child's fingers move. Then the moon shone, and this time there was no mistaking the dark circle in the center of the blanket where Zeev Feinberg's bullet had struck, tearing through the child and then hitting its mother. The land bore the dead girl on its back, and the dead girl bore the dead child on her back, and the arms of each of them were spread on the back that bore them, ten large fingers and ten small ones. The loamy soil was damp and red, and the blood of mother and child was damp and red and still hot, and the tears of Zeev Feinberg were large and hot.

A few weeks later Zeev Feinberg was sent home. He would never be fit for war again. The smell of sour breast milk and rotten oranges was everywhere he went, and it was so strong that he had to burn all his clothes to get it off him. The men under his command quickly put out the fire, but he tried to burn them again, and that happened five times. Finally, the senior commander gave the order to let Zeev Feinberg burn whatever he wanted. Perhaps the commander thought that when the clothes disappeared, Zeev Feinberg's mind would be eased. But it is the nature of the mind to hold on to its pain even when the material substance of it has turned to ashes. The smell of sour milk and rotting oranges only grew stronger, only grew worse. Now it seeped into Zeev Feinberg's sleep. Again and again he woke up screaming because he saw himself drowning in hot, festering breast milk. It did not take long for Zeev Feinberg to stop sleeping because he feared his dreams. To keep himself awake, and mainly finally to remove the terrible smell from his skin, he washed his face incessantly. He scrubbed it with cold water and boiling water, rubbed it with leaves and then with rocks. His skin peeled, but Zeev Feinberg did not stop.

On the contrary. Every time he peeled a layer of dry skin from his nose as if it were wrapping paper he hoped that now, if he scrubbed just a little more, the sour milk and the face of the child who had never known its taste would finally disappear.

When Sonya saw Zeev Feinberg on his return, her scream reverberated throughout the village. Sonya didn't scream because of the way he looked, although at the time his face was an open wound from so much scrubbing and peeling. Nor was it because of the way he smelled, although on his way home he had rolled around in everything he found, if only it would remove the rotting oranges and sour milk. It was because of his eyes. His confident blue eyes now seemed as if acid had been poured on them. Zeev Feinberg looked at Sonya without seeing her, and he refused to look at his son at all. Perhaps he was afraid that he would pollute the child's innocence with his gaze.

Zeev Feinberg didn't tell Sonya about the bullet that had ripped through the baby and its mother. And Sonya didn't ask. At first she told herself that it was for Zeev Feinberg's sake that she wasn't asking, for his own good. Perhaps it would heal the wound. But when sleep released the shackles on his tongue and he began to mutter the horrors of the dream, Sonya covered her ears with trembling hands. She didn't want to hear. Zeev Feinberg screamed in his sleep and Sonya went silently out of the house. Multitudes of stars filled the sky, all of them witnesses to her flight. But she could not bring herself to go back inside. A wounded animal disguised as her husband was lying in her bed. No matter how much Sonya wanted to go back to bed and kiss the man who was writhing in his nightmares, her feet refused to move. When she was a child, standing on the shores of a blue lake, she saw a drowning man waving his arms in the water. The women on the shore screamed and a man hurried into the lake in his clothes. But when he reached the drowning man, instead of pulling him out of the water to safety, he found himself being dragged down into the depths. The drowning man's grip was stronger than his rescuer's and the terror in his heart was very great. In his attempts to climb onto the body of his friend to reach the air he craved, he drowned the man trying to save him. Their bodies were found almost a week later. Even the widows could not tell which of the masses of rotting flesh was the drowning man and which his rescuer. Much time had passed since then. Sonya was not standing near the blue lake, but near white cotton sheets. And yet she was not moved to extend her hand to the man on the sheets lest she find herself dragged behind Zeev Feinberg into the depths.

Sonya was ashamed of herself for her cowardice, and the more ashamed she grew, the greater her fear was. Since she was afraid to talk to Zeev Feinberg about his secret, she tried to talk to him about other things. After all, there was still the sun, and a broken chair leg, and the newspapers. But Sonya very quickly discovered that she could not speak about them either. From day to day Zeev Feinberg's secret grew increasingly larger. Until it grew so much that it blocked the sun's rays. Its shadow covered the home of Zeev Feinberg and Sonya. Again it was impossible to see anything. Again it was impossible to say anything. The secret lay in wait for them behind every sentence. Every word. And if, for example, Zeev Feinberg wanted to say, "You know, soon it'll be spring," there was always the chance that he'd say instead, "I killed a woman and a child, and the woman hugged the ground and the child hugged the woman." So he kept quiet. Sonya did too. And Yair, of the age when children lick their first words with their tongues, looked at his parents and kept quiet as well.

3

YAACOV MARKOVITCH knew nothing about what had happened to Zeev Feinberg after the day they met in the street. He himself was sent to the Galilee several weeks later. It wasn't easy for him to leave. His commanders had to come to his house, wake up that strange man and his gorgeous wife by pounding on the door and demand that he get dressed and come to do his duty. The harder they tried to focus on Yaacov Markovitch's sleepy face, the more their eyes wandered to the breathtaking creature that was Bella Markovitch. Even with a baby wrapped around her neck, her eyes glowed in the gloom and her golden hair was gathered on her head like sheaves of wheat. Forcibly returning their gaze to Yaacov Markovitch, they admonished him: "What's this, why aren't you moving?" although the answer was becoming clear right before their eyes. It was because of that woman standing beside him that he wasn't moving. That woman, who was a head taller than he, who did not look at him even once as he refused to go with them, who did not look at his commanding officers as they raised their voices to her husband, the woman whose eyes gazed far into the night, as if she weren't listening to an argument about life and death here but to the song of the toads.

In the end, the commanding officers threatened to confiscate the house. This land, which Yaacov Markovitch had received many years ago, was not given to deserters. The good people in power had put it in Jewish hands so that it would yield Jewish crops. But Jewish hands are sometimes required to put down the pickaxe and pick up the rifle. Yaacov Markovitch listened and said, "All these years I have grown grapes, and olives, and sometimes apricots. Sometimes the fruit was sweet, sometimes bitter. Sometimes it didn't ripen, sometimes maggots ate it. But never, in all these years, have I ever grown a Jewish crop. An olive remained an olive. A grape could only be a grape. And an apricot—an apricot." The commanders began to wonder silently whether Yaacov Markovitch was even fit to take part in the war. Their eyes returned to the woman. The man had given them a nice tongue-lashing, but one look at Bella Markovitch and they knew that it was a subterfuge. It wasn't because of the olives, the grapes or the apricots that this man was clinging to his land and denying its Jewishness. Was it right that at a time when the soldiers were in their trenches, he himself was entrenched in the flesh of his wife? He would come with them this very minute or he would have to find a new house for himself and his family to live in.

At that moment Zvi Markovitch stopped playing with his mother's hair and burst into loud crying. Yaacov Markovitch took one look at the tearful child and said, "I'll come with you." He turned and went inside to pack his things. The commanding officers remained at the door with the woman and child. When they summoned the strength to steal another glance at Bella Markovitch, they didn't understand what had happened. The golden hair had become a totally ordinary blonde. The sheaves of wheat were only the ends of curly hair, not especially neatly combed. The eyes still glowed in the darkness, but their glow was no different from that of a cat's eyes or a cow's when you come across them in the middle of the night. In summary, the moment Yaacov Markovitch took his eyes off Bella Markovitch she was transformed from an adored idol to a flesh-and-blood woman. Yaacov Markovitch returned and left the house, his rucksack slung over his shoulder. When he kissed the top of the child's head he stopped crying and looked at him, surprised. Yaacov Markovitch had never kissed him before. The dry, cracked lips pressed against a spot slightly above his forehead, imprinting it with heat and longing.

Now Yaacov Markovitch turned and looked at his wife. The commanders held their breath: it was as if someone had put a lighted match to an already extinguished campfire, igniting it all at once. Because now Bella was again the most beautiful woman they had ever seen. How was it possible that earlier her hair had looked absolutely ordinary, when now it was perfectly clear that it was strands of pure gold—according to one of the officers—or definitely dripping honey—according to the other one. While they silently pondered the matter, Yaacov Markovitch took a single step towards Bella Markovitch. The commanders averted their eyes from the scene. A man deserved to part from his wife and son in private, even if he was a deserter. So they kept their eyes downcast, allowing the man and his wife to fall into each other's arms, even to press their lips together, his dry and cracked, hers full and red. But none of that happened between Yaacov Markovitch and Bella Markovitch. They stood staring at one another for a long time, and might have continued to stare at each other for many more minutes if the commanding officers hadn't decided that every emotional leave-taking must come to an end, and began to clear their throats. Yaacov Markovitch turned to them and began to walk away from the house. Every step he took became lighter, less solid. The gravitational center of his existence, the obsession that had become the very marrow in his bones, remained behind in the stone house. And she was surrounded by olives and grapevines and apricots.

*

And so Yaacov Markovitch arrived in the Galilee, fading into nothingness. He fought in pointless battles during the day and wrote pointless letters at night. Bella never replied, but she read the letters with wonder-filled eyes, like a person listening to the song of a bird and not understanding it. Yaacov Markovitch wrote nothing about the war, and not because he wanted to protect Bella from it. He himself never met the war, even though all the days he passed far from home were spent inside it. But the war never touched his being, because he saved that entirely for Bella. People like him move like a beetle on the soil of this country, and they don't care what flag is waving above it. Yaacov Markovitch was clearly not a beetle, but one more Jewish farmer with smuggled weapons and also heroic tales in his bag. And yet he was like a man waking from a dream, his ears filled with the cries of imagined people, and he didn't know whether to listen to them or not. He heard the shouts of his commanders in the distance, the cries of the men in his company, the booming of shells. But they grew increasingly weaker even as he doubted that they were real, because every sound that was not Bella's voice seemed false now. And so Markovitch gradually dropped out of the world, because while they screamed at him and shouted in his ear and shook him, he was thinking about what he would write to Bella when the day ended.

All the days that Yaacov Markovitch spent in the battlefield in the Galilee, Bella Markovitch spent in the battlefield of the village. True, enemy feet never trod on the thresholds of the houses, never even reached the orchards, but neighbors' quarrels were more than enough to make everyone miserable. The women were tired and worried and angry, and the children were nothing more than a reflection of their mothers. Every little thing brought them to tears, and the tears of one quickly infected all the others, passing from child to child like a chickenpox epidemic. During the first days of the war the women still felt as if they shared the same fate, which united them and smoothed out every wrinkle of a quarrel. But as the weeks passed each woman entrenched herself in her own misery, piling on brick upon brick of worry and fear and much uncertainty.

"It's unbelievable that she could make apricot jam now, of all times."

"The smell is all over the village."

"And she never even thought to offer some to anybody else."

But even when Bella went to her neighbors' houses and offered the women some jam, none of them would take any. Though apricots were scarce that year and the smell of it cooking was mouth-watering, they would not eat Bella Markovitch's jam. Because from the moment Yaacov Markovitch left his house, there was no mistaking the change in Bella. Her happiness was too blatant; it screamed to high heaven. Her golden hair dazzled the children and her eyes flashed with such enthusiasm that they sometimes misled the distant troops, which saw them as highly important fire signals. And worst of all—she sang. As long as her mouth was closed, the women could forgive the affront of Bella Markovitch's beauty, which after all was not something she had chosen. But when she sang there was no escaping the fact that Bella Markovitch was literally blossoming. For the first time in her life her beauty was not the result of an external eye looking at her, but emerged from her inner self, and that was something the women could not forgive. It was one thing to glow because men were looking at you, and quite something else when it was a result of your own feelings. Bella Markovitch's beauty stained the entire village.

A man going off to battle—what does he want for himself? He wants the world to stand still. For a man who has buried his friends with his own hands, grain growing peacefully is like a slap in the face. Not to mention a carpet of anemones. What a disgrace. The village land should stop its womb and wait for its owners. But the trees continued to give fruit and the anemones reddened and the grain grew at a uniform pace. Bella Markovitch looked at all that, a song she had written for herself on her lips. She rarely thought of Yaacov Markovitch. The house had divested itself of his image. And his most personal things—the writings of Jabotinsky, for example—had gradually become free of the burden of their owner. Sometimes, when Zvi built sandcastles, her thoughts would wander to the weeks and days ahead. Then she would ask herself if all those days would be like these days, if the prison guard had indeed gone, never to return. And she would remain within these four walls, in the prison that had become a home, and raise this child in blessed, shining solitude.

But Yaacov Markovitch's letters continued to arrive. Sometimes they were so sentimental that, immediately after reading them, Bella had to wash her hands to keep them from getting sticky. Once or twice she was seized by a paroxysm of laughter at the sight of an especially clichéd metaphor. Bella felt guilty about that, but certainly would have forgiven herself if she had known how generous she was in comparison to her husband's fellow soldiers in the regiment. From the first day, they saw Yaacov Markovitch's otherness. They all wore the same uniform, but in that too the others could see, even smell, the strangeness of that quiet man. During the long nights, when the campfire had been doused and their stories had been chewed thin, there was always someone who dared to snatch Markovitch's notebook. Then they all gathered around to hear what he would say to his beloved this time, adding all sorts of moans and sighs that made their ears redden. Yaacov Markovitch begged and pleaded, stamped his feet and shouted loudly, but all that only intensified the soldiers' ridicule the way oil fuels a fire.

One night Yaacov Markovitch looked for his notebook, and it was gone. No sound came from the tents, so he knew immediately that the men had something to do with it. That quiet, which surrounded the entire camp, was like the silence of troops before they fired. From where the men lay in ambush, their eyes studied him. What would he do? Would he run back and forth searching feverishly? Or perhaps he would stay where he was and begin pleading, the best flammable material for heating up a group of bored men? But Yaacov Markovitch did not do either of those things. The minutes passed and he remained standing where he was, uttering not a word. The men's excited anticipation changed to boredom. That night they would have to find something else to amuse them. But as they were still trying to figure out how to tie up the fat private from the adjacent company while he slept, they heard they sound of a rifle being cocked. Yaacov Markovitch stood with his weapon in his hand, and he was aiming it at the bushes where the men were hiding. "The notebook. Now."

Most people can easily distinguish between various sounds. Fewer know how to distinguish between different silences. Yaacov Markovitch's commander was one of them. Not only could he easily differentiate between the cawing of a crow and the courting of a barn owl, he also understood the huge gap between a smiling silence and a terrifying one. The entire time the men had been taunting Yaacov Markovitch, the commander lay in his tent and heard nothing. But the moment Yaacov Markovitch cocked his weapon, the commander sensed the thickness of the air outside his tent. He hurried outside with his gun drawn and found himself facing that private whose name he couldn't remember even at that moment.

"What are you doing, soldier?"

"My notebook disappeared, sir. I want it back."

"And that's why you're threatening the bushes with a rifle?"

"Not the bushes, sir. The people behind them."

The commander squinted at the bushes but didn't see a thing. The men, who had grown silent earlier out of their fear of Markovitch, dared not breathe at all now out of their fear of the commander.

"And how do you know that there are people there, soldier?"

"I feel them, Sir. I feel their ridicule through the leaves."

The commander studied Yaacov Markovitch, noting that sometimes extraordinary talents are hidden in the bodies of very ordinary people.

"Come out and return this man's notebook, you bunch of hyenas. And you—after you write whatever you want to write in it, come to talk to me."

Yaacov Markovitch wrote quickly and then left his tent to go and see his commander. He left the notebook in the open, where it lay, as if tempting the soldiers to dare touch it. When he arrived his commander scrutinized him at length, with considerable disappointment. Seeing Yaacov Markovitch aim his rifle at the bushes, the commander had felt the heat radiating from under the man's uniform, threatening to set it on fire. Yaacov Markovitch almost glowed with anger. But now, having had the chance to pour his heart onto the pages of the notebook, Yaacov Markovitch's anger was dulled, leaving the observer with only the ashes of his face. He had once again become what he was in times of peace: a simple, unmemorable man with an awkward demeanor and watery eyes.

"It must be clear to you that I could have punished you. The rifle in your hands was not intended to threaten our own soldiers."

Yaacov Markovitch hesitated before replying, and the commander was worried that his instincts had been wrong. He had already made up his mind to punish the private if he dared to apologize for his actions. But then Yaacov Markovitch looked directly into his commander's eyes and replied,

"I would do it again."

To Markovitch's surprise, the commander smiled at that reply and ordered him to sit, gesturing cordially.

"Fire, soldier. That's what you have. I may not have noticed it till now, but tonight there was no mistaking it. And with the help of fire like yours, only with its help, will we win the struggle for this country."

Yaacov Markovitch's commanding officer was not the least bit concerned about the fact that the fire he so admired was inspired by a woman and not by the homeland. The source of the fire did not matter to him, as long as he thought he could harness it to his own objectives. Throughout his military career he had collected dreamers and visionaries wherever he went. His colleagues raised an eyebrow, but he knew very well that, despite the ludicrous appearance of his obsession-ridden men, if exploited properly they were an elite company superior to all our forces put together. Apart from Markovitch, he adopted a chronic gambler who had escaped to Palestine from his American creditors. The gambler's Jewishness was rather questionable, but the fire that blazed in his eyes at the sight of a pair of dice caused the commander to keep him close. Even before he met the gambler, he had insisted on adding to his regiment a lame young man whom everyone thought would never make it through a battle. He came from a religious family in Zefat, and was proud that his forefathers had never left the land of Eretz Israel. After the angel Uriel came to him in a dream and ordered him to join the Zionists, he left his home and his city and limped all the way to the military headquarters in the

Jezreel Valley. The recruiting officer laughed in his face, but the commander gave his eyes a quick glance and ordered his men to find him a uniform. Finally he took a merchant from Jaffa, a large-bodied Tunisian who had lost all his possessions and his entire family when he became an alcoholic. The commander met him as he was beating the living daylights out of a barman who refused to pour him another drink. He paid for the drink and promised to pay for many more if only the merchant would come with him.

Markovitch met the three of them shortly after his conversation with the commander. From that day on he spent his time in a separate tent along with the chronic gambler, the lame dreamer and the iron-fisted drunkard. He no longer had to worry about the notebook. The three men had taken a quick look at the notebook and immediately understood that therein resided Yaacov Markovitch's passion. And they respected it deeply, just as they respected their own passions. Yaacov Markovitch was not used to such respect. Admonishments for the way he had treated Bella had been a part of his life for so long that they had already been absorbed into the mix of everyday sounds, like the chirping of crickets or the constant burbling of the brook. And now, in the tent where the commander had put him, there was not a crumb of admonishment, not an iota of condemnation. His comrades in the tent were sociable, even friendly. For the first time in his life Yaacov Markovitch knew the sweet taste of belonging to a group.

At night, when the sounds of laughter and song drifted from the other tents into theirs, the four men shrugged in disdain. Then one of them launched into a panegyric of his passion, and the others listened intently and with great respect. Yaacov Markovitch would talk about Bella's eyes, the Jaffa merchant extolled the velvet of liquor, the gambler waxed poetic about the sides of a die, and the lame man glorified the angel Uriel. Whenever one finished speaking—not because he had grown tired, heaven forbid, because he could have gone on singing the praises of his passion forever, but out of respect for the others—another would take his place. Often they stayed awake until daylight. Then the lame man would smile in satisfaction, straighten his yarmulke on his head and quote from the Haggadah: "The days of your life refers only to the days. All the days of your life includes the night as well." Sometimes the commander came to visit them in their tent, and was much gratified to see how one man's obsession fed those of the others. The four of them spoke pleasantly to him, but were eager for him to leave. From the moment they had found each other, they saw no point in frittering away their time with people who were not ruled by their passion. They never guessed for a moment that, under his uniform and his rank, the commander was one of them. He was a volcano covered with a green carpet of grass, but under the vegetation and the rocks lava was bubbling.

Until one day the volcano erupted. The gambler was just talking about how he had left his house in the hands of a vindictive creditor when the commander burst in, his eyes blazing. "Tonight!" he roared.

"Tonight?" Yaacov Markovitch asked.

"Tonight. We capture the fortress tonight."

Then the commander told them about his passion: a fortress with reinforced walls that overlooked the valley from the west. For ten years he had been knocking on the walls in his mind, but no one answered. He had almost grown used to wanting it from a distance. But now the British had given it to the Arabs, and that was completely unacceptable. He hadn't slept for more than a week; the screams of the stones being ravished under the shoes of the enemy filled his ears. The chances of victory were slight, he wouldn't hide that. But he preferred the torments of defeat to the shame of acceptance. As soon as the commander finished speaking, the lame man rushed over to hug him. The Jaffa drunkard wiped away a tear surreptitiously and the gambler wept unashamedly. "We'll go with you," Yaacov Markovitch said, and the others agreed unanimously. It was a great honor for a person to fight in the service of such a grand passion, even if it was not his.

They attacked the fortress late at night, advancing under cover of darkness. Yaacov Markovitch and the gambler walked in front, their faces sweaty, burnt by the heat the commander emitted. The drunkard walked a little way behind them, carrying the grateful lame man on his back. And perhaps also the angel Uriel, who the lame man claimed was sitting on his shoulder. The rest of the soldiers walked behind those four, holding their weapons in shaking hands. Even while they were being briefed, far away in the safety of the valley, they had begun to be afraid: the Arabs had the high ground, and the shortage of weapons did not augur well.

When the moon came up, silver and traitorous, the faces of Yaacov Markovitch and his four comrades were flooded with bright light. They looked at it affectionately. For it, like they, owed its existence to something else that gave it its light. The moon continued to shine above the advancing troops, and the whistle of bullets was not long in coming. Yaacov Markovitch realized that he was not surprised. From the first moment it had been clear to him that they would be seen. Nonetheless he would willingly have repeated the words he had spoken in the tent, would have again eagerly joined this journey, which was to no purpose, just as it was the purpose of everything.

The fire radiating from the commander, who was charging forward, illuminated Yaacov Markovitch's face, but the terror of the soldiers behind him froze his back. The sounds of running into the distance were louder than the stamping of feet charging upward. Many retreated. Several moments earlier, when the glow of the moon had shone on the commander's crazed face, the rumor spread among the soldiers that he had gone mad. Some of them stayed with him, erroneously believing that it was the commander's passion, not the madness of his passion, that was surging inside him. Others fled and found themselves making excuses for it for the rest of their lives. And Yaacov Markovitch and his comrades charged forward with smiles on their faces, each picturing the fortress as the embodiment of his own passion. The drunkard saw the walls and, lo and behold, they were a giant mug full of sweet liquor. The gambler knew that the square fortress was nothing but a giant die thrown from on high. The lame man saw the angel Uriel looking down on him from the guard tower, and fell to the ground, bleeding when the angel Uriel hit him easily with a sniper's bullet. Yaacov Markovitch saw clearly that the fortress's refusal to be captured was nothing more than Bella's refusal, so he kissed the lame man on the forehead and rushed forward into battle. Close to the walls themselves he stumbled on the body of the gambler, who had erred in calculating the statistical chance that the sniper who hit the lame man would succeed in hitting him too. Yaacov Markovitch closed his comrade's eyes which, though empty, were nonetheless filled with supreme satisfaction, and charged forward. Now he was already inside the fortress itself, fighting his way among the Arabs. Then he saw the drunkard lying on the ground, a bayonet stuck in his heart, his blood flowing like sweet wine.

Yaacov Markovitch pulled the bayonet out of his comrade's body and used it as he used it, and other people's lives were ended. He had slaughtered several of those people when he heard his commander's voice and thought that his hearing had been affected by the whistle of stray bullets. But then the commander shouted the word "retreat" again, and Yaacov Markovitch's face fell.

It was not his comrades' deaths that saddened Yaacov Markovitch but his commander, who fell in the battle between the voice of reason and the voice of passion. At that moment, Yaacov Markovitch thought about Bella asleep in the stone house in the village. Instead of causing him to run from the battlefield, that image made him tighten his grip on his rifle, as if he were tightening his grip on Bella herself. The rest of the soldiers had already begun to retreat but Yaacov Markovitch continued to load his rifle, magazine after magazine, shooting into the darkness as if he were in the grip of madness. When the commander saw Yaacov Markovitch's madness, his own madness erupted again. For long minutes they stood back to back, the tall, strong commander and the gloriously average Yaacov Markovitch, shooting enemy soldiers, smiles on their faces. They were so calm, so handsome and assured that if a painter or a photographer had captured their image, it would certainly have appeared on a stamp. But unfortunately there was no painter or photographer in the fortress at the time, and even if there had been he would most likely have been dead or wounded, since that was the condition of most of the people there when dawn came.

The first rays of the sun astonished Yaacov Markovitch's commander. He hadn't thought for a moment that he would see the next day. When the moon had risen, giving away their position almost five hours earlier, he already knew quite well that the battle was lost. He continued to charge without hesitation, but called for his troops to retreat when he saw that too many of them were lying on the ground, clearly unable to obey his orders. Even then, when he ordered the retreat, he knew that he himself would not go down from the fortress. He didn't hope to fight, but to find himself a dagger to fall upon, as Saul had done in his time. But then he saw Yaacov Markovitch making love to his madness, and was again filled with blazing passion. Those moments when he was shooting in the darkness, his body pressed up against Yaacov Markovitch's body, his face to the mountains, were the most beautiful moments of his life. Yaacov Markovitch's commander did not want the light of the sun to stain those moments with the sight of the enemy's flag still waving above the fortress. Once he had climbed the hill, he could not return to the valley. Yaacov Markovitch felt his commander's body pressing against his for one more moment, and then the commander broke into a run straight into the line of fire in front of him. Yaacov Markovitch felt his commander's body break away from his, but did not turn to look at him. He knew where he was going. He fired four more bullets, one for each of his friends lying on the hill, and then dropped his gun and turned to go down. He passed the commander's body, lying with his face thrust into the ground. The whistle of the bullets pursuing him kept him from turning his commander onto his back, but he knew very well that if he did, he would see a smile on his dead face.

4

WHEN YAACOV MARKOVITCH returned to camp, his legs were tired and his heart was aching. But he could not sleep. He lay on his mattress in the deserted tent for long hours, to no avail. The other mattresses shouted in his ears relentlessly. The Jaffa merchant's bed was still strongly redolent of liquor, and a pair of dice and two decks of cards lay beside the gambler's bed. A prayer book lay open at its regular place on the lame man's bed: "On my right Michael, on my left Gabriel, in front of me Uriel, behind me Rafael, and on my head the divine spirit of God." Now the prayer book was orphaned. As were the liquor bottle and the dice. Yaacov Markovitch thought about his comrades left behind on the hill and knew that the weight of a great mission lay on his shoulders. He picked up the liquor bottle and drank from it. Then he threw the dice and made a bet with himself about the results. When he won, he picked up the prayer book and called out the name of the angels, lingering on the name Uriel and raising his voice the way the lame man had whenever he reached that angel's name. Usually his raised voice was answered by booming laughter from the adjacent tent, but this time Yaacov Markovitch heard nothing, either because the occupants of the tent were too injured to laugh, or because tears filled his ears. And so Yaacov Markovitch drank and gambled and prayed in memory of his comrades for that entire day and the two days that followed, until soldiers

came to the tent to tell him that the new commander wanted
to speak to him.

Over the three days that had passed since he left his comrades
on the hill, Yaacov Markovitch had perfected his new skills to
the level of art. Now he could pray, drink and gamble all at the
same time. First he would take a large swig of the liquor. While
the liquid was still sliding down his throat, he would toss the dice
and immediately begin to pray, wishing with all his being that the
goddess of luck would drop the dice with the number five showing,
the number of letters in the name Uriel. Sometimes his prayer
was interrupted by a hiccup caused by the liquor. Then Yaacov
Markovitch would apologize with all his being to the lame man,
and give the drunkard a small smile. When the soldiers came to
call him, one of those hiccups escaped his lips. The soldiers didn't
understand that the hiccup was nothing but a magnificent monument to the memory of the Jaffa merchant, or perhaps they did
understand but were not great fans of monuments. One way or
the other, one of them reached out to confiscate the bottle. This
time, Yaacov Markovitch did not have to cock his weapon. The
look in his eye was enough to make the soldier withdraw his hand.
On his right the drunkard, on his left the gambler, in front of
him the lame man, behind him the commander, and above him
one passion spread across the sky of the country—that was how
Yaacov Markovitch walked to the tent of the new commander.

"I understand that you are the only one who survived."

The new commander resembled the old commander in almost
everything except that the former was alive and the latter dead.
He had curly hair and a strong gaze. But did a passion haunt his
dreams? That, Yaacov Markovitch could not say.

"Many survived. The camp is full of them."

"The camp is full of men who retreated. But of those who charged forward, of those who committed suicide on the hill, you are the only one left."

"Yes."

Yaacov Markovitch felt a hiccup rising in his throat and began praying to Uriel to block his mouth and betting on the chances that the angel would actually grant his request. But then the commander uttered a deep, echoing sigh, and Yaacov Markovitch's hiccup was swallowed up inside it, leaving not a trace.

"What a waste. What a waste. It was clear that you didn't stand a chance."

Yaacov Markovitch didn't know whether the commander was waiting for an answer, and decided not to say anything. He couldn't provide a logical answer, and the answer he could provide—either a person understood it himself, or there was no point in it.

"And now we have to attack again."

Now Yaacov Markovitch looked at the commander in confusion. It was clear that the fortress did not dominate his dreams, so why would he attack it again?

"Sir, if we don't stand a chance, why try?"

"Because we've already failed. Every one of the men who survived that hill knows that we almost reached the gates of the fortress. If we give up now, if we go on to other hills and other fortresses, the failure will stick to the soles of their shoes and paralyze their trigger fingers."

Yaacov Markovitch thought about his former commander, whose face was undoubtedly still stuck in the mound of sand on the hill. Was his smile widening now? And would his glazed, gaping eyes now close in the sweet sleep of eternity? Thoughts of this kind floated amid the liquor fumes in his mind, and seemed quite logical when he looked at them through the alcohol fog. In fact, the commander's eyes had been closed from the moment he fell to the ground, and the capture of the fortress would change nothing about them, except that the worms living in them would move onward to other corpses. But that thought did not cross Yaacov Markovitch's mind at all, and if it had, he would most certainly have beaten it away. Instead he looked directly at his new commander and said,

"If you want, I'll follow you to the fortress for the second time."

"Usually, when a person is saved from the inferno, he's in no hurry to return to it."

Yaacov Markovitch hesitated before answering. Looking at the face of his new commander, he very much wanted to say that the defense of the northern villages was his main concern. When he looked into the eyes of his old commander and his three comrades, he almost believed that it was a desire to honor their memory that would drive him to the hill. But when he looked into his heart with wide-open eyes he saw that neither was true. It was for his own sake that Yaacov Markovitch wanted to take the fortress, for his own sake alone. When he had stood back to back with the dead commander, firing into the night, Yaacov Markovitch had felt a wonderful serenity he had never experienced before. All the parts of his body pulsed in perfect harmony. For the first time in his life, he was absolutely sure of where he was and why he was there. Now, sitting in the commander's tent with his head spinning, he yearned to feel the same fiery confidence, the stability of his feet on the ground as the bullets whistled around him. Yaacov Markovitch stood up slowly and saluted the commander with a trembling hand.

"When we speak again, sir, the entire valley will be spread at our feet."

They did not speak again. Yaacov Markovitch's new commander fell not far from where his old commander had fallen, except that the new commander fell on his back, facing upward, and continued to gurgle for quite a while. Yaacov Markovitch stayed at his side, trying to extract something from his fragmented sentences that he could repeat to the commander's family: Ducks. Bible exam. Tamara. Ruth. Burning. Burning. Yaacov Markovitch memorized the words because he thought that they might someday give someone comfort. He never met the commander's family, and didn't know what either Tamara or Ruth looked like. But he never forgot the sight of the new commander's face, no matter how hard he tried. The commander continued to gurgle, moaning the words Tamara and Ruth, Ruth and Tamara, and Yaacov Markovitch felt as if his ears would explode. So he began to repeat Bella's name, rolling it around in his mouth the way Arabs roll worry beads with their fingers: Bella, Bella, Bella, Bella, letting the name fill his ears and his mind, raising and lowering the volume to match the commander's screams.

Apart from the commander, twenty-one other soldiers were killed that night. Each one most likely had his own Tamara, or Ruth, or Bella, but Yaacov Markovitch had no intention of dealing with that, because he knew very well that if he did, it would cost him his sanity. So he did the best thing he could do: he stopped thinking about it. Utterly. The new commander and the old commander lay one on top of the other in a mass grave in the depths of his memory, beside the lame man, the drunkard, the gambler and the other twenty-one young men who weren't even given nicknames. Yaacov Markovitch packed the dirt on them and walked onward without looking back. More than a month later, as he made his way along the winding path under the fortress and looked up at the Jewish flag waving above it, he was filled with a strange sadness that pricked his eyes and quickened his steps.

5

Y AACOV MARKOVITCH pushed his past into a corner. Zeev Feinberg lived his past as if it were an eternal, ongoing present. And Rachel Mandelbaum felt that her past was pursuing her, claws extended, almost catching up to her and becoming the future. Again and again she was awakened in her bed by the sound of the old Jew's skull cracking in Vienna. Many years had passed since she had seen the old man's head hit the curb, long years, but since the war had broken out the sickening sound was alive and palpable in her ears. That sound was so close now that she no longer believed it came from the past. Rachel Mandelbaum knew: the war was getting closer to the village. She knew it even though the newspaper headlines said differently. She heard skulls cracking everywhere in the country, and the echo of their cracking pursued her wherever she went. She knew that, now, the sound came from the battlefields in the north, from the ambushes in the south, from the troops charging from the east and crushing everything in their path. The Austrian boys who had shoved the old man from one to the other in their game had now come out in search of her, and it didn't matter whether they wore swastikas on their sleeves or had blackened their skin and hair and become Arabs.

Rachel Mandelbaum continued watering the roses and feeding the baby that had grown into a child, but at the same time her ears were perked to hear the approaching sounds. Often she broke off in the middle of singing a lullaby in order to hear better, and sometimes she did the complete opposite and sang more loudly, the surprised child looking at her and laughing, and her singing was so loud that the sound of the cracking skull almost disappeared. Almost. She told no one about the sounds in her mind. There was no one to tell. Avraham Mandelbaum had been sent to the south many days before, although even when he was in the same house with her the words they spoke to each other crossed vast oceans before reaching their destination. Yaacov Markovitch had gone north and, except for five letters addressed to Bella, they had heard nothing from him. As for Bella—her face glowed, her skin was radiant and she was all happiness. Rachel Mandelbaum did not dare scorch her happiness with her own anxieties. One day she picked up the child and walked with him to Sonya and Zeev Feinberg's house. At the front door she raised her hand to knock. Then she looked through the window and her hand dropped. Zeev Feinberg and Sonya were sitting in the living room, both silent, his eyes staring into space and hers staring at the floor, and between them sat the child, Yair, uttering not a sound.

At night, when the howls of the hyenas rose and fell like the trumpeting of a siren, she waited for the bombs to come from the air. The night silence did not deceive her for a moment. Before dawn, when her body hurt from hours of tense anticipation, she reached down between her legs and sought comfort. She no longer thought about the Austrian soldier Johann. Her dawn reveries were indistinguishable from her daytime nightmares and her night-time anxieties. But after a while, if she persisted, and her touch was desperate enough, she had a few moments of happiness. Her whole body shuddered gently and silenced the voices, if only for a moment.

*

It would be a great mistake to think that Avraham Mandelbaum did not write letters to his wife. True, none of them were ever sent by mail, were not even put on paper, and yet Avraham Mandelbaum wrote letters with unrivaled devotion. He kept a greeting card to Rachel in his pocket, various and sundry objects that told his life story and captured his love. A red oval stone. The pincer of a scorpion that had rotted in the sand. A twig of blossoming acacia. At night, when his tent-mates were engrossed in their letters, Avraham Mandelbaum would take out one of those things and look at it for a long time. The oval stone, for example, held the crimson of the sky over the village at sunset, and at the same time was a beating red heart and a mysterious spot on the forehead of an Indian woman. Avraham Mandelbaum would look at the stone, thrilled by the multitude of possibilities he was holding in his hand. Then he would close his fingers around the stone and imagine Rachel's fingers opening an envelope and finding it inside. Would she understand, would she stop to look at the crimson sunset, or would she toss it into the yard? Actually, if she did toss it into the yard, the stone would find its place. How pleasant that thought was: the stone that had traveled all the way from the sands of Egypt resting now at the threshold to his house. But every time the mail collector came (the envelopes piled on the back seat of a van, the fresh smell of words newly picked), Avraham Mandelbaum changed his mind and left the stone in his pocket. What a shame, he thought, that people had got used to receiving letters that said everything. How nice it would be if they received letters that said nothing, and the reader could guess at everything in them.

Those thoughts would most likely not have come into Avraham Mandelbaum's mind if he had possessed a modicum of writing skill. But just as he was not a man of the spoken word, he was not man of the written word either. Words in themselves made him quite uneasy. Too determined, too sharp, like a pack of drooling dogs or a group of sneering women. He loved Rachel for her many silences, and he loved the desert because words seemed pointless in it. Why bother to say "It's hot today" when the heat melted the sentence that wanted to describe it even as it was being spoken. The wilderness and fullness of the desert divested words of their meaning. The more the other soldiers tried to fill the vast expanse with words and witticisms, shouting vulgar jokes and lewd stories at each other, the faster their voices fell, and they didn't know why. Avraham Mandelbaum looked at the wadis and the mountains, saw the rocky cliffs and the ravines, and felt how the words spoken here fell rapidly to the ground like rotted fruit. Liberated from words, free to shoot, with the oval stone, the scorpion pincer and the blossoming acacia twig in his pocket, Avraham Mandelbaum was happier in the desert than he had ever been in his life.

Sometimes, at night, he thought about his son. In a little more than a month he would be five. Would he recognize his father when he returned? Avraham Mandelbaum never wondered for a moment whether he himself would recognize his face. For he had changed very much.

It was autumn. The sky saw the people's expectations and filled with clouds. The people saw the clouds in the sky and filled with expectation. The expectation weighed on the clouds and cracked them. Water fell from the cracks drop by drop. The people looked up at the sky and said, "rain". The moment they said "rain" the drops stopped falling and the clouds moved onward. After such a false rain, the heat was more oppressive than before. Finally, the people stopped looking up at the sky because they could not bear the expectation. It was autumn, and the expectation stood in the air like the heat of August, like the cold of January. And where the expectation stood there was neither heat nor cold, only hope, which is always at room temperature. And when the expectation and the hope began to rot, like pumpkins forgotten in the field for too long, when the people said that there wouldn't be any rain this year, and didn't even look up with a defiant expression of "I dare you" when the sky became superfluous, simply superfluous—that's when the rain fell and filled the land. And after the rain came the flowers, slowly, hesitantly, having been crushed enough by the burden of corpses the previous spring. And corpses fell on them this time too, first many, then fewer, until one morning the war ended exactly as it had begun, the corpses rotted on the ground and flowers were picked and placed on the corpses. Then Avraham Mandelbaum returned home and found his wife hanging in the butcher's shop.

When her husband found her, Rachel Mandelbaum's stiff corpse had already begun to turn blue. Avraham Mandelbaum stood in the doorway of the butcher's shop and looked at the small, shriveled body, its beauty still clearly visible. The shapely breasts unaffected by gravity, the brown braid almost as thick as the rope wound around her neck. And of course the ears, delicate shells that could no longer bear the sound of the cracking skull, whose pain had ordered her hands to knot the rope and her legs to climb on the stool and her body to lean forward. Because it was now, when the sounds of war had ceased, when the newspapers had taken on a festive look and people danced in the streets, that Rachel Mandelbaum realized that the sounds in her mind would never stop. While the battles were still raging she had hoped that, if only the Jews won, the sickening sound of the cracking skull would stop and she would once again hear other sounds—the laughter of children, the whisper of wheat waving in the wind, the mooing of a cow. But when victory was declared she heard nothing but the familiar sound and knew full well that it would always be with her. From the moment she discovered that the war could definitely pursue her all the way from Europe, she also understood that she would never know for sure that the battles had indeed ended. That she was truly safe.

A person who doesn't know how to live only rarely knows how to die. Rachel Mandelbaum could not have chosen a less propitious time to take her own life. The entire country was borne on a wave of happiness and joy, so relieved that it floated in the air. The villagers greeted each other warmly, smiling even at their most hated neighbors. Cakes were baked, flags were hung, men fell into their wives' arms and children hugged their fathers' legs. Not only was the happiness genuine, it was also what the occasion demanded. Truly a moral obligation. And Rachel Mandelbaum had betrayed that obligation. In the small museum established later near the entrance road, between the falafel stand and the ceramics shop, the newspaper clipping announcing the end of the war was removed. And with good reason: the newspapers lauded the celebrations in the neighboring towns, but in mentioning the village they focused entirely on Rachel Mandelbaum's suicide, which everyone agreed showed a total lack of consideration.

Several weeks later, when the happiness died down and minds became occupied with other things, the villagers began to ask what had actually happened to her, to Rachel Mandelbaum. As long as elation had spread its wings over them the people had taken refuge in its shadow and were a peaceful, unified group. But now the elation had floated onward, and people looked at each other and recalled that they were not at all alike. One woman rediscovered how much she hated her husband's face. Another man remembered how much he hated his job. Forgotten debts, unresolved arguments, hopes and jealousies, all reappeared with the passing of the wave of happiness that had washed over everyone when the war ended. The sweet fullness vanished, and now their mouths were filled with the taste of everydayness, of life getting back to normal. However much they had yearned for that life when the war was going on, however much they had prayed and hoped and anticipated, a nostalgic tone stole into their voices when they spoke of those days now. "Then," they signed at the end of a meal, "then there was 'togetherness'." They looked around and saw no "togetherness", but when their eyes fell upon Avraham Mandelbaum's butcher's shop they knew that if there was a chance of finding it, it was certainly there. And so, after spending the first days of mourning in blessed solitude, Avraham Mandelbaum found himself surrounded by crowds of people who came to ask, to care for, to advise, to rescue, because, after all, "the tragedy is ours too" and "the whole village is with you".

Avraham Mandelbaum did not send them away. Instead, he sent himself away. So bustling were the rooms that no one noticed his absence. For long hours he would sit on the stone steps and watch the sun descend into the sea, his hands drawn to the love letters that had remained in his pocket when he returned from the war. He would move his hand from the red stone to the scorpion pincer and back again, running his fingers over them as if they were a mezuzah. The scorpion pincer gleamed like marble, and the oval stone that had been polished by a sea that no longer existed and winds that had come and gone was rolled again and again between his butcher's fingers, which also had something of the sea and the wind in them, because they knew profound sadness and great longing.

As Avraham Mandelbaum's hands stroked the stone in full wakefulness, his brain was immersed in a kind of torpor. From the moment he'd found Rachel in the butcher's shop his mind had become enshrouded by a thin white fog that blinded his eyes and dulled his ears. He didn't know why she had climbed onto the stool on the day the battles had ended, of all days. She had never told him about the cracked skull that had sent her from Vienna to the village, so he couldn't guess that it was precisely the same skull that had sent her from the village to the stool and the rope. Avraham Mandelbaum thought of other reasons, dark and evil reasons. He still didn't see them clearly because the blessed fog in his mind concealed every sharp insight. And yet, through the white, woolly clouds, he could make out a slowly approaching thought, a large black bear waiting to pounce. Sometimes the fog dispersed a bit, and the bear would come closer to him, and Avraham Mandelbaum would recoil and say to himself: because of me. Because of me. She hanged herself because of me. Because I was coming back.

Then he would pull the white fog over himself again like a child hiding under his blanket from the terrors of the night, reach out for the stone and press it harder between his thumb and forefinger. What sort of comfort it was that he drew from the stone, Avraham Mandelbaum could not say. But when the black bear bared its teeth, or when he was trapped in the talons of a curious neighbor, or dragged unwillingly into a conversation with one of the farmers, his fingers were immediately drawn to his pocket and he felt a slight relief.

But one morning he woke up and the stone was gone. The sun had just risen, and none of the villagers had awakened and come to fill their existential void with a condolence call. Avraham Mandelbaum took off his nightshirt, put on his trousers and reached into his pocket. But this time his fingers did not find what they sought. He froze for a moment, then pulled himself together and reached into his other pocket—perhaps it was there, perhaps he had moved it yesterday in a moment of distraction. But the other pocket was just as empty as the first, and Avraham Mandelbaum's hand found nothing there to hold on to but air. Suddenly a voice came from the yard. Avraham Mandelbaum hurried out without even putting on his shirt. When he burst out of the house, whose windows were shuttered, the strong sunlight dazzled him, and it took him a little while to distinguish between the muttering child and the rose bush. Yotam was half a head shorter than the roses, and the hair on the top of his head reached only the lowest petals. Despite the days he had already spent on earth, he still looked at the roses with a wonder that was never less—or more—than the wonder with which he looked at grasshoppers, people and tea kettles. Yotam duck-walked among the branches, his steps hesitant, as if his legs still hadn't decided whether they wanted to walk or float. His arms extended sideways from his body, and he walked on the surface of the damp ground like an acrobat on a tightrope. Avraham Mandelbaum's eyes were drawn to the small, fisted hand. What was the child hiding? Suddenly he saw a familiar red color between the child's fingers. The stone. In a single step he covered the distance that had taken Yotam at least ten steps to cross. He reached out and picked up the surprised child. Yotam waved his arms in protest, and the rose bush repaid him with a thorn scratch on his hand. Avraham Mandelbaum's oval stone, the sun of an Egyptian desert that he had carried in his pocket and polished with his fingers, fell into the rose bushes.

The child burst into tears, not because of the loss of the stone that had so fascinated him when he woke up at dawn—the world was full of such fascinations—but because the roses had betrayed him. Avraham Mandelbaum paid no attention to the child's crying, nor did he lick away the drops of blood on the small hand. He put his crying son on the ground and began to crawl among the roses, searching for the love letter to Rachel Mandelbaum and not finding it, picking up one stone or another hopefully and throwing it down in disgust. The child cried harder, but Avraham Mandelbaum remained on all fours on the damp ground, his eyes glued to the clumps of sand. Gone. The stone was gone. And with the stone, the blessed fog also disappeared, rising from Avraham Mandelbaum's eyes like the curtain in a theater, revealing what he had not dared to look at until now: Rachel Mandelbaum never wanted him. Never loved him. If there was a reason for her suicide, it was he himself.

Then he looked at the roses with blazing eyes. The pride of Rachel Mandelbaum's garden. The one indulgence she allowed herself. The neighbors whispered that, even on that morning when she plaited her hair into a thick braid, took a thick rope and went into the butcher's shop, even on that morning, she got up early to water the bushes, to caress the leaves. Had she also bothered to caress the boy's cheek that way? Had she ever caressed his cheeks that way?

Many months had passed since Avraham Mandelbaum had ripped out the carob tree in the field with his own hands. Now he ripped out the rose bushes in his yard. Then he had been avenging the affront to his wife at having to give birth alone. This time he was avenging the affront Rachel Mandelbaum had inflicted on him, the loneliness that was spreading inside him, infecting his blood and closing his ears to the child's crying. The thorns protested, painting Avraham Mandelbaum's hands red, and redness also spread over his cheeks. The smell of the blood flowing from his palms blended with the smell of the roses, sweet and heavy in the blazing sun. Yotam kept crying the entire time: at first in surprise, then in anger, and finally in long, uniform sobs.

Avraham Mandelbaum paid no attention to that, just as he paid no attention to the blood and the roses, and simply went back to scouring the ground. Perhaps now he would find the stone. When the villagers came to visit the grieving family they found Avraham Mandelbaum standing in his yard, his hands covered in blood and the roses lying on the ground like corpses.

6

THEY TOOK the child to Sonya. Apart from Rachel Mandelbaum, no one knew that Zeev Feinberg's sadness had expanded to swallow up his spirited wife as well. For the villagers Sonya continued to be what she had always been: a woman capable of bringing a man back from the sea with curses and contempt, whose skin smelled like orange groves and who had enough chutzpah to chase off horse thieves by howling like a wolf. A woman like that, the villagers thought as they carried the weeping child to her, a woman like that would know what to do with a child whose mother had hanged herself in a butcher's shop and whose father beheaded rose bushes.

The sound of hands knocking at the door disrupted the deathly silence that had long since fallen upon the home of Sonya and Zeev Feinberg. The house was so quiet that the flies had stopped visiting because they were embarrassed by the sound of their wings filling the rooms. Sonya didn't open the door immediately. She remained sitting on the sofa for a long while, her eyes staring into space, trying to figure out the meaning of the sounds. But then Yotam's voice rose over the noise of the knocking. A child crying. A child crying in the yard. She hadn't heard her own son, Yair, cry for days. He had been so infected by his parents' silence that he hardly uttered a sound. Zeev Feinberg appeared from the bedroom. Over the last few weeks his sleep had been so chaotic that he couldn't distinguish between day and night, and he lay down on the mattress every time he felt even a twinge of welcome tiredness. He fell asleep for several minutes and then woke up, sometimes screaming, sometimes with his body trembling and his eyes open in terror. He was walking the line between sleep and wakefulness when he suddenly heard Yotam's voice. A child crying. A child crying in the yard. He got up immediately and went into the living room, where he met Sonya hurrying to the door. A child was crying. A child was crying in the yard and they were rushing out to him, but there was no way of knowing whether they were doing it to save him or so that he could save them.

There were four of them. Michael Nudelman held the thrashing child with his hands extended forward, like someone holding a snared fox. Haya Nudelman stood behind her husband, feeling extremely righteous and compassionate. Yeshayahu Ron stood behind Haya Nudelman, pretending to look at the crying child while he was actually studying her rear end. His wife, Leah Ron, pushed between him and the front door, pretending not to notice what her husband was doing. When Sonya and Zeev Feinberg opened the door of their house, all four of them squeezed inside, talking at the same time.

"He went crazy!"

"No question about it!"

"He tore up all the roses!"

"And with his hands, no less!"

"The poor child, growing up without a mother."

"And with a crazy father."

"And there's something's wrong with him too."

"Definitely, crying like that without stop!"

"He cried all the way over here."

"And kicked and scratched, a real wild animal."

"It's a good thing our Michael held him so tight."

"And his wife is so kind-hearted."

"Thank you, Yeshayahu, that's a very great compliment."

As they spoke they examined the inside of the house, for mouths speak only to camouflage searching eyes. Zeev Feinberg and Sonya had many virtues, but cleanliness was not one of them. But the living room held nothing of the motley jumble that had characterized the house in the past. Then, all sorts of objects had been piled on the floor, and though the connection between them was definitely random, they still created a charming mosaic when seen together. A rag doll, patched trousers, three pencils—Sonya had the strange ability to turn all those into something different, more sublime. She never picked flowers and put them on the table—she always returned from the field with something odd in her hand. A turtle shell that became an ashtray, a dry leaf with veins in the shape of a nude woman, a horseshoe that, when held upside down, looked like a smiling mouth. The village women would wrinkle their noses at the sight of the dirt and disorder, but when they returned to their scrubbed, lookalike homes they couldn't help recalling the garlic-clove eyes that Sonya had hung above the smiling horseshoe mouth, a face-talisman laughing at bad luck. Now, with the weeping child as an excuse to examine the inside of the house, they found nothing of that delightful disorder in it. The jumble was still there, but this time it looked like a hill of ruins and not an amusement park. The air seemed to have become thicker when they stepped through the door, and words weighed so heavily in their mouths that they gradually stopped speaking them. Even Yeshayahu Ron felt it, and momentarily removed his glance from Haya Nudelman's rear end to see what was actually going on here.

Though he had very quick hands, both in field work and in the work of love, Yeshayahu Ron's brain was quite dull. That is not to say that he was stupid; he was definitely capable of calculating without using his fingers, and giving fiery speeches that were sometimes more than moderately successful. He could easily identify the moment he stopped loving his wife, even though their love had run around for a while before it grew silent, like a chicken without a head. But when it came to the geology of the mind, to the layers hidden from the eye, Yeshayahu Ron felt as lost as a child. And now, turning his gaze from Haya Nudelman's absolutely wonderful rear end, he couldn't see what was bothering him so much about the inside of the house. He shifted his weight from foot to foot uneasily, like a beast of burden trying to guess at the weight of an approaching load without understanding it. But the place looked as it always had, so why not return to the exciting rear end? What was it in the room that held his eyes, and why did he feel as if he could—if only the others weren't here—burst into tears?

Yeshayahu Ron could feel how oppressive the house was, but the source of that feeling was beyond his ken. And precisely because nothing had changed, precisely because the turtle shell was still on the table and the dry leaf had crumbled on the shelf, precisely because the horseshoe was where it had always been, precisely because of all that, the house was a corpse fossilized in its stagnation. Until the day she had seen Zeev Feinberg walking on the road with acid in his eyes, Sonya had been constantly changing, and the house along with her. Sometimes she would get up in the morning and decide to put the turtle shell on the tree in the yard, perhaps a bird might come and build a nest in it. Sometimes she would move the horseshoe to Yair's room to amuse him with galloping sounds. And there were days when she threw out everything—every bit of decoration in the house—picked up Yair and said, "Let's go find some new things." But from the day Zeev Feinberg had returned with the shame of the dead child filling his mind, Sonya no longer went out to look for everyday treasures, and the treasures in her house turned back into what they actually were—ordinary, charmless objects.

Yeshayahu Ron didn't understand that. Zeev Feinberg and Sonya sensed it only dimly. But the oppressiveness of the house did not bother Yotam in the least because he had been crying for more than two hours now. His throat was dry and a faint fear stirred in the depths of his heart that he might continue crying forever, crying and crying and crying, because, truthfully, he had forgotten how to stop. He didn't remember the roses, the red marvel that had caused him to go out into the yard that morning, or its thorny betrayal and the scratch it had left on his hand. Now he was crying because Michael Nudelman was holding him with outstretched arms, because his father wasn't here, and because his mother wasn't here in another sense of the word, which he had noticed but did not truly grasp. But then, through his tears, he saw something new and wonderful: Zeev Feinberg's mustache. When Zeev Feinberg came closer to look at the child, his magnificent mustache hovered right above Yotam's face. And even though it had become patchy, even ragged, the mustache still managed to do what everything else had failed to do—it made Yotam Mandelbaum stop crying. The child dropped his crying the way he let go of a toy he was clutching when he suddenly saw another toy. The tangle of black hair snaked above him, intriguing and inviting. The child immediately reached out to Zeev Feinberg's mustache and pulled it hard.

"Aie!" Zeev Feinberg cried. And at that moment, with the single blow of that word, the dark sorcery that had enveloped the house shattered. Because Sonya burst out laughing; she couldn't help it. Zeev Feinberg's look of confusion when the child tugged at the glory of his manhood drove her to the floor, where she sat and laughed and laughed and laughed. Zeev Feinberg looked at her and began to laugh too. And Yotam, who had not heard that sweet sound for many days and had already begun to wonder whether grown-ups were even able to produce it, pulled the mustache again and burst with pleasure. Sonya looked at her husband and knew they had been saved. The blue of his eyes, which was not murky for the first time in a long while, was like a window that had been cleaned after too many months.

7

MORE THAN TWO WEEKS had passed since the war had ended, and Yaacov Markovitch still hadn't come home. Nor had he written any letters. Whenever Bella was out in the field she couldn't help turning her head to the road to see if he was there. The more days that passed, the more frequently she looked. He might be returning at any moment. At any moment she might see his puny, bent figure walking down the winding path from the hill. Often her eyes played tricks on her: one morning the old postman's slow gait looked to her like Markovitch's, and it sent her running into the house. Once inside she looked around, confused. After a moment she sat down on the bed, and got her breath back as her heart pounded like a drum. What would she say to him? What would she say to him? She spent quite a while contemplating a large array of possibilities in her mind, until the postman arrived and knocked on the door. Looking at the old man's face, she was filled with embarrassment at her mistake, but on another day she again erred in thinking that Yeshayahu Ron walking in the field with a hoe on his shoulder was none other than Yaacov Markovitch returning with his rifle. This time she did not go into the house but stood firmly beside the stone fence, her entire body tensed as she struggled to restore the cold contempt to her eyes that had been absent from them for so long. Sometimes she asked herself if the eternal flame of hatred could be extinguished. And perhaps, just as time extinguished great love, great hatred could remain only an ember. But the days she spent alone, which had distanced the memory of the sin Yaacov Markovitch had committed, had also given her a taste of freedom. And that taste was so sweet, so precious, that the thought of Markovitch's return had become unbearable.

Yaacov Markovitch did not abandon his passion, did not forget his wife in the village. But he had another, more pressing obligation. He had promised himself that when the war ended, he would first go to the homes of his comrades. To the families of the lame man, the drunkard and the gambler. The longer he wandered, the more frazzled Bella's nerves became. Would he come back or wouldn't he? And as happens often in cases of frazzled nerves, when a person withdraws into a constant, dizzying uncertainty, it was someone else's problems that put an end to Bella's torment. When Bella Markovitch heard how Avraham Mandelbaum had slaughtered the roses and forgotten his son, she hurried to his house. She walked alone on the path leading to the house. The neighbors, who had visited the place en masse until that morning, were now in their own homes, looking out resentfully at the *meshiginner*'s house. When Rachel Mandelbaum hanged herself in the butcher's shop they helped her husband with small talk, consoled him with futile visits. And now he too was losing his mind, losing it with such criminal negligence that they could not blame him, and yet how could they not blame a person who abandoned himself so eagerly to madness, embraced it with arms spread wide and brought total destruction upon himself—yes, yes, brought it upon himself? When a person has the flu the illness takes over his body and he himself is not to blame for anything. But when a person becomes mentally ill we enter into the wonderful world of choice and guilt, because tragedies happen to all of us, but not all of us rip out beds of roses with our bare hands and ignore our crying children as if they were stray cats—no, we would treat a stray cat better. True, Rachel Mandelbaum died a sudden, tragic death. But we've all known such tragedies of some kind, and even small tragedies are large to the people who endure them, like the day little Asher Shahar's puppy died and his weeping shook the village; even tragedies like that are respected here, as long as they're kept in proportion.

From the moment the villagers decided to make Avraham Mandelbaum the reason for his tragedy, they no longer had a drop of compassion for him. They cast him out just as lepers or plague-stricken people—in a different village, at a different time—were cast out. Rachel Mandelbaum's madness was a dead madness. But Avraham Mandelbaum's madness was alive and well. And perhaps contagious. The sort of contagion the village people were deathly afraid of. Contagious things robbed them of their sympathy and ordered them to distance themselves. In vain did they tell themselves that mental illness was different from physical illness. And even when they met someone with a severe physical illness they tried to place the blame on him. "He must have been a big drinker", "or lived an indecent life"; "I heard that he hardly ever washed his hands", "that his house was filthy". So they would speculate and search (maybe he got out of bed too late. Maybe he got out of bed too soon?) until they found something. Oh, then a smile of victory would appear on their faces, for the moment they found a reason for their friend's downfall they felt that they themselves were protected. Because, in the end, the world was a very organized place, and a person didn't fall into a pit unless he'd dug it for himself earlier.

That was why the villagers stayed in their houses and closed the curtains in order not even to see Avraham Mandelbaum's house. And that was why they didn't smell, couldn't smell, the smoke pluming from his yard. Bella Markovitch did smell the smoke, and hurried towards the back of the house, where it was coming from. There she found Avraham Mandelbaum burning all of Rachel Mandelbaum's belongings: five dresses, two nightdresses and many curtains she had made for herself from her past, from the wardrobe she had brought with her from there.

"What are you doing?" Bella Markovitch shouted. Avraham Mandelbaum did not turn to her. He was engrossed in tearing up his wife's nightdress. He had expected the fabric to resist, to scream as he tore it. But Rachel's nightdress maintained the custom of the body that had worn it and, like that body, let go of its existence the moment the pressure was too strong. With no effort at all the nightdress was torn in two by Avraham Mandelbaum's hands and he, furious at its submission, threw the pieces angrily into the fire.

"Because of me. She hung herself because of me. Because she didn't want me to come back." Avraham Mandelbaum's words remained in his mouth, and Bella didn't hear a thing. Nonetheless she understood. She reached out and placed a hand on Avraham Mandelbaum's shoulder. She did so hesitantly, because he was a big man and his rage was even bigger. But at the touch of Bella Markovitch's hand on his shoulder, Avraham Mandelbaum calmed down instantly. Sometimes a broken man needs nothing more than the touch of another person's hand on his shoulder.

While Avraham Mandelbaum was reveling in the touch of her hand, Bella Markovitch saw something that made her spring from where she stood: in the depths of the fire, lying among its flames, was a notebook. It was small and bound in stiff leather that saved it from the flames for a few minutes. When Bella saw the notebook the binding had already begun to surrender to the lashes of the flames, and in another moment the pages and the words on them would turn to ashes. "Bastard," Bella cried. Avraham Mandelbaum looked at her in surprise. A split second ago an angel had placed its redeeming hand on his shoulder, and now a she-devil, her hair glowing in the light of the bonfire, her eyes blazing, was beating it.

"You're burning her diary? Her words? She hardly spoke, that woman, she was so gentle, so closed, and you want to set afire the only words she left us?!"

"But I—"

She would not let him say a word. A man who sets fire to his dead wife's words is forbidden to speak. Bella approached the fire. She turned her head from the flames to Avraham Mandelbaum, from Avraham Mandelbaum to the flames. Her compassion for the grieving slaughterer was now replaced by blazing anger towards this man who would rather burn to ashes every trace of the woman he loved, just so nothing remained of the woman who didn't want him.

Before she realized what she was doing, Bella thrust her hand into the fire and pulled out the notebook. The leather binding that had burnt in the heat of the flames stuck to her hand, leaving a deep, glowing burn. But Bella didn't let go of the notebook until she was sure it was safe, and when she dropped it on the ground she clutched her ruined hand with her good hand and a roar of pain burst from deep in her throat. Avraham Mandelbaum hurried to grab Bella Markovitch before she fell. She didn't fall. She had never been so steady. She stood as she had never stood before, two legs planted on the ground like steel towers. Bella Markovitch looked at her hand, which didn't look like a human hand now. The five fingers remained in place, but the soft, delicate skin had completely separated from the body and was stuck to the notebook binding that lay on the ground. With the skin torn from it Bella Markovitch's hand was nude, a blend of red and purple and yellow, the sweetish, sickening smell of scorched flesh rising from it. The hand of a monster. The hand of a fire monster. How could anyone recognize in it that aristocratic, elegant hand which only had to touch the piano keyboard in order for it to begin to play heavenly music? The fingers that looked so much like pink, elongated petals that if Bella fell asleep in the field, butterflies hurried to alight on them and bees buzzed around them in search of pollen? The hand of a monster. Avraham Mandelbaum looked at the doughy tissue, turned aside and vomited up his guts. But Bella continued to look at the hand, not horrified, but curious. She thought, "So this is what I'm like under the skin," and, "I wonder when the terrible pain will begin," and "Now no man will ever use the word 'perfect' when speaking about me."

A week later, when her burnt hand stopped leaking yellow sap, Bella Markovitch opened Rachel Mandelbaum's notebook. She read it beside the carob tree in whose shadow her friend had given birth, at the foot of the magnificent corpse of the trunk. After Avraham Mandelbaum had ripped out the tree with his bare hands, no one had dared remove it from the path, or even cut its body into firewood. The uprooted tree continued to lie on the side of the road, a silent monument to Avraham Mandelbaum's strength and the madness of his love for his wife. If a villager had to walk past the tree he would quicken his step, and only when he was sure he wasn't within reach of the carob branches would he mumble, "*Meshiginner!*" and continue on his way. But Bella wanted to be near the tree, the way a person who loses a beloved object wants to return to the last place she saw it. And this was the last place she had seen Rachel Mandelbaum before she turned into a pale shadow of herself. So Bella sat on the ground, her back against the fallen trunk, sat Zvi down beside her and gave him two carob pods, rattles to play with, and picked up the notebook. She ran her healthy hand over the leather binding and shuddered, remembering the pain of it on her flesh.

What would she find there, on the other side of the binding that had been twisted in the fire? In all the times the three of them—Bella, Rachel and Sonya—had talked, Rachel had never mentioned that she kept a diary. The very idea that she would keep a diary was a contradiction of Rachel Mandelbaum's existence, which had been so tenuous, hanging by a thread, like those groundsels that turn into white ghost flowers in the summer, and if you merely breathed near them they scattered all around. But words in a diary were heavy, remaining in place even long years after the field and all the flowers in it were plowed and fertilized and abandoned, and many buildings built on it. How then did Rachel Mandelbaum keep a diary?

She didn't keep a diary. When Bella finally dared to open the leather binding (her healthy hand shook, her burnt hand suddenly pinched) she saw short, neat lines written in German. Rachel Mandelbaum's poems. Bella had to wipe her eyes three times before she could manage to read the written words. That woman, who had sworn to speak Hebrew and only Hebrew from the moment she had arrived here, who came to Bella and helped her tame the wild new language so she could use it, the woman whose laugh—rare as it was—had adopted the throatiness of Hebrew rather than the lushness of German, that woman wrote in German. Poems. Rachel Mandelbaum's handwriting on the page was urgent, angular, as if the words were escaping from the left edge of the page to the right edge, hurrying to reach the finishing line before they were caught by their pursuer: Hebrew, the legal wife, which did not tolerate mistresses. That time period—with its battles and declarations, with aphids in the orchard that needed be exterminated and laundry that had to be hung—did not allow for inconsequential poems. The past was a raging bull, every German word a red flag before its eyes, and it immediately gored you with horns of longing.

In the end, Bella Markovitch's tears dried and she finally turned to the poems themselves. But it took only several moments for tears to well up again. Because Rachel Mandelbaum's poems were more beautiful than any poem she had ever read. Compared to them, the words of the poet from Tel Aviv were like the droppings of black pigeons dotting the page. Like alchemists, who knew how to turn flax into gold with their magic, Rachel Mandelbaum had the ability to distill the journey of her days into pure golden tears with her words. Bella sat there the entire day and read Rachel Mandelbaum's poems, her healthy hand holding the notebook, her ruined hand resting on the tree trunk. And when she finished, she knew she would translate them. The thought came so calmly, so clearly that it seemed as if everything she had done until that moment had been meant to bring her to that carob tree where she would decide to translate Rachel Mandelbaum's poems. Bella raised her burnt hand from the tree and ran it across the notebook binding. At the touch of the binding the yellow liquid began to flow once again from the wounds. I would do it again, she whispered to herself, all of it, I would do it again. Because all of it had only one purpose: to rescue Rachel Mandelbaum's poems from destruction, small diamonds of German in the depths of a dark mine that you have to pass through with an agitated mind and weary feet.

Zvi dropped the carob pods and looked at his mother, puzzled. She hadn't turned her gaze to him for a long time now, and the lack of that caressing gaze felt like hunger in his body. He uttered a short, inquisitive cry that had a question mark at its end—are you here? Bella slammed the notebook shut quickly. She was here. Of course she was here. Rachel Mandelbaum's words had waited so long, they could show a bit more patience now. And Zvi, feeling his mother's eyes on him once again, picked up the carob pods, rattled them and banged them against one another to announce loudly to the world that all was well.

8

B EFORE HE WAS THIRTY, the deputy commander of the Irgun
already had three babies named after him. Ephraim Yemini
was born on Kibbutz Nitzanim on 13th June 1948. Between one
labor pain and the next, as her screams were swallowed up by the
boom of mortar shells, his mother decided to call him Ishmael. But
when he was three days old the order came to evacuate the kibbutz
children. The Egyptians were on the way. The exhausted mother
burst into tears and refused to get up. She still wasn't able to walk,
so how could the child eat without her? That evening the kibbutz
members poured a sleeping potion into the children's bottles of milk
before putting them in their mouths. The baby house was bustling
with people because every parent wanted to hold his child's hand,
to see him rocked to sleep one more time before they were separated for who knew how long. And for the children sleep was late
in coming despite the sleeping potion. How could they fall asleep
with their parents beside them, the same parents who normally
left the baby house at night, rebuffing the most desperate pleas,
the ones made with choked throats and wet eyes—Mommy, let me
sleep with you and Daddy—and going home to sleep with heavy
hearts but committed minds. The children looked in amazement
at their parents and the parents looked longingly at their children,
until the sleeping potion overcame puzzlement and all the children
closed their eyes. Then the parents picked them up out of their
beds (so small, so light) and went out into the night air with them.

They walked for almost two hours before meeting the soldiers who had slipped through the Egyptian blockade to meet them. A final kiss, a final hug, shhh! Just don't wake them up! Still asleep, the children were passed from their parents' arms to the soldiers. The parents saw their children cradled in the muscled young arms and asked themselves if they would ever carry the weight of their children again when that war was over. And the soldiers felt the weight of the children in their arms and asked themselves if they would ever get to hold their as yet unborn children like that when the war was over. Only the deputy commander of the Irgun asked himself why he saw only twenty-two babies there when there were supposed to be twenty-three. When he was told that the baby was too young to leave its mother and the mother was too weak to walk he said, "Then I'll go and get both of them," and began to run towards the kibbutz. He came back three hours later, the mother on his back, and in her arms the baby that was supposed to be named Ishmael and would now be called Ephraim.

Ephraim Sharabi was born two months later, though no one would bet on the day or the hour. His father, a first-class sniper, was fighting in the Jerusalem hills at the time. Somehow, rumor reached him that his wife had given birth. To a boy or a girl or a winged monkey—he didn't know. The deputy commander of the Irgun heard about it and ordered the father to return home. He refused. "If within forty-eight hours you're not standing in front of me reporting what it's got between its legs, I'll crack your head open." The father hurried to his home and found that a son had been born to him. He called him Ephraim, rushed back and was killed two weeks later.

Ephraim Greenberg was born in Tel Aviv on a smoggy day in March. He inherited his mother's bulbous nose and unpleasant temperament and his father's skin, which tended to break out into rashes, and his eyebrows, which joined together into a single line. He was quite an ugly baby, although there were undoubtedly others uglier than he. His mother saw him shaking his small fist up and down, and knew that one day he would shake it above a speaker's lectern in the Knesset. So she searched for the name of a great leader to give him. "David" was taken: too many mothers in the maternity ward had coveted that name. "Herzl" was heard ad nauseam in yards and on porches. Yehuda Greenberg stood beside his wife's bed, looking emotionally at his son. The baby began to cry and Fruma gave him a swollen breast. Yehuda saw the huge breast and recalled the whipped-cream breasts she'd had when he tasted them for the first time on the ship bound for Eretz Israel. But when they reached a safe harbor and the divorces were arranged, Fruma chose to have a taste of the country and its men, but in the end returned to him, Yehuda, and married him for the second time. Now those whipped-cream breasts had become breast milk. At that moment Yehuda Greenberg knew that he would give the child the name of the deputy commander of the Irgun, who had sent him on the journey to Europe from which he had returned married. That gesture contained equal parts of gratitude and feelings of inferiority, for just as Yehuda Greenberg appreciated that, in the end, the deputy commander of the Irgun was responsible for his happiness, he also enjoyed imagining himself scolding little Ephraim, who was under his command, "Ephraim! You made caca outside the potty again." To big Ephraim he didn't presume to say anything but "Yes, sir!" Yehuda Greenberg lost no time in suggesting the name to Fruma Greenberg, who thought about it and said, "Yes, he's not a great man yet, but he's definitely on his way to becoming one. Fine, we'll call the baby Ephraim." And the quite ugly baby, as if understanding that he was being spoken about, let out a small fart.

The deputy commander of the Irgun did not speak often about the babies who bore his name. So every time one of his commanders found himself without a worthy name for his son—because "Herzl" was commonplace and "David" was overused, and how much could you honor the three Patriarchs—he immediately decided to call him Ephraim, clearly an original idea. Within six months the deputy commander of the Irgun heard about four more babies, all of whom he had to hug and pick up and stroke, and all the while his mind was occupied with a question about a different child.

The deputy commander of the Irgun had never seen Yair Feinberg. Three months from the day he slept with Sonya, Zeev Feinberg burst into his office with a bottle of liquor in his hand, put it on the desk and shouted, "To my son!"

"Your son?"

"Okay, maybe my daughter. For that, we'll have to wait and see. I swear to God, if it's a girl, and if she has Sonya's scent, I'll have to take machine-guns and grenades from you to defend her against the boys!"

Then Zeev Feinberg burst into thundering laughter that was heard loud and clear throughout headquarters, though not by the deputy commander of the Irgun. The word "son" had settled inside his head, right next to his eardrum, and its body blocked out all other sounds. A son. A child. Growing in Sonya's body was a child. Then Zeev Feinberg opened the bottle and they drank, and then they drank some more. Zeev Feinberg talked about how the taste of Sonya's vagina had changed and was a hundred times sweeter now, as sweet as peach, really. He had never tasted anything like it, well maybe only once, in the past, with that woman from Gedera who had one blue eye and one green eye, and in fact she had twins six months later, one with blue eyes and the other with green ones. Then Zeev Feinberg began to wonder out loud: was it really like a peach, because there was also plum and apricot in it, and how could he describe that sweetness and that texture exactly, and all the while drops of liquor glistened on Zeev Feinberg's marvelous jutting mustache. The deputy commander of the Irgun looked at a drop, and saw two words reflected inside it again and again and again: a child.

Finally Zeev Feinberg stood up and left, but not before he hugged the deputy commander of the Irgun. The deputy commander of the Irgun remained at his desk for a long time, then got up and went to do the only thing he knew how to do: kill Arabs. He killed them in the Galilee, he killed them in Hebron, and in the streets of Jerusalem and the alleyways of Jaffa. Every time the Jewish Yishuv was in need of a retaliatory raid, or defensive action, or—in the interest of historical honesty and accuracy—when they needed to launch a successful attack, the deputy commander of the Irgun was the first to set a personal example. And they named babies after him even before he turned thirty.

Three days after the end of the war, the deputy commander of the Irgun was returning home hungry and tired. So exhausted was he that he didn't notice Fruma Greenberg rushing towards him from the end of the street, so he was easily trapped, like the proverbial deer in the headlights.

"What a miracle, meeting you like this!"

This elicited a polite nod from the deputy commander of the Irgun, who saved the word "miracle" for special occasions, like the day on which he had grabbed a grenade that had landed in the heart of the camp and threw it back.

"Today is little Ephraim's first birthday! It would be so nice if you joined the guests!"

The deputy commander of the Irgun realized that he was trapped. In vain did he point to his dusty, bloodstained uniform and say that it wouldn't be appropriate for him to come to the party like this. Looking at the stains, Fruma's eyes glittered. Her dear husband—a nasty little stone had settled in his kidneys, barring him from any position that had even a drop of heroism in it. Now she would finally be able to show off with a real commander. She put her arm through the arm of the deputy commander of the Irgun and led him to her home. The guests welcomed him enthusiastically. It wasn't every day that a man rubbed shoulders with a great personage on his way to pour himself another glass of lemonade. They asked him about his exploits in the north, interrogated him about his adventures in the south, and whispered above their slices of poppy seed cake—is it true that one night you slipped through the Jordanian blockade to touch the stones of the Western Wall?—but didn't wait for an answer because, for them, there was only one possible answer. The deputy commander of the Irgun smiled politely, letting the stories swirl around him like the mountain encircled by a veil of clouds that adorned Chinese porcelain saucers. But instead of making it clear that they were recounting legends, fairy tales that did not even warrant a reply, the polite smile of the deputy commander of the Irgun only convinced them that their stories were true. It is the nature of polite smiles that people can find in them whatever they wish to find.

"We showed them a thing or two!" a stranger standing beside him roared, dripping sweat and lemonade. The deputy commander of the Irgun nodded. A gesture like that didn't cost money, and it made people very happy. "We drove them out of Lod, sent them packing from Jaffa. And now the land shall have peace for forty years!"

The deputy commander of the Irgun froze in the middle of his nod. "No," he said, "there will be no peace." For even though he was well skilled in nodding and accustomed to feigning heroism when necessary, he was incapable of accepting such self-deception. He himself had seen the eyes of the Arabs of Lod as they packed a few possessions and left on the long march. He saw the blazing sun. Saw a woman trying to nurse a dead baby. And when he looked into her eyes, into the eyes of all the Arabs, it was as if he were looking into his own eyes staring back at him from a mirror. Because he knew that look. Knew the look of a person who had lost the one thing he loved to someone else. When he answered the man dripping sweat and lemonade, it wasn't the landscape of the country or the Mediterranean Sea or Lake Kinneret that he saw. When he answered the man he saw only Sonya's wide-set eyes, and Feinberg's hand caressing the honeyed stomach on which he had rested his head. He saw and said, "How can there be peace in this land?"

Without saying goodbye to anyone, still holding a slice of poppy seed cake in his hand, the deputy commander of the Irgun left the house. The guests looked at him and shrugged. A strange man. He knows very well how to kill, but his ability to take part in an ordinary conversation is no better than that of a grandfather clock. As they were pouring themselves another glass of lemonade, the deputy commander of the Irgun was hurrying to Jaffa. He had to know whether it was true, whether the gaze of an Arab looking at his land was identical to the gaze of a man looking at the woman he loves.

When he arrived in Jaffa he had to walk back and forth in the streets before he found one. He grabbed him by the throat and pressed him up against the wall. Under the pale street light, he looked into his eyes for a long time. If only he would find fear in them. But the Arab returned a different kind of look, one that he knew quite well, and he dropped his hands and let him go. Now he knew that, just as he would smell Sonya's orange scent wherever he went, those people would smell the oranges, the citrus fruits and olives and grapevines that had been theirs, for generations to come.

The deputy commander of the Irgun wandered the streets of Jaffa all night. It was such a long night and the streets were so winding that there were moments when he thought that the sun had set forever, that he would walk those narrow alleyways for eternity, turning right then left, and always finding the same darkness beyond the bend—and another bend after that. Until, at one of the bends, he suddenly saw the sun. Looking at it, he knew that the war had ended. And even though he should have been happy, he was frightened. For the first time in his life he was frightened. The rising sun illuminated the paving stones, bathing the entire street in gold. It was quiet. No artillery shells, no machine-gun bursts, and the whistle of planes and sirens no longer filled the sky. Commanders were not barking orders, soldiers were not muttering prayers. And in that silence, that terrible, horrifying silence, the deputy commander of the Irgun could hear what the war had been kind enough to stifle: Zeev Feinberg telling him that Sonya was with child.

9

IN HIS SEARCH for the families of his dead comrades, Yaacov Markovitch went first to Zefat. He spent a few days with the lame man's family, telling them how he had fought with the angel Uriel before his eyes, and how he died with the song of God on his lips. When they prayed, he prayed with them, and when they blessed the food, he blessed it with them, and when it came time to leave, he understood how much comfort he had taken in those texts and those laws; just as he had books on how to raise citrus fruits, they had books on how to raise people—how they should be fed, what they should drink and how to treat their pain.

From there he went to the home of the Jaffa merchant, where he was welcomed with a glass thrown at the door frame under which he stood. Yaacov Markovitch could not decide—had the glass missed its target, his head, or was this how the inhabitants of the house greeted all their visitors? A jar of olives that hit him squarely in the stomach made it clear to him that this was not meant as a warm welcome. The Jaffa merchant's wife, a skinny creature with steel hands, was throwing a variety of kitchen utensils and food at him. Before Yaacov Markovitch could open his mouth the merchant's wife had already tossed almost half the contents of the house at him, showing no mercy for a very old bottle of wine or a fragrant cake just out of the oven.

"Out! Right now! Or I'll throw knives at you too!"

Yaacov Markovitch considered retreating. He had fought in many battles, but had never experienced the sense of palpable danger he felt when the merchant's wife picked up a pot of boiling milk and waved it in the air.

"Stop! I'm your husband's friend!"

Yaacov Markovitch managed to leap aside before the bubbling liquid could hit him. His shoes were sprayed with white drops, which sizzled for a moment and then cooled.

"Another debt collector? Or some importer of spirits in search of prey? Or maybe you're another one he promised one of our daughters to in exchange for a drink?"

"A farmer," Yaacov Markovitch replied, and that was enough to make the Jaffa merchant's wife put down the basket of eggs she was planning to throw at him. Behind the basket was an angular face and tar-colored hair.

"Do you grow grapes?"

"No."

"Make apple liquor?"

"No."

"Maybe plum liquor?"

"Madam, I have never sold spirits to your husband."

"So did you let him drink for free?"

"No. But I drank to his memory."

Dozens of eggs smashed all at once when the Jaffa merchant's wife stumbled and her legs overturned the basket. Yellow and white blended together on the floor.

"To his memory?" For the first time the harsh voice cracked and shook.

Yaacov Markovitch cleared his throat. "They didn't tell you?"

"People came, but I locked the door and refused to open it. I thought he'd deserted to look for liquor and they came to take him back. I poured boiling oil on them from the roof."

The Jaffa merchant's wife sat down on the filthy floor. Yaacov Markovitch hesitated for a moment, then approached her and sat down beside her.

"Stupid. He was so stupid." Round tears began to rush down her angular face. "And lazy. And unfaithful. Admit it. He was unfaithful!"

Her angular face turned to look directly at Yaacov Markovitch, who shifted uncomfortably until he finally said, "I admit it."

"Unfaithful and a lecher," the Jaffa merchant's wife said, burying her face in her hands. Her wild black hair covered almost her entire body. "And a liar." Yaacov Markovitch lowered his gaze to the floor, where the woman's tears mixed with the milk she had thrown at him earlier and bits of smashed eggs. When she raised her head, he saw that her face was wet with tears.

"You do agree with me that he was a pig?" she said.

"An absolute pig."

"Aahhh!" The woman wailed shrilly.

Yaacov Markovitch stared intensely at a small egg stain on his trousers. He wet his finger with saliva and tried to rub it out. Without success. Not only did the stain refuse to disappear, but his concentration on the stain refused to make the woman's weeping disappear, and it had now become unbearably difficult to listen to. Finally he turned to her and said the only thing he could think of:

"But you should know that he died like a hero."

The Jaffa merchant's wife stopped crying. With a dirty hand she wiped her tears and pushed away the ends of her black hair. When the curtain of tears and hair that had separated them was rolled up, Yaacov Markovitch realized how close he was sitting to the merchant's wife, and drew back slightly. She looked at him mockingly.

"There is no 'dead like a hero'. Dead is dead."

Yaacov Markovitch didn't know how to reply to a remark like that, which might seem simple and fair but still contained a kernel of catastrophe. He decided to venture:

"Even so, there's a difference."

Hearing that, the merchant's wife stood up and went to kitchen. Yaacov Markovitch hurried after her. Most of the utensils and food had already been thrown at the unwanted guest, and only a plump chicken remained on the counter.

"This chicken that I worked hard to clean before you arrived— would you say that it cares whether I make meatballs or cutlets out of it?"

"That's not the same thing, after all—"

"And my husband," she interrupted him, "my stupid, lazy, unfaithful, lecherous pig of a husband, does he care whether they make him into a hero or a villain?!"

She threw the chicken at him too.

Confused and covered in food scraps, Yaacov Markovitch arrived at the American consulate to find out whether his comrade the gambler, whose Jewishness was dubious, had any relatives. He had to wait nearly two hours before he was told that his comrade did not exist.

"What do you mean, he doesn't exist?"

"He's not in our records."

"So look in other records."

"There are no other records."

Stories of the gambler's heroism at the fortress were of no help; nor were heart-rending descriptions of his glorious death. The man might be a hero, the Consul said, straightening his glasses on his nose, but he wasn't an American. When additional investigation at various institutions achieved the same results,

Yaacov Markovitch began to ask himself whether the American gambler whose Jewishness was in doubt had really existed. That he was a gambler, there was no question. But American?

Finally despairing of official institutions, Yaacov Markovitch decided to try his luck with people. Though institutions were more organized, more orderly than people and contained many binders full of facts about people's lives filed alphabetically, it was still possible that the binders and the organization and the orderliness might not know of someone's existence, while people surely did. They remembered him not by his identity number, address or zip code, but by the smell of his body, his diction, the way he shook his friends' hands or struck his enemies. So Yaacov Markovitch left the consuls and the clerks behind and turned to the gambling dens. If anyone knew the American gambler whose Jewishness was dubious, that's where they would be.

His name was André. He was born in France. And America, it turned out, was a place he knew only from pictures. Yaacov Markovitch heard those details from a tall man wearing a shabby trench coat who refused to give his name. Markovitch spent three nights in gambling clubs before he could extract even a sliver of information about his comrade. It appeared that the gamblers were deaf to anything but the clatter of dice. When he spoke to them their eyes glazed over and their mouths clamped shut. Finally, frustrated and furious, Yaacov Markovitch leaped onto a rickety wooden chair and shouted, "I am looking for information about my good friend. He was a gambler, one of you. I thought he was American. Now I'm not sure. He told me that his name was Jacob. I'm not sure of that either."

The gamblers looked at Yaacov Markovitch for a moment before going back to what they were doing. The wooden chair creaked under his weight, and Yaacov Markovitch got off it quickly. That was when the tall man in the shabby trench coat spoke to him. The man's face could be defined more by what it lacked than what it contained: he was missing three teeth. His cheeks were sunken. His eyes were devoid of expression.

"Why do you want information about the American gambler?"

The suspicion in the voice of the man in the trench coat finally made it clear to Yaacov Markovitch why the gamblers had paid no heed to his questions. They almost certainly thought he was a ruthless creditor searching for their friend. So he quickly reassured the man in the trench coat.

"You can be sure that I wish him no ill."

The man in the trench coat looked at him doubtfully. Yaacov Markovitch almost revealed the reason he had come, but after his visit to the Jaffa merchant's wife he decided that, this time, the death announcement would not come from his mouth.

"He was a close friend of mine."

But those words, instead of dispelling the suspicions of the man in the trench coat, only transformed them into terrible anger. The man's entire face reddened and his nostrils widened more with every breath. Unconsciously, Yaacov Markovitch took a step back.

"Close friend? If you were such close friends, why didn't he tell you his real name and where he was from?"

The man's eyes bored into Yaacov Markovitch. His sunken cheeks swelled with rage. Suddenly, Yaacov Markovitch realized that the man standing in front of him was jealous.

"No, you don't understand. We were comrades-in-arms. We fought together."

Now the man in the trench coat looked confused and upset. Before Yaacov Markovitch could understand what was happening, the man had grabbed him by the throat and shoved him up against the wall of the club. None of the gamblers looked up.

Yaacov Markovitch fought to breathe. The thin fingers of the man in the trench coat squeezed his throat like pincers. Blue and purple spots began to appear before his eyes. Beyond them, he caught sight of the gold ring on the man's finger. It was a large ring with a diamond-shaped ruby at its edge. Through his hazy consciousness, Yaacov Markovitch remembered a similar ring worn by the American gambler whose Jewishness was dubious. The man in the trench coat thrust his face to within an inch of Yaacov Markovitch's.

"How can I know that you really were his comrade-in-arms? How can I know that the information I give you won't hurt him?"

With trembling lips and his last ounce of strength Yaacov Markovitch whispered, "Nothing can hurt him anymore."

All at once the man in the trench coat let go of Yaacov Markovitch's throat. When he had got his breath back he looked around and saw that the man with the iron grip was weeping bitterly at the adjacent table. Hesitantly, Yaacov Markovitch approached the table. The man in the trench coat pulled back the chair next to him, gesturing for Yaacov Markovitch to sit down. Yaacov Markovitch hung back for a moment, running his hand over his painful throat, but finally sat down.

"He was such an innocent angel," the man in the trench coat mumbled, "a pure, innocent angel."

Yaacov Markovitch said nothing. Though he loved the gambler with all his heart, a "pure, innocent angel" was not his first choice of description for him.

"So sweet, so pure," the man continued to mumble.

Yaacov Markovitch looked at him, undecided. His common sense and aching neck ordered him to distance himself from the grieving thug with all possible speed. But his obligation to his comrade and his natural curiosity begged him to stay. In the end he gathered the courage to ask, "Did you meet him when he arrived here from America?"

"America? His sweet foot never stepped on American soil!"

"Then where did he come from?"

"Paris. André longed for a croissant worthy of the name every morning of our life together."

Yaacov Markovitch did his best to assemble the various pieces of the puzzle in his mind, to solve on his own the enigma of the American gambler, who it now seemed was not American at all. In the end he gave up.

"Could you please explain to me why, if he was born in France, did say he was American?"

"To throw his creditors in France off the scent. A pack of wolves hunting for prey, that's what they were!"

The man in the trench coat raised his head and pounded the table angrily. The glass of liquor on the table fell and shattered with a crash that frightened Yaacov Markovitch, but made no impression on the other patrons.

"That scum pursued him all through Europe. He finally realized that if he wanted to live, he had to escape from the Continent."

"Why didn't he escape to America?"

"Everyone escapes to America. So he escaped to Israel. Only a madman would escape to Israel."

"And why did he introduce himself as an American?"

The man pulled a bottle of liquor from his trench coat and took a long swig. "Have you ever gambled?"

"No."

"Have you ever wanted something so much that you couldn't let it go, not even if it cost you your life?"

"Yes."

The man in the trench coat gave Yaacov Markovitch a long look and handed him the bottle.

"Less than two hours after he walked off the ship, the minute his hands stopped shaking from seasickness, André was standing at a gambling table with a pair of dice in his hand. And you know how small Palestine is. All the sins crowded together on one miserable street. In no time at all rumors of the French gambler would have spread, the creditors would have come, and André would have found himself hanging from a Jaffa mosque with a bullet through his mouth."

"That's why he pretended to be an American?"

"Before he fell into the trap of lady luck, he was a language teacher. A prodigy with a promising future. He specialized in English and ancient Greek. When he decided to spin a cover story for himself he couldn't decide whether to take on the identity of an American gambler or a Greek philosopher. But the indecision was brief. André admired Hollywood. And despised Greek tragedy."

As he spoke, the man in the trench coat spun the gold ring on his finger. Now Yaacov Markovitch saw how sharp the diamond-shaped ruby was. You could easily slit a person's throat with it. Yaacov Markovitch swallowed his saliva and searched for something nice to say to the man at his side. Finally, he found this:

"I assume that gambling rivalry somehow turned into true friendship for you."

The man in the trench coat shook his head. "I never stood at the gambling table with André."

"Then how did you meet?"

The man pointed to the wall he had pushed Yaacov Markovitch against earlier.

"Here, at that very wall." He went on speaking, stroking the ruby ring with longing. "Even before André arrived in the country, I was hired to take care of an American gambler who had come here to escape from his creditors. For days I lay in wait for him in gambling clubs. Until, one night, I was sure I'd found him: André appeared, rolling the dice and quoting lines he'd learned from Humphrey Bogart movies. When he got up to leave, I grabbed him by the throat and was about to send him to the world where all the dice come up six. But then he started pleading for his life in French. Finally, he convinced me that he wasn't the man I was looking for."

A salty tear fell from the man's eyes and landed right on the sharp stone.

"Of course, in another sense, he *was* the man I was looking for. We spent a whole year together. For his birthday I ordered him a ring just like mine. So he could defend himself in case of trouble. Sweet André! He had a good long laugh at that and said he could never slit a throat with a piece of jewelry I gave him. He was as gentle as a child."

"Why did he leave?"

The moment the words left his mouth, Yaacov Markovitch realized that he'd made a terrible mistake. Curiosity, that sly she-devil, had taken control of his tongue and driven away caution and good sense, the guardians of his life. The hand of the man in the trench coat froze on the stone. He gave him a hostile look.

"He didn't leave. He had to run away."

"Of course," Yaacov Markovitch hastened to agree, "of course."

"One day I came back from a week's trip and found the apartment empty. While I was taking care of a man who had done wrong and run off to Acre, three men from France arrived here. André saw them before they saw him and disappeared. Some said he left the country. Others said he joined the army. But I knew he'd come back. I took care of those bastards and went to look for him among the soldiers."

"You joined the army?"

"God forbid. Exchange my ring for a rifle? Give up intimacy, handmade death, for an alienated, industrial production line? No, no. I was a boutique soldier in a war of factories. My name would never come up at meetings where it was decided who would be awarded a medal of valor, but I swear by this ring that I killed more Arabs than any other soldier. And one officer who was rude to me."

Then Yaacov Markovitch told the man in the trench coat about his beloved's heroic deeds. How he charged the fortress and how he fell, his blood draining out of him. The man in the trench coat listened intently, rubbing his sharp, red ring abstractedly. When Yaacov Markovitch finished speaking he saw the small cuts the ring was making on the man's fingers—tiny drops of blood dotted the table like mushrooms. The man didn't notice the blood. He was totally focused on Yaacov Markovitch's face.

"And after all your comrades were killed, you set out to travel the entire country? A chorus of lamenters consisting of one man?"

"I wanted to know that there was a pair of eyes shedding tears for each one of my comrades."

"Why are the tears for your comrades so important? They're all dead, aren't they?"

"The tears wash away the dust on their names."

The man leaned back, took a cigarette from somewhere in his trench coat. "And did you find the tears you were looking for?"

"I did. The mother of the lame man from Zefad believes that her son is now sitting at the side of the angel Uriel. Her eyes look upward, but her tears fall to the ground. The wife of the drunkard from Jaffa threw knives and eggs and cake at me, but lamented his death before she threw a chicken at me. You thought about cutting my throat with that ring but released me and mourned the gambler. Now I'm afraid that you'll use the ring to cut your own flesh."

The man took a long drag on his cigarette. For the first time he looked as if he too saw the trail of blood drops on the table.

"No," he said, "I won't cut my own flesh. I have to wait for the American gambler whose Jewishness is dubious."

For a long moment they were both silent. It seemed as if there was nothing else to say. Yaacov Markovitch was already thinking about getting up when the man in the trench coat stared at him.

"You said before that you, like him, have something you want so much that you will never let it go. Not even if it costs you your life."

Yaacov Markovitch thought of Bella and replied, "True."

"If so, why didn't you run back to that something, a woman, I suppose? The war went on for so long, and every day you wait, you lose a little more."

Yaacov Markovitch smiled bitterly and replied that a person cannot lose what has never been his. When he finished speaking, even before he had time to see exactly from where, the man took a thick envelope from the depths of his trench coat. "Here." When Yaacov Markovitch opened the envelope the man in the trench coat had handed him, he saw that it contained what men in trench coats usually put into envelopes of that kind: money. But they didn't usually put in so much. The envelope the man handed to Yaacov Markovitch was bursting with bills.

"That money cannot give me back the one thing I want. Who knows, maybe it will give you back the one thing you want."

As he said that, the man in the trench coat stood up, indicating to Yaacov Markovitch that their conversation was over. And so Yaacov Markovitch returned to his home a wealthy man.

10

A s YAACOV MARKOVITCH neared the village, Bella was standing at the edge of the field. Which meant that for a long time she had been searching for a Hebrew rhyme worthy of one of the German rhymes Rachel Mandelbaum had left behind. Whenever she came across an especially recalcitrant line, Bella would stand up from her chair in the living room and pace. As she moved, her skirt would swirl between her legs and sometimes the right rhyme would suddenly come to her in those whispering gusts of wind. But the Hebrew often persisted in its refusal. Then Bella would open the door and go out to the yard for a little walk around the flower beds. The smell of the damp earth usually mollified the words and they deigned to present themselves where she needed them. And sometimes both the flower beds and the smell of the earth failed, and Bella Markovitch had to cross the stone fence and walk in the field behind the house. The distance her legs covered was in direct proportion to the strength of the Hebrew language's resistance to the act of translation. Only several times did she have to go as far as the edge of the field, and only one time did she get as far as the edge of the village before she shouted, "yearning!" and ran back excitedly, straight to her desk.

But there were times when, deeply immersed in her search for an elusive rhyme, Bella would suddenly freeze, tensing at some sound or something she had glimpsed from the corner of her eye. She would hurriedly scan the horizon, the fields, the path leading to the stone house. Only when she was absolutely sure that her senses had misled her, that she was still alone, would she slowly return to her work on the poems, the tip of her nose still quivering with suspicion. Whenever Bella Markovitch turned her head to the path, Zvi would turn his as well. What he expected to see there he didn't know, but the urgency of his mother's movements, that inner chord that suddenly tensed within her, sent his glance to the hill. When Bella was engrossed in translating and he was tired of his games he would sometimes go outside and look at the path, perplexed. Perhaps the thing his mother was waiting for would appear. And he would stand and wait without knowing what he was waiting for. Before he was four years old, he had become a master of waiting. The present was nothing but a corridor he had to pass through on the way to his true, unknown destination. And so, unaware of what she was doing, Bella transferred to her son the same waiting sickness that had haunted her from the time she was a young girl.

The day Yaacov Markovitch returned home Zvi was walking several steps away from his mother, looking with interest at the insects in the field. He had long since learned that at such moments, when his mother paced to and fro, her lips moving soundlessly and her beautiful forehead furrowed with thought—at such moments he must not bother her. Bella stood at the edge of the field, trying with all manner of incantations and oaths to force the words to submit to her, tempting them with promises, to no avail. Through her open eyes she saw only letters, mainly letters, and they were infuriatingly obstinate. But between the letters she suddenly saw someone walking down the hill. Bella let him walk without giving him any further thought. The man walking in the distance was erect, his gait one of restrained power. It could not be Yaacov Markovitch. Bella returned to her pursuit of Hebrew and a few moments later, when it had made up its mind not to acquiesce this time, she turned around angrily and kicked the ground. That kick totally destroyed the small beetle which, for several moments, had been making Zvi's life happy. But the child didn't cry. He knew in his heart that beetles, as delightful as they might be, were nothing more than a cheap substitute, something to pass the time when he wasn't waiting, his eyes on the path leading down from the hill. So he looked at the path again—and saw a man. Zvi quickly turned to his mother, but Bella (furious at her failure, though slightly amused as well) was already nearing the house. So be it. That man walking down the path was clearly not the thing his mother was waiting for. He would simply walk past the stone fence and continue on his way, just as everyone else did.

Nonetheless he looked at him as he came nearer, and every step the man took was like a tiny window opening in Zvi's chest, because the steps reminded him of something he couldn't remember at all, and when the man was only a few meters away from the stone fence Zvi's eyes filled with tears. Because now that man would keep walking, and beetles and toys would continue to change nothing, and there would be only the expectation and the waiting, the expectation and the waiting for he did not know what, which nevertheless compelled him day after day to watch the path and the hill that so many people walked down without ever stopping. But then the man turned and began walking towards the house, and Zvi snapped out of his reverie and ran straight into the surprised arms of Yaacov Markovitch.

Inside the house, through the open door, Bella heard the pounding of Zvi's running feet. From where she stood she couldn't see what had captured the boy's heart. Most likely a bird. Perhaps a cat. One way or the other, when he came back he would have to eat lunch. Bella went into the kitchen and took out two plates, and that's how she was standing, the two plates in her hand, when Yaacov Markovitch entered the house carrying her son in his arms.

A few days later the child was already calling him Papa. Yaacov Markovitch was surprised—he had never spoken that word to the child, and he was absolutely certain that he hadn't heard it from Bella. If so, from where had Zvi dredged up the word Papa, which made him smile whenever he said it and caused small waves of heat to ripple through Yaacov Markovitch's body? Yaacov Markovitch said to Bella, "He must have heard one of the village children calling his father that." Bella stifled an urge to nod. Since Yaacov Markovitch had returned her face had become a frozen ivory mask. It remained frozen even while she slept. Zvi was sleeping less. He'd only just been put to bed, and already the patter of his feet on the floor could be heard hurrying to the sofa where Yaacov Markovitch lay, to make sure he was still there. Sometimes Yaacov Markovitch would be awakened in the middle of the night by the touch of small, fascinated hands exploring his face. Yaacov Markovitch's face, a face universally acknowledged to be lacking in any distinctive features, a face that was forgotten almost immediately by anyone who looked at it—that face was an inexhaustible source of interest and pleasure for the child. He studied the slightly sunken eyes, the sparse eyebrows, the valleys of wrinkles at the corner of the mouth, the hill of the forehead. Yaacov Markovitch abandoned himself to the investigation with every fiber of his being, even when the child pinched his nose or stuck an incautious finger into his eye. Sometimes he thought that, until Zvi had begun his investigation, he had never really known his own face. For Yaacov Markovitch every pat and pinch, every scratch and tickle was further proof of his existence.

From the bedroom, Bella listened to Zvi's nocturnal explorations. She heard his feet padding to the living room and her heart clenched. Though, for a long time, she had wished that the child would finally stop interrupting her sleep with his fears and thoughts, now she hoped every night that he was on his way to her. She wanted to see his round face peering through the crack in the door as he asked, "May I?" then charged onto her bed before she had time to say no. He'd ask for a song or a story, or he'd prattle on about a dream and fall asleep before he could finish. The pleasure her son derived from playing with the face she hated aroused intense emotions in her. Much time passed before she recognized it for what it was. Jealousy. She was jealous of Yaacov Markovitch. That fact seemed so incredible to her, so loathsome, that Bella doubled her efforts to look away from Yaacov Markovitch's face. Yaacov Markovitch noticed it, but nonetheless was unable to take his eyes off her, for she was—still was—the most beautiful woman he had ever seen in his life. Though she was no longer perfect. A large scar covered her left hand, and it was so horrible that even his eyes could find no beauty in it. Several times he tried to ask her what had caused the scar, and each time she replied with a cold look. He decided, therefore, to ask Feinberg. But when he reached his friend's house he found it shuttered and locked.

Ten days earlier, Sonya had appeared in the office of the deputy commander of the Irgun. He was engrossed in a book at the time, and when he raised his eyes he saw her there. As if she had always stood there. As if he had raised his eyes a thousand times in the past in anticipation of that exact sight, and had been forced to make do with only the spareness of the office. He had to lower his eyes to the book again, and raise them a second time in order to make sure he wasn't imagining it. But when he raised his gaze again she was still standing there. Slightly fuller. Very determined. Her gray, far-apart eyes looking directly at him. And for a brief moment the deputy commander of the Irgun thought that, lo and behold, the day had come and he was cured of his love for her. Because when he looked past his desk at Sonya he felt nothing but surprise. His heart did not pound. The blood continued to flow slowly through his veins. His body temperature remained unchanged. Apart from the caw of a crow, there was no sound of birdsong from the street. In short—Sonya's presence in the room seemed to the deputy commander of the Irgun to have no effect whatsoever. But then, like the bombs he had planted in the war, whose delayed fuses allowed several moments before everything burst into flames, the delayed fuse of Sonya's presence in the room came to an end. The heart of the deputy commander of the Irgun began to pound like a rusty plane propeller, his blood surged through his veins, his body temperature leaped upward, and all the birds in Tel Aviv (sparrows in the streets, pigeons in the plazas, blackbirds on electric wires, honey-suckers in gardens, seagulls on the pier and one canary in a brothel) began to sing all at once.

With the birdsong deafening him, the deputy commander of the Irgun asked Sonya why she had come. He was convinced that the noise of the birds had scrambled her words when she replied that she had come to ask him to save her husband. "Save him? Feinberg?" What he actually wanted to say was: you're asking me to save Feinberg? Feinberg, who sleeps with you at night and hugs you in the morning and is entitled, any time he wants—even right now!—to run his finger along your cheek? What exactly is there to save such a man from? What evil could possibly threaten him?

Sonya sat down on a wooden chair in front of the desk and took a deep breath. "Okay, it's like this." And then she told the deputy commander of the Irgun the story of Feinberg's war experience, how he set off to it tall and straight and returned from it a broken man, how sleepless his nights were and how restless his days, how he had scrubbed the skin off his body with sponges and stones, how he started as tensely as a beaten dog at every step and sound, how he tortured himself, writhing and suffering, because of a secret that she dared not ask about, that gave him no rest. "When the boy came, I thought that would save him," Sonya said, and the ears of the deputy commander of the Irgun trembled. But then she told him about the son of some friends who was brought to them after his mother committed suicide and his father was driven mad with sorrow. She said that for several days she had harbored the hope that the presence of the child would be enough to bring him back to himself. But the comfort the child brought with him did not last long, was only a brief respite from the rain, a single ray of sun after which the winter seemed a hundred times colder.

"Now I have two children on my hands. I can't take care of Zevik too. And even if I could, I don't know how." The deputy commander of the Irgun looked into Sonya's eyes. He expected to see tears there, but instead he met only silent, gray, granite rocks.

"What do you want me to do?"

"Once he escaped to your office with Markovitch and asked you to save his life. You sent him to Europe then. So send him to Europe. Do it now too."

"To Europe?"

"The land here is poisoning him."

The deputy commander of the Irgun pointed out that the land in Europe was not particularly well known for its good qualities either, so maybe she should send Feinberg to a sanatorium? Sonya burst out laughing. No, she wouldn't lock Feinberg up with a bunch of emaciated women and hallucinating artists. Just as she wouldn't send a wounded tiger to recuperate on a farm. Not because she was concerned about the animals on the farm, but because the total boredom was liable to damage the tiger.

"He needs a good hunt. He needs something to pursue. Something to hate and something to love, and a clear distinction between the two."

The deputy commander of the Irgun thought about that for a moment. True, the hunting season was at its height, and he had often thought of suggesting to Feinberg that he join the squads that combed Europe for escaped Nazis. But he had rejected the idea time after time. He knew very well that it wasn't to avenge the Jewish people that he wanted to send his friend to the forests of Germany, but because of a pair of gray eyes and a subtle scent of citrus groves, and a child whose face he had never seen but who sent question marks galloping through his mind every time he thought about him. But the situation was different now. Now he wasn't the one who wanted to send Feinberg away, but Sonya herself. Before he realized what he was doing his mouth was already saying,

"On one condition."

Sonya straightened her back, surprised. The thought that the deputy commander of the Irgun might impose conditions had never occurred to her. Nor to him.

"Come to work here, in Tel Aviv. I need a secretary. As long as Feinberg is in Europe, there's nothing to keep you in the village."

"But the house—"

"I'll rent you an apartment."

"I assume that you expect to have a key?"

"I promise that I won't even knock on the door if you don't invite me first."

Sonya looked at the deputy commander of the Irgun and smiled. "I'm sorry, Ephraim. For a minute I made the mistake of thinking that you were taking advantage of my situation."

The deputy commander of the Irgun rebuked Sonya. The condition that he imposed was meant for her good just as much as for his. True, he wanted to see her at his side every day (and every night, and in the oval spaces between day and night and night and day), but she was also too tired to begin waiting on the shore for Feinberg now, night and day, with a baby in each arm. There were children to feed and a routine to maintain, and a woman cannot subsist without a decent wage. So admit it, Sonya, though it's possible to die of love, it's quite difficult to live from it.

"So be it," Sonya said, "I'll come here." But she immediately warned him that she would take apart this office of his because it had been taken over by dust and it rejected sunlight, which made it look more like a mole's burrow than anything else. With every admonishing word the smile of the deputy commander of the Irgun widened. Many hours after Sonya had gone, the scent of oranges stood in the room.

11

WHEN YAACOV MARKOVITCH arrived at Zeev and Sonya Feinberg's house, she was already in Tel Aviv and he was far out at sea. The salty air did him good. The movement of the ship on the water imbued him with serenity. A man escaping from his thoughts should be in perpetual motion. Whenever the memory of the corpses of the mother and child knocked on the porthole of Zeev Feinberg's compartment, he promptly threw it off the deck, and the ship sailed forward on the water. The memory knocked on his stateroom porthole again and again, and again and again; Zeev Feinberg seized it and threw it into the sea below. Until the intervals between one knocking and the next gradually grew longer, and Zeev Feinberg found himself spending entire hours unburdened by pictures of the dead mother hugging the ground and her dead baby hugging her back. He began to leave his compartment. At first, for only a few minutes. He'd look at the sun, the water and the faces of people, then return to his compartment. But soon enough he saw how beautiful the sun, the water and especially the faces of people were, and spent a substantial part of his day outside his compartment.

When he realized that he had indeed returned to the company of people, he wondered when he would return to speaking as well. So much time had passed. Occasionally, when he heard a deck comedian tell an old joke, his tongue danced in his mouth, wanting to break through the wall of his silence. But he refused, fearing that he had already forgotten how to speak to people. Until, one evening, with the help of several glasses of liquor and two giggling young girls, the fortifications of Zeev Feinberg's silence fell. They fell all at once. One moment he was listening to a man at the next table ruin a joke he loved, and the next he was bursting out: "Not like that! You're taking all the punch out of it!" Then he retold the joke to the sound of the young girls' merriment, and did it so well that even the man, angry at first, laughed loudly. Like riding a bicycle, he thought, the body remembers everything. And he went to bed calm and happy, and did not dream about the woman and the baby for a long time.

But the closer they drew to Europe, the more uneasy Zeev Feinberg became. He believed that as long as the ship was moving forward with him in it, he was protected. But the moment they reached land, the moment he stopped moving, the memories he had thrown from the deck would swoop down on him all at once. When they reached their destination he jumped from the ship and began walking rapidly. The people who had come to meet him were obliged to hurry after him. Zeev Feinberg was the only member of the squad who hadn't been in Europe during the war. Before he arrived they were afraid that he would be less motivated than they were. In these kinds of missions personal involvement was everything. But they learned quickly that the opposite was true. Zeev Feinberg did not stop for a moment. In a little more than a month they had covered half the country, scouring village after village, town after town, constantly on the move. Even when the hunt went well, even when they had succeeded in putting their hands on a well-known criminal, Feinberg let no one rest on his laurels. "Let's go. There are others." His comrades on the hunt lauded his determination. No one knew that it was not single-mindedness that drove the mustached hunter, but fear.

Zeev Feinberg pursued because he was being pursued, and that is why only a few escaped him.

The isolated moments of happiness came on the days when the hunt was carried out with supreme speed. Then, with the gas pedal slammed to the floor of the vehicle, with his squad mates shouting at him to slow down, Zeev Feinberg knew that he was indeed escaping for a short time from the mother and baby. The car raced forward, and in that no man's land between times, between the place they had left and the one they would come to, he could finally think about Sonya. He asked himself if now, too, she was standing on the shore, cursing his name with such vulgar words that the sea foam blushed. He tried to guess which words she had chosen, that beloved she-devil, and his mind filled with curses and obscenities that tickled his mustache. Zeev Feinberg would picture Sonya's blazing eyes and chuckle. Then he'd think about how long it would be before he could return to her and grew somber. And all the while the other members of the squad would look at him, their admiration diluted by anxiety, as he scorched the earth of Germany with his driving.

Only one of the squad members was not frightened by Feinberg's speed. Yanosh was a short, thin man of about thirty. More than anything, he looked like a bank clerk. He had no family name. When asked about it he would reply that the Nazis had killed his entire family anyway, and if there's no family   there's no family name. The other men argued with him—even if there's no family, the name remains. To remember them. Then Yanosh would grab the belt that held up his trousers and reply: to remember them, I do other things. Before Zeev Feinberg had joined the squad, Yanosh's belt had already been wound around the necks of twenty German soldiers. The rest of the time the belt stayed around his waist, his button-down shirt shoved under it. Yanosh had struck a simple deal with his commanders in Israel: for every one he caught and turned over to the authorities, he was entitled to kill another one. That way the State of Israel would take its official revenge, and he could take his own personal revenge. Of course, his superiors explained, a deal like that had to remain completely secret if he were caught. But they had nothing to worry about. With his scrawny body, his button-down shirt and shabby belt, Yanosh did not seem at all like the sort of person who committed crimes. Except, perhaps, for tax evasion.

The members of the squad kept their distance from him. He didn't drink, didn't tell jokes, didn't give the others a pat on the back at the end of a successful hunt. He preferred to eat his meals alone. On the other hand, they treated Zeev Feinberg like a prince. The best hunter by day—the life of the party by night. Because from the moment the day's hunt came to an end, Zeev Feinberg feared inactivity so much that his feet compelled him to dance. He would drag all the others with him to theaters in the cities, to inns in the villages, to anywhere a person could move his feet and silence his mind. Yanosh never showed his face in such places, but when the night was over—when the other men wandered to their beds or were hauled to them on someone's shoulders—he waited for Zeev Feinberg near his room. Then they both went out on their silent, nocturnal walk, the thud of their steps echoing in the empty streets. They walked for hours without saying a word, each fleeing his own devils. Zeev Feinberg never asked Yanosh what he was fleeing, and Yanosh never asked Zeev Feinberg.

One night, as they were walking in a dark alley, Yanosh suddenly froze. Zeev Feinberg turned to him in surprise. Yanosh had never stopped walking before four in the morning, and it wasn't even two yet. But then he saw his comrade's eyes, which were fixed on a man crossing the street opposite them, pushing a pram.

"Hermann Ungrat."

And before Zeev Feinberg could say anything, Yanosh had taken off after the man. Feinberg hurried to catch up. After all, they were in the heart of the city, with no back-up. It would be total suicide to try and seize the man now. They would follow him together tonight, and return to capture him tomorrow. Hearing Feinberg's words, Yanosh stopped momentarily, his eyes flashing, his voice trembling. "I would rather die with him here than let that man sleep through another night." Yanosh, with Feinberg at his side, continued to follow the man, who was moving away from them. Now the man took the baby out of the pram and rocked it in his arms, murmuring words that Feinberg didn't understand, but he knew their meaning quite well. He too had walked with his son that way many nights ago, trying to persuade the child with pleas and threats finally to stop crying and go to sleep. The man shifted the baby in his arms and its crying became more subdued. Now he placed it gently in the pram and continued walking. As they followed the father, Yanosh told him about Hermann Ungrat. "The nicest officer in the ghetto. So charming. And cultured. He loved to quote Goethe. In the afternoon, when exhaustion and hunger closed people's mouths, he would say with a smile to anyone he met in the street:

Over all the hilltops
Is rest,
In all the treetops
You can feel
Scarcely a breath:
The little birds quiet in the leaves.
Wait now, soon you
Too will have peace

And my father loved Goethe; he could recite his poems by heart. He always said that love of poetry is the heart's insurance policy. And when he heard Hermann Ungrat recite Goethe, he believed that maybe he would help us."

Now they were standing in the shade of a chestnut tree, watching the man smoke a cigarette under a street light, his left hand on the pram. With his erect posture and pleasing face he looked like a statue. "When the *aktzias* began, my father sent Sarah to him. She was ten. As beautiful as an angel. She knew Goethe by heart. We all looked terrible by then, you know, but Sarah had pink cheeks even in the ghetto. I don't know how, maybe because of the cold. And the hunger made her eyes bluer. I'm not joking. I saw the river in them. No one could harm such an angel. Definitely not a poetry lover. Their hearts are so soft, like cream."

As he spoke, Yanosh pulled his belt out of the loops of his trousers. His button-down shirt was slightly disarranged, one shirt-tail now dangled out of his trousers. "We sent her to plead for our lives. She wore a white dress. An angel's dress. She didn't come back until almost dawn. There was blood on her dress. She could barely walk. My father wailed with fury. Or sorrow. Or guilt. He didn't want to get out of bed anymore. They took him in the next *aktzia*."

All at once, Yanosh leaped from the shade of the chestnut tree and ran towards the man under the street lamp. From where he stood Zeev Feinberg saw Hermann Ungrat, half his body in darkness and half in light, look in surprise at Yanosh. Before Ungrat could grasp what was going on the belt was already around his neck. The illuminated half of his face changed color from healthy pink to red, from red to purple, from purple to gray. Zeev Feinberg left the chestnut tree and walked towards Yanosh, a short, skinny bank clerk who kept pulling his belt tighter and tighter, until it seemed as if the head would separate from the body at any moment. When he was only a few steps from them Zeev Feinberg stopped. He didn't want to interfere. From where he stood he watched Hermann Ungrat, lover of Goethe and ten-year-old girls, fall to his knees. Right after that, from where he stood, he heard the baby cry.

At first he thought Yanosh's ears were deaf to the crying that was coming from the pram. Perhaps they were filled now with the sound of someone else's crying. But when he jerked the belt for the last time, letting the head of the man lying beneath him fall onto the ground with a loud bang, he suddenly noticed the sound. For a long minute Yanosh looked at the baby lying in the pram. And then, his movements mechanical, he removed the belt from Hermann Ungrat's neck and made a very small loop in it.

"No!"

Zeev Feinberg leaped at Yanosh, pushing him aside a moment before he could put the belt around the baby's neck.

"Don't touch the child!"

Zeev Feinberg reached for the bundle in the pram but Yanosh jumped on him. Though Yanosh was smaller and lighter than he was, Zeev Feinberg couldn't shake him off.

"It is sentenced to death, Feinberg; don't try to stop me."

Zeev Feinberg looked into Yanosh's eyes. It was not fear that he saw there, or vengeance, but pure despair. Yanosh would never sleep again if he let the baby live. Just as Zeev Feinberg would never sleep again if he let Yanosh kill it. So they continued to struggle. Zeev Feinberg didn't know how long they wrestled like that, under the street light, beside the crying baby and the cooling body of Hermann Ungrat. Perhaps it was only a few minutes, perhaps an hour. But he knew very well that Yanosh was getting the better of him. He had already broken three of Feinberg's teeth and had beaten him almost senseless when, through the noise of pounding of fists, he suddenly heard the sound of approaching steps. From where he lay on the ground, Yanosh astride him and beating him mercilessly, Zeev Feinberg could see over Yanosh's shoulders that a German policeman was running towards them. A single shot sliced through the night. Yanosh fell on his side.

Zeev Feinberg got his breath back. The policeman, stout and frightened and very red-faced, stood over him.

"What's this? What happened here?"

Zeev Feinberg glanced quickly at the two bodies.

"I was out taking my nightly walk. Suddenly I saw that madman choking that fellow over there. I tried to intervene, but he attacked me too. He definitely would have killed me if you hadn't come."

"And the baby?"

"Mine."

The stout, frightened policeman bent down beside Hermann Ungrat's body. He was looking for some papers that would identify the victim when Zeev Feinberg stunned him with a punch. He looked briefly at the unconscious policeman, the strangled Nazi and the survivor who had been shot. Then he picked up the baby and hurried away.

It was a girl. About a year and a half old. Golden hair, blue eyes and a smile that brought tears to his eyes. He told his fellow squad members that she was a relative. He and Yanosh had gone to get her out of an orphanage. On the way back, they saw a former Nazi officer. Yanosh did his duty, but was shot by a German policeman. Feinberg himself fought with the policeman and escaped. The story was not particularly credible, but Feinberg repeated it so firmly that doubts were silenced. At least for a while. Zeev Feinberg now saved his money, which he had been spending on dances and drink, for wet nurses he found for the baby in the villages they went to. Every time he got out of the car in some village—red roofs, well-tended bushes—he found himself holding the baby tighter because the forces ordering him to drop her were great. He would survey the farmers silently, trying to see which hand held a hoe but sought a trigger. The farmers returned dim, frightened glances that shouted, "I didn't know!" But they had known, Zeev Feinberg thought as he cleaned his gun, of course they had. And that baby girl, the daughter of ghetto officer Hermann Ungrat and an anonymous woman, had also known. If her father and her mother had known, then the baby had somehow known as well, and it made no difference whether she had been a separate egg and sperm at the time.

Under the night lamp, Zeev Feinberg would look at the baby's pink arms, in which pure Aryan blood flowed. And thought about all the arms that had turned blue and gray only because that kind of blood did not flow in them. When he turned off the lamp he was convinced that the next day he would set off without her. He would leave her here. Her golden hair and blue eyes would certainly bring out the kindness of one or other of the villagers. But when dawn came, he wrapped her well and took her with him. Because he had never felt stronger than he did when he held a fatherless Aryan baby in his arms. Even slaughtering Nazis could not compare to its power. The men's satisfaction in taking revenge on an SS officer in his cabbage field lasted only a few seconds, and in those few seconds they saw their image reflected in the eyes of the man pleading for his life, and it was a very noble image indeed. But they knew very well that the officer's eyes themselves had seen countless pleas and, remembering that, their victory turned to defeat even before the blood had dried. But when he held the baby girl in his arms, Zeev Feinberg felt a sense of victory that did not quickly fade. For a man never feels stronger than when he shows mercy to the person upon whose mercy he had previously been dependent.

He no longer went out with the squad members at night but stayed in his room, walking back and forth with the baby girl in his arms, trying to soothe her. Soon enough, he discovered why Hermann Ungrat had gone walking in the dark street late at night: the baby stopped crying only when she was rocked in the open air. Zeev Feinberg, who was used to walking with Yanosh in the small hours of the night, now found himself walking at those very same hours with the baby girl in his arms. And if the dead mother and baby suddenly approached in the darkness of a remote alleyway, he would turn to them with the baby girl in his arms, and they would step back. She was his atonement.

12

THE ENTIRE TIME Zeev Feinberg was pursuing Nazis in the ruins of Europe, Sonya was in Tel Aviv. She left the children in the care of Leah Ron, who agreed—for a small fee—to feed, bathe and put them to sleep, and even play with them a bit. Sonya would rather have left the children in Bella's house, but her friend was immersed in her translation work, and words and small children do not go well together. She didn't want to bring them to Tel Aviv. She knew she would have to work from morning till night, so why leave them in the hands of strangers? Sonya had another reason for not taking the children out of the village: Zvi Markovitch. Yair and Zvi cut their first teeth on the same day. They came down with chickenpox on the same day. They recovered on the same day. They fell asleep at the same time and woke at the same time, and when one of them burst into tears in his house, his mother knew right away that sobs would soon be shaking the house at the end of the street. And so Sonya moved to the city alone, accumulating longing and guilt five days a week and cleansing herself of them with games and special treats on her weekend visits.

She spent her first week in Tel Aviv reorganizing the office of the deputy commander of the Irgun. She cleaned and filed and swept, and felt as if she might die of boredom. In the village she could at least raise her eyes and see large expanses when routine became unbearable. But here you raised your eyes and all you could see were binders. Hundreds of binders. Thousands of pages. All of them waiting only for her. But worse than the binders was the tea. Many people visited the office of the deputy commander of the Irgun, and they all drank tea. One drank it strong, the other weak, one with lemon and the other with milk, one in a glass and the other in a ceramic mug. When the thirtieth visitor arrived and instructed her at length how to mix the sugar in his cup of tea, she could no longer hold her tongue:

"If I may be permitted to ask, how many cups of tea do you drink a day?"

The man across from Sonya was surprised, thought for a moment and replied: five, maybe six. Depending on the weather.

"And the sugar—is it always added for you beforehand?"

"Definitely."

"Let us say, then, that you represent the behavior of the average man in Tel Aviv. Let us also say that there are about 50,000 men in the city who drink five cups of tea a day, which is, if I am not mistaken, 250,000 cups of tea per day. The sugar for those 250,000 cups of tea is added by secretaries, wives, sisters and daughters. Now let us consider what would happen if you added it yourselves. As you spoke. That might be difficult at first, but you would be surprised to discover how quickly the body gets used to this sort of change. Tell me, how many man hours would be gained?"

The man studied Sonya. The deputy commander of the Irgun almost choked, asking himself why, goddamn it, Sonya had to give her cup-of-tea speech now, of all times, in front of the Irgun commander himself. But Sonya did not know whom she was standing in front of, so she stood in front of the commander of the Irgun relaxed and confident, a slightly amused expression in her gray, wide-set eyes. The deputy commander of the Irgun was about to send Sonya out of the office in a tone he hoped would sound admonishing, when he suddenly saw that the commander of the Irgun himself was looking at Sonya with an expression that was no less amused than hers.

"What the hell, Froike, how dare you keep this woman as a secretary?"

The deputy commander of the Irgun heard the words and trembled. His love for Sonya had misled him: it wasn't amusement he saw in the eyes of the commander of the Irgun, but anger at her lack of respect for him. Though the deputy commander of the Irgun was not the sort to frighten easily, he nonetheless did not welcome a clash with the person who was his boss.

As he sought a reply that would reconcile his love for Sonya and his love for his job, the commander of the Irgun continued to fume:

"You lock her in the office, compel her to file documents and send memos; you hide a diamond in piles of moldy binders!"

The deputy commander of the Irgun looked at the commander of the Irgun in confusion, but the latter had already turned away from him and was looking at Sonya:

"What's your name?"

"Sonya."

"Sonya what? I can't order them to print only Sonya on the paper."

"Sonya Feinberg. What paper are you talking about?"

"Your stationery. Sonya Feinberg—In Charge of Integrating Women into the Irgun Workforce."

In addition to the stationery, Sonya was also given an office, a secretary and a free subscription to newspapers. The office was empty, no one ever saw the secretary, and the newspapers were left orphaned on the threshold. Sonya spent her days in the streets and markets, speaking to women and teenage girls, asking questions of old ladies and young women. To those places she had no time to visit she sent her secretary, ordering her to write down what the women knew how to do, what they dreamed of doing and what they actually did. The reports came back to her and she read them until dawn, making notes in her round script, her hand moving so excitedly over the pages that they often tore.

In the evening she waited for the deputy commander of the Irgun outside his office and they would walk along the streets together, Sonya laying out her plans and the deputy commander of the Irgun listening intently, although he occasionally thought that if he were to fall into a deep sewer, Sonya would keep walking and talking without noticing. Her gray eyes looked into the distance, where, through the bus exhaust fumes and the tangle of electric wires, she saw an egalitarian and just Israeli society. She said that without a drop of cynicism, although she was definitely cynical about all the rest: she considered meetings to be nothing more than cracker-devouring festivals. She refused to write memos because they were merely "someone making love to piles of paper, not to reality". Overlong consultations with senior officials made her feet dance under the table, the clack of her heels clearly audible in the room. But no one dared reprove her. The junior staff feared her tongue. The senior staff saw in her an elusive quality that people only rarely come across in such pure form.

Within two months Sonya's name was known to all, but only the deputy commander of the Irgun murmured it in his sleep. For other people that name was now synonymous with uncompromising determination, but for him it was a blanket to wrap himself in. Because unlike the masses, who knew Sonya from her speeches in town squares and tongue-lashings at meetings, he knew the sound of her moans during lovemaking. He knew her throaty laughter. A purring lioness. More than three years had passed since he had held her for the last time, but he could still—if only he were asked—reimagine every single moment of that night.

Sometimes, as they strolled together in the evenings, Sonya would sense the gaze of the deputy commander of the Irgun on her body. Then her legs sent her onward, and her cheeks reddened. Not in embarrassment—a foolish feeling that women tended to wallow in unnecessarily—but in sudden excitement, which she wanted to hide from Ephraim. When the gaze of the deputy commander of the Irgun rested on her with such yearning that it almost left its fingerprints on her body, it would shiver with pleasure. Too much time had passed since a man had looked at her that way. First Yair was born, and her nights moved between his distressing tears and her restless sleep. Then Zeev Feinberg went off to the war, and her nights were spent in loneliness. Then Zeev Feinberg returned from the war, and though he filled her bed, her loneliness only intensified. Now he had gone to Europe, a shadow of a man, and she prayed that he would return a whole person. For all the time that Sonya's body was trapped in constant loneliness, it had almost forgotten that it was meant not only for sleeping and eating, not only for plans, revolutions and speeches, but also for making love. Then came that look from the deputy commander of the Irgun, reminding her body of what hard work, disappointment and longing had allowed it to forget.

Although she quickened her steps, the deputy commander of the Irgun, whose observation skills were unrivaled, could see the flush that spread over Sonya's cheeks. A thousand honey-suckers flapped their wings inside his body. But he pulled himself together immediately: if Sonya knew that he could see the desire aroused in her, she would most certainly distance herself from him. And he himself, though he had yearned for such a moment for so long, had no idea what would happen to him if his wish were granted. So the deputy commander of the Irgun and Sonya continued to walk along the avenue that was shielded from the moonlight by ficus trees, and Zeev Feinberg's presence hovered above them like those bats that suddenly swoop down from the treetops, split the night air with their blind shrieks, then vanish.

One evening, as they walked along the avenue, Sonya saw two young girls move aside at the sight of the deputy commander of the Irgun. More than once she had noticed that women behaved differently when he walked past them. Stories of the heroism of the deputy commander of the Irgun floated around him like the sounds of a flute, even when he was silent, and people followed those sounds as if bewitched. The fact that the deputy commander of the Irgun himself never paid the slightest attention to the effect he had only heightened it. Sonya shifted her glance from the smiling girls to the deputy commander of the Irgun. From where he stood under the street light, she could see nascent flecks of gray in his hair.

"Tell me, Ephraim, why don't you get married?"

This time the deputy commander of the Irgun did not turn his gaze to her as quickly as he usually did. They continued walking along the avenue for almost a minute, Sonya's eyes fixed on the deputy commander of the Irgun, his eyes fixed on the sidewalk, before he stopped and looked at her.

"And why should I get married?"

Sonya was surprised to discover that she was trembling under his glance. "Don't you want a wife? A child?"

The deputy commander of the Irgun looked at Sonya for a long while. "I have a woman. And a child."

And all at once, before Sonya realized what she was doing, she burst into tears. The deputy commander of the Irgun froze. He had never seen her cry. He sometimes thought that those eyes, set one millimeter too far apart to be considered pleasing, were not equipped with tear ducts. And now she was standing in front of him, the salty liquid running down her beautiful, beloved cheeks.

"You knew?"

"I guessed."

"And you didn't say anything?"

"What is there to say?"

Now Sonya was crying so loudly that several of the avenue's residents stuck their heads out of their windows. When she was furious, she devoted herself utterly to her fury; when she loved, she devoted herself utterly to her passion; and now that she was crying, she devoted herself utterly to it. So much so that someone shouted from his balcony, "Call the police!" The deputy commander of the Irgun quickly led Sonya away from the avenue. As they walked through the jumble of alleyways and streets, he suddenly realized that, for a while now, he hadn't been the one leading the way. Through her tears, Sonya had been doing the navigating, and now they were standing in front of her apartment building. When she put the key in the lock, the deputy commander of the Irgun saw that her hand was shaking. That was fine. He was shaking too. A sweet, delicate smell filled the house. As if someone had put a fence around an entire orange grove between the four walls of that one-room apartment. He half stumbled over a monster-sized pile of newspapers—and there he was, inside.

"Sit down. I'll bring pictures."

But before she could go, he grabbed her hand. "There's no point, Sonya. If you're not ready to show me the boy's face, what's the point in my looking at pictures? And if you are ready, if you agree to bring him here, to let me look into his face, to stroke his head—I don't need pictures then either."

When he had finished speaking he continued to hold her hand. He continued to hold it for a long moment. And the moment might have grown even longer, he might have held her other hand as well, even more than that, if there hadn't suddenly been a knock at the door.

It was the secretary, holding a pile of documents. That morning Sonya had instructed her to bring them to her the moment she finished transcribing the breathless handwriting into respectable printed letters. And here they were. It had taken many hours to do, but she managed to finish everything the same day. The woman in charge of integrating women was definitely an inspiration, and when there is inspiration, fingers move more quickly over the typewriter keys. Before that, for example, she had worked for a rather famous lawyer. Inheritances and properties and an occasional real estate transaction. The typing was unbelievably slow then. Hello to the deputy commander of the Irgun. And goodnight.

The secretary left the apartment and Sonya burst out laughing. She's a good girl, she said, even if a bit tiring sometimes. And she has fantastic legs. The deputy commander of the Irgun nodded absently, having barely noticed the secretary's legs.

"You should give her a try," Sonya said. "Before she started working as a secretary, she modeled stockings. Until the new immigrant women from Germany arrived, her legs were considered the longest in Tel Aviv. That's a documented fact."

"If I looked at legs, I'd look at yours."

Sonya tapped her legs and let out a scornful breath. "Two squashes, Ephraim. I expect more from someone with your discerning eye."

She was about to say something more when she suddenly grew silent. The deputy commander of the Irgun was looking at her legs, and she felt her cheeks redden. Her legs were no longer limbs to stand and walk on. Now they were the object of great desire. And that great desire stirred her own desire, for it had been so long since Feinberg had left. And though she remembered very clearly his smell, the weight of his body on her, his sweet moan in her ear when he entered her, she was nonetheless ready to exchange all that for a body with a different weight, a different smell and a different sound of pleasure, as long as it was here, after all the time she had been alone. Sonya extended her hand to the deputy commander of the Irgun and said, "Come."

A delicate scent of soap rose from the sheets. The blanket was a little too heavy. Sonya and the deputy commander of the Irgun lay between the sheet and the blanket, naked and embracing. They lay like that for a long time. Too guilty to continue. Too aroused to stop. Though their bodies were pressed so closely together that not even a pin could fit between them, they were separated by the name Zeev Feinberg, which had not been spoken aloud but still echoed in the room with every breath they took. So they remained as they were, in the intermediate space that was neither unfaithfulness nor innocence, locked in an unmoving embrace. The deputy commander of the Irgun thought about all the things he wanted to do to her if only he dared to move. And Sonya thought about all the things she wanted to do to the body of the deputy commander of the Irgun if only her conscience would let her. They pondered their dreams for hours, until the idea of actually making love seemed pale, inadequate and slightly boring compared to that ongoing parade of thoughts and images. At dawn, Sonya and the deputy commander of the Irgun found themselves exhausted from so much desire, but innocent of having gratified it.

On Friday the deputy commander of the Irgun and Sonya drove to the village. They rode in silence. Sonya was thinking about her son's face and the deputy commander of the Irgun was thinking about his son's face. Sonya had a clear picture in her mind. The deputy commander of the Irgun had a cloudy image of fragmented features in his. When they arrived at Leah Ron's yard, the deputy commander of the Irgun saw a little boy standing beside a pomegranate tree. His heart overflowed. Although baby fat still blurred the boy's face, there was no mistaking the jawline, so similar to that of the deputy commander of the Irgun. And the cheeks, plump and freckled like his mother's, would melt the heart of anyone seeing them. He was about to leap from the car when Sonya said that the boy standing near the pomegranate tree was called Yotam, and he was the son of Rachel Mandelbaum, who killed herself, and Avraham Mandelbaum, who had gone mad with grief.

She was still speaking when a little boy came running out of the house, his face completely hidden by a mop of unruly hair. "Yair!"

And in an instant Sonya was outside the car, hugging the boy hidden under a pile of curls with both hands, and the sound of laughter filled the yard. She immediately rebuked herself, let go of her son and hurried to hug the other, larger child, who continued to stand beside the pomegranate tree, watching her with dull eyes. "Yotam!" But the curly-headed child, refusing to accept that kind of theft, raised his voice in a terrible shriek. So Sonya picked up the two boys together, her back almost breaking under the weight, her heart almost floating with the joy of the reunion. Leah Ron appeared in the doorway of the house, her lips clenched. So, what can you expect from that Sonya, who goes off to Tel Aviv and leaves her children behind, then comes back and lets them yell like that, without a drop of civility, instead of giving them a good slap and putting an end to the commotion right then and there. But when Leah Ron saw the face of the man sitting in the car her lips spread in a broad smile. The deputy commander of the Irgun. In person. What an honor. What an honor.

But before Lean Ron could greet the distinguished personage, while she was still deciding what words would be suitable to the occasion, the deputy commander of the Irgun started the car and drove away. He drove with breakneck speed. Leah Ron assumed he was in a hurry. Sonya knew that he had fled. As he bolted towards Tel Aviv he once again pictured the boy in his mind, a pair of eyes and legs and a pile of curls above a face he had not seen. He hadn't had the courage to see. Because when he saw Sonya pick up the child, when he heard his laughter, he knew that if he only brushed away the curls, if he only looked into the child's eyes, he would not be able to leave.

Several days after the deputy commander of the Irgun fled from the village, Sonya returned to Tel Aviv with the two children in tow. The time she spent with Leah Ron had made it clear to her that it would be better to take the children with her and not leave them with that sourpuss of a woman. She hired a nanny to be with them during the day, and stopped taking walks with the deputy commander of the Irgun so she could be with them in the evening. They met only at meetings, where they smiled politely at each other and took their seats, as far from each other as possible, to keep the deputy commander of the Irgun from smelling Sonya's orange scent, to keep Sonya from detecting the scent of despair that rose from the deputy commander of the Irgun.

13

A WEEK LATER, when the deputy commander of the Irgun returned to his office after an uneventful meeting, he was surprised to find Yaacov Markovitch at his door. Much time had passed since they had seen each other last. As their mouths exchanged polite words, their eyes were busy scrutinizing: the slight tremor above the lip of the deputy commander of the Irgun that gave away his agitation did not escape Yaacov Markovitch's notice. And the deputy commander of the Irgun noted that Yaacov Markovitch's hands were clenched into fists the entire time they spoke, and a clenched fist is a clear declaration: I want something, and I will not leave without it. When each man had assembled a clear intelligence picture in his mind of the person standing opposite, they allowed themselves finally to abandon the empty conversation. Yaacov Markovitch abruptly ended his speech about the disasters of the drought, clenched his fists a bit more tightly and asked, "Have you heard anything from Feinberg?"

The slight tremor above the mustache of the deputy commander of the Irgun worsened slightly. "I sent him to Europe. He's doing an excellent job there."

"When will he be back?"

"Whenever he wants."

Yaacov Markovitch considered that answer before he said, "It's not natural."

The right eyebrow of the deputy commander of the Irgun rose slightly, lending his face an expression of amused puzzlement tinged with a touch of disdain. As a young man he had practiced raising his eyebrow exactly that way in front of the mirror for hours, as if he had guessed how useful that gesture would be to him when he wanted to undermine his opponent's position in an argument years later.

"It's not natural? For a person to avenge the blood of his people, that doesn't seem natural to you?"

Yaacov Markovitch shrank in his chair. Against his will, he recalled the first time he sat in this very same office. How ashamed and timid he had been then in the face of the blazing power of Feinberg and the deputy commander of the Irgun, as if his very existence was an affront to all of human masculinity. Now, facing the slightly raised eyebrow of the deputy commander of the Irgun, he felt small and pathetic, a simple farmer bothering his betters with trivial matters. Nonetheless, he mustered all his strength to go on speaking.

"I saw Feinberg on the day the war broke out. You know what we talked about? His son, who had already learned to walk. About the smell of his feces. Yes, you heard right: about the smell of his son's feces."

The deputy commander of the Irgun raised his eyebrow a bit higher and asked where the hell Yaacov Markovitch was going with all this. Yaacov Markovitch swallowed his saliva and persisted,

"A man like that, who considers war background noise to the music of everyday life, a man like that does not go off to hunt Nazis right after the war ends. He stays home and lives his everyday life. And if he ran away, he must have had a reason."

"And if he did? How does it concern you?"

Yaacov Markovitch leaned forward in his chair. "I'm his friend. Like you were once. I don't know what happened here since I left for the war. In the village, tongues wag a lot but say little. But I understand that something happened. Something bad. And now Sonya's here, in Tel Aviv, and Feinberg is in Europe, and this situation might be very good for you, but it's very upsetting for me."

The deputy commander of the Irgun breathed heavily. The tremor above his lip intensified so much that he had to cover his mouth with his hand. Yaacov Markovitch did not take his eyes off him. He no longer looked so small.

"Send me to Europe so I can bring him home."

"We are an organization working to save the country, Markovitch, not a travel agency."

Yaacov Markovitch stood up and walked to the door. The deputy commander of the Irgun stayed where he was. He heard the door slam and Yaacov Markovitch's feet hurrying past outside the building. He remained sitting for a long time and thought about Yaacov Markovitch, who had come all the way to Tel Aviv from the village and was now returning to it empty-handed. But Yaacov Markovitch did not go back to the village. He went to the port. When he reached the ships, he took the heavy envelope he had received from the man in the trench coat out of his pocket and paid for passage to Europe. Now the envelope was a bit lighter. He dashed onto the ship that was about to leave the port. He had just enough time before it set sail to pay a young man who promised to send Bella a telegram for him: "I've gone away. I'll be back with Feinberg."

Europe confused Yaacov Markovitch from the moment he set foot in it. No matter how hard he tried to hate that dark continent, he remembered that Bella had come to him out of that darkness. He himself had come out of it. He had hoped to find it broken and crushed, perhaps then he could forgive it. He had expected to find piles of ruins, but found paved roads and streets instead. And in the midst of them—many people. He searched the faces of those still here for a trace of the faces of those now gone, and did not find it. His feet trod the cobblestoned streets on which skulls had been cracked but, apart from the thumping feet of children playing hopscotch, he heard nothing. Realizing that, anger raged in him towards this forgetful country. But he was also envious. He swore to spend an entire twenty-four hours on the streets of Berlin without thinking even once of the war. To walk through the alleyways of the city for a full day without bearing the six million witnesses on his shoulders. To peel away, if only for a few hours, his people, his homeland and his past. It didn't work. No matter how hard he tried. Yaacov Markovitch told himself: it is as if I were asking to walk around for a whole day without the smell of my body. But we cannot remove this smell that has become part of us, the smell of the victims.

For the next few days he found himself riding public transportation without paying. With no advance planning, he also began to shoplift sweets and pastries. A number of times he banged into other men on the streets, not unintentionally. It was remarkably stupid, but it gave him pleasure. Once a day he went into a quiet café and knocked a delicate porcelain cup off the table. When the grumbling waitress bent beside him he felt not an iota of shame, only a thrill of pleasure. Not because he could see her breasts, but because she was kneeling before him, her fingers gathering up the cake crumbs. On one of his first days there he hurried to the market with a vague idea in his mind about the stall where breakable glass objects were sold. But at the stall a miracle happened to him: snow began to fall. Yaacov Markovitch walked quickly into the shade of the stall—a large area covered with a cloth canopy and filled with crates: high stacks of lamps, dishes, glasses. Customers who had braved the cold to wander among the crates picked up one item or another to look at it. Whenever someone lifted a glass, a plate or a crystal candlestick it would make a soft sound as it clinked gently against another of the items in the crate. And since there were many people in the roofed stall on that snowy morning, there were many such sounds. No one spoke. Only the glass objects singing to each other, and the snow falling softly, like white ballerinas.

Faced with the miracle of the falling snow and the song of the glass objects, Yaacov Markovitch abandoned his plan. He no longer wanted to smash those glass objects, their undersides imprinted with the date of their manufacture. The fact that such fragile items had outlived their owners no longer upset him. That day, Yaacov Markovitch stopped enacting his poor man's revenge and went back to searching for his friend. So liberated from the magic of this Europe did he become that he was no longer confused by it, as he had been on his previous voyage. Nor was he brazenly disrespectful of it, as he had been on this present voyage. Now he traversed the length and breadth of it without passion or anger, but with one simple wish—to see Zeev Feinberg once again.

When Yaacov Markovitch found Zeev Feinberg, the envelope that he had received from the man in the trench coat was already much lighter. He had never noticed before how quickly money could be spent. Perhaps because, before, he'd had no money. Apart from what he paid for lodging, travel and food, there were other expenses: in post-war Germany, the women were painfully beautiful and amazingly inexpensive. All their faces had the same expression of bewilderment mixed with sadness, as if they had not yet completely internalized their defeat. Yaacov Markovitch had sex with them gently, almost fearfully. He always left more money on the shelf than they had agreed upon. If he felt any guilt, he quickly allayed it in the arms of yet another woman. The same was true of anger. He soon discovered that all the emotions a person is subject to—guilt, anger, sadness, longing—retreated in the heat of passion. When a sheet lay over his body and a woman lay beneath it, Yaacov Markovitch would forget for a while what he wished to forget. It never occurred to him that his moments of oblivion were deeply engraved in the memories of the women who were the instruments of his forgetting. He paid them above and beyond.

Gradually he began to gather information about a squad of Jews led by a mustached giant. He had no doubt that the giant was Feinberg. But when he heard that, in addition to a pistol, the giant carried with him a golden-haired baby girl, Yaacov Markovitch's confidence faded slightly. Nonetheless, he continued to trace the movements of the squad, both because he hoped that Feinberg really was the person behind the information, and because he had no other leads. He finally found him in a small town on the Austrian border so remote that even its residents had forgotten its name. Zeev Feinberg and the other squad members had come there several days earlier in search of a sliver of information that might lead them to their next destination. But so small was the town that rumors of a Jewish gang and the golden-haired baby with them spread rapidly, and the residents kept silent. Since the girl's appearance was so totally different from that of the men, the townspeople were concerned about her identity. None of them believed she was the mustached man's daughter, even though he repeatedly told all the waitresses in the town's only café that she was. It didn't take long for someone to whisper that Passover was coming, and maybe the Jews couldn't find a Christian boy, so they had to make do with a baby girl? And someone else to shush him with a loud bellow: times are different. A Jewish gang is roaming the streets with pistols sticking out of their pockets. The people of the town would do better to look after their own children and not occupy themselves with dangerous speculations about other people's children. The squad members noticed the whispering and were eager to leave, but the baby girl ran a fever and they had to spend several more nights in the town.

During the day Zeev Feinberg raced around the neighboring villages in his car, asking for information, sniffing around people for the smallest hint, but at night he returned with his squad mates to the inn, nodded a greeting to its disapproving owner, and went upstairs to take the baby from the wet nurse. Then Feinberg wrapped the baby in blankets and took her out with him on his nocturnal stroll, the eyes of the townspeople following him like a swarm of lightning bugs as he walked.

On the evening that Yaacov Markovitch arrived in the town, Feinberg was out walking when he suddenly felt as if it was not only lightning bugs that he sensed on the back of his neck. Someone was walking behind him, too far away for him to see who it was, too close for him to ignore. With one hand cradling the baby, his other hand reached for his pistol. The person behind him quickened his steps. Zeev Feinberg cocked his weapon and turned around, directly into the outstretched arms of his old friend, Yaacov Markovitch. "Good God, Markovitch, I almost shot your face off!"

Many days had passed since Zeev Feinberg and Yaacov Markovitch had seen each other last, on the eve of the war. Now they hugged for a long time. Zeev Feinberg held the baby girl in one hand and hugged Markovitch with the other. And Markovitch, despite his impatience to find out who the hell she was, that child, postponed his questions in honor of the occasion. The envelope he had received from the man in the trench coat had bought him many embraces on European soil, but not one of them touched his soul the way Zeev Feinberg's embrace did. Now he knew that he had not made this journey in vain.

Zeev Feinberg let go of Yaacov Markovitch and studied him. "You've become a man."

Markovitch's body was still as thin and his eyes as watery as ever. And yet there was no mistaking the change in him. When and how the change had taken place, Zeev Feinberg did not know. But he did know that the man standing before him now on the soil of Europe was different from the man he had seen on the eve of the war. So different that, for a moment, Zeev Feinberg wondered if he was the same person, but immediately stopped wondering, because who knew better than he that no one returns from war the same person he was when he set out for it.

"And you," Yaacov Markovitch said to his friend, "you, who were a man, what have you become?"

Upon hearing the question, Zeev Feinberg grew serious. A long moment later he replied, "I've become a nomad."

"A nomad? But you have a home. And a wife. And a child."

Yaacov Markovitch had barely finished speaking when Zeev Feinberg turned away to look at a point in the distance. Across the street the houses were preparing for sleep. Lights were dimmed, laughter hushed. The townspeople began shedding the day that had passed, readying themselves for the jumble of night dreams. With his eyes fixed on the windows of the houses, Zeev Feinberg spoke to Yaacov Markovitch in a quavering voice.

"I can't go back there, Markovitch. I can't. I've crushed Sonya's spirit. I never thought there was anything in the world that could crush that woman's spirit. It turns out that there is: me. And the house, it wasn't a house anymore. It was a grave, and the child, would you believe me if I tell you that he stood next to me for days and I didn't see him? That he cried and I didn't pick him up?"

"But now," Yaacov Markovitch persisted, "now you look fine. Why don't you go back?"

Zeev Feinberg sighed. "The minute I stop moving, everything will go back to the way it was."

Yaacov Markovitch heard Zeev Feinberg's last words through the pounding of blood in his ears. His best friend, his only friend, had left the village and its oranges, had left his wife and son, had left him to wander through Europe with a pistol and a baby girl he still had to explain. And he had no intention of returning.

"You're not a nomad, Feinberg, you're just a poor excuse for a man. Wallowing in your guilt and sorrow like a pig in a puddle of mud and leaving everyone else to endure the filth and the stench. What about Sonya? What about Yair? And who the hell is that damn baby girl?"

Zeev Feinberg looked at him, stunned. He had never seen Yaacov Markovitch so enraged. He thought for a moment that his friend would hit him, even hoped he would, because then Markovitch would finally stop talking and the white-hot iron of his words would be removed from his skin. But Yaacov Markovitch did not raise his hand, though he very likely thought about it. Finally, Zeev Feinberg could no longer bear Yaacov Markovitch's shouting. When he opened his mouth his voice thundered through the entire street:

"Who are you to judge me, Markovitch? You, who imprisoned a woman who cannot love you, in your house? I, when I realized I couldn't love anymore, got up and left. What's wrong with that? Who are you to judge that?"

Some of the residents of the houses peered out of their windows at the two men shouting at each other in an unknown language. Yaacov Markovitch wanted to reply, but Zeev Feinberg's booming voice had awakened the baby girl and now she was crying bitterly. They had to walk back and forth and back and forth again almost four times before the baby went back to sleep. They did not exchange a word that entire time. When they finally stopped walking, Yaacov Markovitch said,

"You asked how I could judge you. Believe me, Feinberg, better that I should judge you than you should judge yourself. Because that's what you did, isn't it? You were the prosecutor and the judge, and there was no defense lawyer. You imprisoned yourself and flogged yourself and exiled yourself. I didn't come here to judge you. I came here to free you. I don't know what you did, but no deed could be so terrible."

Zeev Feinberg was silent. They paced back and forth along the street several more times before they went back to the only inn in the town. At the reception counter Zeev Feinberg said, "Goodnight," and went up to his room. Yaacov Markovitch replied, "Goodnight" to Feinberg's back as it moved away, wondering whether he would see his friend again the next day, or he would wake up and find the inn deserted.

The next morning Zeev Feinberg woke up but stayed in bed. He was expecting fear, or guilt, or habit to drive his legs out of bed and back to the chase, to the constant movement. But his legs stayed where they were, and he remained in bed until noon. When the members of the squad knocked on his door he told them that his journey with them had come to an end. He was ready to return home. And then he got out of bed and knocked on the door of Markovitch's room. "I'm coming with you. But the baby is coming with us."

That same day they left the town. With Yaacov Markovitch at his side and the baby girl in his arms, Zeev Feinberg walked to the document forger who had helped a great deal during various hunting missions and asked him to forge papers that would enable him to say that the baby was his daughter. The forger gave him a long look over his spectacles. Throughout the war Jews with their children in their arms had come to him, and with pleading eyes had asked him to perform magic, to stamp some papers and transform those children into Gentiles. And now a Jew with a Gentile baby in his arms had come to ask him to perform magic, to stamp some papers and transform the baby into a Jew? Zeev Feinberg raged and fumed, his mustache quivering as he blustered in anger. How dare the man standing in front of him doubt the child's Jewishness? True, she was an orphan, but absolutely Jewish. And if a Jewish heart beat in the forger's body he would help him right then and there to take her to Eretz Israel.

"A man who makes his living from lies, sir, knows how to recognize one when he sees it. That child is as Jewish as you are Aryan."

Zeev Feinberg sighed. "True. But even so, for me, make her Jewish."

The forger shook his head. "The lies I have told and the documents I have forged—I did it all to save Jews. Why should I help someone like her?"

"Because if you do, you will be saving a Jew."

"Who, exactly?"

"Me."

Four days later they left Europe. The ship's passengers agreed unanimously that they had never seen a father so devoted to his daughter as Zeev Feinberg was to Naama.

14

ZEEV FEINBERG and Yaacov Markovitch were once again sailing across the sea together. When they set out on their first sea voyage, both were single, fleeing to Europe from the terror of Avraham Mandelbaum's knife. When they set out on their second voyage, both were married: Zeev Feinberg was anxious to get divorced and return to Sonya; and the idea of refusing to divorce Bella was ripening—or perhaps rotting—in Yaacov Markovitch's mind. When they set out on their third journey, both were fathers, Yaacov Markovitch of a son he knew was not his, and Zeev Feinberg of a son he had left in Israel and a daughter he was bringing back with him. But instead of musing on the changes that time and accident had brought them, instead of pondering past events or wondering about the vicissitudes of the future, Yaacov Markovitch and Zeev Feinberg were up to their eyes in tending to Naama, a job that was a thousand times more difficult than any previous mission or challenge they'd had to meet. In the face of the crying, the vomiting and the accumulating pile of diapers, the men were helpless. All of Zeev Feinberg's famous resourcefulness faded after the fourth sleepless night because the baby refused to trust the rocking ship and began to scream whenever it swayed slightly. Even Markovitch's emotional strength and dedication failed the test of her crying, which was so continuous and monotonic that he, a normally stable person, almost threw the screaming baby into the sea. Before boarding the ship they had reassured themselves with the firm belief that, on deck, they would find a wet nurse, a nanny or simply a woman whose maternal instincts would lead her to the baby. But whether they were merely unlucky or deliberately cursed, nothing like that happened. The ship was indeed full of women, but not one of them was a wet nurse, and certainly not a nanny. The mothers were busy with their own children, who cried, vomited, ran around and made enough noise to drive any human creature out of his mind. And the young women behaved like young women, namely they talked and laughed and made love secretly or not so secretly, imagining the land at the end of the sea. None of them wanted to give up their conversations, laughter, lovemaking or imaginings to take care of a screaming baby.

Zeev Feinberg and Yaacov Markovitch split the hours of childcare between them so that one rested while the other worked. This division of labor was definitely effective, except for the fact that it totally destroyed any chance that they could have a real conversation. They did occasionally manage to grab an hour together on deck in the evening, the baby sleeping beside them. But most of the time Naama woke up a few minutes after their conversation began, bringing it to an immediate end. When they changed shifts they were able to tell each other a bit about the day's events (number of bowel movements, time of last feeding, the two smiles Naama had bestowed upon the sailor with the parrot on his shoulder), but nothing beyond that. The moment never seemed to come when Yaacov Markovitch could say: tell me, Feinberg, what is it that made you run away to Europe? Just as Zeev Feinberg was always in too much of a hurry to say: tell me, Markovitch, what sort of welcome did Bella give you when the war was over? And although they were eager for the moment they could have a genuine, long talk, something inside them was nonetheless grateful to the baby for her interruptions. For they knew that the moment she stopped crying, they would have to reveal their pain and suffering to each other and look at each other's wounds.

The closer they came to Israel, the more restless Yaacov Markovitch became. At night he would think about Bella. What she would say to him when he returned. If she said anything at all. How many words could a woman not say? He lay on the mattress remembering how indifferent she had been towards him when he returned from the war. No, he corrected himself, not indifferent, for he could easily see through her efforts to remain aloof from him. And such efforts clearly did not suggest indifference. They suggested hatred. That thought consoled Yaacov Markovitch somewhat, since he knew very well that the direct opposite of love was not hatred, but disinterest. Women had been indifferent to him for many years, and their indifference had diminished his existence bit by bit. Bella's hatred, however, did not diminish his existence but actually gave him presence. And though he shuddered in fear at the thought of the stone house in the village, he nonetheless preferred the heat of Bella's hatred to the cool, indifferent glances of all the others.

As Yaacov Markovitch's fears intensified, Zeev Feinberg's excitement increased. He would soon see Sonya. He knew exactly where he would find her: on the shore. Swearing and cursing his name with blazing words and a razor-sharp tongue. Picturing her there, all strife and contention, he felt desire for the first time in a long while. With great effort he avoided speaking of Sonya to Markovitch because he didn't want to hurt his friend with descriptions of a lovers' reunion at a time when Markovitch himself was sailing towards an ice-covered Arctic Pole. Nor did Markovitch mention Sonya to Feinberg, fearing that his friend might ask him what his wife had been doing, and he did not know how he would reply. And so they sailed together for long days, one expectant and the other worried, and the expectations and worries remained unspoken while their spoken words were as insubstantial as soap bubbles:

"Beautiful weather this morning."

"Maybe we should dress her more warmly."

"Tell me, have you eaten yet today?"

And so on and so forth. But just before they reached Israel, when the coastline was already materializing in the morning fog, Yaacov Markovitch grabbed Zeev Feinberg and insisted that he tell him the secret of the baby. Other secrets could wait, since they were preserved deep in their hearts. But the baby girl—something like that could not be ignored. Where did she come from? Why did Zeev Feinberg bring her with him? Yaacov Markovitch did not consider himself to be prying—after bathing and cleaning and feeding and dressing her, he thought he had the right to know. Zeev Feinberg tried to evade the question, complained about hunger, thirst and dizziness, but Yaacov Markovitch would not let it go. Realizing that he could not escape his friend's questions, Zeev Feinberg leaned his arms on the railing and said,

"My cousin gave birth to her, the fruits of her forbidden love for a young German. The mother died in childbirth. The German disappeared. I felt obliged to take her with me."

When Zeev Feinberg looked at Yaacov Markovitch he expected to see him wiping away a tear of commiseration. Instead he encountered a cold, almost scornful look.

"If you plan to stick to that lie, Feinberg," Yaacov Markovitch said, "you should practice it."

Yaacov Markovitch walked off the deck and went up to his room. He was angry at his friend, who did not trust him. He was angry at the baby, for whom he had been half mother, half father for long days without knowing who she was. He was angry at the voyage for being over, at the knowledge that nothing remained for him now but to go home. Now that the battles were done, that the wandering through the country was over, that the search for Feinberg had come to an end, nothing remained for him but to return to being like everyone else. To sow and harvest and sow once again, to go home from the fields and gaze at the back of the most beautiful woman he had ever seen in his life. She wouldn't turn around. She wouldn't speak to him. He would sow and harvest and sow once again. Perhaps he would plant a fig tree, perhaps grapevines. And he would bring her the fruit, the oh-so sweet fruit, but even if she ate it she would not turn around to him. And he would sow and harvest and sow once again. The fig tree would bloom. The grapevines would bloom. There would be days on which he would yearn to hear the whistle of bullets in the air, another war, something that would split open the silence between them. But the whistle would not come. He would sow and harvest and sow once again. And on summer evenings he would sit alone under his fig tree and grapevines, under the burden of his guilt.

Yaacov Markovitch sank into thought and, as frequently occurs, the thoughts turned into troubled sleep. He was awakened by loud knocking at his door. The ship had already anchored. All the passengers had disembarked. Would he be so kind as to vacate his room? Agitated and confused, he walked onto the pier, searching for Zeev Feinberg, scanning the passers-by in the hope of seeing the tip of a thick mustache or the flash of Naama's blond curls. In vain. Then he caught sight of a heavy-set woman with four children whom he remembered from their journey—he and Feinberg had admired the calm proficiency with which she managed those four horsemen of the apocalypse. He asked the woman if she had seen his friend.

"That strapping fellow with the baby girl? Of course. How could I not? He was the first to get off the ship. But he had a good reason. His wife—you must certainly know—he said that his wife has been waiting many months for him. Such a romantic. They let him pass."

Yaacov Markovitch smiled. He bore not an iota of resentment towards Zeev Feinberg, even though he had disappeared without waiting for him. Because that was the man he had missed so much. That was the Feinberg he had prayed for. When he found him in Europe, a shadow of his former self, he longed for the moment his friend would again be the man he had once been: 120 kilograms of vitality. His concern about the moment Feinberg discovered the gap between his expectations and reality was dwarfed by his sense of relief: Zeev Feinberg was once again hurtling through the world like a shot arrow. He had not the slightest doubt that, if it weren't for the baby, Feinberg would have leaped off the ship near the village and swum to shore, driven by the fervor of his longing for Sonya.

15

T IME HAD NEVER seemed to stand still the way it did on the day Zeev Feinberg disembarked, aching for Sonya. The minutes stuck together, as thick as beeswax. The tires of the bus dragged along the half-paved road, so slowly that Zeev Feinberg twice considered jumping off that sick, motorized mule and making his way on foot. He glanced at his watch every few seconds, and what he saw there annoyed him so much that he looked away from it resentfully, like a man angry at a friend who was not meeting him halfway. All the while, Naama gazed at her new country with wide-open eyes. If Zeev Feinberg had paid any attention, he would have noticed that Naama had not cried at all from the moment the ship anchored in the port. But Zeev Feinberg had other things on his mind, and so the baby hung around his neck, her eyes fixed on the bus window, and the eyes of the passengers were fixed on the baby, who was quite adorable.

Finally, the bus reached the spot on the shore where Zeev Feinberg had met Sonya at the end of his previous voyage. Although they were more than an hour away from the village, Zeev Feinberg leaped up. Ignoring the looks of the shocked passengers and the driver's questions, he stepped off the clattering pack animal. With the baby in one hand and his rucksack in the other he plodded through the sand dunes towards the strip of blue sea in the distance. With each step the blue strip grew larger, and with each step Zeev Feinberg's excitement heightened. The closer he came to the shore, the louder the noise of the wind was in his ears. Suddenly he thought he heard Sonya's cursing voice through the wind. He began to run. He was convinced that the breaking of the waves was the sound of her pealing, husky laughter. He would soon see her. He would soon see her standing there. A Canaanite goddess, her thighs firm, her chin held gloriously high. And her mouth—he missed her mouth more than anything. Gunpowder and chocolate. Her angry words spurting from it onto the water, perfect round stones. And she wouldn't know he was there. That he was approaching her from behind. Standing with her face to the sea, never guessing that this time he would come to her from the land, never guessing that his arms were reaching for her from behind to enfold her in a sudden embrace, to stop the stream of invective with a kiss. How surprised she would be. How happy she would be. And even if she was angry he would kneel before her again, as he had then, and let her shower his face with a torrent of curses and profanities, blessed rain on parched earth.

But when Zeev Feinberg reached the shore he found it deserted. Seagulls took off with fluttering wings. Crabs fled to their burrows. Zeev Feinberg stood silently on the shoreline for a long moment—then turned abruptly and began to walk back. How stupid it was to think that Sonya would be waiting for him here. After all, she was no longer a young girl but the mother of a child, and children cannot wait on the beach for days at a time. They had to eat, play, bathe and sleep. The more Zeev Feinberg thought about it, the better he understood that he had made a mistake. Sonya would not wait for him on the beach, but in his home. Their home. The kitchen would be filled with the same familiar aroma of burnt bread and the jam she cooked to camouflage the smell. The sheets would be redolent of oranges. And Yair. How much the boy must have grown. He would have to be careful not to break his small bones with his hug. At that thought Zeev Feinberg began to run, so impatient was he to reach home.

But when he arrived he found the house locked. He stood for a while at the closed door until Haya Nudelman saw him from her house across the street. "Feinberg! You're back! Zahava—look who's here!"

Zeev Feinberg sighed. He had hoped so much that the first face he would see in the village would be Sonya's beloved countenance, and now it seemed that the first thing he'd have to do was deal with an army of prying neighbors. Even before he had time to devise a fitting escape strategy for himself, he was surrounded by women. All the doors in the village seemed to be open, with the exception of his own. Haya Nudelman, Zahava Tamir and Leah Ron—all wanted to welcome him back. And when they saw the baby girl in his arms, their friendly interest—which from the beginning was mixed with a drop of curiosity—turned into a true onslaught. "Who's that?" "What's her name?" "Where did she come from?" Since Markovitch's rebuke, Zeev Feinberg had managed to polish his story, and now answered the women's questions with full confidence: he found the baby girl in an orphan home in Germany. Her parents were Jewish. His heart would not allow him to leave her there. This time his explanation achieved greater success, either because it sounded more credible or because the women's curiosity had been satisfied and they didn't care whether the story was true or not. When Zeev Feinberg finished replying to their questions, he finally dared to ask one of his own: where was Sonya?

All at once the women stopped talking. They hadn't imagined for a moment that Zeev Feinberg had no idea what had happened to his wife after he left home. "Didn't she tell you that she moved to Tel Aviv?" Haya Nudelman asked, bursting with pleasure. "Didn't you know that she became a chief," Zahava Tamir purred. "Chief assistant to the head of the Irgun," Rivka Shaham exclaimed. Zeev Feinberg replied quickly that the duties of his position had prevented him from having any contact with his home, and the women nodded in feigned understanding. "But now that you're back, she'll definitely come back too," Haya Nudelman said. The other women nodded enthusiastically. They wanted that for themselves no less than they wanted it for Zeev Feinberg. The thought that a woman could one fine day be given such a high position was enough to keep them awake nights. Sonya should come back to burn loaves of bread and overcook food and forget her laundry on the line. Perhaps then the woodpecker that had come in her absence to peck away at the hearts of the women, forcing them to ask whether their own lives could be like hers, would fly away.

Sonya admonished the mail clerk until his ears grew red. "Letters, my dear comrade, were meant to be read. When a letter doesn't reach its destination, it's as if it has never been sent. I wonder how many of the letters I sent this week actually reached their destination, and how many of them were lost forever deep down in that bag of yours." The clerk looked at Sonya resentfully. True, he had to admit that sometimes he took a bit too long distributing the mail because of bad weather or when there were especially interesting magazines at the neighboring kiosk. But to be reprimanded like that by a woman? That he could not allow. As he thought about how to reply to that gray-eyed witch there was a loud knock on the door of Sonya's office. The mail clerk breathed a sigh of relief. The woman in charge of women's affairs would finally occupy herself with women's affairs, and he could finally return to his own occupations (which, based on the new magazine he had bought and shoved deep into his bag, also concerned women, although they focused on different aspects).

But Sonya remained standing with her back to the door, her eyes riveted on the derelict clerk. Without turning around she gave her orders: "Put the reports on the desk, I'll read them before the evening meeting." The office door opened. Sonya resumed admonishing the clerk. "If we think about the cumulative delay, then…" But she suddenly stopped speaking, because the sound of the steps behind her did not remind her in the slightest of the clack of her secretary's heels. Three paces were enough for her to know. It would not be an exaggeration to say that Sonya was endowed with an extraordinary musical ear, a true prodigy. Her grandfather on her father's side was a piano tuner with such a delicate ear that on the basis of one chord he could tell the year a piano was manufactured and, on the basis of three chords, he could tell the last piece that had been played on it. Sonya had undoubtedly inherited some of that ability; otherwise there was no explanation for how she could tell from only three steps that Zeev Feinberg was standing behind her.

She didn't turn around immediately. She was afraid to see the face of the man standing in her office. The steps were the same, and that was definitely reassuring. But what about the eyes? The mustache? As long as she stood with her back to him, Sonya could preserve in her mind the image of Zeev Feinberg as she wanted to remember him, an impressive bronze statue cleansed of the stains that the months preceding his voyage had left on him. If she turned around she would have to see his real image. An image she had no control over. And so she waited another brief moment before turning around, and she might have waited even longer if Zeev Feinberg had not taken another three steps and touched her shoulder.

The sigh that came from Sonya's mouth could be heard clearly in the entire building. Secretaries stopped filing and raised their heads. Managers stopped chatting and perked their ears. The cleaning crew froze with a mop or a rag in their hands. The reprimanded mail clerk momentarily forgot the magazines in his bag. They had never in their lives heard such a sigh, an alloy of relief, desire, guilt and yearning. Because the moment Zeev Feinberg touched her shoulder, Sonya knew that he had indeed come back to her, truly come back. Not a ghost of the man she loved, but the man himself, flesh and blood and powerful hands. Zeev Feinberg's fingers were large and warm, and their grip was strong. He had held her with those fingers on their first night, and they had laughed and explored. He had held her with those fingers on all the nights that followed. He had also held her with those fingers when she clawed his body after finding out that, despite all his promises, he had once again been unfaithful, this time with Rachel Mandelbaum, and although his skin bled from the scratches he still held her and promised to return and hold her after the slaughterer calmed down and he could come back to the village. He had come back to her then. She waited for him on the beach and he came back to her. And now, when she had stopped waiting, when the ring on her finger had become a habit, an old memory and nothing more, he had come back again.

Sonya finally turned and stood face to face with Zeev Feinberg. His eyes were bluer than ever and his mustache was brazen. And under his mustache were the same full, sculpted lips. It was almost embarrassing to think that such sensual lips belonged to a man, and perhaps that was why Zeev Feinberg hid them under an unruly mustache. Now those lips smiled mischievously at Sonya. "I'm here."

Zeev Feinberg had barely finished saying those words when Sonya's body pressed against his, her head burrowing into his mustache, his lips, his neck, and he inhaled her fragrance, and she bit his earlobe. The admonished mail clerk stared at this spectacle with considerable interest for a while before he realized that he should slip out of the office of the woman in charge of women's affairs. The women in his magazine could not compare to Sonya's exhibition of passion and desire, but they were well used to being stared at and their painted smiles were an open invitation to all, while the woman in charge of women's affairs might not smile at all when she noticed his presence.

Zeev Feinberg and Sonya remained alone in Sonya's office, embracing and inhaling each other's scents for quite a while, until Sonya suddenly pulled away from Zeev Feinberg and shouted, "Oh my God, I'm late for the evening meeting!"

She was still hurrying out of the door, Zeev Feinberg clutching her arm (lush, plump, like a sweet challah dotted with raisins)— and saying, "Sonyitchka, how can you leave me now? Tell them to hold the meeting without you."

But Sonya extricated her arm from Feinberg's grip and said with a smile, "How can they hold the meeting without me? I'm the boss."

Before Zeev Feinberg could say anything her skirt was already caressing the threshold in farewell, and he was left alone in the spacious office of the woman in charge of integrating women into the workforce.

Several minutes later the secretary came in with a cup of coffee. "Sonya said that you drink it so boiling hot that it burns your tongue."

Zeev Feinberg took a sip of the coffee and returned the cup to the secretary. "Don't take it personally. No one knows how to burn coffee like Sonya."

The secretary shrugged. "Sonya also said that when you finish the coffee, you can go to see your son and the other boy at 48

Trumpeldor Street and send the nanny home. She'll join you when the meeting is over."

The secretary spoke the last few words to Zeev Feinberg's moving back as he left the office of the woman in charge of women's affairs at a run. He raced down three flights of stairs, almost stumbling over the mail clerk, who was furtively reading his magazine, thanked the secretary who had been watching Naama on the ground floor and, with the baby sitting on his shoulder, hurried off to see his son.

16

THE NANNY SONYA had hired scrutinized Zeev Feinberg.
"And who are you, sir?"

She said the words indifferently, as if she couldn't care less
whether it was the King of England or Moses who replied.

"I'm Zeev Feinberg. Sonya's husband."

"Really?"

The nanny's gaze shifted from Zeev Feinberg to the golden-
haired baby in his arms. Zeev Feinberg frowned in annoyance.
The nanny looked at him serenely. She had taken care of cranky
babies for too many years to be ruffled by an angry stranger.
She had a small, wizened face and, above her lips, a mustache
almost the equal of Zeev Feinberg's. She had never married and
had never regretted it. She saw men as baby-making machines,
nothing more, and since her profession kept her surrounded by
babies she had no need of a machine. She loved babies a great
deal more than she loved adults, so she preferred taking care of
young children to making a child of her own, which would of
course be quite adorable at first, but sooner or later would lose its
sweetness and become a real person with large hands and smelly
feet and a mouth with which to ridicule women with mustaches.

"I've come to take my son!"

"Really?"

Zeev Feinberg stamped his feet impatiently. "Look, miss, I am
Sonya Feinberg's husband. I've just come back from Germany.

I know that my son is here, in this apartment. Now let me see him!"

The nanny stood firm. "How do I know that you are really the boy's father?"

Zeev Feinberg's voice thundered in the corridor. "Of course I'm the boy's father! What do you think, that I walk around the streets collecting children?"

While Zeev Feinberg was still shouting, the nanny looked at Naama again. "And who is she? She can't be Sonya's child."

Zeev Feinberg hesitated for a moment before replying. That was enough to convince the nanny to close the apartment door quickly and lock it. Zeev Feinberg knocked on the door with enough force to shatter the entire building. The nanny opened it a crack.

"Miss, it's a long story, but believe me—I'm the boy's father. If you would just be kind enough to bring him here, he'll recognize my face immediately."

Zeev Feinberg was still speaking when he saw his son at the end of the hallway chasing a ball that had got away from him. "Yair! Yair!" Hearing his name, the child looked up. At the far end of the hallway, on the other side of the door, he saw a mustached man, his face red with anger, his expression desperate as he shouted his name loudly. Yair forgot about the ball and began to cry with fright. The mustached nanny hurried to hug the weeping child with her right arm, and with the left she closed the door in Zeev Feinberg's face.

Before Yaacov Markovitch entered his house, he put on his coat. He was convinced that Bella's coldness was infinitely more frigid than the winter winds outside. But when he stepped over the threshold he discovered that the house was heated and warm. Several moments passed before he realized that the heat in the house was not natural. It was excessive. Bella was boiling with fury and the walls of the house boiled along with her. And this time, for a change, her anger had nothing to do with Yaacov Markovitch.

"They rejected it. Without exception. They all rejected it."

She was sitting on a stool on the other side of the room. Her eyes were moist, her forehead furrowed in unhappiness. Yaacov Markovitch's return to his home after two months of wandering had changed nothing in her, except that now she looked at him when she spoke, while previously she had delivered her fiery speeches to the pine cabinet.

"How could they all have rejected it? Those swine, they would reject pure gold if they had the chance."

For another few minutes Yaacov Markovitch listened to Bella's diatribe against swine, dogs and vermin that rejected gold, diamonds and pearls before daring to ask her what she was actually talking about.

"Rachel's poems, Markovitch, they don't want them. Not one of them wants them."

Now Yaacov Markovitch understood what Bella had been working so hard to translate when he returned from the war, and what he didn't understand, she hurried to explain to him. So deeply affronted by the rejection was Bella that she forgot her resolution to exclude Markovitch from her life, to meet all his attempts to speak to her with thundering silence.

"I worked day and night to translate them. Believe me, you have never seen such beauty. Even they, the publishing people, said so. They admitted that they had never seen such poems here."

"If so," Yaacov Markovitch wondered, "why didn't they publish them?"

Bella leaped off her stool. "Why didn't they publish them, you ask? Really, why didn't they?" Yaacov Markovitch was still wondering if she was waiting for an answer when Bella said, "Because she doesn't set a good example!"

"What does that mean?"

Bella did not reply. She flitted around the room like a frenzied moth, from the cabinet to the table, from the table to the window. She was afraid that if she stopped the floor would be scorched beneath her, so intense was her fury.

"They said that a woman like that, who commits suicide on the very day that the Jewish people won their homeland, who writes in the language of the Gentiles, who leaves her young child motherless out of selfishness and weakness—a woman like that does not set a good example."

Now Bella was standing a few centimeters away from Yaacov Markovitch. Her eyes were blazing. "They won't publish them." And she burst into tears. Yaacov Markovitch wanted to take her in his arms, but dared not. She stood there with huge, majestic tears falling from her eyes, and, sniffing, said, "That scum, they won't publish them." Yaacov Markovitch burned with embarrassment and Bella reached out to wipe away her tears with her left hand. Yaacov Markovitch was horrified at the sight of the scarred hand, but said nothing. Her refusal to tell him how she got the scar, her refusal to reveal anything to him was still vivid in his memory. Bella saw Yaacov Markovitch's expression and gave him a broken smile. "It was with this hand that I pulled Rachel Mandelbaum's poems out of the fire. Avraham Mandelbaum wanted to burn them. I couldn't bear the thought that they would be lost forever." As she spoke, Bella covered her scarred hand with her healthy one. "But you see, they're still lost forever. A poem that no one reads turns to dust. If I had let Avraham Mandelbaum burn the notebook, then people would at least have seen the smoke."

Yaacov Markovitch reached into his coat pocket. Lying in the creases of the material was the envelope he had received from the gambler's lover. It was much lighter than it had been on the day he'd given it to him, but was still filled with notes.

"Here." Yaacov Markovitch took the envelope out of his pocket and handed it to Bella. When she looked inside it, her eyes opened wide in astonishment. "If the publishing companies won't publish Rachel's poems, we will."

When Yaacov Markovitch spoke that word, "we", such a pleasant warmth surged through his body that his face reddened. Bella put the envelope on the pine cabinet and took Yaacov Markovitch's arm between her healthy and scarred hands. She held his arm like that for a long moment until Zvi came running in from the field, saw Yaacov Markovitch and cried, "Daddy!"

The next weeks were the most wonderful in Yaacov Markovitch's life. Not since he had fought with his comrades at the fortress had he felt such a union. And that the union should be with none other than Bella was something he had never even prayed for. Together they organized Rachel Mandelbaum's poems according to subject. Together they deliberated on how to begin the collection and discussed which poem would end it. Together they went to the city to look into printing houses and typesetters. Zvi went with them, glancing from his mother to the man he called his father, and from the man back to his mother, as if he was afraid that if he stopped shifting his glance from Bella to Markovitch, from Markovitch to Bella, one of them would take advantage of the opportunity to disappear. His fear was unwarranted—neither of them thought about disappearing. Bella Markovitch had never felt so close to publishing Rachel Mandelbaum's poems. And Yaacov Markovitch had never felt so close to Bella. He still preferred botany books to poetry books, and there was no doubt that pomegranate cuttings were infinitely more meaningful to him than a perfect metaphor, but Rachel's verses were dear to his heart. After all, those verses bound him to the hand that had translated them, the scarred hand of a perfect body.

They realized soon enough that they needed more money. Poetry, it turned out, was an expensive matter. Bella suggested that they talk to Sonya. The woman in charge of integrating women into the workforce would certainly be happy to help publish the poems of a woman as gifted as Rachel Mandelbaum. And so they traveled to Tel Aviv. Sonya welcomed them with warm hugs and effusive words, but explained that she could not help them.

"She hanged herself while her son was playing in the yard. Really, Bella, you can't expect the office that deals with women's affairs to turn such a woman into a symbol."

Bella looked at Sonya, stunned. Had she forgotten the days they had spent together, Rachel, Sonya and Bella, at the stream near the fig tree? Had she forgotten the aroma of the breads Rachel baked—one to eat on the bank of the stream and another for Sonya, who always complained about the cement blocks that came out of her oven?

Sonya's gray eyes looked firmly at Bella. "Good God, until when will you continue to think that a woman's greatest hero-ism lies in baking bread? I'm trying to turn them into teachers, doctors, maybe even engineers, and you come here and ask me to subsidize poetry!"

"But what poems they are, Sonya, if you would only read them!"

"Of course they're tender. And refined. And very, very sad. And they end with loneliness, or barrenness, or a hand reaching for a throat. That's the kind of poets we have. If they would at least beat other people's breasts a little, not only their own."

Bella Markovitch opened and closed her mouth without utter-ing a sound. She was so shocked by the change in her friend. Was this really the same Sonya who had taken it upon herself to raise

Rachel Mandelbaum's son? The same Sonya who had looked after Bella from the day she came to the village? When Bella found her voice, she discovered that it shook. In vain did she try to explain to Sonya that poetry is also a struggle. That a woman like Rachel, who finished mopping the blood off the floor of the butcher's shop and sat down to write, who held a pen in hands calloused from sewing, washing and cleaning, who managed to draw a real poem from her soul through the endless humming of lullabies to a crying child—such a woman is a fighter.

Sonya shook her head. "It is not to such wars that I send my women." They looked at one another, gray eyes staring into gray eyes. After a moment Bella stood up with the calm elegance of an aristocrat. Yaacov Markovitch also stood up quickly. He had been listening to the bitter argument between Sonya and Bella, an argument he did not entirely understand, so he had preferred to observe it in silence. But even without fully comprehending it, he realized that those two women, who had fallen into each other's arms with sisterly love when they first saw each other, were no longer sisters.

Before leaving the office, Yaacov Markovitch dared to ask Sonya where he could find Feinberg. Not a muscle in her face moved when she replied that he should go to 48 Trumpeldor Street.

17

FIFTY METERS from the house, Yaacov Markovitch and Bella already knew which apartment they were heading for. Zeev Feinberg's shouts reverberated through the entire street. "I am a cruel robber! I am a terrible pirate!" The children's screams of pleasure and fear brought a smile to Yaacov Markovitch's face as he knocked on the door. He had to knock a few more times more before Zeev Feinberg stopped his game and grumbled, "Just a minute, I'll be right there." But when Zeev Feinberg finally unlocked and opened the door and saw the faces of his guests, the grumbling turned into thundering joy: "Markovitch! Bella! What a happy surprise!" Bella smiled weakly, still preoccupied with Sonya's refusal. But Yaacov Markovitch smiled broadly, because his best friend was carrying not one, not two, but three children on his shoulders. On his right shoulder sat Naama, her golden hair tied back with a ribbon. On his left shoulder sat Yotam Mandelbaum, his eyes brown, like Rachel's, and his hair black, like Avraham's, but the smile on his face came from neither his mother nor his father. And in the space between his shoulders, sitting on the back of his neck, his small hands clutching Zeev Feinberg's hair as if he were holding a horse's reins, was Yair, shouting, "Giddy-up!"

Zeev Feinberg sent the children to play in the living room. He told Yotam to watch Yair. He told Yair to watch Naama. And he told Naama—who probably did not understand—to watch the rag doll, which wasn't much bigger than she was. Then Zeev Feinberg put a kettle of water on the gas range, and as the water boiled his eyes shifted constantly from the kettle to the children, from the children to the kettle. Yaacov Markovitch waited until Bella went into the living room and then whispered into his friend's ear,

"Tell me, how did Sonya react to the baby?"

Zeev Feinberg shrugged. "You know what kind of heart Sonya has, as large as the distance from here to Petah Tikva. When she realized that I wanted Naama, she accepted her without hesitation."

Zeev Feinberg was not a prevaricator. His perception of reality was usually credible enough. Even now, he had not spoken a lie. The picture he presented to Yaacov Markovitch was like one seen through a steam-covered window, the reality outside concealed by interference from within. Sonya had indeed not tortured him with questions about the baby girl. She had not demanded to know where she had come from and had not insisted on hearing why he had brought her here. But it was actually her calm acceptance of the child that upset Zeev Feinberg. The fact that she did not demand, did not insist, did not even ask, damn it, was what bothered him. Because in Europe, though he had hoped that Sonya would accept the child and ask no questions, though he said that he had no desire to speak about what had happened on the bridge that night, he had nonetheless hoped, from the bottom of his heart, that she would drag the secret out of him. Deep down, Zeev Feinberg wanted to tell Sonya why he had fled the country and why he had returned to it, to rest his head on her breast and talk about the dead baby boy and the baby girl he had rescued from death.

*

But Sonya did not ask, although curiosity consumed her. She feared that her questions would upset the delicate balance that had enabled Zeev Feinberg to return home. She quickly persuaded herself that it did not matter at all where the baby came from as long as Feinberg's arms were the ones that brought her here. And when, awakened in the middle of the night by the sound of faint crying, she went alone to the baby's crib and asked herself about the identity of the baby girl she was diapering, she told herself that Zeev Feinberg also took care of a little boy whose paternity he knew nothing about. That was the way of the world. That was the way for people who wanted to live in the world, to pass through the minefield between the truth and the lie.

Only rarely did Sonya stand over the baby's crib in the middle of the night. Most of the time she slept soundly after a full day of battles and meetings. The crying easily woke Zeev Feinberg, who stood up blearily from the warm mattress and walked to the living room, which became the children's room at night. There he would diaper the crying Naama, soothe Yair, who was awakened by the noise and began to cry as well, and silently thank Yotam for continuing to lie with closed eyes, breathing regularly even through all that noisy crying. For the first few weeks after his return, Zeev Feinberg took a strange sort of pleasure in those nocturnal rambles. He was convinced that he was making his way back into his son's heart. And indeed, within little more than a week, Yair stopped crying in his presence, making do with a suspicious and highly skeptical look. After another week of courting, the child deigned to smile at Feinberg. Three weeks later he was once again the child who was as attached to his father as his father was to his son.

When Yaacov Markovitch and Bella knocked on the door, Zeev Feinberg was a happy man. He was a bandit, a pirate and a giant, all before ten in the morning. But the moment he opened the door he felt that something was bothering him, and he didn't know what. Only when he served the tea to Bella and saw her expression did he realize that he was embarrassed.

"So what's this, Feinberg," she said, "Sonya's running the world and you're taking care of children?"

Zeev Feinberg knew nothing about Sonya's and Bella's conversation, which was why he didn't know that it was Bella she wanted to rile, not him.

"A very temporary arrangement," he replied, "very temporary."

They drank the tea and ate cookies and parted with warm hugs. When the door closed behind Yaacov Markovitch and Bella the children ran to Zeev Feinberg, wanting to continue their games, but he scowled at them. He no longer felt like a pirate or a bandit, but like a person who has had something stolen from him. He wondered now about all the nights Sonya slept when he got out of bed to tend to a crying child. And when Yair was born it had never occurred to him to leave his blanket, so clear was it—to both him and Sonya—that night-time work was her province, just as the daytime earning of their livelihood rested on his shoulders. All at once Zeev Feinberg forgot the pleasure he took in playing with the children, in the feel of their soft skin on his fingers when he bathed them, in the serenity he felt when he managed to put them all to sleep and returned, satisfied, to his bed. The walls of the apartment closed in on him. He wanted to go out. Wanted to brawl or carouse, to see many eyes on him, many mouths whispering: what a man! He wanted to but couldn't, for he had fired the nanny the day he returned, the moment Sonya came home and verified that he was indeed himself. To the sound of Yair's crying as he angrily objected to the stranger that had infiltrated their home, he had told Sonya that, in the future, he would stay with the children. He alone. And she had agreed. She fired the nanny without hesitation. Why should she refuse?

When Sonya returned to their apartment that day she found all her things packed. Zeev Feinberg was sitting on the sofa, surrounded by suitcases, and stood up the moment she opened the door.

"It's time to go back to the village."

Sonya looked at him in astonishment. It was already dark outside. "Now?"

"No. The children are sleeping. We'll leave tomorrow morning. Early."

Zeev Feinberg spoke in a low, decisive voice. In the dark apartment his eyes glowed at Sonya like the eyes of a panther. A panther just returned from Europe that had settled in her apartment and was now threatening to devour everything she had built for herself. Sonya hesitated briefly before replying. She looked at the three suitcases.

"I can't leave tomorrow morning."

Zeev Feinberg did not move. "Then join us at noon."

"I can't leave at noon either. I have a job, Zevik, and you can't pack that into a suitcase."

In the end, they found a solution they both agreed on and hated equally. Zeev Feinberg returned to the village and its fields. His muscles swelled once again from the physical labor. His speeches at the farmers' meetings grew more and more strident. He was once more a man's man, except for the fact that his house was empty half of every week. Without a hot meal waiting for him on his return, without the scent of a woman or the laughter of children. Sonya spent three days a week in Tel Aviv, depositing her children each morning into the capable hands of the mustached nanny and hurrying to her office. Three days during which she cursed Zeev Feinberg for his stubbornness and he cursed her for hers.

The woman in charge of women's affairs managed and organized and planned aggressively, all the while longing for the hands of the mustached giant. And while those hands gripped his hoe and struck the ground forcefully, Zeev Feinberg thought constantly about a freckled shoulder. On Wednesdays, when Sonya arrived in the village with the children, Zeev Feinberg was distant and angry, and she was proud and determined. The frostiness between them melted gradually during the night, and Thursday's morning light found their bodies intertwined or exhausted with pleasure. On Friday they were still gentle and tender with each other, but on Saturday, already anticipating the parting, they were angry and grumbling. The children learned quickly that on Saturday night they were better off playing in the yard because the living room filled with arguing and shouting, and the sound of a breaking dish or two. Purchasing dishes also became the subject of an argument because Zeev Feinberg insisted that Sonya buy them in Tel Aviv, while Sonya maintained that she was too busy and tried to assign the responsibility to Zeev Feinberg, until in the end they ate their meals from one dish after all the others had been shattered on the floor. Their food was tasteless because Sonya burned everything she cooked and Zeev Feinberg refused adamantly to try his hand in the kitchen. Nonetheless, they loved each other very, very much.

Seven hundred copies of Rachel Mandelbaum's book of poetry were printed in soft cover by a small printing house in south Tel Aviv. Yaacov Markovitch handed the owner the envelope of money he had received from the man in the trench coat, adding some money he had been saving for a rainy day. Bella picked up every copy, caressing each of the 700 books in farewell before they were distributed to the bookstores. Two months later, when all hope was gone, they were summoned to pick up the books from those stores, or they would be tossed into the garbage. Seven hundred copies in soft cover that had never been opened. No one bought the book of Rachel Mandelbaum's poems. The day after they had finished collecting the copies, Yaacov Markovitch was working in the field when he suddenly saw a large fire blazing near his house. He threw down his hoe and began to run. When he reached home he found Bella standing beside a pile of burning books. Seven hundred copies in soft cover, the poems rising from them to the sky in a black cloud. The fire burned for more than an hour, and Yaacov Markovitch and Bella stood beside it the entire time, watching the paper being consumed. Yaacov Markovitch wanted to reach out and touch Bella's hand but it was resting on her cheek, salty tears falling onto the burnt, scarred fingers. When the fire died out Bella went into the house. She said not a word to Yaacov Markovitch. He stood in front of the hissing embers for a long time. They seemed to whisper: 700 copies in soft cover have gone up in smoke, along with that one small "we". That togetherness, which you grew and watered and nurtured, which had burgeoned for three blessed months—that togetherness had been consumed in flames, never to return. Yaacov Markovitch went into the house. Bella was sitting at the kitchen table. She didn't look up at him. Each of them was alone once again.

* * *

You might think that they will never grow old. You might even demand it. Such people are not supposed to grow old. Whenever time extends its withered, destructive hand towards them, mythology hastens to ward off its damage. No, not them. You cannot destroy them. Yaacov Markovitch will continue to hold fast to his love and his sin until the day he dies, and the love and sin will remain as fresh as on the day they were born. Bella will continue to be the most beautiful woman he has ever seen in his life, and her hatred of Yaacov Markovitch will be as strong as always. Zeev Feinberg and Sonya will continue to argue loudly and make love even more loudly. And the deputy commander of the Irgun will forever be the deputy commander of the Irgun, never the commander of the Irgun, and certainly not the retired deputy commander of the Irgun. Yes, it is certainly possible to believe that they will never grow old. Nonetheless, they went ahead and grew old. It didn't happen right away. It never happens right away, and therein lies its strength. A person focuses on trivialities—raising children, working to earn a living, eating a good meal or two—and when he suddenly looks up, lo and behold, he's grown old. That's why it's so very difficult to pinpoint the exact date on which passers-by stopped turning to look at Bella on the street, or to find a written record of the day on which the deputy commander of the Irgun went twelve whole hours without thinking even once about Sonya. Historians who labor to unearth papers and documents will never be able to determine whether it was spring or winter when Yaacov Markovitch first realized that his ability to hold on to Bella was dwindling.

Our minds are reluctant to accept all those things, though they happened. Damn it, those people held dragons by their wings, galloped on unicorns, rode lions. They did impossible things so often that the remarkable became the usual for them. It is tempting, too tempting to say that their fall began at the end of the War of Independence. As if the anticipation of a homeland had the power to sustain and nourish them, a power that faded the moment their fervent desire became reality. As if unrealized desires can endure forever. Essentially, the years passed, and feelings, passions and thoughts passed with them. Cells of the body died and were replaced by others. Hair fell out and was not always replaced. Nonetheless, people continued to behave normally. As if the cells and the hair—not to mention the feelings, passions and thoughts—still existed. For if that were not so, people would feel that they are powerless to stop the days carrying them along from horizon to horizon, the way a line of black ants carries an insect on their backs to its bitter demise. And since a blank page will appear in a few moments, followed by the continuation of the story ten years later, we should lose no time in describing several formative events that occurred during those ten years. First, out of respect to the characters, so they will not feel like puppets whose strings are being pulled haphazardly this way and that. Such an experience can be extremely disruptive, psychologically speaking. Second, the need to jump ten years forward does nothing to alleviate the sense of discomfort caused by sharp transitions, because honestly, how can one blank page contain ten full years, as if a person has been launched from one world to another in some amazing machine? And finally it is especially vital to mention several of the events that occurred during those unrecorded ten years to help us distinguish more sharply between the relevant and the irrelevant. If people were slightly more adept at making that distinction, their lives would be entirely different, usually for the better.

So, for example, there is no reason to linger over the day Yaacov Markovitch returned home earlier than expected and found Bella riding a farmer from the neighboring village. Because that ride, and certainly the farmer, meant absolutely nothing. There had been insignificant pawns in Bella's war from the day she first realized that she attracted no glances as she walked down the street. That war occupied most of her time, and was occasionally more intense than Markovitch's war. The only thing more intense than her war was its utter futility. And it is that futility that deserves to be mentioned, for Bella had never felt as hollow as she did when the farmer penetrated her.

Here are some additional formative events worth mentioning:

1. One cold morning in January, when Avraham Mandelbaum knocked on Sonya and Zeev Feinberg's door to ask for his son back. In one hand he held a bouquet of roses and in the other a certificate from the sanitarium attesting to his sanity. Sonya took the roses, refused to read the certificate and called Yotam. Avraham Mandelbaum and the boy moved to a kibbutz in the Arabah, as far away as possible from the village and its whispering tongues. Three years later his left hand was blown off when he accidentally drove over a mine. But he could still slaughter a sheep with one hand.

2. One hot night in August, when Yaacov Markovitch got out of bed, took a long look at Bella's sleeping face, and asked himself what it actually was that he wanted from her. It was clear to him that if she were to wake up now, get out of bed and embrace him, he would run straight out of the house; the situation had been what it was for so long that he didn't know what he would do if it suddenly changed.

3. One hot night in August, as Bella lay in her bed, felt Markovitch's eyes on her, and went on pretending to be asleep. If she had opened her eyes, looked directly at his unreadable face and said, "Let me go," he would undoubtedly have done so.

4. The first evening that Sonya and the deputy commander of the Irgun walked past each other without saying hello. Sonya went back to her apartment on Trumpeldor Street and burst into tears. The deputy commander of the Irgun lay awake in his bed that entire night.

5. The first evening that Sonya and the deputy commander of the Irgun walked past each other on the
   street without saying hello, and without feeling any
   pain about it. Sonya continued on her way, ate cake in
   a café with a girlfriend, and thought about the deputy
   commander of the Irgun only when her girlfriend went
   to the restroom. The deputy commander of the Irgun
   also continued on his way, ate quiche at the home of a
   lady friend, and thought about Sonya only when that
   lady friend fell asleep with her head on his arm.

6. Several unusual sunsets. One hailstorm. Yaacov
   Markovitch's birthday, which he celebrated in splendid
   isolation. A drunken night that Zeev Feinberg spent
   in the arms of Leah Ron when Sonya was in Tel Aviv
   and Yeshayahu Ron in Tiberias. The evening Zeev
   Feinberg tried to bring himself to tell Markovitch
   about the night he had spent in Leah Ron's arms,
   but could not. The tread of the children's feet as they
   grew stronger, alongside the tread of the adults' feet,
   which grew weaker.

AFTER

1

Fʀᴏᴍ ᴀ ᴠᴇʀʏ ʏᴏᴜɴɢ ᴀɢᴇ, Yair Feinberg's skin gave off the scent of peaches. You didn't have to be much of a biologist to understand that the child's smell was a genetic variation of his mother's scent of oranges, just as his blue eyes were a hybrid of Sonya's gray eyes and the fathomless eyes of the deputy commander of the Irgun. But, unlike the color of his eyes, visible at the moment of birth or shortly thereafter, people did not immediately sense the scent of peaches. At first it was so delicate that it was almost imperceptible to people, although it made them smile. They would look at the child and smile without knowing why. As he grew older the scent became stronger, and people would look around as they spoke to him, trying to locate the fruit that was certainly close by. When Yair Feinberg reached school age, all the villagers knew that the peach orchard was located in the child's pores and there was no point in searching the land for it. Everyone loved him. Especially when peaches weren't in season. With his lovely scent and pink cheeks, Yair Feinberg appeared as innocent as an angel. And since he wasn't an angel, but a child, he learned how to exploit his looks to play pranks and get into mischief.

Wherever Yair Feinberg went, Zvi Markovitch could be found as well. They were so attached to each other that the villagers called them Siamese twins, although they did not look the slightest bit alike. Yair was handsome, the perfect poster boy for the village, or for a talcum powder ad. Zvi Markovitch, on the other hand, although he was the son of the most beautiful woman in the village, never escaped drabness. It spoiled his features and made him alarmingly ordinary. Sometimes Bella thought that her son resembled Yaacov Markovitch infinitely more than he did the poet, his father. Such things, though impossible, are quite common.

While Yair Feinberg's scent and sweet face protected him from all evil, the teacher's suspicions stuck to Zvi Markovitch's face the way fingers stick to a honeycomb. When someone locked Schechter's goat in the empty classroom, Zvi Markovitch underwent a fierce interrogation while Yair Feinberg waited for him in the field. And when someone slathered plum compote over the threshold to the teacher's house, it was Zvi Markovitch who scrubbed the sticky, sweet mixture off the threshold to the sound of constant scolding, while Yair Feinberg waved to him from a distance. But one day, returning from a visit to his mother in Tel Aviv, Yair Feinberg didn't find his friend in class. When he asked the teacher where Zvi was, she told him that this time he'd gone too far. A full barrel of cream had disappeared from Strenger's dairy, and that was something she could not ignore. Yair's rosy cheeks grew slightly rosier when he replied, "But what can a person do with a whole barrel of cream? It would go sour in no time."

The teacher nodded and said, "He has the mind of a devil, that Markovitch. After a few smacks from Strenger he confessed that he dragged the barrel to the spring to cool it in the cold water so it wouldn't go sour. God knows where he got the strength to do that all by himself."

Now Yair's face blazed pink and red. "Strenger hit him? But it was my idea! We dragged the barrel together!"

Yair labored long and hard to persuade the teacher that he was indeed confessing to a crime that he had truly taken part in committing. He dashed off to Strenger's dairy and explained to him what had happened, and so pure were his flushed cheeks, peach scent and tears of regret that Strenger handed him a jug of cream to console him. Yair Feinberg went to Zvi Markovitch's house, and together they ate the cream.

A short time after the cream incident came to an end, Yair Feinberg's mischievousness also came to an end. The fact that he was caught playing one of his pranks was not the reason, because all those involved agreed that it was a one-off affair for such an honest, sweet boy. It was the scent of peaches that kept Yair at home. The smell had become so strong that it gave him away even in the middle of the night. He could no longer slip in and out of places under cover of darkness. The scent of his body preceded him with a loud fanfare and trailed behind him like an ongoing whistle. Zeev Feinberg listened to the whistle and frowned. The scent of peaches that his son gave off kept him awake at night. It was unnatural. Something wasn't kosher. For a woman to smell of oranges or cinnamon or even cloves—that was all well and good, seductive and enjoyable. But who ever heard of a man with skin that smelled of peaches? As long as Yair was a child, Zeev Feinberg convinced himself that the smell would disappear when he grew up, like baby teeth or baby fat or faith in a good God—things that a man discards without looking back. But in another few months the boy would be thirteen. How could he keep smelling like a fruit pie? Such things had to be nipped in the bud. Zeev Feinberg got out of bed, woke up the boy and ordered him to take a bath. Such a thing would certainly never have taken place if Sonya had been home, but Sonya was spending that night in Tel Aviv, so she couldn't say anything when Zeev Feinberg scrubbed Yair's skin until it was red. It was well after midnight when Zeev Feinberg gave up the hope that one good scrubbing would be enough finally to cleanse his son of his scent. "Go to sleep," he told the boy, "we'll continue tomorrow."

And they continued the next day. And the day after that. By the time Sonya came back to the village, the boy's skin was already hurting from so many washings and salves. The scent, in any case, remained. "What the hell are you doing?" Sonya shouted when she saw her son completely covered with a green powder that an old Arab woman from Fureidis claimed could remove anything—from an unwanted smell to a bothersome memory. Before Yair could reply Zeev Feinberg himself replied in a firm voice,

"We are removing it from his body."

"Removing what?"

"It."

Sonya looked at her husband's face. Since her weeks had been divided—three days in Tel Aviv, four in the village—she had learned to recognize the look in his eye. A look that said: I'm angry that you're not here. And if you dug deep enough beneath that look, you would find the archaeological treasure that had been completely covered over by the dust of everyday routine—his longing to be with her. But never mind longing—her son was covered in pasty green powder that had to be removed immediately. In no time at all Sonya and Zeev Feinberg were shouting vehemently at each other, she accusing him of being mad, he accusing her of having bequeathed the curse of the scent to her son. Yair slipped out of the room and went to the spring.

For a long time Yair worked to remove the green powder from his body, and now was standing naked, his calves immersed in water, his mind immersed in thought. An unnatural smell, his father had said. A woman's smell. So he went back to submerge himself in the spring, letting the water cover his entire body, fill every crevice. He didn't emerge until his lungs were about to burst. And for a moment, for one sweet moment, he could smell nothing but the scum on the surface of the spring and the unripe figs hanging above him. Then his lungs demanded an additional supply of air, and when he inhaled deeply he knew that he had failed—because the smell of peaches assailed him mercilessly. Yair walked out of the water, dried his body with his shirt and returned home in defeat.

For a long time the spring lay in silence. The water returned the moon's laughing image. The figs swayed on their branches, accumulating the sweetness of that night and of all the nights that would follow. Then the water rippled again at the touch of Naama Feinberg's body. The entire time that Yair had bathed in the spring, Naama had stood hidden by the bushes, watching her handsome, beloved brother. When he left the house she had followed him silently, treading in the footsteps he had left. Skilled, very skilled. She did not hesitate for even a moment, did not wonder for even a moment how her parents would respond if they checked her bed and found it empty. She knew very well that they wouldn't check. Because they loved him more, and she knew it. It wasn't that they didn't hug her. They did. A lot, even. But they waited for Yair with arms open wide, always open wide. And they hugged Naama when she asked them to. Hugged her when she cried. Hugged her when she hugged them. Naama hewed her hugs from stone, but with Yair the hugs were there, waiting for him. A treasure chest of tenderness that he took for granted. Naama wanted so much to hate him. Those plump cheeks, that curly head, and that smell—they gave her no rest. Nonetheless, she never could hate him. Not wholeheartedly. While half of her was ready to kill him, the other half was ready to die for him. And that was reason enough to let him live.

A short time after Yair stepped out of the spring and returned home, Naama took off her nightgown and went into the water. Perhaps a miracle would happen and a bit of that pinkness, of that scent of peaches she so longed for, would rub off on her. She would settle for a different scent, anything from persimmon to plum, if only her skin would lose its dullness, its ordinariness, and finally be like Yair's and Sonya's skin. After all, Yair's smell was nothing but a version of his mother's. While Naama's skin had no special scent. In vain had she rubbed her skin with the peels of citrus fruit. In vain had she thrown away her food and lived for an entire week on oranges alone. Her skin stayed the same. Again and again she immersed herself in the cold spring, took a deep breath and dived underwater, the way Yair had done only a little while before, until the pressure in her lungs overcame her desire and she surfaced. And for a moment, for one sweet moment, she thought that perhaps the scent of the figs around her was coming from her own body. When her lungs demanded an additional supply of air, she inhaled deeply and knew she had failed—because the scent of the figs belonged to the unripe fruit hanging above her, not to her.

Sonya did actually try to love them equally. She truly did try. The way a bespectacled boy vows never to laugh at people with impaired vision, the way a fat girl swears that even if she turns into a swan one day, she will never make fun of an ugly duckling. Because Sonya herself, long before she became Sonya, when she was still six-year-old Sonyitchka, had sworn that she would love her children equally forever and ever. Her mother had given birth to three strapping sons and one ugly daughter, who played boys' games and who had gray eyes that were too wide-set and made her mother uneasy. Sonya remembered clearly how shocked she was when she discovered that a mother could love one of her children more than the others. Until then she had always believed the conventional lie—that a mother loved all her children, each one differently. In the end she realized that, though they had all emerged from the same womb, there were those whose umbilical cord was never really cut. And her mother, who was supposed to divide her love into four equal slices, loved her oldest brother the most. Then her other two brothers. And finally her. Now she herself was a mother. And she loved Yair more. She never said it aloud. She never even let it echo in her mind, afraid that it might be heard. Nonetheless everyone knew it. Naama knew it. Zeev Feinberg knew it. And Yair knew it as well.

2

O N THE EVE of the Shavuot festival, when he was fourteen, Zvi Markovitch discovered that Yaacov Markovitch was not his father. He was walking behind one of the wagons of produce that packed the main street of the village in a long procession. He was holding a large basket of strawberries, which his father had miraculously filled with the fruit. Yaacov Markovitch was the only farmer in the village who believed that the soil in the region was more than suitable for growing strawberries. They told him that he wouldn't be able to grow them, certainly not enough of them. And that, even if he did grow enough of them, they certainly wouldn't be sweet enough. The earth here, they told him, is too hard for growing such sweet fruit. Oranges, yes. Peaches, yes. It takes blood, sweat and tears to grow them, but they're born on high branches that sprout from stubborn tree trunks. And strawberries have neither branches nor trunks. Just bursting red sweetness only centimeters above the ground. The soil you need to grow strawberries has to be mad about its owner, a flirt. Like in America. Huge quantities of strawberries grow in California, and it's no wonder. Everything there grows in huge quantities. A veritable orgy of fruit and natural resources, lots of money. But our soil is not so amorous. You have to work very hard to get a drop of sweetness out of it.

Yaacov Markovitch listened thoughtfully, then went and planted strawberries on the entire northern portion of his land, his son walking behind him and handing him seedling after seedling from the wheelbarrow. His neighbors thought he'd lost his mind. Zeev Feinberg came to dissuade him. "Grow them in your front garden, Markovitch. In window boxes, for all I care. But why in the field?" Yaacov Markovitch listened to his friend and tossed a few breadcrumbs to the pigeons. Ten years had passed, so these were different, younger pigeons. Nevertheless, they were still fond of breadcrumbs in general, and of Yaacov Markovitch in particular. The pigeons congregated around Yaacov Markovitch's feet, and Zeev Feinberg thought that, at that moment, his friend looked like one of those saints pictured with admiring animals gathered at their feet.

"I want strawberries, Feinberg. I want this land to give me strawberries. And it will."

"And if it doesn't, you're condemning all the members of your family to hunger."

But the other members of the family seemed quite relaxed about that possibility. Bella, who never asked Yaacov Markovitch what he planted in his fields, did not deviate from that habit this time either. When the women of the village asked her what plan she had devised to deal with her husband's madness, she changed the subject. Not because she trusted Yaacov Markovitch to succeed. On the contrary, she sometimes wondered if that entire, insane strawberry business was a way of punishing her. But if they discussed what he planted, that would open the door to a discussion of what he picked and harvested, which would then lead to a discussion of the taste of the fruit, the purchase and sales accounts, a bit of politics, a dash of culture, and bam—they would be husband and wife in every sense. And that was something she could not allow. Her beauty was dissipating, dripping away as she slept. She had stopped reading poetry the day she tossed into a fire the poems she had once saved from a different fire. Her hatred of Yaacov Markovitch, though it had faded, was still the only thing she preserved from the passion of her youth.

Zvi Markovitch, on the other hand, trusted his father in everything. If Yaacov Markovitch could have seen himself through his son's eyes, he would surely have been shocked at how handsome he was. His eyes inspired trust. His nose was proud. His chin prominent and his forehead strong. His hands, which so often hung aimlessly at his sides, gripped his hoe the way a soldier gripped his rifle. So marvelous was this image of the father in the mind of the son that we can only regret that, at one time or another, Zvi Markovitch would have to see his father as he was, and not as he wanted him to be. But for now that moment was still far off, and so when Zvi Markovitch heard his friends making fun of his father's strawberry madness he hit them as hard as he could and would surely have returned home with a tooth or two missing if Yair Feinberg hadn't hurried to his side, fists clenched.

Bella was mistaken when she thought that planting the strawberries was a way for Yaacov Markovitch to punish her, a weapon against her hostility. People live alongside each other for many years, look at each other's faces day and night, and still they are blind men in the darkness. Otherwise how can you explain why Bella, a clearly intelligent woman, did not understand that the strawberries were simply a passion that Markovitch had adopted to replace her. For the moment comes when great passions become slightly less great, then small, and then are gone. Yaacov Markovitch, who had loved Bella for more than a decade, had begun to grow tired. The first indications of this were his renewed visits to the woman in Haifa. Ten years had passed, but the woman in Haifa was still the same age and moaned the same moans. Her name, of course, had changed. When he turned to leave she offered him a strawberry, a gift from her previous client. Yaacov Markovitch ate the fruit and his eyes lit up. The moldy taste of the woman in his mouth was replaced by an intense, lively sweetness. All the way back to the village he thought about the red fruit and decided he would grow it in his fields. He saw himself walking through the heart of a red, velvety carpet, picking strawberries to his heart's content.

At night, Yaacov Markovitch would get out of bed to see how the plants were faring. Though he was a naturally serene person, he was now ready to chop up the innards of any rodent that dared to damage his land. He would walk across the length and breadth of the field and, as often happens to a person walking alone at night, he would begin to speak. He told the strawberry plants about his childhood and his parents. He told them about the dreariness of his life. He told them about the moment everything changed, when he saw Bella's face in a crowded living room in a freezing city. And once he began to speak of Bella he could not stop, and recounted the entire history of his unrequited love. He extolled her skin, glorified her eyes, exalted her hair and even described her breasts. The strawberry plants listened in silence, and Yaacov Markovitch needed no more than that. With shining eyes he spoke of her elegant gait, the regal way she held her head, her sculpted nose. The hours passed and Yaacov Markovitch walked and talked, and when he could no longer walk he lay down flat on his back, careful not to crush the plants, and whispered all the rest to the earth. He whispered of Bella's glorious pubic mound, which he had seen for only one blessed moment. Of her stomach. Of the softness of her limbs. And so he fell asleep for a short while before dawn, pouring his passion into the earth, the leaves of the strawberry plants shading his face from the sun.

It did not take long for the entire village to learn about Yaacov Markovitch's nocturnal wanderings. Though many farmers occasionally spoke to their grains, or chatted a bit with their fruit, none of them had turned their nocturnal strolls into a habit. But from the moment Yaacov Markovitch planted the strawberries on his land, he had not spent an entire night in his bed. They said that he read the evening newspaper to the strawberries. They insinuated that he wrote erotic poems to them. They whispered that he sometimes spread his own seed on the ground to bring the promise of a good crop. Yaacov Markovitch shut his ears against all that talk. His long years in the village had inured him to people's criticism. He no longer saw them shake their heads or heard them cluck their tongues. But Zvi Markovitch—his eyes saw and his ears heard, which is why his skin was covered in bruises. He engaged in almost daily battle with one or another of the boys about his father. At any given moment he could count at least five hematomas on his body. He wore them proudly, the way a soldier wears his medals of valor, and he vowed never to tell his father why he had them.

Sixty days after he had begun courting it, the land yielded to Yaacov Markovitch. The strawberry plants, which had listened every night to the determined farmer's erotic dreams, dared not turn their backs on him as well. For sixty nights Yaacov Markovitch had walked among them, had embraced them in his sleep, had entrenched himself in the earth with desire, and now triumph was his. The red fruit came from the earth like a sigh of pleasure after a lengthy bout of lovemaking. Yaacov Markovitch saw but didn't believe, for deep down he had feared that the earth would also refuse him. But instead of refusing, it had offered up a resounding "yes". Yes and yes and another yes, a strawberry and a strawberry and another strawberry, until the entire field uttered a loud, red moan. It was the time of the Shavuot festival, and the moan of Yaacov Markovitch's land could be heard throughout the village. Everyone listened, their curiosity mixed with envy, as a person might listen to his neighbor's lovemaking. Zvi Markovitch walked in the streets with a smile of victory on his face. Now everyone knew how great his father was. On the eve of the holiday he filled a basket with the finest of the fruit, so sweet that they couldn't get through the front door. Every time Bella grabbed a strawberry and Yaacov Markovitch reached out a covetous hand, Zvi Markovitch had to fill the basket again before he could leave the house. "Exceptional," Bella said, and Yaacov Markovitch nodded in confirmation. And Zvi, who couldn't remember when he had seen his father and mother so gentle with one another, hurried out before the moment could pass.

Now he was walking down the main street of the village with the other boys, each carrying a basket brimming with the finest of the season's harvest. Naama Feinberg walked beside him, her golden hair piled on top of her head. Yair Feinberg walked on his other side, his expression serious, pushing a wheelbarrow of pumpkins. He refused adamantly to put even a single peach in the wheelbarrow, and until now had been forced to rebuff a substantial number of well-meaning farmers who wanted to do so. Zvi Markovitch walked between his best friend and his pretty little sister, holding a basket full of strawberries in one hand and feeling something he had never felt before: there was nothing about that moment that he wanted to change. Even the nasal voices of Zahava Tamir and Rivka Shaham, a little ways behind them, couldn't spoil the sweetness of the moment.

"Look at how beautiful Feinberg's children are, beautiful enough to have their pictures in the newspapers. It's too bad that Markovitch's ugly son is stuck between them."

"At least the strawberries in his basket look good."

"Well it's about time Yaacov Markovitch managed to grow something right. If your wife hates you and you're raising a child who's not yours, you should at least know how to earn a living."

*

Zvi Markovitch's basket of strawberries didn't drop out of his hand immediately. He kept walking for another five minutes, his legs like two lumps of dough, like those of the gingerbread boys his mother baked for him when the mood was upon her. And he took step after step with them, feeling each leg collapsing into itself, blending into itself, a gingerbread boy getting burnt, turning black. And all the while Yair Feinberg and his wheelbarrow of pumpkins, and Naama Feinberg and her oranges, walked beside him, both stealing glances at his face to see if he had heard. It was when they said to themselves that he definitely hadn't heard, when they reassured themselves that, miraculously, the words had gone over his head, because look, five minutes had already passed and Zvi Markovitch's face was expressionless—it was then that Zvi Markovitch stopped short and dropped the basket of strawberries. The red fruit rolled on the ground and was crushed by the feet of the marchers. Someone muttered something about the boy's clumsiness. Someone called out—it's a sign of good luck. Zvi Markovitch didn't listen to any of them. An avalanche roared inside him, stone pillars and marble slabs collapsed one after the other, gravel and sand and rocks smashed into bits when they fell. A cloud of dust rose and covered the temple that Zvi Markovitch had built to his father in his mind, now turned into ashes.

Naama Feinberg hurried to pick up the strawberries. Yair knelt beside her. Zvi Markovitch stood where he was, staring into space. Before his eyes, fragments of remarks he had heard at home came together with neighbors' whispers and teachers' looks. Suddenly the knowledge was perfectly clear, as if it had always been there. At that moment Zvi Markovitch realized that he was about to vomit.

He turned and began to run. Far from the wagons bursting with a cornucopia of first fruit. Far from the pumpkins, the oranges and the peaches. Far from the strawberries. A few minutes later he stopped and vomited on the main street. Thick red vomit, all the strawberries he had tossed into his stomach since morning. The red doughy mess on the ground looked like an animal's innards. A nauseatingly sweet taste filled his throat. He vomited again. And again. He vomited for a long time after the nausea had passed. He vomited for a long time after he had nothing left to vomit. Nonetheless, he stuck a finger into his mouth and waited, then vomited again, and forced himself to vomit more because he didn't know what he would do when he stopped vomiting. He vomited again and again, but no matter how much he vomited, he could not disgorge Rivka Shaham's words, which had settled in his stomach and clamped their fingers around his organs. Until other fingers came and clasped his hand, and Naama Feinberg said, "Enough."

Zvi Markovitch pulled his hand away, and once again stuck a finger into his mouth. But before he could vomit again Naama grabbed his hand and repeated, "Enough." This time he didn't pull his hand away. They heard the sound of singing coming from a nearby street. The parade of the first fruits would soon be there. "Come on," Naama Feinberg said to Zvi Markovitch, and pulled him by the hand. He followed her. The first marchers were visible at the bend in the street, and Naama Feinberg walked more quickly. Only when she reached the other side of the cypress-lined avenue did she slow down. She held his hand all the way to the spring. She kept holding it when they sat down on the damp ground, dirtying their white holiday clothes.

"Now ask for it."

"For what?"

"Ask the spring to give you what you want. It grants wishes. My mother told me."

"You're not serious."

"I'm very serious. It worked for me."

"You asked for something and you got it?"

"I asked for two things. I got one. Which means that your chance of success is fifty per cent."

"What did you ask for?"

Naama Feinberg looked at the water before replying. "One thing that didn't happen and another one that did. I'll tell you what did happen—I asked for the figs to ripen."

Zvi Markovitch snorted derisively. "But they would have ripened anyway."

Naama Feinberg's hand clenched in his. "Don't say that."

So he didn't. He sat there silently holding Naama Feinberg's hand, and thought that a spring that grants wishes was the stupidest thing he had ever heard in his life. And thought that grown-ups were the nastiest creatures he had ever met in his life. And thought that Naama Feinberg's hand was the nicest thing he had ever held in his life.

After that day, Zvi Markovitch never held Naama Feinberg's hand again. When the sun set over the spring, they stood up and went to their respective homes. Zvi Markovitch to an empty house (Yaacov Markovitch had gone out to the field and was walking among the strawberries like a drunkard, and Bella, sick and tired of strawberries because for hours all he had talked about was strawberries, had gone out to escape the suffocation of the house with a stroll along the paths of the village), and Naama Feinberg returned to a full house (Sonya had come back from Tel Aviv sooner because of the holiday, and she and Zeev Feinberg were already arguing about who had been in charge of putting a cheesecake on the table: he claimed that she was and she said that he was, and then she picked up the bowl of cheese that was on the kitchen table—cheese that should have been turned into a cake, though it wasn't clear by whom—and hurled some at

Feinberg's face. Cheese dripping from his mustache, he charged at her with a cry of angry laughter.) While Zeev Feinberg and Sonya were going at it, Yair turned to his sister and demanded to know: where did you go? One minute he was bending down beside her to gather the strawberries, and a minute later he found himself alone. Zvi Markovitch had vanished. His sister had vanished. He had looked for them for almost two hours. He asked everyone in the village. And now she just waltzes in, her white dress covered in mud. Her face flushed.

Naama looked at her brother and said that she didn't have to report to him. But she was excited that he had asked her for a report, that he had noticed her dirty dress, her lateness, all the things that Zeev Feinberg and Sonya hadn't seen over the bowl of cheese. His sister's reply made Yair Feinberg angry and he stormed off to his room. Naama hurried after him, determined to make up with him. She suggested that they read a book together, or play with the deck of cards she had once taken from Yeshayahu Ron's disgusting son after he pulled her hair. "Go and play with him if you want," Yair Feinberg said, and slammed the door.

For a while longer Naama stood on the border between Yair's locked door and her parents' quarrel. She could hear the cheery sounds of Feinberg and Sonya's squabble coming from the kitchen. The pungent scent of peaches penetrated Yair's door, an indication that he had taken off his clothes. Naama stood in front of the closed door and inhaled deeply. Yair's peach scent blended with the smell of oranges that spread through the house whenever her mother was in it. Peach and orange. Orange and peach. And the spring that her mother had said could grant wishes. The figs that had ripened. Her skin, still unripe. And she suddenly knew that she could not bear it if Yair's door remained closed. If the peach scent were also taken from her. So she decided that she would never, under any circumstances, hold Zvi Markovitch's hand again.

3

YAACOV MARKOVITCH sold the strawberries at a large profit. For the first time in his life he was able to drive a hard bargain because, for him, parting from the fruit was like parting from a lover. With the money he received for the strawberries he bought Bella a red silk scarf. It didn't take many days for Yaacov Markovitch to discover that Bella had turned the scarf into a dishrag. But instead of shrugging and returning to make love among the strawberries, his passion for his wife grew. A strange thing: the land's submission to his whims had actually strengthened his ability to hold on to Bella. As if the capitulation of the former had proved that also the latter, if he would only persist in courting her, would ultimately give herself to him. And so he courted her again as he had at the beginning, when she first entered his home. But Bella, sensing his desire, grew colder. And for several days they did their little dance, he moving closer, she moving farther away, and so engrossed were they, he in his desire, she in her anger, that not until two weeks after the Shavuot holiday did Yaacov Markovitch notice that his son had stopped calling him Dad.

For more than two weeks Zvi Markovitch watched his parents, scrutinizing them like a researcher observing the behavior of fish in an aquarium. He saw Yaacov Markovitch's courtship dance and the barbed quills Bella raised in his direction. He saw the bubbles of venom she exhaled and the gifts he gave her. In the end, they were no different from the octopus and the sunfish he had seen when his class visited a lab in the Technion. He tried to envelop her with his eight arms, and she was poisonous and evasive. But unlike the octopus and the sunfish, which can circle each other forever, whether in the ocean depths or in front of the astonished eyes of forty boys, Yaacov Markovitch and Bella began to sense the eyes looking at them. Gradually they stopped circling each other, disturbed by the new presence. The boy had never looked at them like that. At first they didn't even know how to define it, how to explain to themselves what it was about his glance that stopped them from moving. Until they finally understood, each one separately, the change that had taken place in the boy's eyes: they had become empty. Zvi Markovitch looked at his parents with eyes devoid of illusions. Yaacov Markovitch no longer glowed with a bright light. Bella was no longer wrapped in a soft, golden halo. He saw them as they were, and that forced them to see themselves as he did. And that hurt.

Soon after Yaacov Markovitch understood that, he also realized that the boy had stopped calling him Dad. Though he didn't discuss it with Bella, he knew that she too had noticed it. She was more circumspect, no longer recoiled from Markovitch with such unconcealed rudeness. As if she feared that if the boy cut himself off from him, Markovitch would renounce him. After all, he was not his father. In this she was mistaken, because he was his father. He had soothed him after nightmares when he was four, and had assembled his bicycle when he was five. He had taught him his first words. He had disinfected every cut and scratch. Markovitch's love for the boy was strong and steady, unconnected to his love for his mother. The new distance between them worried him no less than it worried Bella. Nonetheless, he didn't ask the boy what had happened to him. Every time he saw him the words stuck in his throat, heavy and garbled. Never before had he needed words in his relationship with his son. Perhaps that was why the relationship was so good. Wordlesssly, their sweaty bodies shared the day's work in the field. Wordlessly, they smiled at each other in understanding at the moment of an animal's birthing. Wordlessly, their eyes would meet as Yaacov Markovitch sterilized his son's wounds with practiced fingers, only the trembling of his lips giving away his anger at the boy's injuries. But since Shavuot Zvi Markovitch had not asked his father to bandage a bleeding bruise. All at once the fights had ceased. He no longer fought with the other boys. Now he fought with himself. The bruises, when they appeared, grew inward from his skin, never seeing the light of day. Nonetheless, Naama saw them.

"What do you fight about?" she asked Zvi Markovitch in the schoolyard one gruelingly hot afternoon.

"Who's fighting?"

"You and yourself."

He sniffed scornfully and turned to leave, but Naama, who was already adept at interpreting smells, could tell from his breath that she was right, and sensed the affront to the hand she had not held again. Zvi Markovitch walked away from her and returned to his home and his observations. Twice Yaacov Markovitch had stood at the boy's door, his hand raised to knock. Each of those two times he had dropped his hand and walked away. The silence spun around and around the house like a spider's web.

One day, when Naama, Zvi and Yair were lying in the shade of the cypress trees, Zvi Markovitch finally opened his mouth and said aloud what he had been feeling only in the depths of his heart for weeks:

"I want to get up and go. I want to leave this place."

It was a hot day. The earth was blazing. The shade cast by the cypress trees was nothing more than a dark drawing on the ground. Yair Feinberg turned to look at his friend with languid curiosity. His black curls rested on his forehead, his peach-pink lips opened slightly:

"Where to?"

Zvi Markovitch hesitated. He had struggled a great deal with the question of whether to get up and go, but until that moment he had never asked himself where to. Even worse—he thought he could see a hint of mockery in his friend's eyes, as if Yair Feinberg found it amusing that someone could be so determined to leave a place without having the slightest idea where he would go. After all, Zvi Markovitch thought, when a person sets out on a journey, all he needs is a point of departure. So why Yair's skeptical look?

Yair's look, however, was not directed at Zvi Markovitch but at Naama, whose eyes had been glistening from the moment Zvi had spoken. To get up and go. Why hadn't they thought of that before? The three of them would run away, maybe that very night. If they walked quickly they could make it to Lake Kinneret in a week. They'd eat fish and dates. They'd swim in the lake. No one would know where they were. No one would know that her parents loved Yair more than they loved her. But when she told them her plan, Yair burst out laughing.

"We'll die of sunstroke in less than two hours."

"So we'll go at night."

"Maybe we should ride there," Zvi suggested.

"Ride what?"

"We'll sneak onto one of the produce trucks. We'll get off wherever. It doesn't really matter. And we'll never come back to the village."

His words actually extinguished the spark in Naama's eyes. Never? Beyond the cypress trees, the village was taking its afternoon nap, never imagining the approaching betrayal. Chickens clucked in the distance, the land breathed heavily.

"No," Naama said, "we can't leave the village. No one ever did that. Except for Avraham Mandelbaum, who everyone says was crazy, and a few *chalutzim* who were afraid of malaria, and everyone makes fun of them in our civics class."

Now the string that had tensed in Yair Feinberg's back finally relaxed. He rolled onto his back and looked up at the sky. All was well. His sister was staying here.

But Zvi Markovitch did not relax; he stood up and pleaded, "Why not?"

Yair and Naama Feinberg remained lying on the ground. "Because farmers don't leave their village," Yair replied, "otherwise we'd be like *them*."

4

ZEEV FEINBERG had been relentless in bequeathing his anger at "them" to his children. Against Tel Aviv he had a personal grudge. Since Sonya had made that city her second home, Zeev Feinberg could no longer abide the sight of it. He almost forgot that he himself, newly arrived on the shores of Palestine, had hesitated slightly before choosing a farmer's life. The time that had passed since then had erased the question marks, so that the crossroads looked like straight paths he had taken decisively.

"A bunch of clerks and secretaries and merchants. There isn't a single real man in that whole city."

"Not a single one?"

Sonya's tone was amused, her eyebrows skeptical. Since she had returned to the village the previous evening, she and Feinberg had been constantly fighting and making up. Now, at Friday night dinner, she was in a good enough mood to see that Feinberg's aversion to the city was nothing but a reflection of his love for her.

"Really, Sonya, this boy sitting here is stronger than they are!"

When Yair Feinberg heard that, his face glowed with pleasure. Since Zeev Feinberg had declared a war unto death against the peach scent, he had not praised the boy very much. He ordered him to take long baths and keep the windows open at all times, to prevent the scent from permeating the rooms. Such praise from his father, even if given offhandedly, was of great value. Zeev Feinberg did not notice his son's happiness and continued speaking,

"I'd bet on it, Sonya, you don't have even one real man in that city of yours. Except Froike."

When Zeev Feinberg said the name of the deputy commander of the Irgun, a shadow flitted over Sonya's face. Zeev Feinberg didn't notice it because he was thinking about his friend. Yair Feinberg didn't notice it because he was thinking about his efforts to please his father. And Naama, waiting as expectantly as ever for any leftover affection that Sonya might toss her way, noticed the shadow that crossed her mother's face and stored it away in her mind.

"Yes," Zeev Feinberg repeated, "Froike is a real man."

"Why?" Yair Feinberg asked, determined to find out what it was that turned someone into a real man, raised him from the humdrum world into the magnificent realm of people his father spoke about with admiration in his eyes. Then Zeev Feinberg began to talk about the exploits of the deputy commander of the Irgun, and as he grew more enthusiastic Sonya shrank further into herself. So enthusiastic was Zeev Feinberg that he forgot that he hadn't seen his friend for many years, that he declined every invitation to visit with a variety of excuses. Such things were mere trifles. The main thing was the mix of gun oil and mud, the smell of gunpowder and blood, which were the hallmarks of real men.

"You see, son, a fellow like Froike could crush a British police-man's nose with one hand while he played the harmonica with the other. Any other soldier would take off right after that, but Froike, he would keep playing the song to the end, and only then would he get up and go. Slowly, like a gentleman. And without leaving any traces. They never caught him. Not like you, with that smell of compote. A whole regiment would find you in half a minute."

Upon hearing Zeev Feinberg's last words Sonya shot him an admonishing look, but it bounced off his glazed eyes and scattered. Because Zeev Feinberg had already left the house. He didn't see the wooden table in front of him, but the trench in which he and the deputy commander of the Irgun had hidden many years ago on their way to blow up the walls of a detention center where illegal immigrants were being held. The belts of explosives had embraced their waists like a passionate lover. The proximity of death sharpened the senses and made the world remarkably beautiful. The stars in the sky had never shone above them as brightly as they did that night, when fifty kilograms of explosives rubbed against their skin with every step. Unconsciously, Zeev Feinberg moved his fingers to the faded leather belt around his waist, the belt he had recently added a hole to so he could buckle it. How quickly he would exchange this warm room for that night of silent crawling. But his crawling days were over. Now there were bills he had to pay and broken ploughs he had to fix and children he had to cleanse of their strange smells. For the first time since the night he had mistakenly killed the mother and her baby, Zeev Feinberg missed the war. And, as often happens, his longing for the war took on form and shape: the form and shape of the deputy commander of the Irgun. For while Zeev Feinberg was busy raising offspring and working the land, Ephraim remained as he had been: a soldier. Instead of babies hanging on his shoulder, there was a rifle. He spent his days doing crucial strategic planning. Zeev Feinberg continued to dwell on the image of Ephraim and their joint exploits, and Yair Feinberg listened to the words and burned them into his heart. Now he knew what he had to do, how to finally erase the disappointment in his father's eyes. And so, one Friday evening in August, over a plateful of burnt potatoes, Yair Feinberg decided that he would be a soldier.

The training camp was set up at the far edge of the wadi, and kept secret. Zvi Markovitch and Naama Feinberg were the only other members, and they pledged their total allegiance in an elaborate ritual that included the intermingling of blood and the beheading of a grasshopper. They trained in running and jumping, in laying ambushes and devising stratagems. More than anything, they trained themselves to be angry at "them". They would spend entire nights talking contemptuously about the young men sleeping in their beds now, young men who didn't know how to navigate by the stars or cover their footprints. Young men who would be caught in minutes if they tried to set an ambush. They never mentioned the chances that Yair Feinberg would be caught; he had turned sixteen, and his peach scent was even stronger and wonderfully sweet. Sometimes, when the three of them crowded behind a rock shelf to ambush a terrorist who never came, Zvi Markovitch's arm would accidentally brush against Naama's hand. Those moments, which they never spoke about, were worth all the sleepless nights.

When winter came, Zvi Markovitch expected that they would find other things to occupy them. He quickly realized that he was mistaken. Yair Feinberg considered the cold and rain to be a golden opportunity, tools to toughen them physically and men-tally. Not even the pneumonia they all came down with after he forced them to swim across the reservoir dampened his resolve. Even before his fever went down he began to sneak out of bed for morning training exercises. Zvi Markovitch, on the other hand, stayed in bed, spitting and coughing, long after his friends had recovered, until the doctor said that it wasn't pneumonia he had, but a serious case of asthma. Yair Feinberg heard the news and paled. He knew that serious asthma disqualified his friend from combat duty, forcing him to become one of "them". When Zvi Markovitch got out of his sickbed, none of them mentioned the word asthma again, just as they didn't mention Yair's peach smell or Naama's femininity. Those things, which divided them and kept them from being what they were required to be, need not be spoken about.

As spring approached and the night frost melted slightly, they returned to the wadi and the ambushes. But they soon discovered that they had lost their charm. The sweetness of danger had passed, leaving the bitter taste of boredom in their mouths. They no longer tensed at every noise. They knew that they were only the sounds of night, or at most a couple looking for a place to be alone. Their search for something else that would interest them took them to the other side of the wadi, up the slope of the hill, to the ruins of an Arab village that had been deserted since the war. Then the color returned to Naama's cheeks and the spark to Yair's eyes. "We have to defend this place," he explained excitedly, "to guard it in case the Arabs want to come back." Zvi Markovitch nodded in agreement. At any moment, the village might again fill up with rioting Arabs who would dig in behind the stone walls and riddle the bodies of Jewish soldiers with their hateful bullets. True, three is a frighteningly small number of people to defend such an important strategic asset, but the Jews had always been the few against the many, and the three—though they were only teenagers—were superbly trained and staunchly resolute. Every day they waited impatiently for school to end, then hurried to the wadi. As they neared the village, a head movement was enough for them instantly to crouch down to keep the enemy from seeing the approaching forces. They almost always crawled the last fifty meters between the patch of cactus plants and the first house in the village, and if any of them made the slightest sound when a thorn or a stone pierced his flesh, the other two would give him such a withering look that he would fall silent in shame. When they reached the first house they quickly took cover behind the half-destroyed walls and watched the other buildings through the window. Only when they were sure that no hostile element had taken advantage of the time they were learning math, literature and geography to invade the village did they leave their ambush site. From then until sunset they picked cactus fruit and reconnoitered the other houses. As shadows grew longer they began to feel the unease a person feels as he walks around a destroyed, abandoned village, thinking he hears a mother calling her children for supper, or imagining he sees a man returning from the fields. Nonetheless they would force themselves to stay until darkness fell, perhaps then evil forces would emerge from their burrows. At around 7:30, when it was clear that all further delays would lead to unnecessary questions around the dinner table, they began to run towards the village. Near the cypress fence they parted with a handshake, which they considered appropriate at the completion of such an operation. Yair and Naama turned towards their house and Zvi Markovitch towards his, although in his mind he kept walking beside his friends, one hand on Yair Feinberg's shoulder like comrades-in-arms, his other hand holding Naama's with the sort of comradeship he had not yet dared to define to himself. Even when sitting at the table with his parents he continued to think about his friends, either because thoughts about Naama and Yair were pleasant, or because the presence of Bella and Yaacov Markovitch was unbearable. For many months now he had been aloof from them and they, instead of forcing him to tell them what was troubling him, took refuge in the shadow of his silence.

While silence reigned in the home of Yaacov Markovitch and Bella, the home of Zeev Feinberg and Sonya was buzzing with words. From the moment that the longing for battle had reawakened in Zeev Feinberg he talked about the exploits and escapades of the deputy commander of the Irgun at every opportunity, embracing the memories as if he were embracing the memory of a lover who has slipped away. Yair Feinberg listened in fascination to the story of how they drove a tribe of barbarian

Bedouin from the southern border, listened open-mouthed to the tales of hair-raising battles in the Jerusalem hills. But one night, when Zeev Feinberg was talking about forging a path to the Galilee settlements and heroic deeds on the coastal plain, the boy's expression grew sad. He suddenly realized that everything had already been done. All the enemy forces had been pushed outside the country's borders. Not a single Arab was left to defeat with his bare hands. It was true that, not long ago, the IDF forces had endangered their lives in a war with the Fedayeen, but that war had also ended without his participation. The next day he was silent, his face angry, as they walked to the abandoned village. When they passed the cactus patch Naama and Zvi crouched quickly, but Yair remained standing. "It's pointless," he said to his astonished friends, "there's no one here. And there never will be. No Arab will ever come back here."

And in an instant the magic ended. The shared lie that had united them for long weeks, that had filled them with pleasure and fear and secrets, shattered to smithereens. The dangerous enemy territory in front of them was nothing but a collection of ruined houses. Apart from the cactus plants, there was nothing there that could hurt them. Embarrassed, Naama and Zvi straightened up. Hesitantly they wiped off the sand and dust that was stuck to their clothes. Now they gave Yair a half-questioning, half-accusing look: so what now?

Yair ignored the question and sat down on the ground, arms and legs outstretched, his relaxed body proclaiming his firm conviction that there was no living creature in that place but them. Naama and Zvi sat down beside him. For a long moment no one spoke. In the heavy silence they could almost hear the ground mocking them—what could you expect from an asthmatic boy, a prankster who smelled of peaches and a young girl whose budding breasts were already visible under her blouse no matter how hard she tried to hide them? A great war requires great soldiers. They had come and taken all the glory, leaving nothing for Yair, Naama and Zvi.

Yair Feinberg picked a groundsel and began to tear it into many small pieces. His father would never give him the admiring looks he wished for so much. With glazed eyes, he would speak forever of the heroism of the past. Zvi Markovitch tore off an unlucky three-leaf clover and began to tear it apart. It was over. They would return home that night, never to climb the paths of the wadi again. The center of their lives would once more be the village, with its wagging tongues and judgmental looks, and his house, which stood in it like a throbbing wound. And he loved the destroyed, abandoned, Arab village. It was so far away and nothing could pass through the fence of cactus plants at its entrance.

Naama looked at the two young men taking out their anger on the wild plants, two defeated, hopeless warriors. How could she let Yair abandon himself to a depression that would make his scent even heavier, as heavy as a fruit the moment before its flesh rots? She jumped up and spoke in a serious, determined voice, imitating as best she could Yair's voice when he urged them into action: "Even if everything has already been done here, on the borders of the country there are still other places where heroism and daring are needed." Then she began to talk about the rock castle deep inside the Jordanian desert, dredging up from her memory bits of information she had read in the newspaper, adding necessary bits from her imagination. True, others had been there before them, but not many. The trip was difficult, but they could make it. And when they returned, everyone would know how great is the courage of Israeli youth.

Zvi and Yair looked at Naama open-mouthed. They knew the legends well: the red kingdom hidden in the heart of the desert, across the border. A kingdom that few had attempted to enter, and from which even fewer had returned. Was this golden-haired girl really suggesting that they take those legends and turn them into their own lives? Yes, that's exactly what she was suggesting, and the suggestion sounded more magical, more possible from moment to moment. They were well trained in long-distance walking, well practiced in camouflage, experienced in navigation and carrying provisions. After all their ambushes and operations, after all the tests of their courage, they couldn't simply return to the village, to the existence that was all dreary routine. Yair Feinberg had already begun to paint a picture in his mind of the day they would return from their journey. His tearful mother would throw her arms around him and his father would demand to know where he had been. He wouldn't reply, he would just look at his father with the silent determination of a soldier. Then he would take a blood-red stone out of his pocket (or perhaps even an entire cornice of the castle, if it wasn't too heavy), place it on the dining room table and walk away. Zeev Feinberg would know immediately where the stone had come from—where else could a person find such a red stone—and hurry after his son. With a smile on his face, Yair imagined how his father would beg to hear more details about the daring operation and how he would finally agree to recount them in a quiet, measured voice. After his father heard how heroic the exploit had been he would take the bottle of liquor out of its hiding place above the cabinet and pour a glass for each of them. The truth was that Yair despised the taste of liquor, which made him intensely nauseous every time he dared to sneak a sip from the bottle. But now he was positive that, after he completed his journey and returned with a cornice in his hand, he would become a man and love the taste of the liquor the way other men did.

Zvi Markovitch dropped the clover and also became immersed in thought. The idea of crossing the desert had caused chills to run up and down his spine. He remembered the coughing attack he'd had when the village children went on a trip to the hills around Eilat, the result of the dust on the road and his hurried effort to be the first to reach the top of the hill and wave to Naama from there. But however daunted he was by the thought of the journey, the idea of giving it up was even more daunting. Because Naama and Yair would go without him; the dreamy expression on their faces left no room for doubt. If he decided to stay they would go without him and he would be left behind, alone in the village with his father and his mother and the strawberry plants. Naama's hand would move away from him; when she returned from the journey, she still wouldn't let him hold it. Why should a girl who had experienced such an adventure let him hold her hand? Now he knew that there was no room for hesitation. He had to go with them.

That day, they left the destroyed Arab village long before sunset. With heads held high they walked away serenely, as if they had never made evasive exits from it. As they walked down the wadi, Zvi looked back at the cactus patch dotted with orange fruit. They'll turn more orange, he thought, they'll turn more orange and then red, and then rotten, because no one will come here to eat them. Beyond the patch the houses of the village stared at him through gaping windows and smashed doors. And for a moment he thought that the familiar childish fear had returned. But the devastated village no longer frightened him, it could not possibly frighten him anymore. Just the opposite—he almost found himself missing it. Zvi Markovitch turned away from the abandoned village back to the winding path on the slope of the wadi and knew that he was no longer a child.

5

Y AACOV AND BELLA MARKOVITCH woke up one morning and discovered that their son was gone. That same morning Zeev Feinberg woke up and found his children's beds empty. Until evening, Yaacov Markovitch and Bella assumed that the boy was at his friends' house. Zeev Feinberg assumed exactly the same thing. It wasn't until Bella arrived at Feinberg's house complaining about the dinner that was getting cold that everyone realized their mistake.

"Maybe they ran off to Tel Aviv, to see Sonya at work?" Markovitch suggested.

"Without telling anyone?!" Bella fumed.

"They must have thought they'd be back the same day," Feinberg said. "Sonya probably gave them a good talking to."

But Sonya, when she finally answered the phone in her office, was sure it was a joke. "Very funny, Zevik. Now can I go back to my meeting?"

"They're not with you?"

"Of course they're not with me. Why would they be with me? You're sure you're not making all this up to get me home a day earlier?"

"Sonya, the children aren't here."

They searched for them all night. Zeev Feinberg and Yaacov Markovitch recruited the village men, who went out with them to scour the fields, while Sonya walked through the streets of the city—perhaps they had gone there after all. At dawn all of them were red-eyed from lack of sleep and a tear or two that had been wiped away surreptitiously. At ten in the morning, when Yaacov Markovitch, Bella and Zeev Feinberg sat down to consider their next step, Sonya came tearing into the house. "Tell me they've found them." Zeev Feinberg didn't have to reply; one look into his eyes was enough for her. At eleven the villagers split up into organized search patrols and resumed combing the area. Around noon the police and volunteers from the neighboring villages joined them. They dived into the spring, scoured the wadi, walked through the cactus patch to explore the houses in the abandoned village, and looked at the sea, eyebrows contracted. Every now and then they glanced at one or another of the parents to see how they were holding up. Bella's skin was pale, her eyes vacant. When a volunteer went over to show her a shirt that had washed up on the shore, she collapsed onto the ground. "Does it belong to one of them?" Bella shook her head. Nevertheless, she didn't get up. The fact that the shirt might have been her son's was enough to paralyze her.

While Bella was sitting on the shore, as pale as death, Yaacov Markovitch was more energetic than he had ever been in his life, the blood surging through his veins, driving him this way and that, the volunteers running behind him unable to catch up. After a while the volunteers realized that such a chaotic search was pointless, so they left Yaacov Markovitch and went on combing the area more methodically. Yaacov Markovitch continued to run around in circles, calling out the boy's name over and over again, until he came across Bella sitting on the shore.

"Come on," he said, "we'll keep on searching."

Bella remained sitting, her eyes on the sea. "What if he's there?" she said, gesturing towards the dark water with her head.

Yaacov Markovitch knelt beside her and took her beautiful

head between his hands. "He's not there," he said, "he's somewhere else and we'll find him. I promise you that we'll find him." He spoke the words with such certainty, and they were so utterly baseless, that Bella burst into tears. Yaacov Markovitch took his wife in his arms to comfort her.

Sonya, meanwhile, was negotiating with God. Although at work she was considered a tough opponent in any negotiation, now she was promising everything, without exception, if only the children would come back. Zeev Feinberg, who normally ate a chunk of salami on a slice of bread slathered with butter every morning, now rediscovered the Jewish god. And so they prayed and searched, searched and prayed, until they saw headlights moving in the direction of the village. Since night had already fallen and not many people came to the village at that hour, Zeev Feinberg and Sonya hurried to see if the car was bringing any news. The headlights blinded them, so it took several seconds for Sonya to realize that she was looking straight into the tormented face of the deputy commander of the Irgun.

Zeev Feinberg threw his arms around his best friend. Sonya stood frozen.

"Let's go into the house," the deputy commander of the Irgun said, "it's better if no one else hears what I have to tell you."

From the moment the door to the house opened, there was no mistaking the peach smell. Almost forty-eight hours had passed since Yair Feinberg left home, but the scent of his body still filled the air. Reluctantly the deputy commander of the Irgun turned and looked at Sonya in surprise. He was quite familiar with the orange scent of the woman he loved, but the peach scent was something he could not have anticipated. Sonya avoided the glance of the deputy commander of the Irgun and went to make tea, while Zeev Feinberg inhaled the scent deeply and hurried to close the windows to keep it from escaping.

"I heard about the children on the radio," the deputy com-mander of the Irgun said, "I used all the means at my disposal. Three hours ago a young man from Yotvata got back to me. They're on their way to Petra."

"What?!"

"That fellow, one of the best soldiers I have ever commanded, recently came back from a trip to Petra. You know how it is, the rumor takes off and other young people make a pilgrimage to see him and hear about his experience. A month ago he received a letter from three youngsters from your village—all recently discharged from elite combat units—who asked about his trip. He sent them the details, added a map he drew himself, and wished them luck."

The deputy commander of the Irgun was silent for a moment, and that was enough for Sonya to burst out angrily, "So what? There aren't enough young people in the village who might be interested in such a foolish trip?"

The deputy commander of the Irgun replied without taking his eyes off the wooden table. "Last night, three teenagers arrived at his kibbutz, two boys and a girl. They asked to fill their water canteens and said they were on their way to the hills around Eilat. This morning, when he heard the news on the radio, my soldier was alarmed. He went out to check for their footprints. They led eastward." The deputy commander of the Irgun looked up from the wooden table, straight at Zeev Feinberg. "I think we should go out to search for them ourselves. No army or police, nothing that might make the Jordanians nervous."

Zeev Feinberg stood up and began to pace the living room. He remembered the long nights he had spent telling Yair heroic stories spiced with criticism of him. Now the boy had gone out to find his own heroism, and who could say if he would return? Sonya fixed her gray eyes on Zeev Feinberg. For an instant the same thought that tortured Feinberg crossed her mind—his fault, all this madness, his fault—but she pushed the thought away and stood up to hug her husband. Sonya enveloped the big man in her arms, his mustache scratching her neck, his pained, hot breath on the back of her neck. The deputy commander of the Irgun quickly averted his eyes. He was there only by chance, witnessing an intimate moment between a man and a woman, between the man who had played chess with him on the rickety ship of illegal immigrants and the woman whose scent he could recognize with his eyes closed. A moment later Zeev Feinberg moved out of his wife's embrace, went over to the deputy commander of the Irgun and tapped him on the shoulder. "Let's go. We'll get Markovitch."

They drove silently for hours. Zeev Feinberg thought his thoughts and the deputy commander of the Irgun thought his. In the face of such thoughts spoken words seemed very small, so they both said nothing. Yaacov Markovitch did not say anything either. In another few hours they would reach Yotvata and slip across the border. It was precisely this kind of journey that Zeev Feinberg had talked about so nostalgically around the dinner table when he conjured up memories from his younger days. But now, sitting beside his friend in the car as it raced forward, he felt nothing but the heaviness of his tongue inside his mouth.

When they left Beersheba behind them and Yaacov Markovitch fell into a restless sleep in the back seat, the deputy commander of the Irgun said to Zeev Feinberg, "Tell me about the boy." Zeev Feinberg found that he was grateful for his friend's request. For some time now the silence had been growing thick around his legs, like the shifting sand of this desert. Speaking about the boy might ease the weight of his tongue in his mouth. So he began to talk about how fast he could run ("No one in the village could catch up with him! Not even the dogs!"), about how cunningly he had escaped from the dairy with the barrel of cream, about how cleverly he had always found where the candy was hidden in the house. The deputy commander of the Irgun listened in silence, his face unmoving, except for the slight quiver of his upper lip that had begun the moment Zeev Feinberg had opened his mouth. "You know," Feinberg added, "before he was born, I... I thought that maybe I had a problem with my equipment." The deputy commander of the Irgun tightened his grip on the wheel and kept his eyes on the road. "I blamed Sonya. To tell you the truth, I was pretty nasty. And Bella's pregnancy didn't help. Then Yair came and everything worked out." Zeev Feinberg hesitated before going on. For the first time in his life he had spoken things that he had never dared even to think. Afraid that his words were embarrassing the deputy commander of the Irgun, he turned to look at him. A shout escaped his lips at the sight of the deputy commander of the Irgun driving with his eyes squeezed shut, his lips clenched and his hands clutching the wheel like an animal's claws.

"Froike!"

The deputy commander of the Irgun opened his eyes. "What happened? Are you in pain?!" Feinberg asked.

"No, it's nothing. It passed."

"Do you want me to drive?" The deputy commander of the Irgun shook his head. "You're sure you're okay?"

For a moment the deputy commander of the Irgun contemplated all the replies he could give to that question, but in the end he made do with "yes". They drove in silence for several moments. Then, his voice restrained, the deputy commander of the Irgun said to Zeev Feinberg, "Tell me more." Zeev Feinberg needed no further encouragement. He immediately began to talk about the boy's birth, how everyone agreed that he was the most beautiful baby in the village, how he began to crawl backwards and only later forward. Zeev Feinberg talked and talked, and the deputy commander of the Irgun listened, storing the words in his memory, placing a hand over his trembling lip. Every now and then, to Feinberg's surprise, he added questions like, "Did he cry when he was teething?" Or—"What kind of costume did he wear last Purim?" Zeev Feinberg replied, sometimes at great length. By dawn the deputy commander of the Irgun was already an expert in the life of Yair Feinberg, from his failing grade in Bible class to his fondness for fig jam.

6

Y AIR FEINBERG knew exactly where they had taken a wrong turn. It was at the fork in the road, not far from the acacia tree. He said they had to go left and Naama insisted they turn right, and Zvi sided with her. Even if she had suggested that they dig their way down, he would have sided with her. For a minute Yair thought of turning around and throwing that in Zvi Markovitch's face, but his throat was too parched for unnecessary words. So he kept dragging his feet, busy thinking up an array of well-reasoned insults, which blended with the pulsing of the blood at his temples. From beneath the insults and the pulse the fear was rising. Freezing him, paralyzing him, threatening to throw him to the ground. Yair Feinberg fought it with all his strength but the fear grew stronger from hour to hour, darkening his ingenuity and logic like spreading gangrene. For a moment Yair Feinberg gave in to the temptation to turn around, but jerked his head back quickly. The terror on Naama's and Zvi's faces was clear and unmistakable. And contagious. They all knew that if they looked at each other they would not have the strength to go on walking, so the three of them looked straight ahead and tried to move forward as best they could. None of them suggested going back. They remembered the barren desert all the way back to Yotvata. And up ahead there would be a spring; that's what the map said. If they just kept walking they would reach it. But every step became more difficult. The blood pounding in Yair's temples intensified and thirst made his throat ache. Yair Feinberg had never imagined that thirst could hurt. When he thought about it, the panic slithered up his back like dozens of small snakes. Yair Feinberg struggled to push them away, occupying his mind with complex mathematical calculations: nine liters of water divided by thirty-one hours of walking meant that the three of them were living on 0.290 liters of water per hour of walking, which is 0.096 liters per person. But that calculation wasn't exact because in the last eight hours they had been walking without any water at all, so everything had to be divided by twenty-three hours, and maybe the water they'd drunk before setting out had to be added as well. Those calculations did a fairly good job of subduing the panic, so Yair Feinberg kept at it, and his head was so full of calculations of hours and liters and kilometers that at first he didn't hear Zvi Markovitch fall and Naama scream.

When Yair Feinberg looked back he saw that his friend was lying face down on the ground and his sister was kneeling at his side and shaking him. He hurried over to them, turned Zvi Markovitch onto his back and gently slapped his cheeks. Zvi Markovitch's eyes opened into narrow slits. He uttered a barely audible sound, which was nonetheless unmistakably "water". With their last ounce of strength, Yair and Naama dragged Zvi to the pathetic shade of a lone acacia tree. They panted violently from the effort, causing the pain in their throats to intensify. Now they could no longer contain the panic, which raced back and forth between Yair and Naama, its legs blocking every bit of thought.

"We'll go back," Naama said.

"Thirty hours without water? We're better off continuing."

"But Zvi can't walk."

"I'll carry him on my back."

"Then you'll faint too and I'll carry both of you?"

"You have a better idea?"

Naama was silent for a moment, then said quietly, "Maybe we should call for help?"

"You're not serious. The Jordanians will shoot us."

"Maybe they won't," Naama said. "After all, we're still children." When she said that they both fell silent. This escapade seemed so foolish and impulsive now, a child's journey. Yair Feinberg felt the pain of thirst in his throat diminish in the face of his rising anger. Was that really all he was, a child pretending to be a man?

"You stay here with Zvi. I'll go and get water."

"Have you lost your mind? We can't split up. You yourself said that at every training exercise we ever did."

"This is not a training exercise, Naama. This is anything but a training exercise. We need water. Zvi can't walk, and there's no way we can leave him here. The spring should be close by. I'll run to look for it and then come back."

Naama Feinberg's throat was so dry that she couldn't speak, so she simply shook her head again and again. Yair stood up. Naama shook her head more vehemently but remained sitting.

"One whistle for danger. Two whistles if I find water. Will you remember that?"

Naama kept shaking her head but she knew she'd remember. After all, she was the one who had taught Yair to whistle, torturing him with endless practice until he managed to produce the strong, unbroken sound. How angry he had been that whistling came so easily to her while he himself failed over and over again. And how much she had enjoyed the knowledge that there was indeed something she could do better than her brother. One whistle for danger, two whistles for a happy discovery—that's how they had informed each other that the school principal was approaching, or that a loved object that was lost had been found, or that it was the right moment to sneak over to where the fig jam was hidden. Yair Feinberg began to walk, feeling Naama's eyes on his back all the way to the bend in the stream bed. When he turned the bend, she could no longer see him. Now he was walking alone. A tidal wave of excitement flooded his body. Alone in the desert. Like in his father's stories about his friend Froike, who crossed the sand dunes alone to rescue the besieged members of Nitzanim. Yair's thirst abated slightly and he walked faster. Now he felt stronger than before, although anyone observing him would be horrified at the sight of his sun-scorched face and feverish eyes. Yair Feinberg knew exactly where he was going—if he shortened the distance by climbing the high cliff he would reach the fork in the stream bed where they had gone wrong, and from there he'd turn left to the spring shown on the map. Clear, sweet water awaited him there. At the thought of water he walked even faster, imagining that he was running to the spring, bounding up the hills, leaping over the hilltops. In fact he had tottered a few hundred meters, walking like a drunkard on wobbly legs. But beyond the next bend, beyond the next bend he could smell the spring. He heard the burbling of the water. Yair Feinberg put two fingers in his mouth, getting ready to give two strong whistles.

Yaacov Markovitch saw them first. Two children faint with thirst and heat in the shade of an acacia tree. A shout of joy burst from his mouth, the first sound any of them had uttered for hours. Since setting out they had searched painstakingly for traces of the children, speaking as little as possible. They based their search on the children's footprints in the sand and the map they had received from the young man in Yotvata, a map that was identical—so he said—to the one he had sent the youngsters. But more than anything they based their search on that delicate, almost imperceptible scent of peaches. Almost twenty-four hours separated the children's journey into the desert from their parents', but the hot earth had absorbed Yair's sweat and the stagnant air had preserved his scent. When they were not sure which path to take they stopped, bent to the ground and inhaled deeply. Most times it was Zeev Feinberg who straightened up first and, with a gesture of his head, indicated the direction they should take. It was he, after all, who sniffed his son every day when he stepped out of the bath, alert to any hint of the hated peach scent, ordering him back to wash himself again the instant he caught a whiff of it in his pores. Yaacov Markovitch stood up immediately after his friend and resumed walking, while the deputy commander of the Irgun lingered another moment on the ground, eyes closed, inhaling the memory of the boy's presence.

When Yaacov Markovitch saw the figures lying in the shade of the acacia he began to run towards them, Zeev Feinberg and the deputy commander of the Irgun hurrying along behind him. They were convinced that they would see the missing boy on the other side of the tree, but when they reached the acacia they saw that Yair wasn't there. They gave Naama and Zvi water and patted their faces until they opened their eyes. They were extremely weak and dehydrated, but the shade of the tree had protected them from the lethal heat of the sun. Zeev Feinberg and the deputy commander of the Irgun tried again and again to get the children to tell them which way Yair had gone, but they were too weak to speak. After several moments they decided to separate: Yaacov Markovitch would remain there, with the children, and Zeev Feinberg and the deputy commander of the Irgun would keep searching for the missing boy. The two men immediately bent down to smell the air on the ground. A moment later they stood up in unison and began to run towards the bend in the stream bed and, from there, up the hill. Now there was no mistaking the boy's footprints in the sand. But while the prints were clearly visible, the scent of peaches was growing weaker.

Both Zeev Feinberg and the deputy commander of the Irgun sensed it, and they looked at each other fearfully as they kept running where the footprints led them. Zeev Feinberg and the deputy commander of the Irgun took huge breaths of air, their entire bodies strained to detect the boy's scent. But with every breath they found it harder to smell the peach scent. A moment before the bend in the path they inhaled once more, a powerful, stubborn intake of air. At the very moment they realized that they no longer smelled anything they rounded the bend and, beyond it, saw Yair Feinberg's body sprawled on the ground.

Zeev Feinberg's anguished scream echoed among the hills for hours after the searchers had headed back to the border, bearing the children on their shoulders. Yaacov Markovitch walked behind the other two, his son lying across his shoulder, drifting in and out of consciousness. The blazing son and the boy's weight did not bother Yaacov Markovitch in the slightest because, when he had taken the boy in his arms beside the acacia tree, he had smiled weakly and whispered, "Dad". That word had been sufficient to keep Yaacov Markovitch on his feet despite the arduous trek. Zeev Feinberg walked close to Yaacov Markovitch, carrying Naama on his shoulder. He was convinced that the girl was unconscious throughout the journey, but that was not the case. After Yaacov Markovitch gave her water near the acacia she had begun to revive, but the screams that came from the bend in the road completely paralyzed her. When Zeev Feinberg and the deputy commander of the Irgun came running back with Yair, she closed her eyes to protect herself from the sight. "Quickly," the deputy commander of the Irgun shouted, "to the border. Maybe we can still save him." In minutes the three men were already hurrying back, each carrying a child across his shoulder. The entire time that Naama's eyes remained closed, the words of the deputy commander of the Irgun filled her head: maybe we can still save him. She wanted to sink once more into that hazy, semi-conscious state she had been in when the men found them after God knows how many hours of waiting in the shade of the acacia. But she felt herself growing more alert, more aware with every minute that passed, so she could not fail to notice Zeev Feinberg's sniffling and his heaving shoulders. Even without seeing his face, Naama knew that the man carrying her home cried all the way to the border.

The deputy commander of the Irgun walked fifty meters in front of Zeev Feinberg and Yaacov Markovitch, Yair's unconscious body lying across his shoulder, his arm around the boy's waist. This summer he would be forty-one. In a drawer in his Tel Aviv apartment were three medals of valor and one letter of gratitude from the Prime Minister, its contents top secret. At least seven children bore his name. At least fifty men had died in clashes with him. He had slept with eleven women. He loved one. And he would have given it all away, all of it, without blinking an eye just to bring that boy home alive. Behind him he heard Zeev Feinberg's cries of anguish, but he himself uttered not a sound. Not a word. He shed not a single tear. He simply hurried along, without stopping, all the way to the border. As long as he could walk, as long as he could translate the tempest in his soul into physical action, the tempest would bend to his will.

Z VI MARKOVITCH couldn't say how much time had passed from the moment the IDF soldiers had run towards them to the moment he found himself lying between the starched sheets of the hospital bed. He didn't know when his mother arrived or at what point Naama Feinberg's bed had been placed in his room. When he opened his eyes he thought that a great deal of time had passed, maybe years, because his mother suddenly looked very old. Bella Markovitch kissed her son's face again and again and again. Then she went over and took Yaacov Markovitch's hand and kissed him as well. Embarrassed, Zvi Markovitch turned his head away from his parents and looked at Naama's bed. The girl's eyes were closed, but Zvi Markovitch knew immediately that she wasn't sleeping. Her eyes were closed too tightly, proof of the effort she was making to keep them shut. If she opened them she might find that her old, secret dream had come true—that she was her parents' only child. Naama Feinberg refused to open her eyes, and Zvi Markovitch had no intention of forcing her to do so. Instead he reached out and did what he had been wanting to do for many months—he held her hand.

Yaacov Markovitch and Bella left the room and joined the deputy commander of the Irgun, Zeev Feinberg and Sonya in the waiting room. When the doctor approached they all stood up except for Sonya, who remained seated, her eyes fixed on the linoleum floor. The chances were slight, he said. The boy had a severe case of sunstroke. They could only guess how many hours he had been lying in the blazing sun.

"But maybe a miracle will happen," Yaacov Markovitch interrupted.

"Yes," Bella said, "maybe a miracle will happen."

"Maybe a miracle will happen," the doctor agreed. He always agreed when people spoke of miracles.

In the silence that fell after the doctor had spoken, they all looked at Feinberg and Sonya. But it was the deputy commander of the Irgun who suddenly began to cry uncontrollably. Thirteen years of anticipation and missed opportunities burst from his throat in huge, desperate sobs. Zeev Feinberg looked at the deputy commander of the Irgun, the surprise on his face turning into something darker. Yaacov Markovitch looked at Zeev Feinberg's face and realized that his friend had begun to suspect what he himself had guessed a long time ago. His brow furrowed, Feinberg thought about the questions the deputy commander of the Irgun had asked about the boy on their drive to the south, about his insistence on carrying the boy himself all the way back, and about the stark paleness that had spread over Sonya's face when he burst into tears. Zeev Feinberg turned abruptly and stormed out of the waiting room, Yaacov Markovitch hurrying after him. In the corridor they passed a pregnant woman, a young man with broken legs and four groaning old men without noticing a single one of them. The entrance door to the hospital, which separated the world of the sick from the world of the healthy, shook from top to bottom when Zeev Feinberg rammed it open and burst onto the street.

Yaacov Markovitch continued to follow his friend down the street. He couldn't decide whether to approach Zeev Feinberg in his fury or to let him be, and in the end he chose neither.

Instead he kept walking a polite distance behind him, which enabled Zeev Feinberg to turn around several moments later and speak to him without raising his voice, his face tormented with doubt.

"Do you think it's true?"

"I don't know."

"I didn't ask if you know. I asked what you think."

"I think it's true."

"But why would she do such a thing?" Zeev Feinberg asked the question, but didn't dare to consider the answer that had begun to take shape in his mind.

Yaacov Markovitch was also cautious about saying things that best remained unspoken. "People do different things for different reasons."

"And I," Feinberg asked, "what will I do?"

After a moment's silence Yaacov Markovitch said, "How can I advise you, Feinberg? I can only observe the kind of love you and Sonya have for each other from the outside, the way a person looks at a display window."

"What are you talking about, a display window?!" Zeev Feinberg roared, "that's what love looks like to you?"

"Yes," Yaacov Markovitch replied in a quiet, sure voice, "that's exactly what love looks like to me. Believe me, a man who lives without it can recognize it from far away."

Zeev Feinberg did not reply. The pain and the anger made his entire body shake. Passers-by looked at him fearfully. His blazing eyes searched for something he could take apart with his bare hands. Although he saw several candidates that were clearly deserving— a nearby wooden bench, a fellow with a mean face, a street sign not properly mounted—he nonetheless stayed where he was, fists clenched. He knew that even if he were to smash the entire city down to its foundations, the knowledge would remain in his mind. Yaacov Markovitch looked at his friend for a few moments. Then he turned and began to trudge back to the hospital.

When Yaacov Markovitch entered the waiting room Sonya raised hopeful eyes to him, but when she saw that he had come back alone she put her head in her hands. Yaacov Markovitch sat down beside her, hesitating. The words, as treacherous as always, evaded him. He did not have the faintest idea what to say to her, to that grieving lioness. He finally reached out to put his hand on her shoulder. But another hand, a large, warm hand, reached it first. Zeev Feinberg's hand. Wordlessly Yaacov Markovitch stood up, leaving his seat for his friend. Zeev Feinberg sat down beside his wife without speaking. For a moment his expression remained dark, his mustache jutting out in anger—then he relaxed all at once and whispered, "Sonyitchka." Sonya raised her head from between her hands and buried her face in her husband's chest. Beneath the cloth of the shirt, beneath the dusty curls and the sweaty skin, Zeev Feinberg's heart beat strongly against Sonya's cheek.

So tender was the sight that everyone who came into the waiting room quickly averted their eyes. It was not meant for them. Everyone, that is, but Yaacov Markovitch. He looked at Zeev Feinberg with wide-open eyes. Only a moment ago he was roaring outside the hospital, gripping his pain and anger with clenched teeth. Now he had let it go all at once, leaving the rotting carcass behind, and had returned to comfort his wife. And he, Yaacov Markovitch, had been wallowing in his own pain for so many years, holding on to his protesting wife, refusing to let go. Compared to what Zeev Feinberg had just done, his refusal to let Bella go seemed so pathetic, so pointless. Yaacov Markovitch had been holding on to Bella for so long, and she did not want him. He held her dress in his clenched fist and refused to let go. When he looked at Zeev Feinberg's open hand on Sonya's shoulder, he suddenly remembered the blessing of fingers spread wide. And he wondered if he could still open his hand. But the thought terrified him. Let go? Of Bella? How could he? His fist had been clenched for so many years that his hand was no longer suited to any other work. Refusal had been a way of life for him.

All the way back to the village in the car of the deputy commander of the Irgun Yaacov Markovitch looked at Bella wonderingly, as if seeing her for the first time. The deputy commander of the Irgun and Bella struggled to carry on an ordinary conversation, as if their sons were not in the hospital now, waiting for time and chance to have their say. Yaacov Markovitch sank into the back seat, watching his wife's profile as she said something about the figs, which were late in ripening this year. Some vestige of her regal beauty still remained. But her eyes were framed by the delicate web of thin lines that heralded the wrinkles that were to come. They had already begun to appear at the corners of her mouth. Delicate wrinkles, like the lines of a sketch an artist draws with a soft pencil right before he paints them boldly onto the canvas. Despite the freshness that still flickered on her face, he could already guess how she would look as an old woman. Time would blur the contours of her lips and carve new lines on her forehead. But however much it wrote and erased, however much it rewrote Bella Markovitch's face, it could never erase the expression of refusal that had become second nature to her.

Because neither the wrinkles that existed nor the wrinkles that would come changed anything for Yaacov Markovitch. He knew only too well that he would desire her forever, young or old, blooming or withering. It was not the ravages of time that caused him to shrink into the back seat but the expression of refusal on

Bella's face, the expression that was clear even at that late hour in the dark car. It hid in her eyebrows, was embedded in her cheeks and had been poured into her blue eyes like poison into a glass. Even when Bella Markovitch took Yaacov Markovitch's hand in a surge of gratitude for bringing her son back, even then the refusal had remained on her face. For the first time he asked himself if he would spend the rest of his days looking at this woman who, though she was the most beautiful woman he had ever seen in his life, said "no" to him with every muscle and movement of her face.

The car continued to race through the dark night, and the bonfire of the conversation between Bella and the deputy commander of the Irgun was occasionally rekindled with the gust of a sentence of two, but quickly died out again. Yaacov Markovitch sat in the back seat and asked himself whether his clenched fist could once again become an open hand so arbitrarily, in a momentary decision, and the flickering night lights replied in the distance: just as the "no" was born in you one night long ago, so the "yes" can be born in you now, tonight. The possibility that such an emphatic "no" could wake up one morning and turn into "yes" shocked Yaacov Markovitch so much that he almost didn't notice that they had reached the village, and it wasn't until Bella opened the car door and thanked the deputy commander of the Irgun for everything he had done for them that he remembered to mumble something and get out of the car. Now they're standing at the door to the house, Bella talking about the things they had to organize before their trip back to the hospital, Yaacov Markovitch looking at her in silence, and then they're in the living room, the most beautiful feet he has ever seen in his life flashing briefly in front of him as Bella takes off her shoes before they disappear again into felt slippers. Yaacov Markovitch thinks about Zeev Feinberg's open hand on his wife's shoulder.

Yaacov Markovitch thinks about the eternal refusal on Bella's face. Yaacov Markovitch thinks about the wonderful, miraculous way the "no" might ripen and become a "yes". Finally, Yaacov Markovitch stops thinking and begins speaking.

At first Bella Markovitch thought that the night sounds were deceiving her. The wind rustled through the bougainvillea outside, pretending to be human; in the distance, a jackal howled in a human voice. Yaacov Markovitch had to repeat his words twice before Bella heard them correctly, and even then she still did not believe that they had actually come from his mouth. Yaacov Markovitch saw his wife lean forward to hear him better, and he repeated his words a third time. "I'll give you a divorce if you want one." Bella's expression remained as it was—only her lashes fluttered rapidly, like a bird flapping its wings wildly when the cage door suddenly opens—but she did not move. She stood where she was, motionless, even after Yaacov Markovitch was positive that this time she had heard what he had said. As his wife continued to stand there, Yaacov Markovitch began to wonder if the impossible had become possible right before his eyes. That straw had turned to gold. That the wolf and the sheep were licking each other's faces in affection. That a million dry bones were now dancing their way through the alleyways of Jerusalem in the great resurrection of the dead. In short: could it be that Bella Markovitch, a magnificent, glorious creature that, until now, had been held there by an iron chain, was still standing at the door after the lock had been removed? And who can say, perhaps Bella Markovitch might have stood there forever if Yaacov Markovitch had not decided to tell her of his intention to support the boy whether she stayed or went. Oh yes, Bella Markovitch finally moved from the door then. But instead of going out, her feet carried her farther inside the house. She walked past Yaacov Markovitch to her bedroom. A sob of gratitude was on Yaacov Markovitch's lips when he heard Bella call him from her room—she couldn't find her suitcase.

Yaacov Markovitch took the suitcase out of the closet and lay down on the sofa in the living room. He had spent his nights on it for so many years that he wondered how his back would respond to the touch of the mattress in the bedroom that, starting the next day, would be his once again. He heard the sound of Bella's steps in the other room as she gathered her belongings. The sounds died quickly. Did she have so little here, he asked himself, that she could pack it all in half an hour? She would leave when the sun came up. Her body would still be present in the house for a while longer: a golden hair that he'd find on the mattress, a forgotten sock, her fingerprints on a dish not properly wiped. Gradually they would disappear, until Yaacov Markovitch was left alone in the bare house. He would have to leave the village. Of that there was no doubt. Otherwise the empty house would drive him mad. He would sell his farm and look for another. Or perhaps not. Perhaps he'd follow the pigeons to the city. On his last visits to Tel Aviv, the pigeons had cooed at him invitingly. What would happen to the strawberry plants? Yaacov Markovitch wanted with all his heart and soul to get up from the sofa, take the four steps from the living room to Bella's room and plead for his life. Instead he stayed where he was, his body huddled under the blanket like a ball of tendons, muscles and thoughts. Tomorrow she would be gone. Should he walk her to the door early in the morning? Squeeze her hand? Or should he go out to the field and pound the earth mercilessly as her slim, elegant figure moved away along the path? Yaacov Markovitch suddenly froze. He heard the sound of a suitcase being dragged in the other room. If so, she planned to leave right now. Without delay. Even before dawn. Drunk with freedom, she would rather walk the village streets alone in the cold night than spend another few wretched hours in the same house with him. Yaacov Markovitch dared to open his eyes a crack. The most beautiful woman he had ever seen in his life was standing at the door to the room. He shut his eyes quickly, before they could see her leave.

Suddenly Yaacov Markovitch felt the blanket being pulled from his body, and Bella Markovitch lay down beside him on the couch. Her hands—one perfect, the other scarred—found his trembling hands. "One night, Markovitch. We'll sleep together one night like man and wife." Yaacov Markovitch did not reply. There could be no reply to this moment of grace she was granting him.

8

ALL NIGHT Sonya Feinberg's hand rested in Zeev Feinberg's, his large, warm fingers encircling hers like a cocoon. And all that night Zeev Feinberg's hand sometimes dripped sweat, covering Sonya's fingers with salty wetness, and sometimes was dry. If Sonya felt the weeping hand, she said nothing. Her own hand lay motionless, indifferent to the ebb and flow of Zeev Feinberg's sweat. Zeev Feinberg cried from his hands, and Sonya's hands remained silent. That invincible woman withdrew into an inner cellar and locked the door. A hurricane was approaching the house. The wind roared in her ears. Now she could only wait for it to pass, wait quietly and unmoving in the depths of the cellar. When it was all over, when the roaring moved onward to strike other houses, she would open the door silently and see what the storm had left her and what it had taken with it.

At about 3:40 in the morning, at the same time Bella Markovitch entered her husband's bed, Sonya Feinberg pleaded with the sun to delay its rising. In the hospital corridor the fluorescent lights burned in a constant sunrise, but Sonya narrowed her gaze fearfully at the fading darkness in the window. It would soon be dawn, bringing with it the tidings of a new day. She was sure that her son would not die at night. But in the morning, in the morning she would have to open the cellar door to see if the house was still standing above her or if it had been ripped away by the wind, leaving her amid the ruins. So she spoke wordlessly to the sun, in the language of stars, saying: slower, please, slower. And at precisely the same moment Yaacov Markovitch lay in his bed, which for the first time in his life was also Bella Markovitch's bed, also pleading: slower, please, slower. And the sun, which foolish scientists insist is merely a mass of hydrogen and helium, cannot deny such a plea. For the sun—whatever scientists say about it—loves people with a perfect love, as much as the distance will allow. Otherwise it would not revolve around them day and night with such concern, with a mother's strictness. And even if the foolish scientists say that the sun does not revolve around people, but they revolve around it, and, even worse, that the revolving has nothing to do with love or concern and is caused entirely by physical laws—that would not be enough to refute what the eye sees and the heart knows.

And so newsboys look at the empty horizon with wonder in their eyes. Bakers raise their heads and look at the dark window in surprise. Roosters stamp their feet and stop their cries in their beaks. Farmers toss and turn in their beds, clinging to yet another dream. Because the sun, although the delay causes her great suffering and seriously disrupts time schedules, answers the pleas of Sonya Feinberg and Yaacov Markovitch and grants them twenty whole minutes. For those twenty minutes Yaacov Markovitch lies in bed with his eyes open, inhaling the breath of the woman beside him. For those twenty minutes Sonya Feinberg sits up straight, her hand still resting in Zeev Feinberg's, and does not move. But as the twentieth minute nears its end, the sun can delay no longer. However much it sympathizes with the man lying in his bed and the woman anxious about her son, the good of those two must be weighed against the good of millions of other people who have to work and love and eat and worry and laugh, along with many other things that are best done in daylight. And so at 6:20, a full twenty minutes later than expected, the first ray of sunlight illuminated the village and the valley, the orange groves and the city's concrete fields, the empty home of Sonya and Zeev Feinberg and the home of Yaacov and Bella Markovitch, which had never been so full.

Between 3:40 and 6:20 in the morning Yaacov and Bella Markovitch lay on the sofa, their arms around each other. Yaacov Markovitch inhaled Bella Markovitch's scent, rubbed his cheek on the softness of her shoulder, listened to her breathing. His hands trembled constantly. It was the most beautiful night of his life. At 6:20 Bella Zeigerman got up from the sofa, kissed Yaacov Markovitch on the cheek and left the house.

And at 6:20, newsboys resumed tossing the news of the day at people's doors with a sure hand. Bakers hurried to stack loaves of bread. Roosters finally released their pent-up cries. Farmers opened their eyes. And as they all stretched and dressed and boiled water for their morning cup of tea, the doctor went over to Sonya and Zeev Feinberg and told them that their son was dead.

Sonya realized immediately that she had been mistaken. That when the cellar door opened she did not see the ruins, but the storm itself. The wind roared in her ears, tore her body from within with a huge, gyrating blast. No matter how loudly she screamed, the roar of the storm was louder. The voice of fate rose above her, more thunderous than her own voice. People ran in the corridor. People spoke to her. A white hand in a white coat slapped her. Another hand in a white coat gave her a pill and demanded that she swallow it. But Sonya was swallowed up in the roar of the hurricane, in the storm that shattered everything to bits. Now an enormous force lifted her into the air, and she was surrounded by houses and trees and fruit. From above she saw everything that had been and was now lost, and she yearned for the moment her body would crash to the ground, for, however painful that was, it could never be as terrible as the pain she was feeling now. And all the while she was spinning and whirling, being beaten and battered, she felt Zeev Feinberg's hand far, far away, at the edge of her body, still holding hers. Zeev Feinberg did not let the storm take his wife. It was enough that it had taken his son. He kept holding her hand all that morning. And all the mornings that followed.

As Yaacov Markovitch listened in silence for the sound of the door closing behind Bella, who would never return, and Zeev Feinberg held his wife's hand in the storm, the deputy commander of the Irgun was looking at the rising sun with delirious eyes. The delayed sunrise was a minor detail to him. He hadn't come here to focus on trivialities. He was sitting outside his car, on the top of a gravel hill in the northern sand dunes of Tel Aviv. One day the air here would be filled with the horn blasts of trains in a nearby station and the exasperated cries of drivers on the perpetually congested highways. But at the moment only the rustle of bushes could be heard as a stray rabbit or a timid partridge scuttled through them.

The first gust of wind stirred dozens of grains of sand, sweeping them along the entire hill only to drop them abruptly on the other side. If the deputy commander of the Irgun had known how to listen to the wind, he might have heard the grumbling of the students climbing from the train station that would be built at the bottom of the hill to the university that would be built on the top. But how could someone listen to the wind when internal winds were agitating his soul as if it were a boat of illegal immigrants on a stormy night? And if he did hear—so what? Everyone knows that others lived before him and others would live after him. Such knowledge about the past and the future, though quite interesting intellectually, cannot ease a toothache in the present. And certainly not a heartache. Only a different sort of pain, a greater pain, can mask a heartache. And so the deputy commander of the Irgun sat and waited for the sun to come up, so he could look directly at it.

The ball of fire began to appear beyond the hills in the east, and the deputy commander of the Irgun took a deep breath, preparing himself. The new day would dawn and he would look straight into its core, never dropping his gaze, the way he used to look at disobedient soldiers until they began to cry, the way he used to look at Arab prisoners until they began to talk. He and the sun would look at each other once and for all, and if he lost his sight as a result of his encounter with the great light—then so be it. There are times when a person is better off blind. After all, he would never see Sonya and the boy again.

Now the ball of fire stood above the hills in all its glory. The deputy commander of the Irgun also stood and focused his eyes on the great light, ordering them to remain unmoving even when the discomfort turned into pain, which turned into suffering, which turned into torment, which turned into torture, which turned into scorched eyeballs, which turned into a black, opaque screen.

Nonetheless, they made him Transportation Minister. The dark glasses he had to wear from that morning until the day he died did not detract from his image. On the contrary. They endowed him with a dignity that only enhanced his natural power. Mothers and fathers who had named their children after him when he was only the deputy commander of the Irgun could now nod with satisfaction. And indeed, Ephraim Greenberg did well in life. At the age of two he was weaned from his mother's whipped-cream breasts, though he continued to look at them longingly until his fourth year. When he grew up he became one of the country's leading land appraisers. Ephraim Sharabi received his officer's stripes at a formal ceremony right before Rosh Hashanah, and was killed on the first day of the Yom Kippur War ten days later. Ephraim Yemini left the kibbutz for the city, where he took much pleasure in peeping at women in ground-floor apartments until he was caught, imprisoned, released, found God and peeped only at pages of the Talmud. Other babies called Ephraim grew up and became men called Ephraim, some affectionately and some disparagingly, some tenderly and some reverently. The deputy commander of the Irgun, now the Minister of Transportation, saw them infrequently and showed little interest in them. He spent his leisure time playing correspondence chess against amateur players throughout the world. He particularly liked to play against a Jordanian exile who lived in Paris and sent him letters filled with brilliant moves and elegant insults. He finally married a woman named Edna, though had she been named Hana or Tsila nothing would have changed in the slightest. He treated her with respect, and in exchange she gave him twins. When he walked down the street with them, holding a small, trusting hand in each of his, he felt something that most definitely could be called happiness. If they took a drive on Saturday and happened to pass an orange grove, he immediately ordered them to close the windows in the car. After his death his name came up several times at meetings where new street names were chosen, but was rejected each time in favor of a senior army officer, a poet or another Zionist activist.

It is difficult to know what such a concise description of the fate of the deputy commander of the Irgun can teach us, since the dry facts of a life are no substitute for a flesh-and-blood life. But historical truth requires the admission that, from the day he left Sonya and the boy in the hospital and went to look at the sun, the deputy commander of the Irgun was as tightly sealed as a grave. At his funeral, which was extremely dignified and accompanied by eulogies in the evening newspapers, his wife said that she had never seen him cry.

AFTER AFTER

"THE SHIVAH will be held in the home of the deceased."
Yehuda Greenberg stands in front of the announcement
for a long time, drawing Yaacov Markovitch up from the depths,
dredging up his image, which had grown weaker and feebler and
flimsier from day to day, from month to month, like a notebook
whose pages are flipped rapidly, turning the inanimate drawings
on the lower edge of each page into a single living person. Because
although he had been old forever, Yaacov Markovitch, always an
inanimate picture of wrinkled skin and sunken eyes, had one day
apparently become older than on other days—otherwise how can
you explain that one day he was old enough to die, something he
had apparently not been on the preceding days.

Between the grocery store and the nursery school, another
announcement of Yaacov Markovitch's death demands to be read.
Yehuda Greenberg has almost forgotten. Only ten steps from the
previous announcement, and already the shopping list and the
hefty electric bill that had to be paid and a brief reverie about
sex. All those seem embarrassed in the face of the black-rimmed
announcement. Because how can he even think about Fruma's
breasts, hanging like suicides above her navel, pale white skin,
citron nipples, when the decaying Yaacov Markovitch has moved
from now to then, and he wonders when Yaacov Markovitch last
touched breasts, if he ever had touched them.

It isn't nice to have such thoughts about Yaacov Markovitch, but neither is it nice to put up so many death announcements, as if deliberately intending to annoy, on one small street. Someone has been over-eager about the task. But suddenly he feels a twinge of sadness: perhaps it was Yaacov Markovitch's grandchildren, if he had any. Perhaps they, haunted by guilt, have filled the live street with their dead grandfather. When he was still alive they never walked the one endless kilometer from his house to the park with him, and now they have walked down the very same street, putting up monuments of paper and Scotch tape every meter. Yehuda Greenberg stops in front of the next announcement and reads carefully: Yaacov Markovitch had three grandchildren. But it was clear nonetheless that they were not the perpetrators. It was too boring a job for youngsters, too exhausting for their parents. A blank-faced errand boy is filling Yaacov Markovitch's street with announcements, hurrying to get the job done and be on his way.

For confirmation you need only turn into the side streets, and you'll see that the fences around the houses are free of any trace of Yaacov Markovitch, and there are only two announcements on the kiosk: a twelve-year-old girl who wants to babysit your children, and a dance class opening in the community center. The noise of the errand boy's motor scooter fills Yehuda Greenberg's ears as it sails off to a different neighborhood, another pile of announcements in its box. Hearing the loud noise of the engine, Yehuda Greenberg can only cling anxiously to Fruma's breasts and their citron nipples, to the sweet smell of perspiration and perfume, beneath which lurks a different smell, the smell of a decaying body.

Yehuda Greenberg's anxiety might have diminished somewhat if he had known that, on the morning of his death, Yaacov Markovitch woke up with a song in his heart. He can almost smell the bread on the stairs or in the elevator they finally installed, and from there he has to walk past only three buildings to reach the grocery store. And look, despite the rheumatism and the freezing floor he gets out of bed, he actually gets out of bed, hallelujah, and begins to dress. He brushes his teeth, careful not to look in the mirror. In the elevator on his way down Yaacov Markovitch gives thanks for that miracle: a small cubicle enveloping him like a womb, and there he is, Yaacov Markovitch, suspended in the air, being lowered gently by steel cables all the way to the ground floor.

Now the street. Hotter than yesterday. In the winter there were no mistakes, but the summer was fickle. Yaacov Markovitch shuffles his way down the street, only two more buildings to go, and on the way he recalls a sentence he once clipped from the papers—"Cherry trees in blossom do not signify the spring; cherry trees in blossom are the spring." Although he didn't understand it, he hung it on his refrigerator door with a magnet.

He loves the refrigerator door more than anything else in the house. Hanging on it, side by side, are words that comprise the essence of wisdom, words he has laboriously distilled from books, newspaper supplements and political speeches. Words left unread lose their point, a tree that falls in the forest rots without being seen. But the refrigerator—such freshness, such an endlessly vibrant dance: when you take out the milk for your morning coffee, when you put your newly purchased items inside, when you sneak another spoonful of jam before lunch. Each time, another line catches your eye. Sometimes Ben-Gurion, sometimes Weizmann, sometimes you finish the last pickle in the jar to the heat of Jabotinsky's anger.

Finally he reaches the grocery store. The radio hums him a greeting. In the back, the owner is unpacking crates. Although he knows what he wants, he looks around. Colorful candy wrappers surround him. Red and green and yellow and blue, ridiculously cheerful. Only the drably colored breads are fragrant. A loaf of bread, yes a loaf of bread. That's what he has come for. That's what he has found. Four-seventy on the counter. Hallelujah.

He turns to leave the grocery store, and there are a woman and her daughter. The woman smiles brightly at him. Yaacov, how are you; it seems that she and his son were once friends. He looks intently at her, searching for something familiar in her face. But the face remains beyond his reach. The hair is dyed, the curls might be real or not, he can't tell, dark sunglasses cover her eyes. But the lips beneath the lipstick. Yes, Yaacov, enter there. And as he looks at her lips he has a dim memory of them contorted with tears as she slept in a hospital bed next to his son. And he, Yaacov, sat beside her and told her about faraway countries and nearby princesses. And when she fell asleep he straightened the blanket around her body, happy and a bit sad because he could have told her more.

Now the woman kisses him on the neck and tells the little girl to give Grandpa Yaacov a kiss. And he, seeing the child draw back, says quickly, "There's no need, no need." He already knows: he has an old-people smell. Children can smell it. So can adults. Except that they are not supposed to show it. He is as tired of the little girl's revulsion as he is of the mother's politeness. He takes his loaf of bread and leaves.

On the way to the park the loaf of bread brushes against his thigh in its rustling bag. He sees parents taking their children to nursery school, mothers and fathers on the way to work, hurrying, all of them hurrying. He is surrounded by fragments of sentences hastily spoken: don't forget your sandwich, I'll be back at noon, but why, stop arguing, I'll pay the maid. Yaacov Markovitch listens to them as if to a familiar song on the radio, he can almost hum the melody. So we'll talk later, so I'll see you at lunch, I'll call in the evening. An entire present speaking in the future tense. Only

Yaacov is present, so very much present, and look, he's made it to the park fence, peers inside and keeps walking. Inside he catches a quick glimpse of a sight that fills him to bursting point: two children looking with utter concentration at a turtle.

An old man walks past Yaacov Markovitch and nods in greeting. He nods back. He doesn't remember the old man's name, perhaps he never knew it, but a year ago, when he suddenly stopped seeing him on the corner, he felt as sad as if he had lost a friend. Several days later the old man returned and Yaacov Markovitch almost spoke to him, almost broke ten years of amiable silence, but fortunately stopped himself—the pigeons are waiting. And truly, there they are at the entrance to the park, cooing to him a soft melody of hunger, demand and gratitude.

After the cold floor, the miracle of the elevator, the vividness of the grocery store, the song of the street, Yaacov Markovitch sits down on a wet bench. The well-trained pigeons gather around him in a semicircle, disciplined children at the feet of the rabbi. And he hums words and sounds at them, grumbles briefly about the early hour, tells them briefly about his walk there, and asks briefly how they are, mainly out of politeness. A passer-by—if one had passed by—would have filled with compassion for the old man talking to the birds in Hebrew and Yiddish. What a waste of compassion. Fortunately, the park is deserted. It will be at least another hour before the children arrive, wearing their gym clothes, for their morning run. He likes to look at them in the morning, trying to capture the exact moment the change begins—when the gaze sets, the clay mask solidifies, the child becomes a teenager. He misses it time and time again, as if he is watching a magic show and forever fails to see the sleight of hand. There was a bird there, I swear, so how could it have vanished into a hat? He can never put his finger on it, understands it only in retrospect. The freckled boy who one day stopped trying to swing on the branch of the pine tree, or the pudgy child everyone doted on at the beginning of the year and now finds tiresome.

The first pigeon dares to step out of the circle and actually stand on the bench. Its comrades look at it, stunned. Yaacov Markovitch smiles at its courage and offers it an especially large crumb. Another pigeon lands on the bench. And another. And another. The sound of flapping wings fills the park in general and Yaacov Markovitch in particular. It saddens him that he hasn't brought another loaf. So it is every day, it saddens him that he hasn't brought another loaf. But the pigeons suddenly take off skyward and he is alone on the bench, looking around: who has driven away the moment of grace in his day? There are four of them. Three men, one bride. One of the men is holding a video camera, one a stills camera, and the third is holding the bride's hand. They immediately break into a complex dance: the two men with the cameras circle the bride and groom, who circle each other, and none of them notices the loaf of bread, the pigeons or Yaacov Markovitch.

Yaacov Markovitch crushes the dough in his hands, digging deeper and deeper into the injured loaf—perhaps the baker has hidden a miracle in it for him. A lone pigeon lands on the bench: Yaacov Markovitch recognizes the brave one from earlier and promises that it will father a large dynasty of spirited, intrepid pigeons. A sharp cry drives the pigeon away and interrupts his prophesying. The bride's gown is stained with resin, probably from when she posed with one arm around a pine tree. The men croon consoling words to her, but she refuses to be consoled—it cost 5,000 shekels just to rent the dress, God knows how much they'll charge for the damage. Yaacov Markovitch asks himself how many loaves of bread he could buy with 5,000 shekels. As he calculates, one of the photographers comes over and asks him if he can move, just for a few minutes, the last photo session is on the bench. Yaacov Markovitch wants to say: of course, there's room, sit next to me and take pictures to your heart's content. But he doesn't say that. Why stain their festivity with his old age? Suddenly he understands: two and two are four. The sun sets in the west. Soon he will die.

Now Yaacov Markovitch, more alone than ever, gets up from the bench, crushing the remains of the bread in his hands. The park is still and silent, and Yaacov Markovitch allows himself to be angry. His anger is great and terrible, the ground threatens to split asunder. Then Yaacov Markovitch allows himself to be envious. The bride's skin is rosy and lovely, and his envy is burning. Finally, he allows himself to love. The sky does not grow bluer, but his eyes are moist. Perhaps that is why, at first, he doesn't see the pigeons. Blue, purple, gray, red. All of them coo to him in a single, clear voice. Yaacov Markovitch tears off a bit of bread and reaches out. The bravest of the pigeons alights on his forearm. It doesn't eat the breadcrumb, but tears off a bit of Yaacov's flesh. Yaacov Markovitch is reduced to a crumb. Another pigeon arrives. And another. And another. Yaacov Markovitch thinks about the refrigerator door, then about Jabotinsky, then about the resin stain on the bride's dress, and then he thinks about the most beautiful woman he has ever seen in his life. Finally, he thinks no more. The flock of pigeons completes its work and flies away all at once. Yaacov Markovitch ascends to heaven in a whirlwind. Hallelujah.

Acknowledgments

With thanks to:

Eshkol Nevo, for the four seasons of the year.

Yigal Schwartz, who himself is a mythological figure from a book.

Netta Galinsky-Galili and Esti Halperin-Maimon for their acute judgment and comments.

Dorit Rabinyan, who taught me how to delete.

THE WORLD OF YESTERDAY

STEFAN ZWEIG

'*The World of Yesterday* is one of the greatest memoirs of the twentieth century, as perfect in its evocation of the world Zweig loved, as it is in its portrayal of how that world was destroyed' David Hare

JOURNEY BY MOONLIGHT

ANTAL SZERB

'Just divine… makes you imagine the author has had private access to your own soul' Nicholas Lezard, *Guardian*

BONITA AVENUE

PETER BUWALDA

'One wild ride: a swirling helix of a family saga… a new writer as toe-curling as early Roth, as roomy as Franzen and as caustic as Houellebecq' *Sunday Telegraph*

THE PARROTS

FILIPPO BOLOGNA

'A five-star satire on literary vanity… a wonderful, surprising novel' *Metro*

I WAS JACK MORTIMER

ALEXANDER LERNET-HOLENIA

'Terrific… a truly clever, rather wonderful book that both plays with and defies genre' Eileen Battersby, *Irish Times*

SONG FOR AN APPROACHING STORM

PETER FRÖBERG IDLING

'Beautifully evocative… a must-read novel' *Daily Mail*

THE RABBIT BACK LITERATURE SOCIETY

PASI ILMARI JÄÄSKELÄINEN

'Wonderfully knotty… a very grown-up fantasy masquerading as quirky fable. Unexpected, thrilling and absurd' *Sunday Telegraph*

RED LOVE: THE STORY OF AN EAST GERMAN FAMILY

MAXIM LEO

'Beautiful and supremely touching… an unbearably poignant description of a world that no longer exists' *Sunday Telegraph*

THE BREAK

PIETRO GROSSI

'Small and perfectly formed… reaching its end leaves the
reader desirous to start all over again' *Independent*

FROM THE FATHERLAND, WITH LOVE

RYU MURAKAMI

'If Haruki is The Beatles of Japanese literature,
Ryu is its Rolling Stones' David Pilling

BUTTERFLIES IN NOVEMBER

AUÐUR AVA ÓLAFSDÓTTIR

'A funny, moving and occasionally bizarre exploration of
life's upheavals and reversals' *Financial Times*

BARCELONA SHADOWS

MARC PASTOR

'As gruesome as it is gripping… the writing is extraordinar-
ily vivid… Highly recommended' *Independent*

THE LAST DAYS

LAURENT SEKSIK

'Mesmerising… Seksik's portrait of Zweig's final months
is dignified and tender' *Financial Times*

BY BLOOD

ELLEN ULLMAN

'Delicious and intriguing' *Daily Telegraph*

WHILE THE GODS WERE SLEEPING

ERWIN MORTIER

'A monumental, phenomenal book' *De Morgen*

THE BRETHREN

ROBERT MERLE

'A master of the historical novel' *Guardian*

COIN LOCKER BABIES

RYU MURAKAMI

'A fascinating peek into the weirdness of contemporary Japan' Oliver Stone

TALKING TO OURSELVES

ANDRÉS NEUMAN

'This is writing of a quality rarely encountered… when you read Neuman's beautiful novel, you realise a very high bar has been set' *Guardian*

CLOSE TO THE MACHINE

ELLEN ULLMAN

'Astonishing… impossible to put down' *San Francisco Chronicle*

MARCEL

ERWIN MORTIER

'Aspiring novelists will be hard pressed to achieve this quality' *Time Out*

JOURNEY INTO THE PAST

STEFAN ZWEIG

'Lucid, tender, powerful and compelling' *Independent*

POPULAR HITS OF THE SHOWA ERA

RYU MURAKAMI

'One of the funniest and strangest gang wars in recent literature' *Booklist*

LETTER FROM AN UNKNOWN WOMAN AND OTHER STORIES

STEFAN ZWEIG

'Zweig's time of oblivion is over for good… it's good to have him back' Salman Rushdie

ONE NIGHT, MARKOVITCH

AYELET GUNDAR-GOSHEN

'A remarkable first novel, trenchant and full of love, highly impressive in its maturity and wisdom' Eshkol Nevo

MY FELLOW SKIN

ERWIN MORTIER

'A Bildungsroman which is related to much European literature from Proust and Mann onwards… peculiarly unforgettable' AS Byatt, *Guardian*